HUNGRY GHOST

HUNGRY GHOST

a novel

KEITH KACHTICK

To Wendy,

You're a wonderful yoga teacher!

Namaste,

Keith Kachtick 12/10/04

HarperCollins*Publishers*

HarperCollins books may be purchased for educational, business, or sales promotional use. For information, please write: Special Markets Department, HarperCollins Publishers Inc., 10 East 53rd Street, New York, NY 10022.

FIRST EDITION

Designed by Christine Weathersbee

Printed on acid-free paper

Library of Congress Cataloging-in-Publication Data
Kachtick, Keith.
Hungry ghost : a novel / Keith Kachtick. — 1st ed.
p. cm.
ISBN 0-06-052390-5
1. Americans—Morocco—Fiction. 2. Germans—Morocco—Fiction. 3. Photographers—Fiction. 4. Catholics—Fiction. 5. Buddhists—Fiction. 6. Morocco—Fiction. I. Title.
PS3611.A44 H8 2003
813'.6—dc21 2002038765

03 04 05 06 07 ❖/RRD 10 9 8 7 6 5 4 3 2

For Plaegian

For the more there is of self, the less there is of God.

—Aldous Huxley, *The Perennial Philosophy*

HUNGRY GHOST

I

GRETA IS NAKED AGAIN. A blue-eyed, thirty-one-year-old sous chef from Berlin, goat-beard wisps of blond hair beneath her arms, she drops her black bikini top and diaphanous, wine-colored sarong onto her towel, strides across the damp sand, and dives into the breakers. Sitting up straight, you gape at the slope of Greta's breasts and run the back of your wrist across your mouth. Until she disrobed, you'd been lying flat against a dry dune near the Sendero cabañas, a short Frisbee toss from Greta's towel, presumably undetected in the shadows of the deserted cove, hands clasped behind your head, your attention directed chiefly towards the cloudless blue sky and a lone schooner bobbing in the calm, gold-flecked Pacific waters a few hundred yards offshore.

Over the last three days you've come to think of this long-legged German woman in specific physical terms, individual pieces of an exotic, big-boned puzzle. Greta is taller than average, heavier than average, ample but in an understated, competitive-sculler sort of way. A pre-Raphaelite mop of sandy blond hair. Broad shoulders. Muscular calves. Collarbones you could rope a horse to. A drowsy, full-souled smile. (Last night, drinking cuba libres and playing chess by the driftwood campfire, as Greta forked your queen with that deliciously slow grin of hers, you thought how perfect is the Spanish word for smile: *Sonrisa.* Sunrise.) You can't get enough of her smoky German accent. At times she works so hard at finding the correct word in English, her wide, Old World face scrunched from the effort, that you want to take her hand. But you haven't—not once. And thus far you've managed to stay out of her cabaña, too.

Today is the final day of your three-day shoot. All of your photo gear has been repacked in the brushed-silver Anvils in preparation for tomorrow morning's departure. Less fruitful than it might have been (you exposed only nineteen rolls of film out of the fifty you brought), this unexpected "adventure travel" assignment in southern Mexico will nonetheless pay much of the balance due on your new $2,900 Minolta laser printer and last month's $1,800 rent on your East Village apartment. Despite the half-hearted professional effort, you're in no hurry to leave—the warm winter weather has proven intoxicating. For three days you've remained barefoot, worn the same pair of oversized Abercrombie & Fitch canvas cargo shorts, stayed either high or within arm's reach of a frosty Negra Modelo, and been surrounded by comely beachcombers wearing little more than coconut oil and toe-rings. Your arrival here back on Tuesday now seems like someone else's dream: New York to Mexico City to Oaxaca on increasingly smaller planes, five hours by rickety bus along the winding mountain roads of the Sierra Madres to the fishing village of Puerto Escondido, hitchhiking to San Augustinillo and then crossing by foot the beachfront dunes that lead, ultimately, to this hedonistic Pacific-coast sanctuary.

Zipolite is located on the tip of the country's southernmost peninsula, about as far from the United States as one can get and still be in Mexico. "A hidden, bohemian paradise with unpaved roads and dreadlocked shopkeepers, shaded by palm trees and *palapas* and thatched-roof bungalows, Zipolite is an international rainbow of Lonely Planet travelers, Amsterdam meets the Garden of Eden, a tropically exotic and decidedly Dionysian love song." This is the first line of the 2,700-word article penned by a *Details* writer named Sandy Tesoros (who you correctly assume is a woman), which you were hired and sent to Mexico to illustrate with your photographs. The sentence, you feel, is an apt description for how you've come to regard this place—and for the quality you attempted to capture with your cameras. There are no ringing phones or buzzing alarm clocks in Zipolite, no sunburned tourists camcording the pelicans. Here there are tattooed chests and pierced belly buttons, long moonstruck nights of reggae and mescal on the beach. Here all of life seems tribal.

For three days you munched watermelon and papaya and mango for breakfast, and at night, by votive candle under the thirty-foot-high thatched roof of La Chosa—the open-air restaurant so close to the ocean you could feel its salty spray on your cheeks—savored seared red snapper topped with prawns the size of lobsters. You meditated each morning, hidden behind dunes taller than your outstretched arms. You spotted a stray dog with his ears dyed purple (trying to get him to sit still for a shot, you pined for Marley, your camera-friendly Rasta-mutt extraordinaire, who at this very moment is gnawing on Mrs. Pierno's winter galoshes back in Manhattan). You exposed an entire roll of film on a young Mexican girl selling fillets of iguana from a bucket balanced atop her head. You slept dreamlessly in your own palm tree–shrouded Sendero cabaña, 100 pesos a night (roughly $12), monastic and seductive with its whitewashed walls, slow-turning ceiling fan, gauzy mosquito net, and pine-planked porch from which you flung sand dollars into the ocean. You built a bonfire with a South African motorcyclist awaiting, without complaint, the arrival of a brake-pad for his Ducati for six months now. You discovered the sound a palm tree makes before dropping a coconut.

For three days you wandered from one end of Zipolite's half-mile beach to the other, blissfully stoned, photographing with either your new Mamiya M645 or your rugged little Canon Elan, discreetly and usually with permission, the occasional semi-naked woman lying on the dunes. You discovered that among the semi-naked women you photographed were a Honduran dive-master, a Franco-Czech painter with a name you couldn't pronounce, a journalist from Wales covering the Zapatista rebels in the neighboring state of Chiapas, and Greta, a dripping-wet sous chef from Berlin whose body is so sun-darkened that the palms of her hands seem to glow, and who—eyes lowered, arms crossed—is presently hauling herself from the roaring, early-evening surf back to her towel.

What to do? As another high-tide wave unfurls close to your restless, lust-prickled toes, you lean over and secure yourself higher on the dry dune, your water bottle and black North Face book-bag stuffed an hour ago with your seduction supplies: travel-size chessboard, pack of Marlboro Lights, Spanish-riddled Cormac McCarthy novel (which, due to your dyslexia, you've struggled with for nearly a month), Sony Discman and pair of miniature speakers, five self-mixed, computer-burned, thematically titled CDs (*Caligula, Dharma Groove, Faster Pussycat to the Library, Crash & Burn*, and *Music for the Bong*), $100 in pesos, deck of Red Bicycle playing cards, and what's left of the quarter ounce of marijuana you brought from New York. You turn back to the cove and size up Greta's curvy shoulders beneath her refastened bikini top. Seated and facing the horizon, heels digging into the wet sand, thighs and shins covered again by the maroon sarong, she shields her eyes from the setting sun. The prickling rises up your brainstem. *Oh man—what was my sex vow again? Respecting the Six Perfections seems so much easier when I'm sitting cross-legged on a zabuton.* Struggling neophyte Buddhist that you are, you push a hand through your hair, blow out a breath, and dutifully remind yourself about the cause-and-effect reality of karma, and the Buddha's maxim that sensual pleasure is like saltwater: the more you indulge, the more the thirst increases.

"Puh—it is so hot," Greta declares, kicking up beach sand as she marches past you up the dune towards the rustic Sendero compound. Your head swivels as she works her way over the dune's bosomy crest into the palm-tree shadows around her cabaña, drops her sandals onto its sun-bleached porch, and disappears behind the cabin's swinging door with a fleeting smile aimed your way. You glance back at the ocean and scratch your skull. *Did she know that I was sitting here all along?*

You first laid eyes on Greta shortly after your arrival in Zipolite Tuesday afternoon. Trudging from the Sendero registration hut with your backpacks and photo equipment, already sunburned from the hour-long hike along the beach from San Augustinillo, you caught sight of her swinging in a hammock and reading a paperback novel. You paused before unlocking the neighboring cabaña, jiggling your oversized key to get her attention and conspicuously tilting your head in order to see the book's title. Without saying anything, she straightened the cover for you. Rainer Maria Rilke's *Die Aufzeichnungen des Malte Laurids Brigge.* "Ah," you responded knowingly, though the only book by Rilke you've read is *Letters to a Young Poet.* "Do you speak English?"

Greta's blue eyes returned to the weathered pages. With the hint of a smirk she replied, "That depends to whom I speak."

That night, showered and dressed in your multipocketed cargo shorts, mala beads, and a new Hugo Boss ocher-colored, short-sleeved linen shirt purchased expressly for the trip, the loaded Elan slung low around your neck, you joined her for dinner at the beachfront La Chosa Restaurant—its wooden tables set up directly on the sand, the waves breaking fewer than ten meters away—a boisterous, eclectic-looking group of European backpackers and local artisans eating seafood and drinking cuba libres from plastic cups. A boombox hanging by rope from the thatched roof blasted American rock music. Everyone at the table was barefoot and tan. Most smoked cigarettes. Several were already drunk. Though you were the oldest and palest of the assemblage, after two drinks you felt comfortable. To your right sat a woman named Kaja, an amber-eyed vendor of Mexican silver in Austria who wore a green halter top and a black headband high on her forehead, her tousled brown hair erupting skyward like the plume of a volcano. To your left sat a young Oaxacan painter named Morro, almost feline-looking with his black goatee and ponytail, who warned you of the dangers of Zipolite's notorious surf: "Every day someone gets in trouble with the undertow," he said. "We average here at least one drowning a month."

Between mouthfuls of red snapper and steaming corn tortillas, you slurped *sopa de mariscos* from an enormous bowl that appeared before you out of nowhere. While at La Chosa, in part because of the noise and commotion and free-flowing rum-and-Cokes, you failed to keep your "meal mindfulness" vow (suggested by your ailing Dharma teacher, Christopher Wolf, whom you plan to join on retreat later this month), to always lower your spoon or fork between bites. (To be mindful is to be full of Mind—Buddha Nature—your higher, omniscient Self. The nature of Mind is like pond water, Christopher had explained: unstirred, it remains clear. And you've been stirring relentlessly for years.) You were further distracted by the spectacle of Greta, laughing and drinking with the South African motorcyclist at the far end of the table. Wolfing down another tortilla, you sized up Greta's tight white T-shirt and faded jeans, the beaded necklaces, the loose blond braid. You stared and stared until you finally made eye contact. The blue-eyed Berliner responded with a coy smile and subtle nod and shortly came around the table and demanded that you join her with the handful of others who had begun to dance in the sand.

The dinner and dancing lasted until well after two in the morning. Once most of the candles guttered and the music died down and the few revelers who remained at the restaurant were either napping or drinking coffee, you asked Greta—who had mentioned during a slow dance that she played chess—if she had enough energy left for a quick game.

"Do we play for money or for fame?" she replied, catching her breath back at the table, squinting at you a little drunkenly as she accepted another Marlboro Light.

"Both—come," you said, rising. "Walk with me and we'll go get my chessboard."

After a silent, self-conscious stroll up the empty, unlit stretch of beach to the Sendero compound, you ushered Greta past the smelly communal bathroom, up three steps, around a hammock, and through the swinging door of your cabaña. "Puh—Carter, you have so much . . . *stuff,*" she announced, tiptoeing over a folded tripod and a stack of film canisters. A dozen lenses and four camera bodies spilled from the two opened Anvil cases onto your unmade bed. Your unzipped Tumi duffel bag lay on the pine floor, surrounded by neatly flattened shirts, pants, and boxer shorts.

You tossed the Elan onto the mattress. "I like things to air out," you explained.

With her dark, blond-wisped arms crossed at her belly, her braid further loosened from the walk, Greta stood before you, waiting expectantly, close enough in the cramped cabin space for you to feel her breath on your face, inhale in its warmth the cuba libres, and smell on her damp skin the odor of sweat and cigarettes and the sea. She was almost as tall as you, her sleepy blue eyes looking at you with curiosity. Both of you wondered why you'd invited her to walk back to the cabañas. The cock of her head, the exposure of her neck, the vaguely amused smile all suggested that she was game for whatever you desired. For several tense moments you listened to each other breathing, your indecision palpable. "Do I want to be a bodhisattva or nibble on those Saxon breasts?" you asked yourself. "Couldn't we fuck *mindfully?*" Despite your bristly tumescence you refrained from touching her, and when she moved closer to the bed you took a protective step backwards.

Seeing among the camera bodies a small plastic baggie containing marijuana, Greta asked in a whisper, "You smoke the mota?"

"On occasion, yeah. You?"

Greta held the baggie up to the bare bulb dangling from the slowly rotating ceiling fan. "No. It makes me—hmm—how do you say—daft. Crazy. In Germany, people who smoke to get high, you know, smoke the hashish." She scrunched her nose and returned the baggie to the mattress where she found it. "You have no worry to be arresting?"

"To be arrested? No. Not really." You shrugged, cleared your throat. "I mean, I wouldn't take weed into someplace like Africa—they catch you carrying dope in Africa, they'll throw you in a dungeon. And I *never* try to bring it back into the States. Never. If I have any left, which I usually do—I don't smoke all that much, really—I just give it away. I'll travel with—at most—at *most*—a quarter ounce, which is *more* than plenty for a week or two." You winced at how defensive you sounded. "It's not a big deal."

Smiling opaquely, Greta continued staring at you until you grabbed the chessboard. You averted your eyes from the straining white cotton of her T-shirt, leaned towards the unlatched door, cleared your throat again, and asked, eyebrows raised, "You about ready?"

In February you'll turn thirty-nine. Five years ago a female editorial manager at *Elle* told you over dinner that she thought thirty-six was the red-flag age for never-married heterosexual bachelors, a red flag (as you understood her explanation) that signaled in most females' eyes a man's fundamental difficulty with commitment and perhaps even an unhealthy regard for women. In a word: broken. You've questioned for half a decade whether this assessment is true of you. Though you've not had a steady girlfriend in three years, you feel okay about your love life, which you would semi-seriously describe as semi-serial monogamy. All in all, your life is . . . okay. You've been told that you're handsome, and no longer need constant confirmation that it's true. You sleep well. You rarely get sick.

You volunteer at the Chelsea AIDS Hospice. You hope one day to be a father, and understand that to be a good father you must first be a good husband. And for the last six months you've been attentive to your daily Dharma practice, which consists of a self-concocted pastiche of cardiovascular exercise, seated meditation, mantra chanting, precept vows, and (with an increasingly strained rationale) moderate marijuana consumption.

In fact, the shot of yours that will eventually be chosen to accompany the *Details* article was taken less than an hour after Wednesday morning's palm-shaded meditation. You would like to think the two events were connected. While trolling through Zipolite for more pictures, a little bow and Buddha-like half-smile bestowed upon everyone who crossed your path, you came upon the Franco-Czech painter with the unpronounceable name as she practiced yoga on the beach. The moment you looked through the Elan's viewfinder at the small Sanskrit tattoo between her shoulder blades you knew that this would be the image. Indeed, the shot that will be printed in the magazine was the first exposure of the first roll of the two you devoted to her waterfront Hatha postures. 50-speed Fuji film, exposed at f/2.8 with a shutter speed of 1⁄90th of a second. Though you won't like the art director's final cropping (her legs get cut off too close to her sand-covered gym shorts), the original asymmetrical composition—her lithe back to the viewer, arms akimbo, her blue tube top a shade darker than the aquamarine bay, the hillside Sendero cabañas hovering in the frame over her right shoulder, a pair of pelicans positioned so perfectly beneath a lone cumulus cloud you feared they would look digitally manipulated—will be maintained and work effectively, you'll feel, with the stylized tone of the article. "It's the symbol for the mantra Om," the painter explained of her year-old tattoo over the crabmeat *quesadillas* and Negra Modelos with which you repaid her, twisting her shoulders sideways to give you a closer look. Greta watched the two of you from behind her sunglasses and Rilke novel at a corner table.

"My boyfriend says he wants me to get his initials tattooed on my ankle. I think he might be serious."

Late Wednesday afternoon you caught your first sight of Greta skinny-dipping in the breakers. Early Wednesday evening you invited her to dinner. By midnight, before a small driftwood campfire on a quiet dune near the Sendero compound, you and Greta found yourselves squared off again across your chessboard, a peso and a surprisingly savvy hermit crab serving as White's two missing bishops. Greta was in her purple sarong and the same white T-shirt from the previous night, with a light bone-colored shawl pulled over her shoulders. Between moves you discussed German fashion designers and your favorite non-American films—*The Bicycle Thief, Nosferatu, Lawrence of Arabia.* By the beginning of your second game—you lost the first one, Greta explained, because of your overly aggressive rooks—all of the open-air cafés on the beach had turned their lights off for the night.

Though neither of you revealed much during your two hours together on the empty, moonlit beach, you learned that Greta had apprenticed as a sous chef in one of Kaspar Reist's first restaurants in Barcelona and, prior to this trip to Mexico (she'd been working her way along the Oaxacan coast for the previous two months), was employed in Berlin's four-star Kresbach Kaffe. Already two pawns down, you tried to distract her with questions about life in the kitchen.

"So, what's your favorite taste?" you asked.

"My favorite taste?" she repeated absently, her eyes scanning the board. "Hmm . . . I love much the taste of a fresh strawberry filled with Campari. I love all foods that must need both of the hands to eat."

As Greta looked up after her move to see your response to your now-forked queen, both of you turned your heads towards the barking of beach dogs on the southern end of the shore, your attention drawn to a ragtag gang of *federales* approaching your campfire with flashlights and loosely slung rifles. "Shit," you muttered, quickly burying in the sand the joint you'd hoped to smoke with Greta before the evening came to a close.

"Should we go from the beach, Carter?"

You shook your head and tried to slow your breathing. "No. If we run, they'll think we're doing something we're not. You're not carrying anything illegal, are you?"

Within moments you were surrounded by the six Mexican soldiers or policemen—you were unsure which—one of whom gestured with his rifle for you to stand. Though the *federales* wore military-style boots and green camouflage fatigues, two of them were in T-shirts, and one had a pistol casually tucked into his waistband. All of them smelled of alcohol. You suspected, correctly, that the men had snuck off from their barracks in Puerto Angel to shake down dope-toting backpackers here in Zipolite.

You knew the routine. Without prompting, you interlaced your fingers atop your head and spread your legs. You tried hard not to look down at the black boot crunching sand within inches of the hidden pot, but this meant either closing your eyes or squinting into the flashlights. Greta remained seated while one of the men toppled the chessboard with the butt of his rifle and then rummaged through her straw bag. Another wet his lips and ogled her body. Half hidden in the darkness, their eyes shining red in the firelight, the agitated beach dogs continued to bark.

"¿Usted habla español?"

You nodded at the smallest member of the gang, the one carrying the enormous pistol in his waistband, apparently the leader, and frowned as he rabbit-eared your front pockets. *"Sí,"* you mumbled. *"Un poco."*

After sniffing your money-clip for the smell of cannabis, he shone his flashlight in your face and demanded, *"¿Porqué usted necesita este dinero en la playa?"*

"Para cervezas," you explained, your heart thumping against your rib cage. *"Para comida."*

"Tiene su pasaporte?"

"No."

Your heart began pounding even harder: a pinched end of the white, pinkie-sized joint had emerged from the sand.

"Es un americano?" the pistol-toter demanded with an aggressive, upward thrust of his chin, his eyes glassy and filled with liquor-fueled anger. The guy's pissed off at the poor pay of his day job, you figured. Pissed off that he's a foot shorter than the average American male.

"No," you lied. *"Yo vivo en el Canadá."*

After squeezing your back pockets, the fellow grunted, gave your eyes a final scan with his flashlight, and tossed your money onto the chessboard.

"¿Estamos bien?" you asked, relaxing a little.

"Está bien."

Your heart slowed once the men and their flashlights disappeared around the northern point of the beach, the dogs no longer barking. Hands still interlaced on your head, you glanced down at Greta, who hadn't moved and looked shaken up.

"You okay?"

There were tears in her eyes. She covered her mouth as her shawled shoulders began to shake with frightened, uncontrollable laughter. "Oh my God, Carter. Who *were* these men?"

You ran all ten fingers through the length of your hair and shrugged. "I'm guessing a bunch of sailors from the naval base over in Puerto Angel. Either that or La Chosa's kitchen staff is really well armed." You held a hand out for her. "You about ready to call it a night?"

After gathering the chessboard and empty beer bottles (and discreetly returning the crumpled joint to a back pocket), you kicked sand over the dwindling fire and quietly escorted Greta back to the Sendero compound, half disappointed that you hadn't gotten arrested.

"May we finish our game tomorrow?" she asked at the unlatched door to her cabaña, shivering a little, her shawl pulled tight, her eyes gazing into yours.

You felt feckless and more self-loathing than usual. "No," you answered with a friendly smirk: you both knew that with a forked queen you would have resigned had the game not been interrupted. "Sleep well." Giving Greta's upper arm a reassuring squeeze, you winked and departed to your own cabaña to smoke the joint, and maybe another, and nap for the few hours that remained until dawn.

Thursday afternoon, shortly after lunch, you exposed four final rolls of color film in Zipolite's village and then packed your gear for Friday's departure. You'd not seen Greta all day. Intent on finding a dinner companion for your last evening in Mexico, you showered, shaved, brushed your teeth, stuffed the North Face daypack, and, leaving your mala beads on your makeshift altar (consisting of a small Manjushri statue, a picture of the Dalai Lama snipped from the fall issue of *Tricycle*, and a white seashell), set off down the beach in your cargo shorts and the last of your new linen shirts. For an hour you prowled the beachfront cafés in search of the dark-eyebrowed Franco-Czech painter (whose name, as best you could figure out yesterday, is either Martinovka or Marovtinka), before spotting Greta and her book on the empty shore near the Sendero compound. Rather than wave, you decided to perch yourself on a dune behind her—the better to keep your dining options open.

You spied on Greta for almost an hour before she disrobed and plunged into the water to cool off. And after she marched past you en route to her cabaña, dripping wet and surprising you with her coy smile and comment about the weather, you remained on the dune for another fifteen minutes, flat on your stomach, alternately staring at Greta's white towel and damp black bathing suit draped over the railing, and her shadowy movements behind the shutters.

In recent weeks you've wondered if it isn't better for people to always think of themselves in second person, to fully disassociate their awareness from the obstructing, lower-self "I" that thinks in terms of "me" and "mine" and "may I unbutton your blouse now, please?" You tell yourself again that to spiritualize your desires, you must desire to be without desire. That the spiritual path takes willpower. In your heart you know the truth of this, that you're the captain of your fate, that who you are right now is based on what you did in the past, and that who you'll be in the future is determined by what you do next. Nevertheless, you sigh and flip onto your side, scratch your belly, and stare hungrily at the partially opened door to Greta's cabaña, the warmth draining promptly from your heart into your loins, the lust suctioned southwards so forcefully that you sit up, remove your sunglasses, and let out a long, miserable groan.

Ten minutes later you bang on Greta's door with the side of your bare left foot. Day bag slung over your shoulders, chessboard in one hand, an ice-chilled six-pack of Negra Modelos in the other, you beam broadly as your blond-haired prey swings open the portal and invites you to enter.

Twenty minutes after your arrival, two beers already under your belt, your rolling papers and lighter tossed on the mattress, you lean back in the cabin's one chair and watch Greta examine the labels of the self-mixed CDs you brought for the Discman, now unpacked and positioned strategically with its two miniature speakers on her bed's headboard. Most of Greta's dark, dewy skin is now hidden beneath the sarong and a man's long-sleeved cotton shirt. Apple-scented lip balm adds to her smile a sexy shine. While you crumble the biggest, red-fringed bud from your baggie into a snorkeling mask secured between your knees, Greta flips over and reads the band list for *Dharma Groove*: "Big

Head Todd. Portishead. Morphine. Soul Coughing. What is this Soul Coughing?"

You pause from rolling the joint and open for Greta a second beer. "Nasty funk."

"No—what does it mean? 'Soul coughing'?"

"I guess it means a really deep cough."

Greta nods unsurely and continues reading: "The Charlie Hunter Trio. Cocteau Twins. Erykah Badu. Mmm—I like her. The Latin Playboys. Thievery Corporation. Carter, I know none of these bands. Are they American?"

"Some. You've never heard of Portishead?"

Greta shrugs, sips the new beer, and shakes her head. Spotting the red Bicycle deck among the items tactically extruded from your bag onto her bed, she asks, "Do you play the cards?"

"I do. Wanta see a trick?"

"Yah—of course. Please."

You scoot your chair closer to where Greta sits on the bed's edge. Joint lit but as yet unoffered, you shuffle and then nonchalantly cut the deck with a single hand, fanning the cards face-down with a graceful, "ooh"-inspiring sweep. "Pick a card," you tell her. "Any card." Made nervous by your card-handling skills, Greta examines and cautiously inserts her selection back into the deck. You shuffle the cards three more times, flip the deck over, and present her with the bottom card: the Jack of Clubs. "Is this your card?"

Greta shakes her head. "No."

As you show her each of the next three possibilities, you ask, "Is *this* your card?"

"No," she replies repeatedly, unsure if the trick is unfolding as you intended, though confident that her card is not among the four you place face-down before her on the mattress.

You hand Greta the remainder of the deck. To verify that her selection is not among those you've shown her, you reveal the four cards again, confirming with each as you turn it over, "This is not your card—correct?"

"No," she replies, crossing her arms and shaking her head. "None of those are my card."

You arch an eyebrow, make a show of rolling up your nonexistent sleeves, and dramatically extend for inspection your empty palms. "Choose a number between one and four."

"And tell you?"

"Mm-hmm."

". . . Three."

Pointing to the row with an index finger, you count from right to left to the third card. You take a long, theatrical breath, administer with your fingertips an ambiguously magical *smack*, and with a flourish flip the card over to reveal that—voilà—it has become the card she'd selected: the Queen of Hearts.

Greta clutches her chest and instinctively leans away from you. "Oh, my God—Carter. How is this so?" Mouth gaping, eyes wide, she inspects the remaining three cards with disbelief. "How did you do this?"

You answer darkly, "Magic," promptly gathering and returning the repacked deck of cards to the depths of your bag, as Greta grabs your arm and implores you to show her another of your tricks.

"Please," she begs, but you lower your eyes and wag your head: a good performer always leaves his audience wanting more.

You sigh with satisfaction, thoroughly delighted with yourself, and then take a long, deep drag of the joint, exhale a stream of smoke towards the ceiling fan, and ask, "You wanta try some of this?"

Thirty minutes later the two of you are naked and in bed. Six empty bottles of Negra Modelo are clustered in the corner behind your discarded shirt and cargo shorts. The tangled mosquito net lies on the floor. Greta moves onto her stomach on the mattress beside you, wearing nothing but her beaded necklace, lightheaded from the beer and her first puffs of marijuana in two years. Eyes closed, she rolls her head and hums along with Erykah Badu.

You start with Greta's neck. Pushing aside her hair, still damp from the ocean, her face sideways on the pillow, you lean over and press your lips against the very top of her neck, right at the base of her skull, her skin smelling faintly of salt and brine. With your lips you press large moist circles down the bones of her neck, a lazy roll of warm water that causes her shoulders to tighten and her eyes to clamp even tighter.

You gaze at Greta's feet, at her hips lifted slightly from the white sheet, at her arms crossed above her head and the blond hair under her arms, moist with sweat. Seagulls squawk over the breakers. You dislike that the shutters are open—you see down the beach, a quarter mile away, a handful of young, dark-skinned, bare-chested boys playing soccer. Even with your face returning to her neck you can smell the scent of her arousal, your lips wet against her ear, pushing your mouth closer to the trembling quickly spreading through her shoulders.

You hear yourself whisper, more breath than voice, "Does this feel good?"

"Mm-hmm."

You kiss her shoulder blades, her neck. "How about here?"

"Mm-hmm."

You raise yourself to your knees and sit prayer-rug fashion between Greta's long legs. You trace a finger down Greta's back, along the flare of her hips, the tight muscles of her bottom clenching as your finger touches her tailbone—lightly—then lifts away from the moisture between her legs and retraces the path again, slower this time. Greta looks over her shoulder at you with deep, almost childlike attentiveness. On your knees, aroused, you gaze with interest at Greta's profile, her long thick lashes upturned, her chin raised, lips parted as her breathing intensifies, her damp blond hair swept back against the pillow. You reach up, stretching towards the rackety ceiling fan, and then move your legs forward, hands on her hips, sliding your left thigh against her crotch. Greta laughs softly, startled by the presumption of your touch, but she pushes back, gently, shy, testing herself, moving with a sigh and the slightest widening of her legs against your thigh muscle, wetting your skin with her movement, three or four inches in both directions, her hungry breathing louder now, her arms and hands working against the mattress, helping her push against your leg, her back arched, her head raised slightly, eyes clamped again, breasts brushing—just barely—against the pillow. She murmurs German words you don't understand, the trembling moving through her hips, her legs tensing, her toes curling. A coconut tumbles through the palm tree branches above the bungalow, crashing through the leaves onto the sand with a dramatic thump. You both pause, look at each other wide-eyed and chuckling, before Greta bites her bottom lip and continues pushing against your leg, groaning, the movement a slow dance to slow music as she now imagines it, no one else on the dance floor, not even you, oblivious to the rising breeze and the drumming lifted from somewhere down the beach, oblivious to the growing volume of her own breathing, her back arching deeper, her breasts swaying fully against the mattress, sun-freckles on her shoulders, her shoulder blades moving under her dark skin, forming and then re-forming perfectly symmetrical angles—her muscles and bones so sharply defined that you reach for them, aching with desire, pulling her up by the tops of her arms with more force than you expect.

"Look at me," you whisper.

In the same motion Greta rolls over and faces you on her back, belly against belly now, eyes focused and locked. You smile conspiratorially at the heat and self-awareness of your arousal, but you refrain from going inside her, your motion slowing into a more tender grinding, stomach against stomach, Greta shifting her hips a little, your cheeks touching, your eyes closed, your movement ritualized and yet—you try to convince yourself—somehow uncharted. With your lips you touch Greta's chin, her eyebrows, the hollow of her throat.

"Kiss me," she murmurs, and your mouth falls against hers, the taste of beer and cigarettes hardening the kiss, heating it into something less tender, less affectionate. You feel a flicker of sadness as her arms reach across your back, hugging you, pulling you so close that you feel her heartbeat in your chest. The quivering in Greta's shoulders spills over her throat and stomach and loins, and with your tongue you move down her neck to her breasts, her belly, the blond fuzz-line beneath her navel, back up her belly to her breasts, the right breast and then the left breast, circling each with tiny, light licks. Greta's weight is on her elbows, head tilted back, eyes closed, her midriff rising and falling, her hips lifting to meet your mouth as you work your way down to the soft brown hair between her legs, untrimmed, your hands kneading her bottom as you hold her aloft, tasting the sand and saltiness of the beach unwashed from her skin. The trembling grows more violent. She tenses through her thighs, through her hips, a deep shuddering which makes you hold her to your mouth more firmly, and with a groan she collapses flat on her back. "Puh—wait—please, please," she laughs breathlessly, but you continue until the trembling returns and Greta's fingers claw the tangles of your hair. Her left hand soon leaves your skull and searches for a spot on her stomach, just below her navel, where with three fingertips she pushes in small circles deep into the muscle, a countermotion to the movement of your mouth, rubbing her stomach as you work your tongue deeper within her, remembering the touch of her first boyfriend's lips, a boy from high school, the smell of his skin, the taste of his mouth, *his* hands guiding her hips, the motion faster until—gasping—shaking her head to fight back the sound rising in her throat—she comes, the trembling dissolving into a splash of icy water against her spine, her skin alive, eyes opening, straining to focus, jaw thrust forward, breathing hard through parted lips, searching for your face, though you have not risen, and she clutches your head with her hand as she continues to come, wave after silent wave.

"Are you hungry?" you ask sleepily, as the two of you pull yourself from her bed and dress on opposite sides of the one-room cabin.

Greta shakes her head.

"I'm gonna go get something to eat," you tell her. "Do you want anything?"

After lowering herself onto the edge of the mattress, her back turned to you, Greta sighs but remains silent.

The moon is out by the time you return to Greta's cabaña with two more Negra Modelos and a plate of four fish tacos, the rolled-up soft flour tortillas steaming, the shredded shark meat inside smelling of cilantro. Though your head has begun to ache, you are foolishly pleased with yourself—not for bringing the food or for seducing Greta but for ending your stay in Zipolite without having sexual intercourse with anyone.

Back in her long-sleeved shirt and purple sarong, silent, even more pensive than when you left her, Greta stands smoking one of your cigarettes by the screenless window as you enter without knocking, set the plate of food on the wobbly wooden table, and resume your seat in the room's lone chair. The ceiling fan and Discman have been turned off. The bed is made. The mosquito netting is nowhere in sight. Unsure why you refused to make love with her, she feels queasy, her mouth dry and her eyes reddened from the cannabis.

Because you're chewing the first fish taco and already thinking of the next, you don't see that Greta is near tears. Because you have not bothered to ask, you're unaware that she has come to Mexico seeking respite from the pain of losing a miscarried child, buried in October, fathered by a boyfriend to whom she said nothing about the pregnancy for fear of jinxing it, an architect who routinely beat her in chess and who drove away with their four-year-old Audi when he moved out, without explanation, the Sunday before she lost their child—a boy she planned to name Rainer. You're unaware that on the plane ride to Oaxaca, Greta promised herself not to drink alcohol before dark or while alone, and to do her best not to fall in love with anyone—especially not a handsome American photographer who dances like a teenage boy and speaks in a sultry baritone. You're unaware that the false promise implicit in your short but intimate time together will help her decide to leave Berlin for good, to start elsewhere what she hopes might be a better life, that she will eventually marry a wealthy estate lawyer in Paris, fifteen years her senior, with a thirst for saltwater worse than yours, that because of her marriage to this man she will never again work professionally as a chef, a loss that will lead her to give up on her drinking vows altogether, and that she will die while scuba-diving alone in the Mediterranean Sea on her fortieth birthday.

You're halfway through eating a second fish taco before you speak. Wiping your lips with a finger, you notice the line of ants crawling across the straw mat beneath your feet. "You okay over there?" Greta nods but remains turned towards the darkened sky. You glance at her opened duffel bag, at the stack of her paperbacks leaning against the wall. "Would you like to see a picture of my dog Marley?" Before she can respond, you withdraw from the back pocket of your cargo shorts your passport holder, and from that a wrinkled 3" × 5" self-portrait of you and your shaggy, eight-year-old mongrel—adopted from the pound shortly after your arrival in New York City in 1994—dressed as Batman and Robin for last Halloween's East Village street festival. Marley, looking up goofily at the automated flashbox, wears four little green boots, a red cape, and a crooked gold mask. Greta smiles politely, the image bringing more tears to her eyes, which force her to blink and tilt back her head lest they spill.

"He is a cute dog, Carter," she says, stepping away. "He looks like he is a good friend to you."

You lean back in the chair even further, returning the picture and passport to your pocket, the pond water stirred once again, willfully oblivious to what Greta is feeling, and give the North Face bag—half hidden beneath the bed—a nudge with your toe. You fear Greta expects you to spend the night with her.

"I like your hair, Carter," she says wistfully, turning back after wiping her eyes, gamely trying to change the subject as she reaches down to touch your bangs. "How do you make it to do this?"

"Turn gray?"

"Puhh—no, it's so—mmmm . . . how do you say, it's—"

"Messy? I don't do anything, really. It just comes out this way."

Arms crossed below her belly, she asks, "What will you do with the pictures you took of me?"

You clear your throat and think hard for a moment. "I don't know," you answer, which is more true than not. "I just messenger all the rolls to my editor."

"You are a photographer for newspapers?"

"No—for magazines. Nothing serious. If they use any of my shots of you, they'll let you know. They'll probably mail you a couple of contributor's copies."

Greta gazes out the window at the ocean and moon. Dogs are barking on the beach again. "Hmmm. I have to smile about myself some—I *hate* being looked at with a camera. It takes your soul, you know? It possesses you. And I saw you with so many other women."

You look down at the plate, which now holds only one of the original four fish tacos. You smack your lips and wince, tasting in the back of your throat the biliousness, the weakness, that would lead drunken *federales* to menace a woman on the beach, and begin to understand why Peter O'Toole's self-hating Lawrence, bloodied by a battle wound, would nod and mumble, "Good, good." With an embarrassed shrug, forearm drying your chin, you smile feebly and extend the plate towards Greta—but it's too late: arms still crossed, she's turned fully to the sea and sky. She's no longer listening to you. She's no longer thinking of you. She's no longer even in the room. She's in the future. And the future, she realizes, has not come out quite as she had hoped.

2

THE SECOND WEEKEND AFTER returning from Mexico you head by train from Grand Central Station north along the Hudson River to an area near Woodstock for a two-day meditation retreat titled "Compassion and Wisdom: The Path of the Bodhisattva." The nineteen rolls of unprocessed film have been delivered by bike messenger to your editor at *Details*. Your sunburned nose has finished peeling, and your bowels no longer grumble when you drink draft beer. Your cantankerous, seventy-four-year-old neighbor, Mrs. Pierno, once again agreed to keep Marley in her apartment while you're out of the city, the seventh time you've asked her to do so in the past twelve months. (While you were on assignment for *Maxim* in Jakarta last May, Mrs. Pierno was stuck with Marley for seventeen days, six days longer than she'd expected.) Ten minutes before leaving for Grand Central on Friday afternoon, you bestowed upon your bathrobe-clad neighbor a droolingly out-of-breath Marley, an already-opened ten-pound bag of his poultry-flavored Power Dog mix, his water and food bowls, a rubber ball, and a $20 bill for "emergencies" (namely Mrs. Pierno's thirst for Gallo wine coolers). "Where's his friggin' leash?" she demanded, her gravelly voice inflected with more Italian than genuine anger, reaching up to smack your shoulder with her rolled up *Post* loud enough to make you wince.

Your chief rationale for not paying your widowed neighbor, much less for hiring a professional walker, is that Mrs. Pierno initially *volunteered* to care for Marley, claimed that she was more than happy for the company, and seemed genuinely saddened to give him back after his first couple of stays. Although you usually bring her a token of your appreciation (most recently a turtle made of painted seashells purchased at the Mexico City airport), and assume that she would say something if she didn't enjoy your dog's company (and he *does* give her some exercise), you still feel pangs of guilt for taking advantage of her. You know that it can't be easy for a four-foot-nine, seventy-four-year-old woman with stage-two osteoporosis to follow the forty-pound Marley behind his leash up and down five flights of stairs and around the block twice a day, especially when the sidewalks are covered, as they are now, with slushy snow and ice.

"You're a sweetheart," you assured her, bags in hand, bopping *her* shoulder with the retrieved leash. "I'll be back Sunday night."

With a tug to his collar, Mrs. Pierno shepherded Marley through the door and into her den, muttering over her shoulder, "Yeah. I'll believe it when I see it."

Though this will be your second Buddhist meditation retreat, you're still uneasy about sitting and chanting with a *sangha*, most of whom, you assume, are more advanced than you. But you've been told by Christopher that meditating with others is so essential to the Dharma (the Sanskrit term for the doctrine of Buddhism), that the *sangha*—any community of Buddhists—is considered one of the Three Jewels used to reach enlightenment.

This weekend's "Compassion and Wisdom" retreat is being led by Christopher's "root guru," (a reincarnated Tibetan *tulku* named Jamyang Khyentse Rinpoche), on the one-hundred-acre grounds of a former Catholic monastery thirty minutes by cab from the train station nearest Woodstock. Night has fallen by the time you arrive.

You're bundled in your only non-leather winter jacket, the Tumi duffel bag in one hand, a small photo case slung over the opposite shoulder. Eventually you find the registration desk in a lobby near the snow-covered chapel. With some trepidation you note in the registration folder that Saturday night there will be a formal Manjushri empowerment. Behind you in line you recognize from your previous weekend retreat a handsome African-American woman, in her early thirties, you estimate, with light-brown eyes, a backpacker's physique, and mala beads looped around her neck. She returns your hello with a silent, uninterested bow.

Folder in hand, you search out your room. Down the corridor you smell incense. Sniffing—it's jasmine—you poke your head inside the empty, candlelit chapel and see that the space has been converted into a makeshift shrine room: meditation cushions in place of pews, a large green *thangka* tapestry hanging above the sacristy, a gold-leafed statue of the Buddha serving as the altar's centerpiece. You're not certain what to make of the fact that sixty Tibetan Buddhist meditators have taken over a Catholic monastery in upstate New York for the weekend, though you think it speaks well of both religions. (You remember a news clip of the Dalai Lama preparing to deliver a teaching at the Rosicrucian Temple in Helsinki in 1988 by making three prostrations towards the seat from which he'd speak, behind which stood a life-sized statue of Christ.) You pass only one other retreatant as you leave the chapel, glancing up at the steeple and cross as you tromp through the snow and enter the adjacent building. The red-carpeted hallway in the men's dormitory is lined with faded paintings of stern-looking cardinals and saints. The single-room "cell" you requested (shared rooms were only $40 less expensive) is on the dormitory's second floor and consists of a small, very firm bed, a musty closet with two wooden hangers, a portable space-heater, a nightstand, and a low-wattage lamp. The door has no lock. The men's communal bathroom—presently empty—is directly across the hall.

Unnerved by the monastery's silence, barefoot and cross-legged atop the bed, duffel bag and cameras stowed in the shadows beneath the table, your "travel Buddha" (a gift from Christopher) resting on the windowsill beside the lamp, you peruse the precepts page in the registration folder, which states formally that retreatants must not use alcohol or drugs nor engage in sexual activity for the duration of the weekend. In addition, retreatants take a Vow of Noble Silence and should refrain from reading, writing, listening to music, or speaking to the other retreatants, even during meals in the dining hall. Already you miss your stereo and bong. You sigh and stare through the frosted glass at the stars and snow-covered pine trees.

Christopher Wolf's biography on the back page of the booklet catches your eye. He is one of three Western teachers assisting Jamyang Khyentse Rinpoche this weekend, and your friendship with him is the chief reason you're attending. "Born in London, UK, in 1947 to Protestant missionaries. Grew up in rural province of northern China. As teen in China took Refuge Vows and, later, at Queen's College in Cotswold, earned degree in Tibetan Buddhist Studies. From 1975–1979 studied in Burma as ordained monk under guidance of Sayadaw U Pandita. Fluent in Tibetan, Sanskrit, and Mandarin Chinese. Since 1990 has taught in the United States and England with His Eminence Jamyang Khyentse Rinpoche. Well known for his sense of humor, Christopher is a much beloved Dharma teacher!"

Over the last six months you've heard some amazing things from Christopher, especially since his last hospitalization, about Jamyang Khyentse Rinpoche, who some believe is a fully realized Buddha, which means—if you understand the term correctly—that, although still a human being, he is omniscient and without any semblance of an ego. Born in Tibet, Jamyang Khyentse Rinpoche is a meditation master in the Nyingma order, whose lineage of *tulku* incarnations can be traced back to the sixteenth century. Since his imprisonment by the Chinese from 1962 until 1971, he has resided in India and France, and twice a year travels to North America to lead meditation retreats. According to the retreat's schedule, His Eminence will personally perform Saturday night's Manjushri empowerment.

After a bland vegetarian supper in the full but eerily quiet dining hall—some of the retreatants lifting their forks and spoons in what looks to you like ultraslow motion (to a visitor, you decide, a silent Buddhist retreat must look like an insane asylum on mute)—you venture to the reception area outside the shrine room and nervously sip a cup of peppermint tea as you await Friday evening's final forty-minute group meditation. Once most of the other retreatants file past, you remove your shoes, bow deeply and somewhat self-consciously at the threshold of the shrine room, and secure a cushion on the pale wooden floor a few feet from the back wall. Grimacing with the effort it takes to sit and fold your legs into a half-lotus position (a posture you rarely attempt at home), you inhale the familiar smell of Nag Champa incense wafting from the altar, take a few deep breaths and look around. On the wall to your left hangs a blue-and-gold silk-framed Manjushri *thangka*.

Last Sunday, during your weekly dinner, Christopher explained that Manjushri is the Bodhisattva of Wisdom. As is the norm with a depiction of Manjushri, the deity's right hand hoists a double-edged sword with which he "slices through the darkness of ignorance." In his left hand he holds a blooming lotus, which symbolically ties him to "the wisdom of the sutras," the teachings of Siddhartha Gautama, the historical Buddha, who lived in India six centuries before the birth of Christ. When you asked if Manjushri is considered a god, Christopher assured you that images of the Buddha and other Buddhist deities shouldn't be viewed as images of divinities ("Most bloody Westerners don't realize that Buddhism and Hinduism are no more polytheistic than Christianity") but rather as visual reminders of our "own Buddha Nature."

"Think of the Dharma in terms of dancing," he told you with a playful exaggeration of his Chelsea-influenced brogue. *Tombs of dawn-sin.* "You know the heebie jeebies most of us get when we first stumble onto the dance floor? That's the ego-driven *shit* we feel through much of our lives. Ham-fisted. Trapped in our bodies. Face like a wet weekend from all the worry about how we look." *Hah way luck.* "But if and when we allow ourselves to breathe deeply, to let go and not give a bloody toss, by the second song our muscles have loosened and we close our eyes and lose ourselves in the flow of the music. That second song is the Dharma."

So, what *is* Buddhism exactly? You often wonder about this when you sit down to meditate back home. If it's true that the Buddha isn't a god, and that one can practice the Dharma and also be a Christian or Jew or even an atheist, should Buddhism be considered a religion? What are the implications of a belief system having survived, essentially unchanged, for twenty-five centuries? You've even heard that Albert Einstein was an advocate of the Dharma. And what's with the "Bardo Realm" and the "Six Realms of Rebirth"? Is there *really* a hell? And what exactly is a *tulku?* For the last six months you've been a fish-eating vegetarian and have read a dozen books on Tibetan Buddhism, but sometimes you feel as if you're drowning in all the terminology. Christopher suggested that you quit reading spiritual texts for a while, though the very next book you bought offered helpful advice: "Do not struggle to place your mind around a concept of the Divine. Rather, rest in the knowledge that the Divine is all around you." Go figure.

You glance across the shrine room at a shelf holding flickering votive candles, fruit offerings, a statue of White Tara (a symbol of the feminine aspect of one's Buddha Nature), and a framed photograph of the Dalai Lama. "All humans by nature are Buddhas, as ice by its nature is water," Christopher once said. "Buddhahood is like the sun, and the ego is like a dark cloud blocking the view. Even though you might not see the sun in the sky, it's always there, Carter. That's what 'Buddha' means—to have awakened to this truth. Everyone has the potential to become a Buddha. Everyone. Even you, love."

You notice that most of the other retreatants have brought their own zabutons. Most congregate near the dais. A stylishly disheveled lot, you observe, many of your fellow Buddhists stream into the shrine room for this last sitting of the retreat's first night wearing baggy yoga pants and untucked silk blouses. One or two perform full, almost languorous prostrations before the altar—a genuinely respectful gesture that you nonetheless dismiss as extravagant and showy. You watch these other Buddhists, noting their subdued and reverent air, the confidence with which they adjust their meditation cushions and silently perform their Refuge Vows. You sigh and wipe your moist palms on your knees.

The forty-minute meditation does not go well. Though you keep your eyes shut and count breaths until a thrice-rung bell brings the session to a close, your brain bounces from one worry to another, and continues bouncing long after you return to your cell, curl up on your tiny bed, and with a weary groan reach over and kill the light.

Saturday morning you skip breakfast and wander through the snow-covered woods taking pictures. Saturday afternoon you skip the second of the day's two teaching sessions to stay in your cell and finish reading the Cormac McCarthy novel you smuggled in. Saturday evening—despite still feeling self-conscious meditating in the company of others—you resolve, reluctantly, to get dressed and attend the Manjushri empowerment.

The wordless commotion of the growing crowd in the shrine room has a gentle, excited energy to it, accentuated by the hypnotic chiming of Tibetan singing bowls piped over a hidden sound system. You return to your place near the back wall and take a seat on the same red cushion as Friday night. Despite the vow of silence, an elderly man sitting on the zabuton beside yours whispers to you in broken English that he flew to the United States from Portugal expressly for tonight's empowerment ceremony. "I know Rinpoche on six years," he tells you, holding up all but four fingers. "Rinpoche is a Buddha." You return the old man's boyish, yellow-toothed smile and move your cushion to the left to give him a bit more leg room. His spiffy blue vest and thin black bolo tie are wonderfully over-the-top, you think, as is his Thunderbird sweep of pomaded gray hair. If the opportunity arises before the weekend is over, you'd like to approach the fellow about taking a few pictures.

Sitting directly in front of you is a diminutive brunette in an oversized black turtleneck and faded jeans, her left wrist draped with wooden rosary beads—a young woman from Austin, Texas, who will soon make your life considerably more interesting. When she turns her face in profile you note the fair, almost ghostly pallor of her skin, the intelligent cock of a black eyebrow, her long thick eyelashes, a nose so delicate and slim it appears to have been pinched by a clothespin. There's just a touch of red in her cheeks, but she wears no makeup around her eyes, and her lips seem drained of color altogether. Very serious-looking, you think—a definite book-reader. When she turns her attention back to the dais, your eyes trace the contour of her shoulder blades pressing against the black sweater, which is essentially the same color as her ponytailed hair. She has short, unpainted fingernails—a feature you've always found oddly attractive—and despite the winter weather is barefoot. On her right hand—yes, the right hand, you confirm—she wears a gold wedding band, the loop so huge against her long, slim fingers it slips loosely between the knuckles. You look again at the little crucifix around her left wrist. An attractive, unmarried, barefoot Catholic who meditates with Buddhists. How intriguing, you think, your belly percolating with the possibilities.

You will eventually discover that the young woman was originally named Tristes Matya Kelly (after Lévi-Strauss's autobiography, *Tristes Tropiques*) by her father, a tenured anthropology professor at Tulane—a handsome, teetotaling, manic-depressive, Irish atheist who, during her youth, slept most nights alone on a cot he kept in his campus office. "Matya" was his concession to the child's mother, a Hungarian-born, promiscuous, alcoholic dancer, sixteen years his junior, whom he wooed one summer in Budapest, married in a perfunctory civil ceremony in New Orleans after she got pregnant, and who begrudgingly gave birth to their one and only child—a colicky, six-pound girl—whose strongest memories of childhood are of mixing her mother's martinis (starting at age five), playing with her mother's tarot cards, and listening to the Louisiana rain. Despite being free from physical abuse, hers was nonetheless a childhood marked by isolation and neglect. Tristes Matya Kelly legally changed her name to Mia Malone two weeks after she turned eighteen, three years to the day after her father's suicide. Though she has no idea how she came up with "Mia," Malone was the maiden name of her paternal grandmother, a quiet and earnest Episcopalian schoolteacher, who lived in nearby Baton Rouge, from whom she first learned about religion and art, and whose gold wedding ring she has worn ever since the grandmother's death in 1994, at the age of eighty-one, after fifty-seven years of marriage to another equally quiet and earnest Episcopalian schoolteacher who died in his sleep six weeks after his wife's funeral.

A Cancer, some days Mia feels confident and bright. Her father told her more than once that she had an IQ of 146, and, without tutoring, she scored 1450 on her high school SAT. Other days she feels "dysfunctionally intellectual," her mind so active with questions and concerns about the world that she finds it difficult to sleep. Meditation and yoga have helped, though she's uncertain thus far about Buddhism, which she has sometimes referred to as a "cotton-candy religion."

Mia likes the definition of meditation she read recently in Thomas Merton's *Thoughts in Solitude*, a book lent to her by the monsignor of Austin's Holy Trinity Church, whom she befriended shortly after starting graduate school at the University of Texas: "All good meditative prayer is a conversion of our entire self to God. It is not a vision face to face, but a certain presence of self to Self in which, with the reverent attention of our whole being, we know Him in Whom all things have their being." For Merton and Mia Malone—good Christians both—Buddhist meditation is not unlike contemplative prayer. From a Buddhist perspective—and, if she understood the *Bhagavad Gita* correctly, also from a Hindu perspective—she's determined that "Buddha Nature," or Mind, or Brahman, or whatever one wishes to call it, is God. She hasn't a clue, however, what to make of the notion of reincarnation. And though she's comfortable meditating among these Dharma practitioners, she's decided not to partake officially in the rituals of the Manjushri empowerment.

Yesterday, when Mia arrived at the retreat with her friends from Boston, she felt like an adventurer. This morning, after praying alone in her room in the women's dormitory, she felt blue and lonely. Now, sitting comfortably but nervously in a full-lotus position on the green cushion directly in front of you (she had hoped you would end up sitting near her), she feels like a teenager with a crush.

When, from a distance, Mia first saw you arrive at the monastery Friday evening, she thought you might be the movie actor Jeff Bridges. Watching you slog outside in the snow this morning with a pair of expensive-looking cameras, she thought you might be the photographer Peter Beard. Tonight, as you entered the shrine room with a quick bow and lingered self-consciously nearby, she quickly made her hair more presentable by gathering it as best she could into a ponytail.

Up close you appear to Mia youger than she initially guessed. Thirty-five, perhaps? Feigning interest in the *thangka* hanging behind you, she looks over her shoulder at you (twice), both times returning your polite smile with one of her own. Although she still finds you attractive, in her estimation you smell too good and are too tan to be trustworthy, you expose a bit too much chest with your loosely buttoned shirt (a gray, untucked, long-sleeved Andrew Fezza from Barney's, which she likes), you keep your hair unkempt on purpose, you know that you have nice hands, and you really need to shave. Mia also senses that you are fairly new to Buddhism. Too restless on the cushion. Too curious about the Tibetan iconography. Still, she relishes the hope of learning more about you, and shifts around with pleasure, feeling your eyes on her back.

From Tibet House, a Buddhist culture center in Manhattan, you recognize a bearded psychiatrist and his wife, and a redheaded choreographer and her willowy boyfriend, clustered near the dais, all of whom—like you and the crucifix-wearing brunette in front of you—suddenly grow silent, and stand and bow as His Eminence enters the hushed shrine room.

You know little of Jamyang Khyentse Rinpoche, this bright-eyed, radiantly smiling Tibetan, beyond what Christopher has shared with you. Imprisoned by the Chinese for nearly a decade; reportedly capable of dissolving his body into "rainbow light" during meditation; disciples who are rumored to have become enlightened merely by being in his presence. According to Christopher, the essence of His Eminence's practice can be distilled into a single word: Compassion. "On my first month-long Vajrayana retreat with him in India," Christopher told you last Sunday, "we meditated from dawn till dusk on nothing but *bodhicitta*—the awakened heart of compassion. Between the mosquitoes and all the bloody love in the room, a few of us pretty much got the whirlies." Rinpoche (literally "precious one," a Tibetan honorific for an incarnate lama, or teacher) is a short, round-faced man with dark hair cropped close to his scalp, and pursed lips so red they seem painted. Despite his tiny frame, his burgundy silk robes fit snugly against his chest and belly, and as he flicks the *damaru*—a tiny drum banged by two bone-chips tied to strips of leather—back and forth he patiently adjusts the microphone clipped to his clothing. A monk attendant in silk robes distributes to the *sangha* small pictures of Manjushri to be held during the guided meditation. Each cross-legged retreatant accepts his or her tiny paper portrait with a bow of thanks. Mia bows, but refrains from taking one. A Tibetan-born English translator, wearing slacks and a brown sweater, sits to the side of the dais with a hand-held microphone.

The empowerment ceremony—scheduled to run two hours—begins with the recitation of several prayers, including the Four Immeasurables. The translator leads the *sangha* with an English translation of the Bodhicitta Prayer: *Thus, until I achieve enlightenment, I perform virtuous deeds with body, speech, and mind. Until death, I perform virtuous deeds with body, speech, and mind. From now until this time tomorrow, I perform virtuous deeds with body, speech, and mind.* Almost everyone in attendance knows the Tibetan version of the Short Refuge Prayer, which is chanted, with growing volume, three times and concludes with the line DRO LA PEN CHIR SANG GYE DRUB PAR SHOG. *May I attain Buddhahood for the sake of all sentient beings.* You lower your eyes and try—as you do every time you've meditated at home over the last six months—to truly feel in your heart the implications of this pledge. You chant silently your vow to uphold the Six Perfections: generosity, patience, morality, meditation, devotion to the spiritual path, and mindfulness about life's transient nature. You silently take refuge in the Three Jewels: the Buddha, the Dharma, and the Sangha.

By the second hour your half-lotus posture has begun to take its toll on your knees, and you lament having left your plump, cotton-stuffed zafu cushion back in New York. Your attention strays. You remind yourself why you're on this spiritual path, why you're at this retreat, why this very moment is so important. If for no other reason, you're here because you're tired of not knowing how to connect with people, tired of believing that intimacy, by definition, is a killjoy. Despite yourself, you keep envisioning Marley curled up and drooling in front of Mrs. Pierno's television. And once the formal empowerment begins, you fail miserably to keep your eyes off the fair-skinned Catholic's thick black ponytail, so close to you that whenever she stretches you can smell in her hair her strawberry shampoo.

Sunday morning, right outside your cell's frosted window, the predawn silence is cleaved by a clanging cowbell in the fist of a hapless do-gooder who volunteered to rouse everyone for the six A.M. meditation. ("It's the crack of a sparrow's fart," Christopher might say of the early hour.) You wake up with a groan and blow out a long, despondent breath. After your eyes unclench, you focus in the dim light on the water-stained ceiling and wonder why in your last dream the circus monkeys drowned in a vat of maple syrup.

This final day of the retreat proceeds slowly for you: two forty-minute group sessions of silent meditation, an hour-long teaching on "The Thirty-seven Practices of the Bodhisattva" by Jamyang Khyentse Rinpoche, whose translated Tibetan proves too tedious for you to follow, interspersed by a half-dozen cups of lukewarm herbal tea. Because of the snow and wind, most of your fellow retreatants stay huddled inside the main building, shuffling through the dormitory's red-carpeted hallways in thick woolen socks, silently nodding to one another.

Before lunch, restless, humming loudly enough for her to hear, you hover over the shoulder of the ponytailed Catholic as she thumbtacks a piece of notebook paper onto the community bulletin board near the entrance to the dining hall. You return her shy grin as she departs for the food line, and then lean forward and read the neatly handwritten letter. It's in cursive, and addressed "Dear Fellow Truth Seekers." The writer introduces herself by name as Mia Malone, thanks Rinpoche for his morning teaching (a nice touch), and explains that before returning "south to my studies in Texas," she has "dared" herself to visit New York City. "It will be my first time." Her note concludes, "If circumstances allow, please share with me any recommendations you might have on where in the Big Apple one might procure an inexpensive hotel room, ideally with a kitchenette (I am on a limited budget), as well as any and all 'must-see' art exhibits. Provincially yours, Mia."

Twenty minutes after gobbling up your vegetarian lunch, you thumbtack to the bulletin board a penciled response—smudged gray with erasings, twice-edited, and tightly folded—that reads:

> Dear Ms. Malone,
>
> Alas, I fear that you will not be able to find a safe, inexpensive hotel anywhere on the island of Manhattan, but I am happy to give you my thoughts about current art shows. My e-mail address is written on the flipside of the card I've enclosed.
>
> By the way: You didn't happen to *drive* to the retreat, did you?
>
> If so, may I tag along when you venture into the city? The train ride is so boring.
>
> Cheers,
> Carter Cox (the tall guy
> with the maestro hair who
> sat behind you last night)

At one P.M. the first afternoon teaching commences with three muffled gongs of a small brass singing bowl. Mia Malone is nowhere to be seen. The sixty-minute Dharma talk, followed by questions posed by the three dozen retreatants who've gathered in the chilly, candlelit shrine room, is led by your friend Christopher Wolf. This is the first you've seen of him all weekend, and he looks more frail than he did a week ago. Throughout his talk Christopher sits facing the assemblage, his long thin body hunched, trembling beneath a maroon shawl you recognize from his Chelsea apartment, his watery red eyes and palsied fingers making him look much older than his fifty-two years, though his illness does not diminish his wit nor dull his mischievous, Cheshire grin. A lay teacher (having "put down the robes" long before his move to New York a decade ago), Christopher nevertheless wears a saffron-colored blouse beneath the monkish maroon wrapping. During much of the cockney-flourished talk, he massages the crown of his shaved head with the palm of his right hand. Before he takes questions, he concludes the lesson with a few hoarse but spirited words on "karma," his favorite Buddhist subject.

"Karma is the Sanskrit term for action," he reminds everyone. *Tum fuh auction*. "The law of karma meticulously accounts for every thought, every word, every deed. This means that everything, absolutely everything, we do with our body or mind has a corresponding result. Our actions, good or bad, will eventually ripen into fruit—or the dreaded lurgy." He gives a little cackle, which breaks off into a fit of coughing. When he finally continues, still patting his chest, his voice is lower, more subdued. "Recall what His Eminence said during his teaching this morning: there *are* no accidents. If we examine all that occurs in our lives, we will see this mysterious and yet profoundly simple law of karma at work. As the Buddha said, 'All that we are arises from our actions. Speak or act with an impure mind, and trouble will follow just as surely as the wheel follows the ox that draws the cart.' The spiritual path is a bloody tough yomp, no doubt about it, but what's the alternative? And remember: selflessness—love, compassion, acts of generosity—will always, *always*, ripen into joy and freedom. Think of the Six Perfections as a shovel with which to scoop out the ego-muck from our daily lives. With the Six Perfections we create *bodhicitta*, and with *bodhicitta* the Buddha Nature within our hearts can awaken. Let us sit."

Christopher chimes the brass singing bowl—a sound that always makes you feel lighter—closes his eyes, and leads the group in a short meditation. Right hand cupped by the left palm in his lap, thumb pads touching, Christopher straightens his bony shoulders and then surrenders his body to gravity, allowing what little weight he has left to settle into his stomach and emaciated haunches. The silence in the shrine room is palpable. Within a few breaths Christopher's trembling disappears, the only visible movement of his body the gentle rising and falling of his bellows-like belly.

You close your eyes and clasp your hands and take refuge in the Buddha, in the Dharma, and in the Sangha. You gaze into the peaceful darkness behind your eyelids and recall Christopher's advice to you about sitting: "Meditation is chiefly about letting go, slowing down, and focusing lightly on the breath. Chin steady, shoulders back. The tip of the tongue resting on the roof of the mouth behind the two front teeth. You're not taking a nap, you diamond geezer—you're sitting on a throne. Be relaxed and focused both. It's like this, mind you: Poetry is the silence *between* the words. Likewise, meditation is the emptiness—the openness—between the thoughts. Rest in that emptiness, and you're resting in your omniscient Buddha Nature. Allow Buddha Nature to rise naturally during your meditations, and Buddha Nature will teach itself."

For a few delicious minutes you feel there is nothing in the universe but the sweet smell of jasmine incense and the gentle beating of your heart. A second chime from the brass bowl draws the teaching and meditation to a close, and the warm stillness in the room gradually dissolves. Opening your eyes, stretching your arms and shoulders, you discover that Christopher has made an early exit, and that beneath a corner of your cushion rests a purple flower and a small white envelope. The thrice-folded, handwritten note within reads:

Dear Mr. Cox,

Thank you so very much for your kind message. I was feeling pretty low today, and your missive, though brief, made me smile. Despite the bleak news about lodging, I still plan to venture into the city! (If this is not already abundantly clear: I've never been!) I'm sorry, however, that I cannot offer you a ride back. The couple I arrived with are driving us upon the conclusion of the retreat straight back to their home in Boston. I won't actually get to New York until next week, and then most likely by bus or train. If I may, though, I would like to phone you from Boston to solicit some advice on art galleries.

I'm budgeted (post-retreat) for $275. Is it absolutely impossible to live in a Manhattan hotel for three nights (provided that I consume nuts and berries) on that amount? Are there hotels in Brooklyn? Harlem?

Thank you again for taking the time to write back.

Sincerely,
Mia (Malone)

P.S. I "borrowed" the tulip from the dining hall.

P.P.S. Are all Buddhist retreats this tough on the knees?

You hop up and glance around the emptying shrine room, but neither Mia nor her green meditation cushion is anywhere to be seen. As you leave, you almost forget to turn and bow to the altar. Shoes back on, heart thumping with renewed vigor, you hurry upstairs to your cell, the flower and secret note hidden beneath your sweater. You shut the door, flip off the lamp, light a candle, and spend the next hour atop your bed writing a response, the risky end result—composed in loose iambic pentameter and illustrated with a miniature lotus blossom—folded and promptly pinned to the center of the community bulletin board.

After the next group meditation in the shrine room, which Mia does not attend, you trudge once again to the brown-corked message wall. At last: a thumbtacked message awaits you beneath a pair of stapled notes for Jamyang Khyentse Rinpoche, "Carter" written in small, childishly neat red felt-tip in its top left corner.

Sniffing, you bring the letter to within an inch of your nose: the yellow loose-leaf paper smells faintly of roses. You glance over your shoulder, hiding the note as one of the elderly, white-aproned kitchen workers shuffles into the dining hall carrying a rattling green rack of empty coffee mugs. With your back turned, you read and immediately discern that the course you opted for with Mia in your last communication was not the correct one:

> Dear Carter,
>
> I very much appreciate your note—in verse, no less!—and sweet invitation to "explore with me after a cup of tea" in the woods, but after giving it considerable thought I determined that we should not go for a walk together, nor should we speak to one another while here. You and I took a vow of silence for the duration of the retreat. If we break this vow, a relatively easy one, how will we keep harder, more important vows in the future? I hope you understand.
>
> Sincerely,
> Mia

A tumble of thoughts and feelings. It's difficult for you to tell from the tone of her prose just how offended she felt by your proposal. "Should I take personally her absence at the meditation session?" you wonder. You pinch your lips and look for clues in Mia's handwriting, which seems decidedly smaller than before—cooler, less embellished. You sniff the paper again and convince yourself that its flowery fragrance is the result of a formal spritzing. "Surely a perfumed note implies interest."

With little to lose you send a third note to this ponytailed Romanist:

> Dear Mia,
>
> I just want to say that I have no desire to disrespect nor violate your Noble Silence. A shared walk on the grounds

does not necessitate speaking. If you want to walk in silence or do not want to walk at all, that's okay. Regardless, even though we haven't formally spoken, I feel we've spoken a little.

Am I correct to assume your interest in Buddhism is anthropological in nature? I'm guessing you're working on a Master's Degree in philosophy or comparative theology at the University of Texas. (I love Austin, by the way—I photographed Stevie Ray Vaughan swimming in Barton Springs for *Rolling Stone* a few years back.) Did you come all the way to Woodstock expressly to see Jamyang Khyentse Rinpoche, or are you connected to this Catholic facility in some way? You also mentioned in your note that you were feeling poorly this morning—are you doing better? Perhaps while in New York we could cross paths for a bite to eat, etc. Do you rock-climb? Play chess?

By the way: when meditating, if you keep your hips higher than your knees, your legs and back won't cramp up as much.

My Buddha statue holds your flower.

Peace,
Carter

You're pleasantly surprised to see that Mia is willing to play. Until the final circle-talk in the shrine room brings the retreat to its official close late Sunday night, you and she continue exchanging notes, most of them composed with a question-and-answer format, the folded letters dropped onto the other's meditation cushion, or slipped into a discreetly outstretched hand while passing in the hallway. Over the course of the afternoon and early evening you learn that Mia Malone, who is indeed working on a graduate degree at the University of Texas (though in art history), was invited to the retreat by friends of her late father, both of whom are "long-time Dharma practitioners." Born in Louisiana, she is twenty-six years old—two years younger than you thought. She doesn't play chess ("I dislike games in general"); prefers opera to jazz; studied ballet during high school, and goes swing-dancing every Tuesday night at an Austin "honky-tonk" called the Continental Club; once flirted with becoming a nun; "adores" Aquinas, Augustine, and Thomas Merton; has never been married nor engaged, though periodically has "friendly dates" with a thirty-two-year-old Lutheran minister with a parish in Bastrop; and is now convinced, chiefly because of the teachings at this retreat, that despite their decidedly different cosmologies Buddhism and Christianity can comfortably coexist.

For the retreat's concluding circle-talk, Mia arrives late to the shrine room and secures an empty cushion directly across from you. Once seated, suppressing a smile, she avoids making eye contact by drumming her knees and inspecting the ceiling beams. Though mildly disappointed that Mia is again wearing the modestly oversized black turtleneck, you like that she remains barefoot and that a couple of stray tendrils are defying her ponytail's rubberband. Guessing, correctly, that Mia prefers conservative attire, you've worn brown corduroys and a beige Kenneth Cole sweater. Watching her from thirty feet away, you realize that you've fallen hard for those beautiful green eyes of hers, so bright and clear—the same vibrant color as the silk Manjushri *thangka* unfurled against the wood-paneled wall above her head. Mia's expressive black eyebrows remind you of Audrey Hepburn—especially as Holly Golightly in *Breakfast at Tiffany's.* It's easy for you to imagine Mia alone in a university library on a Saturday night, drinking black coffee and chewing a pencil as she reads a biography of El Greco. She seems to you equal parts Laura Wingfield and Joan of Arc, at once shy and supremely confident. You wonder how much of this paradox has to do with Mia's Catholicism.

Night has long since fallen. Because of the owl-hooting darkness outside, the votive candles lining the walls cast large, flickering shadows across the shrine room's wooden floor. His Eminence Jamyang Khyentse Rinpoche sits on a zabuton before the altar, the translator to his left, two shave-headed Tibetan monks to his right. Christopher is the only one of the three English-speaking teachers not in attendance. Because of the late hour, some of the retreatants have already left the monastery's grounds for home. The two dozen of you now facing one another on zabutons in this lopsided circle—the extra cushions stacked against the shrine room's back wall—three sticks of Nag Champa incense burning atop the dais next to the gold-leafed Buddha—have been instructed by the translator to pass the cordless microphone, one to another, counterclockwise, and briefly share your thoughts or feelings about the weekend's activities.

After nervously accepting the microphone from the translator, the dapper Portuguese gentleman (whose portrait you never got around to shooting), clears his throat and in a halting voice thanks His Eminence for "a very magnificent retreat." The retreatants applaud politely. As the microphone works its way around the circle, the translator occasionally whispers to His Eminence, who smiles and nods. Mia speaks sixth. "This was my first Buddhist retreat," she says with a hint of a Louisiana drawl, "and I very much appreciate how at ease everyone has made me feel. I've learned a great deal these past three days. I would like to thank the teachers for their generosity and kindness." Palms pressed together, Mia offers a short bow and a beautifully embarrassed smile before passing the microphone. Nicely done, you think. The African-American woman you greeted at the reception desk recites an original poem. A blushing, self-described "construction Joe" scratches his neck and says, "This was a pretty intense weekend, but I survived." A middle-aged chemotherapy patient, her bald head covered by a red bandanna, her pale face blue-tinted, shifts her weight on her cushion, clutches the mala beads draped around her neck, and murmurs into the microphone, "Thank you, Rinpoche. Thank you for your inspired teaching of the Dharma. Thank you . . . for not letting us give up our faith." As the woman's voice catches, a hush ensues. Not needing a translation, His Eminence—still smiling—raises a hand in blessing.

You take a deep breath and eye the microphone as it's passed to the elderly Parisian woman immediately to your left—a frail but serene-looking octogenarian with thinning gray hair, sitting beneath a homemade afghan. She clutches the microphone with both liver-spotted hands, closes her eyes, and sings, in French, off-key but heartfelt, a "hymn of thanks that my mother and father taught me" that leaves several retreatants, including Mia, wiping back tears.

Your heart is racing as you accept the microphone from the woman with a grim smile. "As some of you may know," you say, your voice echoing over the sound system, "one of our teachers this weekend—a good friend to many of us—Christopher Wolf—has been under the weather—seriously so—for several months now." You sigh and look in turn at each of the other retreatants, including Jamyang Khyentse Rinpoche and the monks and lovely Mia Malone, and say to them all, your voice quavering with emotion: "Let's keep Christopher in our hearts after we return home." You close your eyes for a couple of seconds before glancing over at Mia, whose head remains lowered. "Thank you."

You unfold Mia's concluding note as you hike through the snow and slide with your duffel bag and photo gear into the idling taxi. The letter awaited you beneath the door to your room after the conclusion of the circle-talk.

Dear Carter,

I hope I didn't make you feel you must offer to share your apartment, but I certainly will be pleased to stay on your couch on a friendship basis. Thank you in advance for your generosity. My plan will be only for one night, and then into a hotel or hostel, so I won't be in your hair TOO much!

I've very much enjoyed our delightful written interaction and look forward to seeing your photographs and hearing more of your voice, which proved to be as sultry as your smile.

Until I see you in the Big Apple next week . . .

Yours truly,

Mia

The express train back to Grand Central takes just over three hours, and when the cab you catch at the station finally arrives at your East Village apartment it's almost two in the morning. Wearied, sore in the knees, conflicted about the turn of events over the weekend—"didn't I go to the retreat to meditate and expressly *not* pick up women?"—you check your mail, throw the Tumi and camera case over a single shoulder, and haul yourself up to the sixth floor. The eighty-year-old building smells mustier than usual, and your hallway's light seems dimmer, paler. You pause and catch your breath and listen for a moment in front of 6B, Mrs. Pierno's apartment. Her TV is still on. "Shit," you mutter. You fear, correctly, that the old woman has stayed up well beyond her usual bedtime, waiting for your knock. "*Shit.*" You dread the prospect of getting up at the crack of dawn to walk your dog in the snow. "*Shit, shit, shit.*" With a doleful sigh and scratch of your unshaven chin, you decide to let Marley spend the rest of the night with your neighbor. "Hell, she's probably fallen asleep on the couch," you say to yourself. But you're wrong: having downed a third cup of instant coffee, Mrs. Pierno sits in her lounge chair, arms folded, staring at a forty-year-old rerun of *The Dick Van Dyke Show*. Slowly—stealthily—wincing more from your broken promise than from the click of the key—you unlock your door and slip into your unlit apartment, vowing that first thing tomorrow—or at least before lunch—you'll fetch Mrs. Pierno a bouquet of red roses, and Marley a new rubber bone.

3

NINE MONTHS FROM NOW you'll be either dead or engaged. Not recognizing this, of course, after dinner with Christopher you skip your evening meditation and spend much of this Sunday night, seven days after the Woodstock retreat, discussing with a pool-playing buddy your burgeoning interest in the fair-skinned art-history student.

"This gal's bright, *really* bright," you tell your friend Nick, a charming but self-loathing thirty-year-old bartender who never finished college and thus spends much of his time seducing financially successful women. For reasons you don't fully understand or appreciate, it's only over this particular pool table, shared with this particular male companion in the back of this particular West Village lounge, that you'll discuss your romantic relationships, or—more often and less romantically—your assorted sexual imbroglios. "She doesn't put off much heat though," you add, lining up a tricky seven-nine ball combination. "She wrote in one of her notes that she's considered becoming a nun."

"Buddhists do the nun thing?"

"No—a Catholic nun. She's twenty-six, though, so I assume her get-herself-to-a-nunnery days are over. Wouldn't you think? I mean, how's that work . . . age-wise? After a certain point convents won't take you—right?" You do some quick math. In four weeks you'll turn thirty-nine. Mia Malone is thirteen years your junior. Realizing that Mia was in grade school learning cursive about the same time you were declaring yourself a photography major pulls your shot wide.

"I don't think there's a cut-off age," replies Nick, chuckling and shaking his head at the easy shot you've left him. "I got a cousin who just joined a convent in Vermont, and she's pushing fifty. Our Lady of the Sacred Ski-Lift or something." Nick blows green chalk dust from the tip of his cue. "You know, my aunt says that Catholic nuns actually *marry* Jesus. Go through a wedding ceremony, wear a gold band, the whole bit."

"With a honeymoon in heaven. No—my sense is that this gal will end up being an art-history professor." You recall with considerable relief from one of her last notes Mia's explanation that the gold wedding ring she wears was a gift from her grandmother. "She *looks* like a young art-history professor. Yo—did you call that pocket?"

Nick snorts, chalks his cue again, and continues shooting. Waving a hand through the cigarette smoke filling the tiny lounge—a musty, hippishly ancient NYU hangout with red vinyl booths, Elvis memorabilia, and a sticky wooden floor—you return to your bar stool as an old Van Morrison song starts up on the jukebox. With a wet smack and an audible belch you finish your third Rolling Rock, glance beneath the stool, and give your book bag a nudge with your heel. Along with your money-clip, numerous credit cards, and keys, inside the bag you have an EOS autofocus, a freshly purchased Pentax IQ zoom, a new rubber toy for Marley, and the twelve-count gift box of Belgian chocolates you bought for Mrs. Pierno on Tuesday. (Though Monday morning Mrs. Pierno begrudgingly accepted the day-old daisies and mumbled excuses you gave her for failing to retrieve Marley the night before as promised—"bad snow storm" blah blah blah, "train derailment" blah blah blah—she closed her door behind you loud enough to suggest that you'd burned your bridges with her as a dog-sitter. Another token of your appreciation couldn't hurt.)

"What're you keeping from me?" you ask, leaning over and sticking your nose in Nick's red-and-white Gourmet Garage shopping bag, half-hidden beneath his black motorcycle jacket.

"Get outta that. I got a date."

"Oh my." You lift from the sack a jar of salsa, a bag of blue-corn tortilla chips, and a shrink-wrapped tray of pork sausage patties. "What date is this—the *ninetieth?*"

Nick chuckles. He returns to the pool table after finishing his beer and calls over his shoulder, "Hey—here's one. How do you titillate an ocelot?"

You smirk and request another round from the bartender, a thirty-year-old musician who wears an undersized brown Wilco T-shirt, thumb ring, and Pete Yorn haircut. Suddenly you vow to refrain from replying to Mia's very sweet e-mail message from Boston for at least twenty-four more hours. "Haven't a clue."

"You oscillate her tits a lot."

"Brilliant. You gonna hit that clean?"

Nick shrugs. "What're you talking about?"

"The shot you're lining up."

"I'm not lining anything up. Just considering my options."

"Yeah. Whatever. If you hit the eleven without calling it, it's a scratch."

"Duly noted."

Leaning low over the faded-green felt, he makes the shot and then moves to the opposite side of the table, chalking his cue some more and grinning cruelly as he scopes the easy eight-ball "gimme." You still can't decide if you like the year-old dragon tattoo on display below Nick's rolled-up shirt sleeve. As tattoos go, you feel it's nicely done—stylized, Asian-influenced, solid black detailing. But still, it's a tattoo, and it's a tattoo that takes up almost all of his forearm.

"So, where was this Buddha-thing again?" he asks. Both of you look sideways as a serape-wearing brunette, fragrant with perfume oil, leaves the unisex bathroom and crosses past the jukebox, smiling at the bartender.

"The retreat was up near Woodstock."

"I thought you said it was in Mexico."

"No. I had a photo shoot in Mexico."

"Okay—so *that's* why you're peeling."

Exhaling with exaggerated concentration at the eighteen-inch shot, Nick needlessly topspins the cue ball, freezing theatrically low over the table in mid-follow-through. With a delicate click, the eight ball rolls forward, hesitates, and disappears with a clunk into the corner pocket.

"Doctor Touch."

"Thanks," he says. "One more?"

The bar is picking up—the other seven barstools are now occupied, only three by males. You glance at your watch and nod. You've lost the last four games, but you're enjoying the music, the slight beer-buzz you've got going, and, as usual, the panache with which Nick does just about everything—including paying for this round of beers from a silver money-clip of folded twenties.

"Very nice," you say, pinching and rubbing Nick's vintage shirt's shiny blue fabric. You've been practically salivating over its sheen since arriving at the bar. "Where'd you get it?"

Nick looks down at the white stitching and customized buttons. "A little place in Williamsburg. So, this Catholic girl's coming for a visit, huh?"

You sniff, shrug. "Yeah. Tuesday. She's crashing with me while she looks for a hotel."

"Smooth."

Despite yourself, and hoping that Nick doesn't notice, you

replace your cue with a lighter one in preparation for the final game, your third time to trade sticks. You rack the balls—the loser's responsibility—with a flourished spin of the wooden triangle and return to your seat. Facing the pool table, side by side on the bar stools, your respective cues held lance-like in your respective left hands, you and Nick eye the two petite, pierced-nosed, parka-wearing NYU coeds cuddling in the nearest booth. Nick clinks your sweating beer bottle. As he gets up to break, he says, "A good craftsman never blames his tools, Mr. Cox."

You came to Buddhism gradually, an evolution that began with your birth in Sacramento, California, to Unitarian parents on February 20, 1962, the same day John Glenn circled the earth, and accelerated during your teens with your family's seasonal camping trips to Yosemite. As a UCLA undergraduate, after a near-fatal overdose of Jim Beam and codeine ("it was kinda cool, actually"), you discovered tai chi and yoga and grew to appreciate the meaning and significance of prayer. But to whom? Where *is* God exactly? The weekend Christianity of your parents and three sisters provided more questions than answers: If God is love and love is blind, then how does he see me kneeling before him? Where was I before I was born? Why does my body feel like a guest house?

Although you were already committed to the spiritual path, several of your more corporeal fetishes (German camera bodies, hydroponic cannabis and Hawaiian coffee, custom-made suits) were exacerbated by your move to consumer-friendly New York City seven years ago. Most troublesome for your checking account (still) is an expensive weakness for things technological, especially since you billed only $11,500 last quarter, your lowest quarterly gross since 1994. Though it's easier understood than acted upon, you now agree with Christopher—as well as your father (a recently retired high-school history teacher)—that "money doesn't make you happy—not *needing* money makes you happy."

You moved from California to the East Coast in the summer of 1994 with romantic hopes of living the artist's life. With the scruffy East Village appealing to your bohemian tastes, you took up residence in a one-bedroom apartment in a former tenement building near the corner of Avenue A and Sixth Street, a short stumble from Little India (a row of roughly two dozen Indian restaurants squeezed in between First and Second Avenues), McSorley's Old Ale House (the oldest Irish pub in the city), and the infamous Tompkins Square Park. The New York chapter of the Hell's Angels is located nearby, on First Avenue and Third Street. You sip your morning espresso and read the *Times* in coffeehouses frequented in the 1980s by artists like Keith Haring and Jean-Michel Basquiat, and now often by struggling musicians strung out on heroin purchased over on St. Marks Place. Neighborhood lunches are had at Alphabet Kitchen, Damask Falafel, or Benny's Burritos. Your late-night carousing often concludes with stops at music venues like CBGB's or the Mercury Lounge, or down on the Bowery, or with a final shot of Johnny Walker Black at the Cherry Tavern.

Your apartment's initial "classical gypsy" aesthetic (a velvet matador painting above the bed, beaded curtains between the kitchen and breakfast nook, a pricey flea-market dining table with multihued chairs) has given way in the last few years to Crate & Barrel bookcases, Pottery Barn dishes, Calvin Klein bedsheets, a Danish-designed computer "hub," a multi-tiered 300-watt Japanese sound system, and six of your own framed black-and-white photographs. Upper East Side conventionality has swept away the downtown scruffiness and dirt, at least within the walls of your apartment. When in 1994 you purchased from the East Village Emporium a 3-inch porcelain Buddha figurine, still tucked among the bookshelf speaker and ashtray on your bed's headboard (the tiny statue one of the few decor leftovers from your first year in New York), you knew next to nothing about Buddhism—you just liked the way the little fellow looked. But now you believe that it was that porcelain Buddha's presence in your bedroom that eventually—karmically—led you to meet Christopher Wolf.

Prompted by your new acquaintanceship with the former Buddhist monk, you attended your first weekend-long meditation retreat five months ago in rural Connecticut. There you were taught that health and "enlightened happiness" come through a blissful detachment from the material world (symbolized in a Buddha statue's closed eyes and tranquil half-smile), that desiring and clutching *things*—a thinner body, a younger car, a plusher mate—lie at the heart of life's sufferings, even illness and death. You liked that Buddhism takes no stand on the existence of a creator God. That it *encourages* skepticism and embraces the Golden Rule. You learned that meditation does not necessarily mean sitting cross-legged on the floor—the Buddha taught that meditation is *any* experience cultivated with selfless, mindful attention. Jogging, cooking, even taking photographs can be an exercise in Buddhism.

A Condé Nast art director you've worked with claims that his Dharma practice changed his life. "Before leaving for my honeymoon in Italy in 1996," he told you, "I asked a friend, who meditated, for advice about how to stay present. I was in love and going to one of the most beautiful places in the world and thought it would be a shame to go there and not be *fully* there. My friend's advice was to sit, look in a mirror, and breathe for five minutes a day. I thought this odd, but I tried it the morning of my wedding and found it very powerful. Now a deep breath can bring me back to the present anytime I choose. When I'm with my wife and one-year-old daughter, I'm really there with them. My experience with Buddhism over the past five years has opened my soul and is utterly inexplicable. Words diminish it."

Within hours of your return home from Connecticut you purchased from Zen & Now, a spirituality shop around the corner on Avenue B, a foot-high Javanese statue of Buddha Shakyamuni, your first sandalwood mala beads, and matching red zafu and zabuton cushions. The next morning in a corner of your den you created a small shrine, before which you have vowed, with some degree of success, to meditate for at least thirty minutes every day.

Despite your own budding spiritual practice, you know in your heart that compartmentalizing your life continues to blind you to much of its beauty and meaning. You're a travel photographer who hasn't recognized that travel is indeed a fool's paradise. You've overlooked the possibility that life's most rewarding trip is into the depths of a single experience—and that life's most rewarding experience is unconditionally loving someone other than yourself. From a Buddhist perspective, a compartmentalized life is an unenlightened life. And you, Carter Cox, compartmentalize almost as easily as you breathe. One moment you're chanting "Om Mani Padme Hung" before your altar, the next, driven by techno-lust, you're leafing through *PC World* hunting for bigger motherboards and more powerful processors. Often you don't taste your food, so busy are you desiring the next bite. In the summer of 1995 you twice slept with three women in a single day. You're addicted to marijuana, caffeine, alcohol, adrenaline rushes, salt, sugar, orgasms, nicotine, and hot showers. Though you're uncertain how or when you became enslaved by sensual pleasures, you think that your inability to figure it out might be symptomatic of the problem.

Mala beads—you own three strands of them—are worn not only to help count breaths or mantras during meditation, but as a visual reminder to live mindfully: implicit in the wearing of a mala is the vow to treat anything and anyone you come into contact with as sacred. You usually remove your beads when you defecate, drink alcohol, or smoke pot. You've also started removing them whenever you become aroused, the gesture a compartmentalizing concession to what you thick-headedly believe is the inherently selfish nature of sex. The first (and only) night you spent with Rhonda Warren, the forty-year-old store manager of PhotoPeople, she sensed the implications when you discarded your mala beads alongside your shirt and trousers—and she called you on it. "What's up with *that?*" she remarked. You shrugged sheepishly, unsure what to tell her, chiefly because you knew that speaking the truth would most likely bring the unzipping of her skirt to a grinding halt.

Tonight—collapsed lengthwise along your couch, home alone an hour after winning the final game of pool with Nick (he scratched)—six Rolling Rocks and two ounces of Cuervo Gold gurgling in your upset belly—you again ask yourself: What's a Buddhist bachelor to do—truly? What's the answer? You have an untamed libido, but you desire to do the mindful thing—if only you knew where the line should be drawn. Arousal isn't the culprit, you convince yourself, already aroused from this month's issue of *Score*, its nineteen-year-old cover model lying sideways on the floor less than a foot from your nose. Arousal is essential for perpetuating life! Some of the past Buddhas had *consorts*, for Christ's sake. Either way, how can indulging in something that *quenches* arousal be bad? And sexual quenching is certainly not limited to restless, freelance picture-takers penned up in their apartments on a snowy Sunday night: your ex-girlfriend Ursula owned so many X-rated Rocco Siffredi videos that she alphabetized them.

To date, you're nine weeks and two days into your vow to abstain from erotica for a year. As if in AA, daily you remind yourself of Christopher's challenge: "Making a vow takes strength, keeping a vow *gives* you strength. You can put on airs and graces, Carter, but it all boils down to willpower and motivation and surrendering to the higher Self. The universe *wants* us to be strong—she *wants* us to win—and she'll help us, if we let her." Nevertheless, the promise of abstinence degraded three weeks ago into a decision not to *own* erotica, allowing for the occasional guilt-ridden adult DVD rental. You rub your itchy toes against the couch's armrest. Licking your dried lips, you glance at your PC's lava-lamp screensaver, over at the DVD-remote tossed to the floor behind your 65-inch Toshiba "Theaterwide" High Definition TV, and then back down at *Score*'s teenage cover model.

The erotica vow was prompted, primarily, by reading a newspaper article claiming that the majority of women who appear in pornographic movies were sexually abused as children. The apparent cause-and-effect chilled you, so much so that later that night, while sitting in meditation before your Buddha statue, you swore to forego further involvement with the world of cinematic smut, and before bed dutifully tossed down the trash chute the pair of Tiffany St. Cloud videotapes you'd kept hidden under the guest pillows in your linen closet.

Yet—and only 168 hours since the Woodstock retreat—"I'm a fucking junkie," you groan, lumbering over to your computer console—you venture into the Hungry Ghost realm lurking deep in your PC at a Web site you discover online called Lust Palace. After lighting a cigarette and untucking your shirt, you shake your head and chuckle apprehensively at the six categories of photographs available to you within the site's inner sanctum: Celebrity Flesh. Amateur Heat. Fetish. Hard-core. Group Sex. Barely Legal. Three minutes later you quit breathing. You stare, open-mouthed and a little dizzy, at the fifth or sixth thumbnail series of grimly lit snapshots of some poor father's naked daughter sprawled with studied abandon on a cushionless green couch. "Oh God," you mutter. Though leaning away from the computer screen, you promptly return to the main-menu page, for there are one, two, three, four, five, six, *seven* more categories of naked daughters to be downloaded.

An hour passes. The sensations now in your body have little to do with arousal. Despite your mildly thumping heart, your hands are cold, your mouth tastes of metal, and what little tumescence you might have initially experienced has been transformed into a kind of seedy impatience. The "devil itch" is now rooted so deeply within your loins that it's no longer a physical sensation. It's raw greed. For sixty minutes you've glanced at the computer screen for little more than a second before hungering for something else. Click. A smiling, freckle-faced redhead is replaced by an interracial threesome. Click. A Russian brunette with bad teeth is replaced by a skeleton-thin and frightened-looking "young Chinese whore" pounced upon by three faceless males, one of whom clutches the girl's long black hair like the reins to a horse. You touch your chest and wonder, "Who *are* these girls? And why are so many of them from Eastern Europe?" Click. *Enough.* You push away from the PC, suddenly more disgusted with yourself than with the images.

Whatever sustenance you drew from Christopher and Jamyang Khyentse Rinpoche and the demure Miss Malone, has managed, in just seven nights, to give way to something rotten and hollow—and perhaps, you fear, beyond your control. You close your eyes and squeeze your temples, two or three of the more gruesome snapshots lingering in your brain like a septic stink. Regardless, your body still hungers for *something.* "Fuck, fuck, fuck." You grunt, light another cigarette, then wander zombie-like in your socks and sweat-dampened shirt through the den into the kitchen, the cluttered sink smelling of soiled dishes and spoiled milk. You open the refrigerator door, its fifteen-watt bulb cutting a narrow path across the cold linoleum floor. You stand there, looking in at the contents with your weight hanging fully on the door, a dairy sourness breathing out from the interior, chilling your exposed chest, the refrigerator's top shelf bare except for two dozen black canisters of film, a carton of milk, a half-eaten wedge of brie cheese, a quarter-gallon can of V8 juice with two identical triangular clefts going rusty-red around their edges. What to do? You feel famished—but for what?

You remind yourself that five dollars spent renting a pornographic DVD is a five-dollar endorsement for the world of pornography. Indeed, could not a case be made that the act of renting a pornographic DVD might in some small way actually contribute to child abuse? Even in your darkest fantasies, you refrain from imagining sexual scenarios involving minors. You fancy yourself a progressive-minded male. You've read *The Beauty Myth.* You do your best not to objectify women. You've had only a handful of one-night stands—and you're certainly not going to phone up someone at this hour on a Sunday night for a quick roll in the hay.

With a suctioned *thump* you close the refrigerator door. "Of course," you rationalize, "there is a *hierarchy* of erotica. Pornography is bad the same way bad art is bad. Gynecological close-ups filmed by someone wearing a coal-miner's helmet-lamp is bad art. No question about it. But what about *good* erotica? *Henry and June*, for example. Or some of those slow-motion, big-budget affairs directed by Andrew Blake? What kind of karma is generated from watching languorous, pool-side sex among consenting and generously compensated adult-movies stars? Especially with the understanding that the DVD(s)—rented, not owned—will be immediately returned tomorrow morning after just one viewing. One could not ask for safer sex." You recall that many of the women in Andrew Blake's movies are Scandinavian and thus presumably more open-minded—indeed *healthier*—in their approach to erotica. "None of that ugly sex-as-a-tool-for-vengeance stuff that ruins domestic porn. Hot but tasteful. Maybe I could even rent something directed by a woman. How about something directed by a *Scandinavian* woman? Mmmmm: Yes, that makes *a lot* of sense." Instantly the prospect of spending the remainder of this unforgivingly cold January evening under the covers watching Scandinavian women having fully consensual Scandinavian sex moves you to depart from the kitchen, sock-slide to the bedroom, throw on a pair of shoes and leather jacket, leash Marley (who's been whining and scratching at the door for half an hour), grab your wallet, and hop down the stairs and into the chilly night.

Within a few steps you and Marley are breathing steam. Although it's no longer snowing, the frosty air is so devoid of moisture that after only a block your sinuses burn. You zip your leather jacket up to your chin, grumble at Marley for taking so long to lower his hind leg at the slush-covered curb ("Whenever you're ready, dude"), drop your head, take an immediate right, and virtually drag the panting mutt along the icy sidewalk to First Avenue. You glance at your watch. It's almost midnight—you fear that the video store will be closed. Light-headed, your face prickly, you freeze at the red light and glare impatiently at the traffic blocking your way, the whooshing tires from the endless stream of yellow cabs sloughing mist, their low-beams splashing orange light across the wet pavement.

You turn the corner, hesitate for a few seconds at a shed-sized newsstand, the opening to which is draped with soggy, clothes-pinned copies of *Stroke* and *Juggs* and *Just Eighteen.* You debate whether you should go ahead and buy another pack of cigarettes. The bundled Pakistani magazine-peddler within the kiosk continues to jabber on his cell phone without acknowledging your presence. "Fuck it." You spin to your right. The unlit front window to Manny's Tobacco Store is devoted entirely to men's magazines—the three from which you've received paychecks in the last year all sport on their covers pouting blond females in various stages of undress.

You cross Eleventh Street against the red light and steer towards the entrance to the fluorescent-lit East Village Videos, dismissing a honking yellow cab with a swish of your hand. You reach for your wallet. You want to be in and out of the store as quickly as possible. Since renting a DVD or video will necessitate a return trip, you decide that tonight—and tonight only—and only because you have not done this for a while—you will *buy* a DVD. Something inexpensive. Something disposable. Something you can watch once or twice and then throw away.

You shield your eyes from the blue lights as you stare through the video store's frosted front window. The adult section takes up fully one-third of the interior. "Where the hell is the goddamn for-sale bin?" You pull your leather jacket tighter and try to ignore Marley's nose probing against your crotch. "Disposable sex. Unfucking-believable. What would the Dalai Lama say about this?"

You move with a sigh towards the entrance, sensing that this is how unloved women must feel darting into D'Agostino's at midnight to buy a pint of Häagen-Dazs. You grab the silver door handle and yank. Hard. The cowbell hanging from the door frame clanks against the glass, and you squint and turn your face, fearing it might shatter. Again you pull the door before realizing your error. With a snort you *push* your way inside the store, the fumey heat from the fluorescent-lit interior hitting you in the face as the glass door pulls itself shut behind you. Fists stuffed into your pockets, shoulders hunched, tugging at Marley's leash, you slip through the velveteen curtain separating the adult videos and DVDs from the adventure section, and hastily start inspecting titles on a carousel marked PRE-VIEWED: FOR SALE.

When you return home to the warmth of your apartment, *Night Flesh* and *EuroAngels 4* hidden beneath your leather jacket, the chug-chug-chug of your computer, followed by a chimey "You've got mail," moves you to click open and read the freshly received e-mail message:

Subject: Knock. Knock. Excuse me. Do hope I'm not disturbing you.
Electronic Mail Sent: 11:58 PM, Sunday 21, January 2001
From: Mia Malone
To: Carter Cox

Dear Mr. Cox,

I certainly don't mean to rush you. I can quite imagine the full life you lead and so wouldn't expect that e-mail should rate among the top entries in your list of priorities. I was however half-expecting that I might have received at least some little swish of your sword in acknowledgment of my perhaps rather lame attempt at witty repartee this past Thursday. I do hope nothing I wrote offended you, at least to any appreciable degree. And I did so enjoy your notes this past weekend. My daft effort at being arch should for the most part, and particularly where you're concerned, be taken as a compliment to the other's intelligence, and as an expression of blossoming excitement at the prospect of again seeing (and hearing!) you this coming Tuesday. If I have in any fashion repulsed or displeased you, please do me the kindness of letting me know in order that I might straightly set myself toward making amends.

And with that, looking a bit crestfallen, she bows low and slips out of the room.

Yours,
Mia (Malone)

You glance down at the two shrink-wrapped DVDs and then over at the remote control still lying on the floor. For the better part of a minute you stare at your altar. You gaze at the Manjushri statue under the *thangka*, at the brass Tibetan singing bowl and the three strands of mala beads draped around the Javanese Buddha statue. "You can put on airs and graces, Carter, but it all boils down to willpower. The universe *wants* us to be strong—she *wants* us to win—and she'll help us, if we let her." You turn to a Thomas Merton quote randomly copied from *Thoughts in Solitude* and thumbtacked on the wall above the laser printer—the passage put there expressly for Mia's upcoming visit. With a sputtering of your lips, you drop the DVDs, unopened, into the wastebasket beneath the computer console, sigh, and run your thawed-out (but still reddened) hands through the mess of your hair.

After showering and changing into a pair of blue UCLA sweat pants and a moth-nibbled sweater, you turn off the computer and desk lamp and all of your apartment's overhead lights. You burn a stick of Nag Champa incense and put on a Tibetan chant CD.

Before lighting the trinity of votive candles in the center of your small altar, you lower yourself onto the meditation cushion and pull your bare feet into a half-lotus position. Tongue lolling, Marley ambles over and rests his wet nose against your thigh. "I'm sorry that I snapped at you, boy," you tell him, scratching his ears and reminding yourself that he's not yet gotten his new rubber bone. You remove one of the cedar malas from the Buddha statue's round shoulders and loop it three times around your left wrist, drawing in long deep breaths, one after the other, until your body begins to relax. With each exhalation you surrender more of your weight to the pull of gravity. Your belly softens. A gentle half-smile plays on your lips. Eyes shut, you place the palms of your hands together, bow your head, and whisper to that dimly flickering spark in your chest, "I take refuge in the Buddha. I take refuge in the Dharma. I take refuge in the Sangha."

4

Mia buzzes your apartment from the street-level intercom Tuesday night at nine-thirty, precisely one hour later than you expected her. Remaining seated on the couch, you gulp one last swig of your Glenfiddich and water before buzzing her up. It's been a long day: a shoot for *New York* fell through, and your computer keeps crashing. You press your forehead against the door and wait for Mia's footsteps on the stairs, though when she knocks, you keep your head pressed to the wood and count to ten before unbolting the door. Marley has joined you in the foyer, ears perked, whining at the movement in the hallway, circling between your legs as you check your teeth in the mirror. When you open the door, a bundled and beaming Mia steps forward, a bouquet of yellow tulips—clutched with both hands—extended, as if for protection, towards your apartment's interior. Behind her in the hallway sits a faded green, snow-moistened, army surplus backpack, almost large enough for your five-foot-four guest to crawl inside and hide.

"Hey there," you say in a Glenfiddich-slowed voice, kissing Mia's flushed cheek and squeezing her arm. "What's shaking?"

"I'm sorry that I'm late," she responds, still out of breath from the hike up the stairs.

"Come on in."

"I got so confused on the subway. When I arrived at Grand Central Station, I took an uptown express train rather than a downtown local train and found myself up by the Guggenheim before I realized what I'd done. I'm still a little . . . overwhelmed. Hello there, dog. How're you doing?" *Dawg. Dew-in.*

"This is Marley."

"Hello, Marley," Mia says, squatting down to rub his pink belly.

You help Mia take off her blue hooded parka, and she steps back into the hallway to stomp the snow from her rubber boots, which she removes and places heels-first against the foyer's nearest wall. You are smitten again by her voice, which is surprisingly deep but stretched into a lilt by the slight southern accent. In a confidential tone you assure her, "I get lost on the subway all the time. I'll be reading a book on the F train and next thing I know I'm in Brooklyn Heights." The warmth beneath Mia's white pullover sweater lets loose a scent that reminds you of the carpeted hallways of the Woodstock monastery. "These are *pur*-ty," you say, taking the flowers. "Thank you much."

Mia clears her throat, nods shyly. She blushes but returns your smile, unblinkingly, as the two of you make and hold for several moments your first eye contact unrestrained by a precept vow of silence.

Chuckling as you step past her, you struggle to hoist her backpack over a shoulder and gasp, "Man, what's *in* this?"

"Monographs mostly. I'm . . . behind." Mia shrugs and, sniffing, follows you into the den. "Your apartment smells nice. What kind of incense is this?"

"Sri Kresna. From Indonesia."

Pausing, glancing wide-eyed around the den, Mia suddenly gushes, almost cathartically, "I am *so* excited to finally be in New York City, Carter, I can't tell you. I've wanted to come here ever since I was a little girl. Every year I'd watch the Macy's Thanksgiving Day parade on TV and dream of floating off the Empire State Building holding on to the Bullwinkle balloon."

"Well . . . now you're here."

When you return from the bedroom, empty-shouldered and tulipless, you find Mia—fingers interlaced behind her back, head lowered, pert bottom extended—leaning towards a wall containing three of your framed black-and-white photographs. Her thick black hair is still pulled back in that no-nonsense ponytail of hers from the retreat. More so than you remembered, and even more appealing now than you'd originally thought, Mia possesses the milky-white skin and praying-mantis beauty of someone who haunts museum archives and listens to Chopin while baking bread. Beneath the baggy, ivory-colored sweater she wears new, fairly snug blue jeans and thick white athletic socks. And those green eyes. You forgot—or perhaps hadn't realized—that Mia has such pretty teeth. And a dimple when she smiles! What else? Prominent ears (which caused teasing from her childhood classmates), trustworthy eyebrows, little makeup and no jewelry save for a pair of tiny gold earrings and her grandmother's wedding band. Marley—tail wagging—clearly approves: sniffing her intertwined fingers while she examines your pictures, he's completely ignored you since your return to the den.

"Interesting," Mia mumbles of the nude "body study" of a Banana Republic catalogue model you dated briefly in 1997. Moving sideways, pointing to the grainy, early-morning shot of Mount Agung, an active volcano near the northern coast of Bali, she says, "I like this middle one very much." She strolls past the big-screen television and DVD player, leans her head sideways to look at your book titles, sniffs a candle on the altar. You like how comfortable she seems, her interest and seeming familiarity with your belongings and space. "This is the largest stereo I have ever seen, Carter. And—wow—you have a lot of computer . . . stuff." Mia grins at the thumbtacked Thomas Merton quote above the printer.

"So."

". . . So."

"You hungry?"

"A little," she replies, turning. "You?"

You pat your belly. "Starving."

An hour later you and Mia check your coats and scarves and are escorted to a corner table in Opaline, a dark, cavernous, underground bistro located on Avenue A, designed in the fashion of a turn-of-the-century Parisian absinthe bar, which you frequent on first dates. "Good to see you again, my friend," the bald, African-American maître d' whispers as he leads you and Mia to a dimly lit booth near the bar. Jazzy Spanish guitar music trickles down from the speakers. An antique ceiling fan with six-foot balsa blades rotates slowly overhead. The Tuesday-night bartender—a muscular Andalusian woman wearing a tight black T-shirt and red lipstick—looks up from the sink while washing a highball glass and nods hello to you over Mia's shoulder.

"Well then," you say, situated comfortably with your back against the booth's cushioned partition, opening the enormous green menu, though you already know what you intend to have, "any tattoos I should know about?"

Mia shakes her head. "None I can show you."

"Any piercings?"

"Just the one in each ear, thank you."

"Excellent . . . excellent."

"Do you *like* piercings?"

"I'm not sure how I feel about females and piercings," you reply. "The subtext always seems to be: Ask me about my parents' divorce."

The Glenfiddich is beginning to wear off, so you order a bottle of '96 Merlot along with the sauteed monkfish in caper brown butter. An arugula salad to start. Mia orders goat cheese ravioli, the least expensive entree on the menu. No appetizer. As the waiter returns with a basket of sourdough bread and bottle of Evian, within your unzipped black North Face bag your cell phone twitters loud enough for the neighboring four-top to look up from their plates.

"Do you need to answer that?" asks Mia between twitters.

"Nah. My answering service will get it. Eventually."

After her first sip of wine, Mia daubs her reddened lips with her napkin and asks, "Do you have family, Carter?"

"Indeed, I do. My parents—good people, both—live in the Sacramento suburbs. I have an older sister in Tucson, and two younger ones in Atlanta. Both married to partners in the same *very* successful architecture firm. You wrote that your father—before he died—was a college professor?"

"Yes. A professor in Tulane's anthropology department. My mother's a house-mom. Hasn't remarried yet. I don't know if she will." Another wine sip and daub of the napkin. "Growing up in Hungary, she was a ballet dancer, apparently a fine one. I try to get her to teach, but—oh—how is that Cormac McCarthy novel? Is it the last one of the trilogy?"

You do a calculated double take and glance down at your opened shoulder bag, its contents strategically exposed. "It's the last one, yeah. It's terrific."

Self-mockingly, Mia remarks, "Most recently I was perusing *The History of Byzantine Art and Architecture, Volume Four.* Or, more precisely, I was turning the book's pages and highlighting all of the thousands of footnotes. I fear that I've lost the joy of reading." She shudders. "My academic life makes no sense."

You pour more Merlot into Mia's three-quarters-filled glass. "What do you plan on doing once you finish up with your master's?"

"Oh, ask Mr. de Montebello if he'd allow me to take over his position and curate the Met."

Chomping the monkfish and nibbling on the ravioli, you and Mia chat about recent movies, other novels ("I generally dislike the moral timidity of contemporary fiction," she informs you), the Woodstock retreat, Christopher Wolf's declining health, your recent photo assignments (you don't mention, however, what happened this morning with *New York*). Though she claims to have mixed feelings about graduate school, she says that she loves living in Austin.

Despite yourself, you continue to evaluate Mia's physical appearance as she sits perched across the table, squinting at you over the candlelight with a smile that is coolly attentive and kind and yet, you think, somewhat impersonal: Mia seems in the restaurant, but not of it. From three feet away, her features seem enigmatic, almost contradictory: girlishly soft chin, sharp feline nose, long black hair pulled back so painfully tight the style seems penitent. If only Mia would let her damn hair down, you muse irritably over the dessert menu, suddenly restless from the wine and an hour of the Gypsy Kings, half-tempted to reach over the table and unleash the ponytail yourself. With her hair untied she would transform from something pretty into something stunning. How can she not know this? And when the conversation returns to your photography career, Mia begins to drink in your words as if they were dipped in ambrosia. Surely, you think, she can't find my thoughts on photo scanning and contract lowballing *that* compelling.

Well, yes and no. With the curiosity of an anthropologist's daughter, she's studying you—watching the way you use your hands, noting your tendency to clear your throat after making a point—though with growing fondness and affection, especially for the "gentler you" she sees flickering deep within the light behind your eyes. She finds it cute that you chummy up with the waiter, charming that you stand when she leaves the table to go to the ladies' room. And she *does* know that with her hair down she looks more seductive.

Without consulting your dinner companion you order another bottle of Merlot and two plates of something called Death by Chocolate. As the waiter departs, Mia widens her glistening green eyes and whispers: "Beware of the Buddhist who drinks red wine after midnight."

You jiggle from your opened bag a half-empty pack of Marlboro Lights. "Cigarette?"

"No thanks."

You lean your head back and exhale the first stream of smoke towards the ceiling fan. "You don't indulge in coffin nails?"

"Rarely. Are you okay?" she asks, gesturing to your vigorous hand-scratching.

"Yeah. Just a little itchy."

By now Opaline has emptied considerably, the relentless Spanish guitar music punctuated by muffled plate-clattering from beyond the swinging kitchen doors. You're embarrassed that the place where you've brought Mia is so dead, but you remind yourself that it's a snowy Tuesday.

"How often do you read the Bible?" you ask, stretching back against the booth's partition, bloated, letting out a breath, trying without much success to relax your belly. You look around to see if anyone else thinks the restaurant has gotten uncomfortably warm.

A tendril of Mia's dark hair comes loose, and she blows it from her cheek with a sideways puff. Her eyes are dancing a bit from the first bottle of wine. "Pretty much every day," she replies, smiling strangely and looking down at her silverware.

You flick your cigarette, raise your glass and peer at her lowered eyes through the candlelight shimmering in the red liquid. A goodie two-shoes? You don't think so. More like a sprightly, sexy saint. Emily Dickinson with a pulse. Someone spiritually and intellectually at peace with herself, someone who knows wrong from right, a "truth seeker" dancing barefoot from the confessional to "the Sultans of Swing Night" at the Continental Club to Boston to a Buddhist retreat to a date with a stranger in lower Manhattan. "And how does that work exactly? Do you look for a particular passage, or do you just pick it up and start browsing?"

"One time I read it through from start to finish, which was utterly fascinating—especially the Old Testament. But it depends. Sometimes I'll spend a month rereading the same letter from Paul, or *all* the letters by Paul, and sometimes I'll just focus on a character like King Solomon or focus on a specific theme and meditate on that. I fancy your mala beads, by the way."

Glancing down at the three beaded loops partially hidden beneath the cuff of your left shirt-sleeve, you extend your arm across the table. "Smell. They're made of sandalwood."

Mia takes your wrist, holds the beads to her nose. "Nice."

"They're from Nepal."

After another sniff Mia releases your arm and, for courage, takes a slug of wine. "So, Carter."

"Yes ma'am?"

". . . Have you ever been married?"

You give Mia a long, sideways look, suddenly struck by the thought that it will be in this lovely lamb's heart that you might finally find sanctuary. "Never even come close," you reply, and then you ask, cautiously, leaning closer to the table's edge, "How old do you think I am?"

She squints at you. "Before you smirked, I would have guessed no younger than seventeen."

". . . No idea?"

Having altered her estimation of your age since her arrival in New York, she says, "If I *have* to guess, I suppose I would say somewhere between thirty-five and forty."

"Ouch. How about you? Ever come close to marriage?"

"Not yet. Someday. Maybe."

"What about this minister-boyfriend of yours? He's . . . not a priest, right?"

"No," Mia answers with a sigh. "He's Lutheran. His name, by the way, is Brian. His parish is a little town east of Austin called Bastrop. And we're just good friends—dancing buddies." Mia takes a sip of her water. "If he were a priest, Carter, I wouldn't be dating him. And if he were my boyfriend, I wouldn't be here with you."

Mia leaves the bathroom and ventures good-naturedly through your den, still strenuously brushing her teeth. "How'd you sleep?" she asks around a mouthful of Crest as you slurp coffee in the kitchen. She's dressed in blue sweatpants, a blue hooded sweatshirt, and a soft gray snowboarder's cap. Her cheeks are red from the cold. Her running shoes and socks are by the door. You deduce, correctly, that Mia awoke around eight, jogged with Marley along the East River, and returned home before you—still asleep on the couch—knew that she'd left. You blink groggily and smile, though not at her question. You can't take your eyes off Mia's skin, which is so jaw-achingly fair, especially in the morning light from the window, you want to throw your head back and howl.

"What's today?" you ask.

"Wednesday." *Winsdy.*

You'd planned to take Mia with you to the New York Sports Club. Now what? Scrap the gym? Play lunch by ear? Perhaps if you asked her what *she* would like to do . . .

"So, Miss Malone—how do you want to spend the day?"

"I'm game for anything," she calls to you from the bathroom. "If you need to work, I can be a tourist on my own."

"No, I'd *like* to show you around."

As Mia returns to the den, her mouth rinsed and smelling of spearmint, she asks, "What's this?"

"That's a CD-burner."

"And this?"

"A faster CD-burner."

Mia roams over to the kitchen table, taps your coffee mug with the salt shaker. "You're such a *boy*, Carter—all these high-tech doodads and computer gizmos and your fancy stereo and that silly photo album with all the snapshots of your girlfriends."

"You looked through my photo album?"

"It was wide open on the nightstand."

"Ah."

Before preparing breakfast—French toast, sliced cantaloupe, fresh orange juice—you show Mia the galleys you just got for an article to be published in *Men's Agenda*, a feature on Latin American street children, illustrated by four black-and-white portraits you took of a human-rights activist, his shelter, and three young *resistoleros* huffing glue in a Guatemala City alley. Though you say nothing, you think the shots are among the strongest you've taken since becoming a freelancer. Pretending to adjust the coffee machine, you spy on Mia, curled up on the couch with the galleys in her lap, as she scrutinizes your pictures and reads the exposé in its entirety.

You and Mia get ready to leave your apartment shortly after ten. In preparation for a long day of walking, you dress in waterproofed hiking boots, a pair of new charcoal-gray wool pants, black turtleneck sweater, black leather gloves, Gigli Massimo pea jacket, and black "homeboy" sock cap. Bundled for the cold (according to NY1, the temperature will hover around thirty), Mia also wears a turtleneck—a navy blue alpaca, a shade darker than her parka—along with her rubber boots, mittens, and yesterday's jeans, which you think are decidedly tasty.

As you secure your book bag over your shoulder, Mia asks, "Can we take Marley?" *Kin we take MAHR-lee?*

The dog is planted squarely in the foyer, eyes riveted to Mia's mittens, tail thumping against the throw rug.

"Sure," you say. "It's all good."

The first half of the day you and Mia take turns holding Marley's leash as he waddles five feet ahead of you along the snow-cleared sidewalks of Little Italy, Greenwich Village, and SoHo. To your surprise (and with more embarrassment than you reveal), your hike from Prince Street to far west Chelsea proves correct Mia's assertion: "I think, Carter, that most of the art galleries have moved up to the meat-packing district." Indeed, you discover that the Gagosian, Barbara Gladstone, and Matthew Marks galleries now line Twenty-fourth Street, between Tenth and Eleventh Avenues, in a row of renovated warehouses. *How could I not know this?* After leaving Cheim & Reid, you meander up to Thirty-third Street and share a sandwich and vanilla milkshake at the Silver Unicorn. Before hailing a cab and taking Marley home, the three of you cut through the aspen-laced, southernmost stretch of Central Park, stopping periodically to take some pictures.

After a brief rest, leaving Marley in the apartment, you and Mia continue your journey through the city by plowing your way through the Fauvist exhibit *Painters in Paris: 1895–1950* at the Metropolitan Museum, a retrospective of Sol LeWitt sculptures and murals at the Whitney Museum, and, finally, at the Museum of Modern Art a show titled *Open Ends*, which includes Cindy Sherman's "Film Stills" and Gerhard Richter's paintings based on the photographs of the Baader-Meinhof terrorists. The tour confirms for Mia how little she cares for contemporary art—and how extraordinary is the work of her favorite painters: Titian, Brueghel, Rembrandt. The only living artist Mia really cares for is Andrew Goldsworthy, a little-known Englishman who makes outdoor installations with natural materials: snow, ice, leaves, stones, feathers, petals, twigs. The bulk of modern art, she silently laments, is too much about its own size, too ego-fueled, too lonely.

More than once over the course of the afternoon, Mia leans against your shoulder—briefly, lightly—while pausing to peek through a bookshop window or stare up at the stained-glass steeple of a church you'd never before noticed. Neither of you has mentioned finding her a hotel room.

Though you have a coffee-stained contributor's copy somewhere in your apartment, you purchase from a Lexington Avenue newsstand a second copy of *DGF*'s February issue, which you roll up and secure in your book bag.

"You don't get high, do you?"

Mia removes a crumpled dollar from her parka. "No," she replies, giving the bill and a hopeful smile to a female panhandler shivering in the snow.

As you reenter the East Village, Mia asks, "Are there many scam artists in New York?"

"You mean like guys playing three-card monte?"

Mia nods.

"Yeah, sure. Every once in a while you'll see a dude set up a box in the touristy areas—Midtown, sometimes over in SoHo. Actually—see those three kids across the street at the ATM? They're scamming people right now. Those candy bars they're selling are all shoplifted. 'Would you please make a dollar donation to help pay for our school's basketball uniforms?' Right. Each of those Milky Ways is pure profit. I bet they pull in ten, fifteen bucks an hour when they're really doe-eyed about it."

Mia wonders whether you would feel the same way about the teens were they not African-American. Or whether what you say is sad but true—that, generally speaking, minority kids in New York City are afforded fewer opportunities to learn about ethics. Recently she read that there are now more black men in American prisons than in colleges. "Where *do* young guys like this get their morality?" she asks herself. "From TV? Video games? That *Sex and the City* poster on the bus?" She deplores the fact that public schools won't touch spirituality—her high school in New Orleans certainly didn't. Now that she thinks about it, there are only a handful of black teens among the congregation of her church in Austin—and only two African-Americans attended the meditation retreat in Woodstock.

"It's not right that these kids don't get a fair shake," you tell her, sensing her unease with your initial assessment, "but that's the way it is. There's so much nihilism here. Less so than there used to be, but still *way* too much. Everything works backwards from an understanding of death. Without an understanding of death, life makes no sense. We blow our life on drugs and ridiculous diets and $200 Nikes."

Or $200 Italian leather gloves, thinks Mia. "That's pretty morbid, Carter."

"'Do everything as if it's the most important thing in the world, all the while knowing it doesn't matter one bit.'"

"Yuck."

"'Hope for nothing. Fear nothing.'"

"*That's* nihilistic."

"No, not at all. Just the opposite. 'Life is best lived with a combination of love and sublime indifference.'"

"I don't see how that's possible, Carter."

"I don't see how it can be otherwise."

Despite Mia's proclaimed distaste for competition, the day ends at dusk with a chess game at an empty table in the back of the Cherry Tavern.

"The goal is to keep control of the board," you explain, rearranging Mia's black king and queen once your portable board is set up. White's bishops, lost in Mexico, have been replaced by two roasted peanuts. "To force your opponent to respond to *your* moves."

Mia offers a knowing smile. "No wonder you like this game."

Twelve moves later, winning handily and sensing Mia's ebbing interest, you suggest, "Maybe we should call this one a draw. You getting hungry? I am."

After a sushi dinner and two bottles of hot sake across the street at Mokohato's, the two of you wrap yourselves back up in your coats and scarves and venture into the night. There's no sign of further snow, but the temperature has dropped into the teens. Though exhausted and sore (you and Mia walked almost ten miles today) both of you are fueled by a combination of growing expectations, deepening pleasure in each other's company, and the warm rice wine.

Smiling again at Mia's childlike mittens, blowing vapor, you traipse through the slush from Avenue B to a dimly lit bar on Ludlow Street, called Barramundi. Even though it's only ten o'clock, the place is packed and smoky. A late-seventies song you recognize, by the Ohio Players, blasts so loudly over the sound system that the bass thumps in your chest. Sidling around Mia as you steer towards the back room (still lit with strands of red and green Christmas lights), you take her hand and make a beeline for an old threadbare couch positioned perfectly before the crackling fireplace.

"Bingo."

Soon slouched shoulder-to-shoulder against the cushions, dripping boots extended towards the flames, you order a round of Irish coffees, loll your head sideways, inhale the powdery fragrance of Mia's reddened cheeks, close your eyes, and groan at the warmth of her breath. Mia gives your shoulder a gentle nudge, her eyes moist and glimmering from the sake and her first sip of the steaming coffee. "I apologize if I was relentless with the galleries today," she says. "I'm not certain how daytime dates are supposed to go. What the expectations are." She leans closer and whispers a little too loudly in your ear, "I'm not a particularly *active* dater."

"You wanta see something?" you whisper back. Removing from your bag the rolled-up copy of *DGF*, you direct her attention to an article titled "Children of a Dying Land," written by a staff writer named Carlos Otera, and accompanied by three of your photographs from last year's trip to Peru. All three shots are of indigenous Peruvian children. "I thought you might be interested in this. It's this issue's token sensitivity piece."

"You have a good eye for kids," Mia says, holding the magazine up to the red table-lamp for a better look.

"I was on an assignment for *Men's Agenda* to hike the Inca Trail and shoot Machu Picchu. The hike took four days. We almost got lost the second day—in the middle of the friggin' Andes. When I got back to Cuzco I spent a day wandering around exposing film.

I bet I shot fifty rolls. Mostly of the people. All of it black-and-white. It was just luck that *DGF* could use these." You lean across Mia's lap and gaze at the red-lit pictures. "That little boy's cute, isn't he?"

"He's angelic."

Returning the magazine to your bag, you pretend to discover that you just happen to be in possession of a deck of playing cards. "Hey—wanta see a trick?"

"As long as I don't have to stand."

The couch area is too cramped to allow for a full fanning of your deck, which you nevertheless continue to cut with two fingers and a thumb until Mia, melting with relaxation and warmth against the back of the softly cushioned couch, finally notices.

"Pick a card," you tell her. "Any card you want."

Mia slides further down against the couch as she examines her choice, revealing it over her shoulder to an empty-trayed waitress who has stopped to watch your performance. After Mia's card is returned to the deck and thoroughly shuffled with the others, you cut the deck again and present her with the bottom card: the Nine of Spades. "Is this your card?"

"Mmm . . . nope."

As you show her each of the next three possibilities, you ask, "Is *this* your card?"

"No sir," she replies repeatedly, growing concerned that she's done something wrong, though confident that her card is not among the four you place face-down on the cocktail table.

You hand Mia the remainder of the deck. To verify that her selection is not among those you've shown her, you reveal the four cards again, confirming with each as you turn it over, "This is not your card—correct?"

"Nope. Nope. Nope. Mmm . . . nope."

You arch an eyebrow, make a show of rolling up your sweater's sleeves, and dramatically extend for inspection your empty palms.

"Okay? Now choose a number between one and four. And tell me."

"Tell you?"

"Yeah, say it out loud."

". . . Four."

"No." You shake your head. "*Between* one and four."

"What's wrong with four?"

A wave of neural alarm rises through your solar plexus. You bring a fist to your lips and clear your throat.

"Oh. Did I say four?" responds Mia, barely able to suppress a smile. "I meant two. Two, please."

"Thank you." Pointing to the cocktail table with an index finger, you count from left to right to the second card, tap it, flip it, and mutter, "Voilà."

"Yep . . . there it is. The Two of Hearts."

The waitress gasps, "Man, how'd you *do* that?"

You gather and toss the repacked deck deep into your bag of tricks. "Magic," you mumble. "Would you bring us a round of tequila shots, please?"

On the bar's sound system seventies funk gives way to contemporary Indian music. Zakkir Hussain on the tabla. Ravi Shankar on the sitar. Both you and Mia gaze into the toasty, crackling fire at your feet. You're halfway through a second Rolling Rock, feeling good, fully in the moment, no worries, your arm slung nonchalantly around Mia's shoulder. Mia is still nursing her first Irish coffee, more comfortable with you now than she's been at any point since her arrival—indeed, since meeting you.

"So, Mia. Why'd you change your name?"

She blows on her coffee. "I don't know," she says, shrugging. "Combination of reasons, I suppose. Too much time on my hands."

"You changed it legally, right?"

"Mm-hmm."

"Did you have to change your Social Security number?"

"No. I just went to the federal courthouse there in New Orleans. Met with a very nice judge, who took me into his office and asked me some questions. Wrote a check for $150. Had to run a notice in the *Times-Picayune* for three weeks, in case MasterCard was looking for me. And then I was legally Mia Malone."

"Very cool."

"I don't know how 'cool' it was. My mother's not forgiven me."

"Perhaps that was the point?"

"No—I hope not." Mia shakes her head. "That's not what it was about."

"When did you become a Catholic?"

Mia looks sideways at you. "Goodness. Is there a tape recorder in that bag too?"

"No biggie. Just curious. Just wanta know you a little better."

Mia sighs. "I guess five or six years ago."

"You didn't grow up in a Catholic household?"

"No. I was brought up by atheists."

"Really? What led you to Catholicism? I assumed Catholics always had it imposed upon them."

"When I was in high school I realized that I was more interested in spirituality than my parents, but I wasn't sure which path was best suited for my particular tastes and inclinations. I researched the Aztecs, the Hasidim—"

"The Aztecs?"

"—Siberian shamans, the Zulu. Oh yeah. I dabbled with raja and kundalini yoga. Tried aikido. And I very much love the light that shines through all of those belief-systems and experiences. But from very early on—perhaps even when I was a wee five or six—I was most drawn to Christ and Christian prayer. Ever since, that's been home base for me. After college I spent several years researching the various Christian creeds: what it meant to be a Methodist versus a Presbyterian versus a Congregationalist—that sort of thing. And then I read Thomas Merton's *The Seven Storey Mountain*, which changed my life. It was Merton who got me interested in meditation."

"How close did you come to being a nun?"

"Pretty darn. When I was a tot, my mother was into various fashion statements for me. Every season there was a new line. Summer of '79 was a gypsy flower dress she made. Fall of '80 was Scottish tartans. Spring of '81 was this navy blue pleated skirt." Mia shakes her head and giggles. "I was a fairly *odd* little girl, you should know—I used to hang out alone in my bedroom for hours, pretending to be Abraham Lincoln or drawing with my red felt-tip pen *hundreds* of little stars on the ceiling. The night after my mother presented me with the navy blue pleated skirt, I put the thing upside down on my head and pretended I was a nun. This went on for maybe a month, but then . . . regardless, I was hooked—mostly on the idea of living the rest of my life either in a church or on a houseboat with Jesus."

"Did you pray?"

Mia finishes her Irish coffee and dries her lips. "Oh, certainly."

"When did you consider becoming a nun for real?"

"Two years ago, shortly after I made the break with a beau *de jour.* I had just completed the First Rite of Initiation as a catechumen."

"What's a catechumen?"

"A neophyte Catholic."

"Did you go as far as looking into convents?"

"Mm-hmm. I seriously considered joining an order in New Orleans. And that's still a possibility. But I fear I might be too selfish to become a nun. I want to have horses and dogs and children. And I like running my own schedule. Though I'm fairly monastic by nature, I'm deeply moved by people—in that department I'm *very* romantic. So, for the moment, I've chosen the life of a grad student. We'll see how long I can hold out."

"So, this could still turn out to be a full-time gig for you?"

"Possibly."

"Wearing a habit, the whole bit?"

"The whole nine yards. I'm serious about it, Carter. I took a vow of chastity when I was thirteen."

"Huh? As in—no sex?"

"That's what chastity is generally considered, at the minimum, to entail, yes."

"Wow. So, what prompted *that?*"

"The vow?"

"Yeah."

"Well, as I understood it, chastity is God's request of His children, and I wanted to respect that."

"At thirteen? That's awfully young, isn't it?"

"I don't believe so. I had already reached puberty. Like you, I assume, I wondered why God would give us hungers that He wants us to ignore. But I realized, Carter, that we're not *supposed* to ignore them, but rather fulfill them at the right time and with the right person, so that we can most fully appreciate them. In high school many of my female friends were misusing sex, and it saddened me. We were all so *desperate* for intimacy, but we were short-changing ourselves and didn't know it."

"So, you're a virgin. That's—that's pretty amazing. Has keeping the vow been difficult?"

"Yes and no. Yes, superficially, from the standpoint that it's led to a certain amount of loneliness. And a twenty-six-year-old virgin looks to the outside world like someone who's gone nutty. But from another standpoint no, not at all. In fact, it's proven to be very helpful. It separates the wheat from the chaff in terms of learning who really cares about you."

"And this is a decision—your vow—that you feel good about, right? It's not the result of some sort of childhood trauma? You weren't sexually abused?"

"Not that I know of."

You look at Mia with growing disbelief. "Are you *certain* that you haven't repressed something? I mean, thirteen is *awfully* young to be taking a vow of chastity. And I ask this, because—sadly—it would not be that uncommon if you had. I would say maybe a third of the women I know were sexually abused as children."

"No—I had a relatively normal childhood. My parents loved me as best they could. Though neither of them was involved with the church and they were a tad moody and independent—Dad would often spend the night on a cot in his faculty office—Mom drank too much—still does—my parents were both pretty good to me. As far as abuse—a boy who lived across the street once shot his pellet gun at me, but I repressed *that* trauma for all of a month."

"How old were you when your father committed suicide?"

"Fifteen."

"Have you ever talked to a therapist?"

"*No*, Carter. Listen, I appreciate your concern, but—"

"Do you masturbate?"

"Excuse me?"

"Do you allow yourself to indulge in *any* sexual pleasures?"

Mia's cheeks turn crimson. "Aren't there better things to do with one's time?"

"Have you ever experienced stigmata?"

Mia chuckles and offers you a look of profound patience and kindness before replying, "Please don't be this way. I *have* sexual desires, Carter. I'm not made of wood." She gives your mala beads a tweak. "Did I mention that I pray a lot?"

You order a third Rolling Rock and for Mia another coffee and bourbon. Her tequila shot remains untouched on the cocktail table. Although you've needed to urinate since arriving, you refuse to move from your seat before the Barramundi fireplace. Warm and sleepy, you can't tell where the left side of your body ends and the right side of Mia's begins.

"I routinely hear or read, Carter, how we Catholics regard sex as having the nature of sin. How marriage can be a sacrament if sex is a sin, I will leave for others to determine. And I disagree passionately with the Buddhist notion that the world and the flesh are evil. *Things* cannot be evil. You Buddhists have it backwards: The work of heaven is material, the work of *hell* is entirely spiritual. May I have one of your cigarettes?"

Suddenly flushed with desire, you shake out one of the Marlboro Lights, lean closer and whisper into Mia's ear, "Sometimes when I meditate, my Buddha statue animates. It begins to breathe."

Mia shivers after the first puff of her cigarette. "Do you smoke pot before you meditate?"

". . . Not always."

Three puffs later Mia closes her eyes. Her face has taken on a bit of a sheen: a long day of walking, the sake, the Irish coffees, the loud music, and now the cigarette have left her light-headed.

"Are you okay?" you ask.

Mia opens her eyes, smiles, squeezes your arm.

"Tell me," you continue in a gentler, more earnest tone. "Do you believe that a fledgling Buddhist, someone who likes kids and does volunteer work every Sunday evening and meditates pretty much every day—and for the sake of argument we'll call meditation 'prayer'—so he *prays* every day—he's a truth seeker—someone who aspires to a life filled with love and patience and who *tries* to conduct himself by a moral code that's fairly Christian in nature—will that person, despite his pursuit of those goals, be condemned to hell solely because he doesn't believe that Christ is God?"

"Any person who truly loves will go to heaven."

"Who then goes to hell?"

"Someone who imposes hell on himself. Someone who says that he wants to have no part of God, no part of love, no part of joy. It's all about the disposition of the heart, Carter. God is, quite literally, love."

"Okay, but if God is love, why would He allow *anyone* to burn in hell?"

"He's given us free will."

"But why even make hell an option? How can God be both love and all-powerful and allow *any* of His children to descend into hell?"

"Because He respects our free will."

"But, Mia, nobody actively chooses to go to hell."

"Some people love hating God."

"You said earlier that God resides in heaven, that He wants to win us over, which seems to anthropomorphize Him. Is God a *being?*"

"Yes."

"A being."

"Yes. God is a being, not a thing. Man and woman are made in the image of God, not the other way around."

"In my ear, heaven and nirvana sound more similar than different. They're *realms.* States of divine, transhuman bliss, where there's absolute freedom and no suffering. Buddhists believe that one reaches 'heaven' by dissolving the ego, the artificial self."

"I don't believe that self can dissolve self. Who is capable of dissolving the self?"

"A Buddha."

"But you're not a Buddha."

"Ahh—yes I am. And so are you. We're *all* potential Buddhas."

"Okay—in that sense I don't necessarily disagree with you. But Christians see that as the *true* self, the self which is grounded in God, who is love. It's the true self that does battle with Brother Ass, as Saint Francis expressed it. The battle between Good and Evil. In the New Testament, it says that all Christians are saints. We're born with sainthood potential. It's the same principle. One becomes a fully realized saint, if you will, when she drops her selfish pursuits and fully opens herself to God. Thomas Aquinas says that when one *knows* something—when one, say, knows a coffee pot—one *becomes* the coffee pot."

"That's Buddhism."

"That's Christianity. They're apples and oranges. They are very different religions. But you know what, Carter? Quite frankly, if I weren't a Christian, I'd probably be a Dharma practitioner."

"Yeah?"

"Or a Taoist, though Taoists can be pretty eccentric. No—surprise, surprise—I very much *appreciate* Buddhism, Carter. I like Buddhism's essential framework, which seems fairly compatible with Christianity. The rituals and sense of community. The Dharma is very beautiful. It's loving and compassionate and respectful and gentle and *very* philosophical. And I agree with you—the similarities between Christianity and Buddhism are striking. St. John of the Cross talks about arriving at the liberty of the divine through the dissolution of the self. The prayer of St. Francis and the bodhisattva vows both encourage us to dedicate our blessings to the benefit of others. But I'm *not* a Buddhist, and I'm not a Buddhist primarily because I know the *person* of Jesus Christ, who is God, and Buddhism doesn't offer that."

Mia's face is now no more than six inches from yours. You stare into her green eyes, into the hazy reflections animating their depths. A kind of holy smoke fills your body, your heart, and you realize with breathtaking intensity—you *know*—that it will be with this woman that you either find or lose your soul. Muzzy from the alcohol, eyelids beginning to droop, you decide to bring your time on the couch to a close. Making something like a sigh, you kiss Mia's cheek, give her ponytail a playful tug, and ask, "Would you like to forgo searching for a hotel and stay with me—as friends—until you return to Texas?"

With surprising and touching formality, Mia offers a little bow and with a shy smile replies, "I think I might very much enjoy that, Carter. Thank you."

• • •

Delivered to your apartment building by gypsy cab twenty minutes later, you and Mia fumble with the front door and then, hand in hand, creak up the wooden steps to the sixth floor. It's almost three in the morning. As you unlock the two dead-bolts securing your apartment door, Mia rests her cheek against your shoulder. You can smell—almost taste—the Irish coffee on her breath.

With a shake of your head you brush away an observation that pops unbidden into your brain: in less than thirty-six hours Mia Malone will return, perhaps forever, to her life in Austin, Texas, two thousand miles away.

Once inside the darkened, warmed den, lit moodily (and not unexpectedly) by the red undulating lava lamp on your computer's flat-panel monitor, Mia allows you to remove her parka and with a contented groan collapses onto the end of your couch. The steam radiator across the room shudders with heat. A faint lavender fragrance from the stick of Sri Kresnan incense, burnt after breakfast over half a day ago, still hangs in the air.

"You want anything?" you ask from the foyer.

Mia shakes her head. "I'm terrific."

When you return from walking Marley around the block, Mia is sitting up and leaning towards the end-table's reading lamp, studying again the *Men's Agenda* article on the Guatemalan street children. Her rubber boots have been placed against a wall by the front door. Her mouth smells of toothpaste. Her long black hair—made even longer and minklike by brushing—is down and draped in a thick *S* over her left shoulder.

"You wanta make out a little?" you ask.

Though Mia smiles demurely and accepts your outstretched hand at the suggestion—she's wanted to be kissed by you all day—she's surprised when you tug her from the couch and lead her into the bedroom, where the pair of Japanese paper lamps flanking your bed are already lit. So is a candle on the headboard, she notes, hesitating for a moment by the door before stepping into the shadowy orange light. Silently she joins you cross-legged atop your lilac silk Calvin Klein comforter.

"We can stretch out in here, be a little more comfortable," you explain, taking Mia's hand again. "I thought we'd just cuddle some. Sleepy?"

Mia nods. "A little."

"Drunk?"

"No."

"Good. Let's take this off," you suggest, carefully lifting the blue alpaca sweater over Mia's head and up her reluctantly surrendered arms. You sigh and kiss her cheek, ingest deeply the aroma of her skin. Beneath the sweater Mia has on a faded white Continental Club T-shirt, purchased the first month she moved to Texas, which she wears over her bathing suit top when riding her bicycle to Barton Springs. You lean back on your elbows and smile. Her goose-fleshed arms are thin and pale, though she has surprisingly well-defined biceps—chiefly from carrying the backpack full of textbooks. You look at her hips, her throat. She's built like a bird, you think. Mia thinks this as well. She considers herself skinny and embarrassingly small-chested, the chief reason you've not seen her wear anything other than big turtlenecks and baggy running sweats. Self-conscious, she lies down next to you in her jeans and untucked T-shirt, her hands placed prayer-fashion between her cheek and pillow as the two of you lie on your sides facing one another. After a few moments of silent staring, you reach across Mia's chest and dim the Japanese paper lamp.

Aglow in the soft, ocher light, Mia watches you nervously. She is, in fact, more intoxicated than she initially realized, the room wobbling, her eyes—straining to remain focused—glistening with excitement, fear, and arousal. The Lord's Prayer passes her lips like the tail of a falling star. She can't decide whether God has sent you into her life as a test or a gift. "Today was wonderful," she murmurs, struggling against the mattress in an effort to sit up. "Thank you for being a lovely host."

"My pleasure—hey—yo—off the bed, dude." You give Marley a gentle shove—Mia petting his hindquarters—his presence relaxing her a little—before the dog descends to the floor and curls up beside the dresser, his snuffled wet nose turned back towards the comforter.

You and Mia begin to kiss, and the kissing is good. Splendid, in fact. This is not what you anticipated. Not at all. Lovely Mia Malone, the book-smart virgin, firmly presses her stomach against your stomach, her legs against your legs, her long black hair cascading luxuriously across the pillows. You close your eyes as her fingertips caress your cheeks. You glance down at the curve of her breasts beneath the stretched cotton, smile at the faint sourness of sweat under her arms. With a groan you position her on top of you—her legs straddling your hips—and kiss her deeply again, her thumbs secured around two of your belt loops, your shirt untucked, quickly losing yourself in the heat of her mouth, in the weight of her body. Her lips and hair brush against your neck, your throat, your ear, her breathing so accelerated—so forceful—that you pull back for a moment to make sure that she's okay.

"Hey—Mia," you whisper, "look at me. Open your eyes. Are you okay with this? Are we going too fast?"

"Yes," she answers, out of breath, looking down at you with flushed cheeks, her palms pressing against your chest as it rises and falls. "And yes. I *want* to be here, Carter. I'll tell you if I feel uncomfortable."

With perked ears Marley watches you and Mia continue kissing on top of the comforter. For the next hour and seventeen minutes, you kiss and moan and laugh—fully clothed, chaste and affectionate, and yet more soulful and profoundly pleasing than you imagined mere kissing could be. Occasionally Mia utters a gentle "No,

Carter" when your hands find their way to the buttons of her jeans. But these admonitions only accentuate your pleasure, and the warmth and tenderness of her touch.

Eventually you see that Mia has fallen asleep. After kisses to her cheek and forehead, you pull yourself from the bed, lean Mia's backpack against the dresser, turn off the light, snuff the headboard candle, lead Marley (who doesn't want to leave the bedroom) by the collar, and depart for the den, quietly closing the door behind you.

After making a pot of peppermint tea, you move in the dark to your meditation cushion. With a pack of matches from Barramundi you light the three votive candles on the altar. You take your time drinking the tea, exhaling with each sip before swallowing, enjoying the warmth in your belly, the warmth of the mug between your palms. As your shoulders continue to relax, you wonder: Have I developed a crush on Mia despite her virginity or because of it? After Marley plods over from the kitchen and lays his head in your lap, you clasp your hands and bow towards the shrine, whispering, "I take refuge in the Buddha. I take refuge in the Dharma. I take refuge in the Sangha." It's been a good day, you tell yourself, going back to the beginning and then replaying as many moments as you can remember until you arrive at the present.

In the candlelight, you focus your attention on the Buddha statue, the centerpiece of your modest altar. Made in Java, the seventy-year-old, cocoa-colored Buddha Shakyamuni, with his symbolic earth-touching hand gesture, cast in stone and gesso-coated, stands just over 11 inches high from his lotus-crested pedestal to the top of his elevated crown chakra. You feel there's something very precise and gentle about this particular depiction of the Buddha. His elongated ears. His lowered lids and peaceful half-smile. His cheeks and jawline are soft, almost chubby, and there's little if any muscle definition in his exposed shoulder and outstretched arm. But his chin is held high, his countenance decidedly regal. The beige-washed red and gold of his robe, the faded green trim along the pedestal, the earthy color of his skin, which seems at times to mysteriously expand and contract with your own breathing—all of the Buddha's details give a depth to your open-throated silence, and to your blossoming attraction to Mia. You close your eyes and, only twice losing track, count the next three hundred breaths.

A half hour later you bow again to the altar and open your eyes. Marley snores against your thigh. The candle flames dance with colors, and you inhale deeply again to get what's left of the incense. You uncross your legs with a low cry—both have fallen asleep. You lean forward, rubbing your calves, your attention gradually drawing back to the altar, specifically towards the Buddha statue. You lean closer and squint in the flickering candlelight. How weird, you whisper to yourself. You verify what you see with a touch. You run a hand through your hair and lean back for a different perspective. Could it be? Either the blemish has been there all along and you're just now noticing it, or it appeared during the past thirty minutes. You recall the antique gold band Mia wears to confirm the significance of the defect's location. Yes, there's no question about it: the fourth finger of the Buddha statue's right hand—his outstretched hand—is now chipped precisely in the shape and placement of a wedding ring.

5

THIRTY-TWO WEEKS AGO—roughly seven months before the shoot in Zipolite, and eight months to the day before your thirty-ninth birthday, which officially begins at midnight—you first visited the Greenwich Village office of New York City's Volunteers in Action, a nonprofit community-service placement agency, ripe with a sudden and mysteriously acquired altruism. You had no idea about what motivated the impulsive (and unprecedented) civic-mindedness to commit one night a week—"a tithe of my time"—to those in the city less fortunate than you, the spontaneous vow made out loud while eating a second serving of dessert at Odeon with a bemused first date named Belinda Witherspoon. That night you slept alone and dreamed of hang-gliding over Sacramento. The next morning you marched up NYCVA's three flights of stairs and declared yourself a "ready, willing, and able volunteer" to a plump, bespectacled, sixty-three-year-old African-American woman talking on the phone beneath a pink-and-blue "Have a Heart" poster. Even though the three windows of her cramped office were closed, the briny tang of uncooked seafood in The Lotus Café's kitchen on the brick building's first floor wafted up like a vaporous fog. A rattling, wall-mounted air-conditioner's blue-tasseled breeze forced the woman to keep a hand on top of the fluttering yellow papers stacked in her "out" basket. The woman seemed not to notice you. With a sigh, she eventually hung up, swiveled around in her chair, and looked at you as if you might be hiding a firearm. Pushing a clipboard across her desktop, she virtually growled: "Driver's license, please."

Her first and only question made it clear that she assumed you were another low-level criminal, sentenced to her office by the municipal judges. "A sweet-smelling cookie like you—I'm guessin' either shoplifting or cheating on your taxes, right?" When you told her no, this was not the case, not the case at all, the woman lowered her glasses and squinted at you anew, explaining forlornly, "We don't get many folks come off the street. And mosta our male volunteers are servin' the public by court order. I apologize."

"No sweat," you replied, "it's all good," pleased at apparently being an exception to the Hobbesian norm. "I'm just interested in helping out somewhere."

"Well, let's see what we got for ya today." The woman—who you noticed had freckles, despite her dark skin—straightened her glasses and dutifully flipped through a cream-colored file containing three sheets of tea-stained paper. "We got some azalea bushes in a community garden up in the Bronx that need trimmin'," she suggested. "We got some crack babies that need holdin' at Roosevelt Hospital Saturday mornings. And we got a hospice group over in Chelsea that needs someone to fix Sunday dinners for an old fella with the AIDS. What's your pleasure?"

That next Sunday evening you arrived with sweaty palms and butterflies in your stomach at an apartment on Eighteenth Street and Eighth Avenue, essentially ground-zero for Manhattan's gay population. Dreading the prospect of experiencing firsthand—or, more accurately, secondhand—the stink and clammy touch of death, you'd downed a quick shot of bourbon at the first Chelsea bar you saw and then further armed yourself with additional entertainment supplies from a nearby Korean deli. On the stoop you checked the address again and held your breath as you pressed the button for apartment 3C with an elbow, the brownstone's street-level door buzzing and unlatching before you could change your mind. In the stairwell you heard Louis Armstrong's scratchy trumpet coming from the third floor. You were surprised to be greeted, as the apartment door swung open, not with the stench of the morgue but with the fragrance of sandalwood incense and a throaty chuckle at your effort to balance in your arms, pyramid-fashion, a stack of magazines, a chessboard, and a large, grease-stained sack of maki rolls. "You didn't have to make a mither," the apartment owner—a tall, completely bald "Buddyism teacher" (so said his NYCVA file) named Christopher Wolf—remarked over the music in a shaky voice straining to be heard but clearly clipped with a cockney accent. "The bloke who used to come—he'd just leave a can of Campbell's on the doorstep and toddle off without a word."

Though still cheerful, Christopher had already grown physically frail and stooped and nearly blind. Until he told you the date of his birth, you overestimated his actual age of fifty-four by two decades. For the first hour of that first Sunday you sat on the couch next to him watching *60 Minutes* and eating the take-out sushi in awkward silence, trying not to glance over at the odd fellow's green silk pajamas and aviator sunglasses. "Sorry I'm still in my scruffs," he said eventually. "At least I got my choppers in." He smiled, and tapped his dentures with the tip of a chopstick. You could think of nothing to say. Nothing. Though she knew your "service recipient" solely from his file, Mrs. Williams over at the NYCVA office had advised you to "always encourage the dying person to talk, and then just listen, and receive what he has to say in silence. Pray with him if he's gotta pray. Just try to make the fella feel comfortable and secure. You don't have to be no expert. Just be a friend." Fortunately for you, Christopher needed little nudging to talk. The moment *60 Minutes* concluded, he flipped off the TV with the remote control, turned to you with his Cheshire Cat grin, leaned forward—so far forward, in fact, that you could see your panic-stricken face reflected in his sunglasses—and whispered, "If it's true that all suffering comes from the desire for our own happiness, then it's also true that selflessness leads to peace."

You nodded, discreetly checked your watch, and mumbled, "I'll take that under advisement."

By the end of the third Sunday evening with Christopher, you knew that your impulse to give back a little something to the world had already been repaid tenfold. Gradually, and almost always with information you solicited from him—he seldom proselytized—Christopher introduced you to the world of Tibetan Buddhism. Before volunteering to help cook dinners for this self-described "willy woofter" Brit dying of AIDS, you knew nothing about Siddhartha Gautama. You knew nothing about karma. You knew nothing about the intricacies of rebirth. Christopher was guiding you through *tonglen* "compassion" meditations that left you in tears (you never told him how extraordinary a feat that was), and with remarkable patience—especially in light of his physical discomfort—explaining for hours what he merrily called "the magic of the Noble Eightfold Path, *bodhicitta*, and the awakened heart of unconditional love."

It didn't take too many Sundays for you to wonder who was helping whom.

"'Know ten things, tell one,' Tibetan elders say." (This was the first entry you wrote in your Dharma journal.) By cultural and spiritual inclination Buddhists, especially Buddhist meditation masters, reveal little of themselves or their practice. The biographical information you got from Christopher over the months came in spurts—in fact, it was only on seeing the Woodstock retreat booklet that you learned that he was fluent in Sanskrit. When he moved to Manhattan in 1986, after taking off his monk robes ("for reasons too numerous to even *begin* to discuss"), supporting himself for a while by teaching math at a public high school in Brooklyn, he became increasingly enamored of Mahayana Buddhism (the bodhisattva's way of "universal liberation") and the teachings of Jamyang Khyentse Rinpoche, with whom he eventually studied and served as a lay teacher.

In 1993 Christopher tested HIV positive during a routine screening at a community blood drive sponsored by a Chelsea hospice, and almost immediately his health—in particular his eyesight—began to deteriorate. Before your first visit to his apartment last June, he'd already been taken to the emergency room three times. Just before January's retreat in Woodstock, he returned to the hospital with a case of shingles. His growing brittleness and failing eyesight made it difficult for him to venture far from his apartment, or even prepare food, but still you sensed that it was only with great reluctance that he accepted the offer from NYCVA to have someone provide his Sunday dinners. Friends from several cross-sectional communities, both local and distant, regularly visited Christopher during the week, but he was obviously pained by the attention. "Given a choice, I'd rather worm out from help such as yours, Carter," he confessed. "I'm still too vain, too full of myself to surrender to the care. I'm tight as a gnat's chuff when it comes to accepting kindness. But a blind man with pride will one day burn down his neighbor's apartment. Even in this, I must let go."

In addition to recurring incidences of Kaposi's sarcoma, Christopher battled cytomegalovirus retinitis, the potentially sight-ending infection of the eyes common to AIDS sufferers. "Nearly fifty percent of us are affected by the blasted condition," Christopher explained with little self-pity. "Antiretroviral drugs helped at first, but the ophthalmologist decided to go with ganciclovir eye implants—a tiny device surgically inserted within the eyes that supposedly delivers the drug around the clock. I can't say that it's helping. I don't know if it much matters anymore."

More than once while in Christopher's presence you shuddered at your own Faustian arrogance: "Who am I to assume that this illness will pass me by?" You're a bachelor, almost forty years of age, and have slept with more women than you can count. "It's this skin-bag of ours that gets us into most of the trouble," Christopher warned, poking at your chest and arms with a bony finger. "Better to stay home and bash the bishop than shag someone you'll never see again. Better still," he advised with a wink and pinch of your bicep, "just leave the bishop alone and go take a seat on the cushion."

In addition to the wisdom Christopher dispensed, one of the chief reasons you enjoyed your Sunday evening pilgrimages to Chelsea—to your "dinner *sangha* of two," as Christopher referred to the weekly three-hour get-togethers—was exploring the strange interior of his two-bedroom apartment. "Is 'Tibetan kitsch' a term?" you once asked him, joking about the red-velvet furniture, the dark, wood-paneled walls decorated with campy art nouveau pieces, porcelain poodles, silk *thangkas*, and framed photographs of Jamyang Khyentse Rinpoche and the Dalai Lama. Christopher's zabuton cushion was canary yellow. An old chain-pull toilet was the centerpiece of "the loo." Candles flickered through the smoke rising from dozens of perpetually burning sandalwood incense sticks, and until you sat and began each week's meditation session, his wireless radio in the kitchen was almost always playing old jazz or Italian opera. The spare bedroom, transformed into an ethereally illuminated shrine room (dubbed by Christopher "the death sanctuary"), looked to you like an opium den: mosquito netting, oversize throw cushions, Malaysian shadow puppets, a pair of smoky, silk-fringed oil lamps flanking his Buddha-mounted altar. "I know, I know," he replied, chuckling. "This place has become a bizarre hybrid of Tibet House and an Amsterdam café circa 1940. What can I say, Carter? I'm as camp as a row of tents."

It didn't come as a complete surprise when Christopher mentioned late one Sunday evening in November that he'd begun experimenting with "God-enabling" entheogens, mind-altering chemicals—namely, psilocybin mushrooms, which he referred to as "the Medicine." Save for the occasional Buddhist retreat or conference, Christopher's days at that time consisted chiefly of long stretches of meditation: a potentially injurious five or six hours at a spell on the cushion were not unusual for him, he admitted. And he'd begun fasting, sometimes for two or three days, limiting his daily intake of liquid to a meager teaspoon of lemon juice. "I agree with Plato," he announced that cool autumnal night, almost feverishly, his cockney accent strangely amplified: "Heaven-sent madness is superior to man-made sanity. The things I've *seen*, Carter—awesomely beautiful. Did you know that the Aztecs called mushrooms 'God's flesh'? It's true, true. Huxley, William James, Huston Smith—they were fearless, those chaps. *Fearless.* They *know* that there's most certainly another reality—a *perfect* reality—that leaves this one in the dust. The Medicine doesn't *cause* visionary experiences—it *reveals* them. It loosens the valve and lets the Absolute freely flow."

You wondered whether Christopher's mind had begun to slip, or if in fact his proximity to death was making it ever more lucid. And how a nearly blind, fifty-four-year-old former Buddhist monk acquired psilocybin mushrooms, you had no idea. Had they been delivered? Christopher flicked his wrist and said, "This is New York, Carter. If you use your loaf, you can find anything." When you asked about the possible danger of mixing psychedelics with ganciclovir, Christopher shrugged and said cryptically, "Oh—I plan to die *before* I die. And don't give me that look, love—I would never commit suicide."

The first time you witnessed one of Christopher's "Medicine journeys," as he referred to them, it was clear that he was transported. Shortly after consuming the mushrooms, he creakily assumed a half-lotus position on his bright yellow zabuton, surrounded by candles and incense and a scattering of Buddhist icons—statues of White Tara and Manjushri, a drawing of

Padmasambhava, the eighth-century Indian who brought Buddhism to Tibet—and gently requested that you stay by his side. Traditionally, Tibetan Buddhists meditate with opened eyes, and you soon saw that Christopher's pupils had dilated. There was reddening of his skin. Facial contortions. His bald head and temples began to pour sweat, and fine muscle tremors rippled through his upper body. "How often has he done this?" you wondered nervously. Though his mouth remained closed, every few seconds he would groan. At one point he muttered several garbled sentences, followed by a prolonged gasp of your name—"Carter . . . Carter"—which trailed off into silence. You checked his pulse periodically, and after two or three challenging hours, sensing that things were slowing down, you lowered him onto his right side, as he'd earlier requested, into what Tibetan Buddhists call the Lion Posture: head slightly raised on a cushion or pillow, right hand cupping the face, left arm extended down the left leg—the sleeping position most conducive to lucid dreaming.

Long after midnight, when he finally came around, Christopher opened his dry mouth, blinked hard several times and, as if with overwhelming relief and gratitude, reached his hand to touch yours and immediately began to weep. His strange tears continued for several minutes. He was unable to recall (or perhaps unwilling to provide) the details of his experience, but it was clear that the drug-induced journey had left a powerful, perhaps even profound mark on him. "Awesome, awesome," was all he would say as you sat with him in his kitchen afterwards, sipping hot chamomile tea.

How much of his six-hour mushroom trip was truly mystical and how much was the deluded vision of a man confronting the specter of death you could only guess. Holding your shoulders as you were taking your leave, his face still contorted and discolored, Christopher looked you in the eye, leaned close, and with great passion whispered in your ear, "Burn the self until it's no longer there. *Incinerate* the self, Carter. Then there'll be nothing to separate you from the Great Perfection."

Christopher never encouraged you to try an entheogen, or criticized your reluctance to "give yourself over," as you put it. Nor did he ever make you feel compelled to mention the near-fatal drug overdose of your youth, or how much you feared the terror and possible irreversible transformation that might come with surrendering yourself—your *self*—to an experience as powerful-seeming as his. Nor did Christopher explicitly reproach you when you announced, during what would prove to be one of your last dinners together, that young Mia Malone (whom he remembered, with a knowing smile, from the Woodstock retreat), had recently departed your East Village apartment after a three-day visit. At the news that Mia was both a Catholic and a virgin, Christopher looked intently at you with his left eye (his right was patched with white gauze), and you feared that you glimpsed a direful warning flash like lightning across his face. He responded, "And I suppose that the two of you continued your vow of Noble Silence during her stay?" For several moments you stared down at your plate of reheated spinach lasagna. "Tonight I don't think I'll be up for any photos," he continued in a lowered voice, apparently disappointed in you. "Sometimes I feel I'd rather stick a sewing needle through my heart than pose for your bloody cameras."

"You'll notice, Chris, that tonight I didn't *bring* any cameras."

"Ah, so you haven't."

"Do you disapprove of my involvement with this woman because I met her at your retreat? Is that it? Or because she's considerably younger than I am?"

"I don't disapprove of anything, Carter. If the teacher is wrong, the teacher is also right, and if the student is right, the student is also wrong."

"Whatever."

"After it pains you long enough, you'll grow tired of it, and then it will stop."

"I'm not *in* pain, Chris."

"Oh?" Christopher sighed. His unpatched eye shimmered chaotically, as if full of broken glass. With the palm of his hand he flattened his napkin. "Each of us is a vessel, a lantern aglow with the spark of divinity. But that divinity is so obscured by human frailties—human *hungers*, Carter—so smudged up with grease and soot that the light's only minimally discernible." Christopher reached over the table and placed his fingertips to your chest. "Keep your lantern clean, my handsome friend—love fully, let go fully—for no one knows when death will arrive."

The morning of your thirty-ninth birthday deteriorates quickly. After a miserably cold trudge around the snow-covered block with Marley, you settle down in front of one of your computer screens with a lukewarm mug of Fairway's southern-pecan coffee and check your e-mail. The first one leaves you aching wistfully enough to rub your chest:

Subject: Halloooh from Texas
Electronic Mail Sent: 8:22 AM, Tuesday 20 February 2001
From: Mia Malone
To: Carter Cox

Dear Carter,

You may remember us sitting shoulder to shoulder one lovely evening in Manhattan during my visit there centuries ago, bantering about a matter I referred to as "habits of being." I asked you point blank who the most spiritual person was—to describe him or (alas) her—that you'd met along your travels, because I assumed that the description would assist me in understanding your vision of

Spirituality. I believe you mentioned an old fellow in Jakarta or Sulawesi (I apologize for not remembering which), and how everything he did or said appeared to issue straight from the core of his being, that his heart and mind were single, unlike the rest of us who possess "crumbling minds and murky spirits."

Well, what you said struck me as absolutely on target. There is a saying in the Mundaka Upanishad, perhaps you know it: "Take the great bow of the Upanishads and place in it an arrow sharp with devotion. Draw the bow with concentration and hit the center of the mark, the same everlasting Spirit. The bow is the sacred Om, and the arrow is our own soul."

For me, of course, you would replace the Upanishads with the Holy Scriptures, the Spirit would be understood as the Triune God or the Holy Spirit, and Om would be rendered instead as Abba. Beyond such differences, the spirit/intention is the same. My point: Your wonderful words (and photographs) inspired and have stayed with me over these past few weeks. Thank you. I'm a very hungry young woman, and I find inspiration a powerful delicacy. I suppose all this makes me sound like a fool. So be it. I never promised you I was a saint, much less an angel. I live on the hope that Christ will one day be able to say of me, as of the woman in the Gospels: "But she loved much."

Thank you again for your hospitality and friendship, Carter. I trust we will stay in touch and perhaps one day (as you put it) "cross paths," be it on the high road or the low one.

I think of you often, and with all my heart I wish you a happy, happy birthday.

Yours,
Mia (Malone)

The contents of an earlier e-mail you now open elicit from you a howl let loose so loudly and despairingly that Marley comes running from the kitchen. Sent to you late Friday afternoon from the folks at *Men's Agenda*, the short missive went unchecked for three days for precisely this reason—somehow you knew. You stare at the computer screen, shaking your head. The 6,500-word story scheduled for *Men's Agenda*'s April issue has been killed—and with it, of course, all of your accompanying photography. It does not help that you're told of the story's termination by the art director's twenty-three-year-old assistant, who offers in her e-mail no explanation for the decision other than a perfunctory "The executive editors felt uncomfortable with the writing." What a shame, you mutter. The galley layout had included (*featured*, Mia assured you) four Carter Cox photos, all of which you thought looked terrific. To boot: as stipulated in your contract, the kill fee will be only one quarter, $2,500 of the full payment you assumed you'd be receiving—and in fact have already spent.

Concerned about your moaning and the fact that your head is now hanging between your knees, Marley approaches the desk and tentatively gives your left cheek a lick. You rise up, sigh, and give your loyal companion a half-hearted scratch behind the ears.

The story, for which you and an assistant flew to Guatemala City (the ugliest, most frightening place on earth, you decided) and spent a harrowing week photographing dozens of wild-eyed street children while they huffed cans of hardware-store glue, would surely have drawn secondary press. The article explicitly accused a Fortune 500 American chemicals company of *aiming* the sale of its toluene-based cobbler's paste to this street-kid market—of essentially peddling an addictive narcotic to tens of thousands of Latin American children. Though an awful experience for you, the seven days in Guatemala City had produced some powerful images. What you'd seen at night in the barrios had shocked you: ragged and malnourished homeless kids piled up like shivering puppies in garbage-strewn alleys and unlit city parks. One feral-looking boy, paralyzed from months of sniffing the sweet-smelling but toxic toluene (one of the Ts in TNT, you learned to your dismay), dragged himself through the puddles among the fruit vendors' stands on a flattened cardboard box. Returning to the relative safety of New York, you felt renewed appreciation (and hope) for the power—perhaps even the magic—a camera can wield.

You glance across the den at the twin-lens Rolleiflex, your very first camera, given to you as a birthday present by your mother twenty-seven years ago today, collecting dust on the bookshelf next to the unopened UPS package containing an unneeded CD-ROM drive for your new laptop computer. "Don't just capture the thing itself," your mother—an ambitious amateur photographer—had said in a calm, soothing voice, when you showed her your earliest efforts. "Look and find the thing's sum and substance. And be more gentle with natural light," she would encourage, "but more ruthless with your framing. Make *art*, Carter. You have it in you."

As a young man you aspired to do that—to capture a subject's spirit, its very essence, with the in-breath of a shutter: to wield your camera like a magician's wand. Poof! Another ghost would mysteriously appear in the developer. How marvelous the process seemed to you! You felt like a sorcerer. Your favorite place in the world was in the red-lit stuffiness of a darkroom, with the delicious stink of all those exotic chemicals and the sight of your wet 5" x 7" prints dripping from wooden clothespins above the sink. At first you did portraits, and your best pictures captured, as if with divine help, the pure joy animating your three sisters as they glanced up, giggling, one after the other, from their row of coloring books. These early images could hint at the sad narrative of a widower neighbor's alcoholic stare. They gave life to the complicated history behind your father's forlorn smile as he watched, barefoot and alone, those beautiful California sunsets every evening on the back porch. The opening-night reception for your debut show at UCLA—an undergraduate group exhibit in the Union Café, earnestly titled "Visions of Time"—is to date perhaps the most glorious three hours of your life. Initially you *did* make art, you tell yourself. You truly did. And even after your move to New York, your best commercial work (at least in the beginning, you'd like to think), still had some spirit. But $1,800-a-month rent and print-lab fees and health insurance and the computer upgrades and the twice-weekly dinner dates soon transformed your magic wand, by financial necessity, into a cold, gray gun for hire.

You stare down at your coffee mug. *What's going on? What have I done to deserve this?* Your last two assignments were a lowly camping-gear-catalogue shoot and a series of headshots for a fledgling soap-opera actress. Upon opening your contributor's copy of *Eastern Horizon* yesterday, you'd discovered with a shock that there in the sky, hovering shamelessly above a self-absorbed rap star you'd photographed in his million-dollar Gramercy Park loft, was a computer-generated full moon. Disgusting. And now *Men's Agenda* had dropped the ball. Granted, you remind yourself, the trip to southern Mexico last month was a good gig, but assignments like that are coming around less and less often.

Your art is now your job, you lament, and how magical can one be with camping gear and pouty rap stars? And when you *do* get a chance to make art—to throw yourself into a terrific project, to possibly even make the world a little better off for your efforts—you get an e-mail on your birthday notifying you that it's been scrapped.

You kill the computer and phone Christopher to see how he's feeling (he'd been in especially poor shape this past Sunday evening), though he deflects attention away from himself and back towards you. You can hear Cole Porter's "Easy to Love" playing in the background. "You sound a bit *off*, Carter—anything the matter?" You hang up after several minutes of chatting without mentioning that you turned thirty-nine today, or that the only person who's invited you to do anything by way of celebration is your philandering pool-buddy, Nick.

Skipping your nightly meditation (you're too agitated to stay seated), decked out in a red turtleneck and the new black Armani sports jacket you gave yourself as a birthday gift, you hail a cab and meet up with Nick around eleven at a bar he suggested near Washington Square Park, called Club Foot. This being a Tuesday night, the line behind the velvet rope at the door is short and consists primarily of bored-looking NYU coeds. The young, steam-breathing woman directly in front of you, wearing brown corduroy pants and a Himalayan fur hat with ear flaps, rhythmically clomps a pair of oversized, block-heeled "Franky" boots in the snow, apparently to stay warm. She returns your smile with a barely perceptible nod. Her eyes are red. Her jacket smells of marijuana.

Feeling overdressed and a tad too gray for Club Foot's twenty-something scene (on the phone Nick had described Club Foot as "Balthazar on acid"), as soon as you enter the throbbing darkness of the "bistro funk-lounge" you reruffle your hair, remove your jacket, and slip your titanium-clasped Seiko into a front pocket. Thirty-nine is not yet forty, you remind yourself, and tonight you have absolutely nothing to lose.

Before you begin searching for Nick, you head straight for the bar, money-clip in hand, order and knock back an ounce of Johnny Walker Black, and ask for a cigarette from the extraordinarily tall woman standing beside you. After the first long drag, you lean back on your elbows and look around. You like the feel of the place. The decor—a pressed-tin ceiling, smoky mirrors, endless rows of green Perrier bottles—gives the lounge an oddly European flavor. Though the two bartenders wear short crimson jackets and black bow-ties, many of the patrons are in hip-hop gear: sock hats, unlaced Timberlands, puffy coats. Several feet away from you an Asian woman, whose black hair is piled atop her head beneath a pink-tipped lotus blossom, nods along to a song by Spring Heel Jack. Another woman wears sunglasses and a light-blue feather boa around her bare shoulders. Every few seconds the overhead lighting bounces unnervingly from a pulsating yellow strobe to a purplish, sixties-style black light. The blouse on the towering woman next to you momentarily glows white. In the ten minutes you spend smoking your cigarette, the disc jockey's selections shift dramatically, jarringly, from the frenetic Spring Heel Jack dance number to salsa to a narcotically slow tune by a band your most recent photo-assistant introduced you to, called Shudder to Think. The dance floor, presently unused, is surrounded by a dozen or so metal-and-glass tables and a series of alcoves, partitioned off from the bar by metal walls containing colossal, blue-lit aquariums.

You eventually spot Nick ensconced in one of the alcove's corner booths, conversing with a small crowd of people, mostly women, all of whom have their backs to you as you approach. You note that Nick has on his blue-velvet, vintage-store cowboy shirt, its sleeves rolled up to his elbows (to show off the dragon tattoo, of course), and that he's grown a neatly trimmed goatee. The veins in his forearms suggest he's been hitting the weights since you last saw him. The smallest of the females, wearing a fringed leather jacket, has her black hair pulled back in a ponytail. Your heart surges with a two-pronged prospect: Good Nick has arranged a surprise birthday party for you, and—is it possible?—Mia has returned to New York for the festivities.

You hold your breath and take a tentative step closer. "Yo, doggie dog!" shouts Nick over the music, beer bottle raised high. Your lips have already curled into an embarrassing, fatuously expectant grin, as five pairs of strangers' eyes simultaneously swivel in your direction. Your disappointment feels like a fist-blow to the sternum. Stupidly—*pathetically*, you think—you offer the group a peace-sign salute and attempt, unsuccessfully, to keep from wincing as Nick pulls himself to his feet.

"Brother Nick," you mumble.

"Brother Carter." Throwing his arm around your shoulder, the sweat from his beer bottle soaking through your turtleneck, Nick barks, "Everybody—this is my man Carter. Carter, these are my pals Marika, Jerome, Karen—"

"Carolyn."

"—*Car*olyn, and Hannah."

With a quick reorchestration of seats, Nick shifts places and squeezes you into the booth between Hannah, a bosomy redhead with long, thick eyelashes, and Carolyn, a rail-thin blonde who appears to be recovering from the flu. Both women are fashionably underdressed and slouched dramatically low against the red-vinyl cushions. Responding to an earlier comment from Jerome—one of Club Foot's two owners, with the tail-end of a skier's tan, whom you vaguely recognize and already dislike—Nick shrugs and snorts, "Hey, I can be a gentleman. When a chick goes into the kitchen, I'll hit the pause button without her even asking." Jerome and Nick guffaw uproariously. You wait for a minute or so, but neither of the two women flanking you initiates a conversation. After ordering another Johnny Walker Black, you lean across the ashtrays and sticky tabletop, and with forced enthusiasm address the petite brunette with the ponytail and leather-fringed jacket. "Marika, is it?"

Marika sniffs, nods.

"Pretty name," you say. "Russian?"

"Czech."

You mimic her bored head-movement. She no longer reminds you of Mia. "Czech, huh?" Even though you don't detect an accent, and despite her growing less attractive with each slurp of her cosmopolitan, you offer a meager smile and inquire, "How long have you lived in New York, Marika?" As you ask this, you notice the Himalayan fur hat with ear flaps resting in the lap directly to your right.

Marika sighs, continues nodding. "Long enough."

". . . Okay." You turn sideways to your neighbor Hannah, whom you didn't initially recognize from outside, and give her shoulder a bump. "I dig the hat. Very Elmer Fudd-meets-the-Panchen Lama."

Though her cannabis-reddened eyes remain transfixed on a yellow sunfish doing laps in the aquarium, the auburn-haired woman—whose age you correctly estimate to be twenty-five—offers an amused smirk.

"Are you a Dharma practitioner?" you ask.

". . . A what?"

"A Buddhist. A meditator."

"Oh . . . nah. I'm pretty much a pagan."

You nod appreciatively. "Hannah, is it?"

"Mm-hmm."

You decide that you're attracted to Hannah's paradoxical good looks: the robust complexion and the bloodshot eyes, the full breasts and the boyishly short haircut, the faded and ripped brown corduroys topped with an expensive-looking green cashmere V-neck sweater. You wonder if she's one of Nick's girlfriends. You ask, "Are you and Nick buddies?"

Catching his name, Nick stops in midsentence and glances across the table.

Hannah chuckles ambiguously and meets Nick's silent glare. "I hope he and I will *stay* buddies, yeah."

Blond and sniffling Carolyn laughs blithely in response to a question from Jerome about a mutual friend's increasing dependence on heroin. Both you and Hannah turn and stare at her. To no one in particular you say, "I'm curious. What makes the heroin experience—the heroin high—appealing enough to risk addiction? And surely everyone who shoots heroin knows it's addictive."

Jerome answers, "That first high. It's . . . perfect. Heroin. Slows. You. Down. *Good.*"

"Most definitely," concurs Marika with another slug of her pink cocktail.

"High's not the right word though," Carolyn interjects. "It's more of a . . . return. You know? Your life's so fucked up it takes smack to do what—what a beach or a picnic should do. It totally sucks. But it's there. And it's cheap. And we're lazy." Straightening against the seat, she lapses into a sad silence, wipes her nose with a tissue, and adds, "But only junkies mainline. Most people snort it."

"Hey—guess what, everybody," Nick exclaims to the table at large. "It's Carter's birthday. At the stroke of midnight he turns forty-five."

Jerome raises his highball glass. "Hear, hear."

Smiling sleepily, her attention returning semi-fully in your direction, Hannah asks, "Really?"

"All day long."

"You're not forty-five, though. *Thirty*-five, maybe."

"Bless you." Despite yourself you glance down at Hannah's cleavage. You note despondently the rush of greed already spreading through your loins, the familiar hot itch in your toes and fingers. Regardless, you take the impulse by the horns and ask, "Are you a student, Hannah?"

"Mm-hmm." Hannah sighs and turns back to the aquarium. "Grad. Classics. What's your last name, Carter?"

"That would be Cox."

"Carter Cox. Are you famous?"

"Oh, yeah. Big time."

"Carter Cox," she repeats dreamily. "Mmmm—I like this song. Do you feel like dancing, Carter Cox?"

You slump down in the seat, copy her dreamy smile, and rub your belly. "That would depend, Hannah, on whether you have any more weed."

The next six hours float by in a haze. You can't remember if you and the three others walked to Nick's apartment or took a cab, though you know you've wondered more than once since collapsing on his couch: *How the hell does Nick, on his bartender's salary, afford a two-bedroom spread decked out with Italian leather furniture, walnut bookcases, and a Bang & Olufsen sound system?* Since polishing off the champagne, you've been crammed atop the crinkly white cushions between Hannah, Nick, and the long-legged, cigarette-dispensing woman from the bar, who in fact turned out to be Club Foot's other proprietor—and since last week Nick's "main squeeze"—her entrepreneurship presumably more enticing to Nick than her black fingernail polish or lanky physique. A former runway model, she claims to be on a modeling "sabbatical," but looks at least forty. (If she's telling the truth, you tell yourself, she definitely needs to cut back on the unfiltered Camels.) Not exactly your type, you think, but what the hell. Her name is Preta, and her white silk shirt is now unbuttoned to the waistband of her black leather pants, revealing a sheer, blue-lace bra and an unnaturally ample bosom. Glancing down in the general direction of your crotch, you note with foggy interest the silver rings on each of Preta's black-nailed fingers as they crawl up your thigh.

Hannah has fallen asleep against your other shoulder. Her lips are parted slightly, and her green cashmere V-neck has twisted sideways, revealing freckles on her collarbones the same color as her short auburn hair. Her boots are piled in a far corner of Nick's apartment, along with her Himalayan fur hat, your sports coat and scarf, and Preta's motorcycle jacket. You close your eyes and swallow thickly. The five Johnny Walker Blacks, and the joint shared with Hannah back in Club Foot's bathroom, and the already-opened bottle of champagne Nick pulled from his refrigerator ("Happy birthday, dude!"), and the snorted line of white powder you trust was just cocaine, and the stink of Nick's hair gel, and the incessant African drums and Middle Eastern whoops and whistles flooding from the CD on Nick's enormous stereo, and poor snoring Hannah's smudged lipstick, and the black-nailed claw inching its way towards your lap, have collectively taken you by the heart and are making you *very* dizzy. You're having trouble breathing, and your mouth tastes more and more like metal. You groan, "Oh . . .

that's, that's not what I want to be feeling." Perspiring, head swaying, you push your shoulders against the back of the couch and hold on tightly as the walls of Nick's apartment spin counterclockwise in slow, loopy circles.

When your eyes open back up twenty minutes later, you have to keep one shut for the other to remain focused, though there seems to be a bit more air to breathe. The African drums have given way to Miles Davis's trumpet. The table lamp is off. The champagne bottle has rolled under the couch. Preta's white blouse and Nick's blue-velvet cowboy shirt are on the coffee table. Someone's hand is massaging your chest beneath your turtleneck. "You are so fucking hot," Nick growls to Preta, kneeling on the carpet before her as he buries his goateed face in her bared belly, which appears in the dimmed light to possess some sort of multilooped navel ring. You squint an eye at Nick's pomaded hair, his bulging arms, his tattooed dragon. As the room gradually ends its gyrations, your attention returns to your left hand, which is flattened, palm up, between the leather cushion and Hannah's brown-corduroyed bottom. Despite some lingering dizziness, your carcass feels aroused. Tingly. Hungry. Your jaw thrusts forward. Your guttural breathing has become as loud as Preta's. You shake your head, but your heart refuses to quit pumping erratically. *Why am I betraying myself like this? What would Christopher say about the light in my lantern now?* But before you can even consider the possibility of offering an answer, you clutch Preta's forearm and turn your face to Hannah, who is still asleep, and with a despairing, barely audible moan lower your parched mouth against the moist, pale flesh of her throat and begin to feast.

6

It's the last Monday in March, roughly two months since Mia's visit, and for the first time this year the temperature in New York City has broken into the sixties. Though it's overcast and breezy, the dewy, midmorning air feels mild enough during your walk with Marley for you to venture off to your shoot thirty minutes later wearing only a hooded sweater and khakis. The relative warmth almost makes you forget that today's assignment is for Eno & Tuatara, a midtier girl's clothing company based in Jacksonville, Florida, specializing in "sophisticated prom wear," with pretensions of becoming a player on the East Coast.

Because of your gear, you splurge on a cab. Packed in the pair of Anvil equipment cases: your Mamiya M645 pro TL camera body, your Fuji medium-format, your Hasselblad 501 CM single-lens medium-format (already loaded with 70-mm perforated film), a strobe light, filters, assorted lenses, and fifty rolls of both color and Tri-X film. You gather around ten-thirty at a rented trailer, double-parked on the east side of Hudson Street, with your phlegmatic assistant, a curvaceous teenage model, and a makeup artist who introduces himself as "Shawn*tell*—as in William" and who reeks of gin. Joining you shortly is the account director from the Borkhardt Group, a fifty-year-old woman wearing a Yankees cap and black ski vest—a crease-faced, ad-agency warhorse, you think. With ingratiating calm, you smile thinly and get to work.

The shoot itself takes place behind several handsome, ivy-blanketed nineteenth-century brownstones, in a quiet and fully concealed public yard known locally as St. Luke's Garden. You've used this outdoor location before, but only during the early-summer months, when the grass was green and the dogwoods were in full bloom. Now the yard is brownish-yellow and the only thing flowering is a potted cactus behind the benches. Josh Villard, the Borkhardt partner who hired you and for whom you've done print ads twice before, professed to like the idea of using the garden, though his directions for the photos proved confusing: "I want Hollywood circa 1940," he explained on the phone, "with a twenty-first-century industrial edge."

The shoot is a moderately budgeted print ad for Eno & Tuatara's latest perfume, a $100-an-ounce, citrus-smelling concoction that will neither be named nor shown on the magazine's page. The first two hours of your work with the model—a coltish, high school–aged blond borrowed from J. Crew's stable of lacrosse-playing youths—take place at the north end of the garden, on a bench shaded by a magnolia tree and a large, red-bricked wall. Atop one of your Anvils, your 45-watt Amnitron boombox plays a homemade CD featuring an Italian aria introduced to you by Christopher. Despite having already exposed eleven rolls of film, you still can't figure out precisely what Villard wants the photos to accomplish, and both the inebriated makeup artist and the young model—shivering and goose-pimpled in a strapless black $450 Eno & Tuatara "evening sacque"—have begun to peer at you mistrustfully.

Hearing the Borkhardt Group's account director clear her throat for the third time, you sigh and select a ring-flash to gently flood the girl's upturned face with what you consider to be a softer, more glamorous light. You recall from almost three decades ago your mother's sage advice: "If your pictures aren't interesting enough, honey, then chances are you're not close enough." You raise high the ring-flash and lean forward. But your move leads to louder throat-clearing. You lower the Hasselblad, pinch your nose, and for several seconds pretend to examine the dead grass. The skin of your cheekbones tightens as you feel yourself teeter between embarrassment and anger. Still kneeling, your hooded sweater damp with sweat, you swivel your head and lock eyes with the Borkhardt woman, who stares back at you with a mirthless smile, unblinking, her hands clasped just below her vested bosom, as if entranced by your ineptitude. "More sheen," she commands, albeit quietly, in a raspy voice, directing your yawning assistant to spritz the model's face and shoulders with a plastic water-bottle that appears out of nowhere. "More sheen, less sweetness. This isn't a portrait—it's an attitude. And do you mind if we kill the Caruso?"

You stand up and glare at the woman. She refuses to lose her cool, however, and steps closer, cocking her baseball cap before taking your arm, leading you away from the magnolia tree, and explaining with a disarming smirk, "Villard can be pain-in-the-ass cryptic, I know. My sense, Carter, is that he wants the ad to acknowledge our target customer's buying power without acknowledging that she probably lives in a Jacksonville suburb. A cross between a poor-man's Rita Hayworth and a poor-man's Jil Sander."

After another clothes-changing break, your assistant—an I.C.P. intern with bad skin and a Che Guevara T-shirt beneath his jean jacket—eventually returns from a liquor store on Barrow Street with the wine glass and bottle of Burgundy the account director has requested. Breathing hard, he hands her a receipt and the change from the hundred-dollar bill she'd slipped in his jacket's pocket. With veteran indifference to the attention she's drawn, the woman uncorks the bottle with a pocketknife pulled from her ski vest, and suggests to the model, whom she has covered with a blanket from the trailer (and who's now wearing a black E & T bandeau and white leather pants): "Pretend it's the 1940s, dear. Drink a full glass of this stuff as pre-War ladies used to—that is, without a pause, in twenty or thirty little sips. Innocent but coquettish. Self-consciously self-conscious." Returning the pocketknife to her vest, the account director whispers conspiratorially in your ear, "Perhaps, Carter, if you can catch something in the *sipping*."

Eyes watering, color spreading across her cheeks, mouth childishly purpled, the young model works her way through the first glass of Burgundy. "Like this?" she asks breathlessly between swallows.

Your assistant hands you the freshly loaded Mamiya. Behind you, beneath the magnolia tree, the account director studies a still-developing Polaroid you've given her for inspection. "Yes—*there,*" you encourage the model, your voice reorganizing itself at a lower pitch. You start snapping again, quickly composing shot after shot. "Yes—yes. Again. Good. *Very* good. Again, just like that. A bit more flirtatious this time." You grab the little silver Contax draped around your assistant's left wrist and direct him to find the strobe in the stack of equipment cases. Out of the corner of your eye you see the Yankees cap nodding with approval.

After almost five hours sequestered in the cool shade of St. Luke's Garden, the shoot finally wraps. It's approaching four o'clock. Your stomach grumbles from hunger as you clean up the dozens of yellow film wrappers scattered across the grass, gulp down the Gatorade offered to you by the sobered and now flirtatiously obsequious makeup artist. Though your knees ache, you feel that the day has been a success. You leave the extraneous equipment in the care of your assistant, deposit twenty-nine rolls of color film and twenty-one rolls of Tri-X in the twice-ticketed trailer, and depart by cab after receiving a kiss on the cheek from both the model and the account director, whose creased face, you've decided, has taken on a certain perspicacious beauty beneath the hazy, late afternoon sun.

Anvils and boombox in hand, you climb the stairs to your apartment, which still smells of the frozen strawberry pancakes you toasted and scarfed for breakfast. You're starving and, despite the relative triumph of the shoot, a little irritable. You ignore the flashing red light on your answering machine, flip on the stereo, grab a lighter and the remains of a joint from an ashtray on the coffee table, leash Marley (who is both whining and wagging his tail), gently tug him back down the five flights of wooden steps, out the front door, and straight to the curb where, with a brusque downward shove of his bottom, you command through the first puff of pot: "Go."

The second puff, held deep in your lungs, brings a thrush of warmth through your upper body. Your eyes redden. The pleasant acceleration of your pulse softens your shoulders, relaxes your jaw, and tickles your lips into a lazy grin. That a police officer, who is watching you from his three-wheeled patrol scooter idling at the corner, rolls down his window and motions for you to approach should probably concern you more than it does.

"What'cha got there, bro'?" he calls.

You lift Marley and cross the street, planting your feet no more than a yard from the side of the patrol scooter, which patters like a riding lawnmower. You continue to hold your breath as you inspect the cop's blue-and-gold shoulder patch, the shotgun secured next to his two-way radio. "A *very* small amount of marijuana."

"Hmm. Not good."

You turn your head and exhale a cloud of redolent smoke into the dog's snout. "It's not mine. It's his." You stroke Marley's ears. "He's got cancer."

The cop cocks his jaw as you take another puff of the joint, snuff the cherry with a thumb and forefinger, and flick the stub over the scooter's blue-and-white roof, unsure whether he should break your nose with his truncheon or smile in appreciation for the size of your balls. "Are you an idiot?" he asks. "Do you *want* me to bust you?"

You exhale towards the curb. "You do whatever you gotta do—*bro*."

"Put the dog down and step away from the vehicle," he tells you, shoving the door open and pulling himself with some effort from the scooter's interior, right hand on his unfastened holster, left palm extended. You lower Marley and lift your arms skyward in mock surrender, refusing to move backwards until the cop's hand makes contact with your chest. "You gonna think it's funny when I run you for warrants, wise-ass?"

You close your eyes and drum the top of your head as you begin to return to your senses. "I guess we'll just have to wait and see."

"That your music blasting out that window up there?"

You refuse to turn around, more embarrassed for playing Fiona Apple than for having the volume loud enough to hear while walking Marley. "Yeah. My bad."

"Any noise that can be heard one hundred feet away is subject to a citation for a 40-2 violation." The cop gives you a thin, cruel smile. "You got any ID?"

In the cramped hallway, after the trudge back up the stairs, pink carbon-copied tickets in hand ("possession of marijuana, littering, disturbing the peace"), you and Marley encounter Mrs. Pierno, who carries the day's mail and is dressed in fuzzy bedroom slippers and an old, blue, cotton shift so faded it seems to you to possess no color at all. Her eyelids look pink and rubbed. She stands just under five feet in height (her nose barely comes to your sternum), and beneath the hallway light her uncombed gray hair is thin enough for you to see her scalp. Though she gives your dog's belly a kindly scratch, your neighbor sniffs and acknowledges your hello with little more than a grunt. You wonder if she'd seen from her apartment window your encounter with the cop. Behind you, both of the Cisneros toddlers burst into tears as you make bloodshot googoo eyes at them over your shoulder, darting into 6D ahead of their baby-sitter, a nineteen-year-old Fordham freshman who in three years will marry her Psychology TA.

You peer at the tarnished 6B on the door behind Mrs. Pierno and wonder if perhaps the old woman is sore that you haven't given her anything for keeping Marley last Thursday night. Since returning Friday afternoon from the two-day shoot in New Jersey for Master John's Ice Cream, you keep forgetting to buy the loaf of sourdough bread from McInerney's Grocery that you promised her—and you still can't recall where you put the Belgian chocolates purchased for her back in January. As well, in your refrigerator is a roll of unprocessed film containing almost a dozen shots of your tiny neighbor, dressed up and coiffed for church, taken unbeknownst to her as she strolled arm in arm with her two firefighter sons along Avenue A one Sunday morning last month. You'd planned on framing the best of the images and surprising her with it as a gift. *Why have I been so remiss? Am I intentionally undermining my relationships with* everyone? "Anything good?" you ask, nodding towards the armful of bills and catalogues cradled against her chest, trying to smile despite the disagreeable odor of her liver-spotted skin and the audible gurgling in your belly. Mrs. Pierno glances down at her mail and expels a snort of air through her nose. "Just people who *want* things from me," she croaks, disappearing behind her door, which she quickly bolts.

Around six, as the cannabis begins to wear off, a pair of yellow-eyed Nigerian deliverymen in matching black T-shirts show up with a $2,400, pearwood-finished Rigne Loset loveseat, recently ordered on-line one night while you were high. The French-designed leather loveseat—not quite as gorgeous in person as it appeared in the Web site catalogue—proves too fat to make it by your foyer's ceiling-high bookshelf, which would have to be emptied and disassembled to move out of the way. "Damn it," you grumble, checking your watch. "I *told* the guy on the phone yesterday. I said it had to pass through a thirty-six-inch hallway, and he *assured* me that you guys could do it." You whip out your tape measure and confirm what you already know: the loveseat is 38 inches tall, 39 inches wide, and 41 inches deep. Neither of the Nigerians is impolite enough to state the obvious, though the older of the two clears his throat. "I guess you'll have to take it back," you say. "Either that or we *force* it through." You poke the left arm's dented leather, already creased from the initial efforts. "Nah. You guys are gonna have to take it back. Sorry." The deliverymen look alarmed. "Here, take my card—if your boss gives you a hard time, have him—or her—call me and I'll make it clear that you did your best. Okay? This was *my* bad, not yours." You hand both men, who show some relief by your promise, a sawbuck for their trouble and pat their backs as they maneuver the loveseat out the door and up the hall towards the stairwell.

After wolfing down another dry ham sandwich and lukewarm cup of reheated lentil soup, you turn your attention to tonight's main event: a third-date dinner to be prepared and served (as is the calculated norm for your third-date dinners) en route to what you assume is a mutually anticipated, introductory sexual encounter. Feed 'em, then eat 'em, Nick has crudely joked of his and your shared tactics. But the strategy seems to work. It's been your experience that few things prove more seductive to an adult female than a man appearing to be at ease in his kitchen. Indeed, over the years, most of your initial conquests have followed the making of multicourse meals.

Tonight's guest: an attractive thirty-two-year-old real estate agent named Visheen Asrani whose chief appeal to you thus far is her exotic New Delhi looks and a proclaimed (though unverified) interest in tai chi and yoga. Date One with Visheen occurred on Tuesday, March 9th, a week after you introduced yourself to her on the Times Square subway platform, and was pleasant enough for you to suggest another. Date Two: margaritas and salsa dancing at S.O.B.'s this past Wednesday (the eve of your departure for New

Jersey), which concluded with a soulful kiss on the stoop of her West Village brownstone and you asking (almost wincing at your predictability), "Hey—how would you feel about me cooking us some dinner next week?"

Visheen arrives at eight o'clock sharp. Though your hands are dry and you've prepared nothing that requires cutting, you open the door carrying a kitchen towel and a paring knife. You kiss both of her cheeks and with a palm to your heart, accept the brown-bagged bottle of Pinot Noir she presents to you. As Visheen wiggles out of her coat, you steal a glance at the substantial curve of her breasts and a flash of her dark flat belly. You also notice the very long, very red fingernails she was not in possession of during either of your first two dates. Visheen notes but says nothing of the five or six candles burning behind you in the bedroom.

"I hope you came with an appetite," you say, returning dutifully to the oven.

"Stah-ving," she coos with an exaggerated British accent, and heads straight for your stereo. "Mind?" she asks, replacing your Pat Metheny CD with a radio station blasting "Let's Get Busy" by Lizard Soul.

While you move about busily in the kitchen, your guest watches from the dining table, set in advance with a vase of white tulips, a half-loaf of pumpernickel bread, and a saucer filled with extra-virgin olive oil sprinkled with paprika. "Carter, your pad is so . . . occupied." Unsure if this is a compliment, you shrug and pour yourself a second glass of the Pinot Noir. "Most men care so little about decorating," she laments over the music, leaning across the silverware towards a shelf containing liquor bottles and a small, framed self-portrait of you on a 1996 assignment in Portugal. "Are you always this neat?"

You offer another self-deprecating shrug and respond, "Neat maybe, but not particularly clean. You'd be appalled if you looked under the rugs."

In lieu of the habitual third-date lasagna, tonight you've opted for barbecued chicken breasts, braised cardoon, and a large bowl of spinach salad, into which you add with a flourish a measuring cup's worth of Bacon Bits and garlic-flavored croutons. Waiting until Visheen turns her attention back from the liquor shelf, you pour onto the spinach leaves, from a tureen held several inches above your forehead, a half pint of homemade ranch dressing. "Mmmm. What is that *smell?*" she asks, sniffing, in an apparent swoon as you pull the blackened, Reynolds-Wrapped casserole dish from the broiler.

"That would be a chicken breast barbecued so tenderly you shan't need a knife," you reply, confirming after a surge of panic that you did indeed wash the cardoon stalks. Once the plates are ready, you dim the overhead light, unfold, with a pop, a white cloth napkin, and spread it with such care across Visheen's lap that she shuts her eyes and lets out a prolonged, toe-prickling groan.

An hour later the two of you are in bed, and little more than an hour after that, with correlative excuses about it having been a long day and how tomorrow's work starts early, et cetera, you both turn your backs and silently get dressed, exchange a dry kiss at the door, and promise to stay in touch. You bolt the lock before Visheen makes it down the hall to the stairs. Almost immediately you're overwhelmed by fatigue and sadness. You wag your head at the sight of yourself in the hall mirror: your shirt buttons are out of alignment, your tangled hair looks like a parody of tangled hair, and your cheeks are swollen and bright red—less from a day in the sun than Visheen's acrobatics. Again you wince at the odd cramping deep within your bladder and convince yourself (accurately, at least this time) that the pain has nothing to do with your romp with your dinner date. You sniff gas and realize with a jolt that you've forgotten to turn off the oven. Glancing at the dirty dishes still on the table, the guttered candles, the empty wine bottle and lipstick-stained glass flanking your toaster, you decide with a weary wave of your hand to deal with the whole mess in the morning.

With tonight's guest fed, bedded, and ushered out the door, Marley ventures from his crate with a leash in his mouth, though you make him sit whimpering in the den while you take a shower. Once out on the sidewalk, you find that the mild March afternoon has turned into a very chilly March night, and you rebuke yourself for not covering your wet hair with a hat. You take your irritation out on Marley with a leash-jerk emphatic enough to produce a yelp, for which you instantly kneel down on the sidewalk and apologize. It's well past midnight as you strip again for bed. After flipping off the remaining apartment lights, shivering, your head throbbing, the bladder-cramping gone but your stomach now sour, you see with a sigh the blinking red light of the unchecked message on your answering machine. "Surely they're not already calling about the overdue MasterCard bill," you mutter to yourself. Curled up on the throw rug by the dresser, Marley watches you tiptoe naked from the bed to the machine. With a whirl and a click, the tape rewinds and spews out the nasal voice of Harold Ticket, *Men's Agenda*'s wunderkind art director, who—judging from the echo—apparently called and left his message to you shouting into a speakerphone: "Carter—this is Hal Ticket. Give me a ring, would you, at your earliest convenience. I have a deal for you."

When you eventually get through to him on the fourth attempt the next morning, the art director—who is ten years your junior—picks up halfway through the second ring. "Speak to me."

"Harold? Hey, what's shaking? This is Carter Cox. You called?"

"Carter. Yeah. Hold on for a second, Peterson's on the other line." A beep, and the phone goes quiet. You fear that you've been disconnected. At last, though, Ticket returns, his boyish voice deepened as he shouts from across his office into the speakerphone: "Carter, listen, we're in something of a bind here. In February we farmed out a couple of peachy photo-assignments to Max Lorrie. Did you know Max?"

"Yeah, he and I've crossed paths once or twice."

"Well, old Max hooked up with Reuters for a gig in Liberia last week and got himself shot. Apparently he was trying to take a picture of Charles Taylor, and some of Taylor's people didn't much appreciate it, and—well—they shot him. So, I need a replacement for him on these two assignments. And we're *definitely* behind schedule."

"Is Max okay?"

"Negative. The assignments are both in Morocco, so it's two birds with one stone. The first is a fashion shoot in Marrakesh or Fez. Your call. The models—chicks all—will be coming down from a shoot in Spain. The boys we're using are from some semi-pro Moroccan soccer team. We're putting 'em in the summer lines from the usual folks—Joseph Abboud, Calvin Klein, Louis Vuitton, a few others. Outdoorsy stuff. Bright, exotic colors. Camels and cobras and dudes wearing turbans in the background. You know the routine. It's about the clothes, not the boys. The second shoot is in some place called Essaouira—I *think* that's how it's pronounced—which is apparently some hot-shit windsurfer place on the Moroccan coast. Last year's windsurfing world-champ—some French kid named Matrit or Matret, something like that—"

"Michel Motroet."

"Right. Well, he lives there, or trains there, or he does something there. Anyway he's *there.* Peterson's running a thousand words on him, and we need two or three tasty Carter Cox shots of the dude. The contract would be the same as the Guatemalan street-kids photos, which were really solid, by the way. It sucks they killed the feature. Really. So: five nights in Morocco, airfare, car rental, food, lodging, blah blah blah—bring an assistant, that's cool. The models and a location scout will meet you in Marrakesh. Do one shoot, then the other, in whichever order you want. You're the boss. Just call the travel office, like last time. We need proof sheets by April 20th—earlier if possible. I can messenger the contracts, contact numbers, and a copy of the windsurfing story to you this afternoon. You game?"

"Umm, I think I can swing that," you reply, turning your head from the phone as you clench and pump your fist before exhaling, silently giving thanks to the photo gods above. "Let me check my calendar, Hal, and I'll get back to you within the hour."

Later that day you learn that Christopher has died. Thursday night, gorged on take-out food from Indian Oven, drowsy and dim-witted, more from enervation than the three Tanqueray and tonics you've gulped since returning home from the two-hour memorial service at Tibet House, you indulge this rare sensation of sadness until your heart feels filled to bursting. Though you disposed of the three grease-stained white cartons over an hour ago, the den still smells of *saag paneer* and the *pista kulfi* you gobbled for dessert. For the past thirty minutes your CTX's red lava-lamp screensaver has been the only light in your elegiacally darkened, noiseless apartment. Marley has long since fallen asleep on a blue Oaxacan throw rug next to the graywashed, accordion-like ribcage of the steam radiator, finally silenced and cooled with the arrival of spring. Despite the late hour and mild temperature, you remain dressed in a single-breasted black wool Helmut Lang suit and a loosened silver-gray Jacques Yormad tie, both purchased expressly for tonight's remembrance ceremony. You're fairly drunk. You're on the verge of tears. You're in need of a shave, and, as of about three minutes ago, a looser belt. Slumping against the computer keyboard, you breathe noisily through your mouth and stare at the three wedges of lime shriveled among the melting ice cubes at the bottom of your empty highball glass.

You can't figure out why Mia won't return your calls. Your invitation to her to accompany you to Morocco went out by e-mail Tuesday evening, almost forty-eight hours ago. You need to leave for Casablanca on Monday, April 9th, which means booking a flight with *Men's Agenda*'s travel-office by tomorrow afternoon. With a groan and a hand on your belly you rise up, click online again, and squint at the Incoming Messages quadrant of the computer screen, pleading with it to issue forth a response. In addition to the e-mail, you've phoned Mia twice at her apartment in Austin, leaving requests on her answering machine for her to call back as soon as possible, no matter the hour. Earlier today you went online and checked with the official University of Texas Web site and discovered that the graduate school spring break coincides with your intended departure and return dates. You even called the school registrar to see if Mia might be holed up in a TA office somewhere.

With a sigh so dramatically forlorn that Marley looks up from across the room, you scroll through your saved messages and find the most recent one written by Mia. You check the date. This last e-mail was sent to you almost a month ago, roughly a week after your birthday.

Subject: Moved to Tears
Electronic Mail Sent: 11:33 AM, Wednesday,
28 February 2001
From: Mia Malone
To: Carter Cox

Dear Carter,

I received your photographs of the Resistoleros this morning, and found the images even more extraordinary than those originally included in the lay-out galleys. The haunted looks on those children's faces! God bless them all. To think that the glue is manufactured here in America, and that the company knows all these homeless waifs abuse it as a narcotic makes my blood boil. I was moved in particular by your nighttime portrait of that British human rights worker, all those little boys clinging to his legs, so clearly desperate for his affection, that wonderful halo-effect you managed with the street light. It's a haunting image, Carter.

With these pictures you have made great art. Whoever is at the helm of *Men's Agenda* is a fool for not using them, but I know in my heart that they will eventually find a home. They are too powerful not to be published. Americans need to know about what is going on beyond the palace walls!

Again, thank you so much, Carter, for taking the time to share them with me. I will return them post-haste (the SASE was a considerate touch). Please keep me up to date with what happens to them—and to you.

With deep affection,

Mia

Four weeks since you received this. "Why didn't I respond?" you wonder. "Arrogance? Fear?" Palm moving from swollen belly to aching chest, you swing around heavily in the computer-lit murkiness and peer at Mia's photo, the little black-and-white print cloistered in a black-lacquered frame, perched these past two months since her departure on the bookshelf beside your mother's dusty twin-lens Rolleiflex. Taken while walking Marley in Central Park the second day of Mia's visit, it's the only photograph of a romantic interest (if indeed the situation is romantic) on display in your entire apartment.

You inhale deeply, nostalgically. You can still remember the fragrance of Mia's fair skin as she posed for the picture. She'd proven to be a natural model—loose, carefree, with an easy smile, responsive to (though vaguely amused by) your posing suggestions, indifferent to the stares of passersby, patiently indulging you in the snowy park for the better part of an hour. "Why *that* camera?" she asked near the end of your picture-taking. "What makes you choose one camera over another?"

You looked down at the chrome-and-black Leica, an original twenty-nine-year-old M4, elegant and straightforward with its brass gears and beautiful build quality, one of the classiest cameras of all time. "Despite all the techie junk in my apartment, I suppose I'm pretty conservative when it comes to photo equipment," you answered, "if conservative means to conserve tradition. This M4's a classic. I love it. When I use the 28-mm it brings up the framelines for the 135-mm, so if I use the border of the viewfinder I get perfect framelines. It's heavy—it has some gravitas to it, you know? Nice, loud, smooth clicks. It's the camera I use when I feel strongly about my subject—as I do today."

Mia raised both black mittens to her heart and stared straight into your eyes. It took you several seconds to realize that she wasn't making fun of you.

"Let's move over there to those aspen trees," you directed for the shot you eventually framed: a close-up of Mia's face, slightly turned away from the camera, eyes lowered though fully focused on something at her feet, the background a lovely black-and-white crosshatching of snow-covered branches. You'd used a standard lens. No filter. Such old-fashioned grace, you mused, staring at Mia's slender profile through the viewfinder. No melodrama. No pretense. Her eyes sparkling in the frigid January air. A mitten raised to brush away a stray hair from her braid. A little out of breath as she bent over to rub Marley's belly, Mia had asked teasingly, "Will any of these find their way into the Carter Cox scrapbook of 'lady friends'?" *Click* and again, *click*. There. Goodness, you said silently, staring at her with both eyes opened as you lowered the camera to your chest, repeating the word almost audibly before responding to her question with a shake of your head and a decisive, "No. I promise."

The decision to invite Mia to join you on the five-day trip to Marrakesh and Essaouira both surprised you and somehow didn't. You'd known soon after returning the signed contract to Harold Ticket that you would rather lug your own equipment and load your own film than spend five days under the African sun making small talk with the insipid I.C.P. intern. Your previous two assistants from the Dalmar Agency had fled to the West Coast to pursue acting careers. Whom could you hire? Several years ago, you'd asked Nick if he'd be interested in assisting you on an assignment in Montreal, but he'd dismissed the proposition with a disdainful cackle, snorting, "Brother Cox, I gave up being a caddie in high school." Even if you offered to pay them, none of the three or four women you'd dated since meeting Mia seemed desirable candidates—a couple of them no longer even spoke to you. You'd flirted for all of ten seconds with the possibility of asking Visheen Asrani, who surely would have been willing to sweat a little in exchange for a free trip to the wilds of Northern Africa—but you couldn't get past those scary red fingernails of hers, or the fact that during your one and only sexual encounter she kept grabbing your hair and wailing, "Good boy—that's a good boy."

You click the computer to get back to the incoming-messages screen. Nothing. The realization that things might not work out with Mia results in another wave of gin-lubricated sorrow. You run a hand across the back of your neck and blow out a long, bitter-tasting breath. You remove the tie, toss it to the couch. You've always hated funerals, the chilly reality of death hovering over the proceedings like a contagion, and tonight's memorial service for Christopher proved no exception. Despite your fondness for him (deeper than you'd allowed yourself to acknowledge), the prevailing emotion you experienced while sitting in the back of the Tibet House art gallery had been dread. Dread mixed with regret and guilt for how selfishly—how foolishly—you're living your life.

You'd received word from your supervisor at NYCVA that Christopher had died Tuesday evening, the phone call coming only moments after you finished composing your e-mail invitation to Mia. You were told that Christopher had passed away at his Chelsea apartment, peacefully, surrounded by his sister and three or four of his closest companions, that the ashes of his cremated remains had already been scattered off Chelsea Piers into the Hudson River. Tonight's service at Tibet House was attended by twenty or thirty of Christopher's students and Dharma associates, only a few of whom you recognized. Jamyang Khyentse Rinpoche, who had flown with his translator to New York from a meditation retreat in Vermont for the service, spoke last and lauded Christopher's great gift of teaching and his never-ending curiosity about life. Everyone in attendance chuckled with appreciation when the translator explained that Christopher's final words as he died had reportedly been: "Well, *this* should prove interesting."

For much of tonight's service you'd wondered about death—the mechanics of it. The last breath. The spirit loosing itself from the body's grip. You'd assumed that one's Buddha Nature exits the body through the mouth, blown out into the cosmos with the concluding lungful of air, until Christopher had explained a few Sundays ago that, ideally, it is through the crown chakra on the top of the head that the Buddha Nature's spiritual essence—what he referred to as *rigpa*—fueled by its karmic winds, would depart. One's *rigpa* will leave from the most karmically appropriate site, Christopher warned. "Good luck to him or her," he laughed, "whose angry spirit is farted out the arse."

During your final Sunday evening with Christopher he'd seemed transported, as if he'd already begun to let go of his body. His skin looked jaundiced, his eyes rheumy, and though his raspy breathing was clearly causing him distress, he seemed peaceful. Dressed in those emerald-green, silk pajamas of his, Christopher hobbled from couch to cushion to kitchen, a hand on the nearest piece of furniture, his brogue taking on the quality of a tired traveler. "Calm down," he whispered, as you yanked the burned casserole dish from his oven. "Don't get yourself in a paddy. It's just lasagna." Two hours later, as you steeled yourself to say good-bye and leave his apartment for what you sensed might be the last time, he sat you down for a talk. Leaning over from the couch,

Christopher lit with trembling fingers another stick of sandalwood incense and remained silent as the smoke wisps initially trailed through the darkened, candlelit apartment. *Tosca* played faintly on the kitchen radio.

"The cancer has spread through my pancreas and liver," he announced in a quiet, detached voice. "As of last week I've ceased taking medicine. No more trips to the hospital. No more entheogens, no more antiretrovirals, no more painkillers, no more aspirin. For things to go smoothly, I should be more *attentive* to what I'm experiencing."

"Chris, you can't just give up," you urged, though your voice was almost as subdued as his. Even when you'd first arrived that night, you could tell that it was a done deal—you saw in Christopher's eyes that he already had one foot out the door. With the dish of frozen spinach lasagna in hand, you had stood uneasily in the darkness, several feet from where he rested, wheezing, on his couch. It hurt—physically *hurt*—to look at his haggard face. You'd been warned by NYCVA that the end was coming, but the palpable reality of Christopher's dying was more than you had bargained for.

Finally stepping closer into the candlelight, you were taken aback by the sight of what appeared to be a long blade of grass, perhaps three or four inches high, bright green and clearly genuine, which seemed to sprout from the top of Christopher's shiny bald skull. "What *is* that?" you gasped, leaning closer. You declined his invitation to touch. Chuckling weakly, he whispered, "Oh, don't look so alarmed, Carter. It's not uncommon at this stage of the process for a hole to dilate in the fontanel. The grass keeps the hole open. Frankly, anyone can do it. Anyone can do *anything*—that's the great secret. Though it is decidedly *not* easy, I assure you, to find a healthy blade of Saint Augustine grass in Manhattan."

"Does it hurt?"

"Yes, a bit, but I'm fine." Christopher sighed again and, wincing from the effort, resettled himself among the pillows. Two hours later: "For heaven's sake, Carter, sit down, *please,*" he commanded with sudden vigor. "You're making me nervous." After you joined him on the couch—the apartment smelling more from the incense and less, thankfully, from oven smoke—he turned to you and continued after a prolonged silence in a quieter, dreamier voice, "I've been thinking a fair amount about dying, I must tell you. I can *feel* death seeping into this body. In here—in the chest. It's a strange, though not entirely unpleasant sensation. A bit like a broken heart. A tremble in the breastbone. Do you know the feeling? Have you ever had your heart broken, Carter?"

You thought for a moment. "I believe so, yes."

"Truly?" replied Christopher, lifting his eyebrows. "I would think you'd not allow yourself to get in a situation where you were that vulnerable." His yellowed fingernails clicked against the top of the coffee table. The candlelight shimmered against his pajama top's green silk. "Did you know that when it dies, with its last ounce of strength, the great white whale springs from the water and ejaculates? You have to admire the chutzpah. I fancy I'll be whimpering like a baby."

"No, don't say that."

Christopher grinned oddly. "Have we discussed what happens during the transference of consciousness at the moment of death?"

You shook your head. You could feel Christopher studying your face, and it made you uneasy.

"It's like something out of Dante, though more personalized. As the Bardo of Dying dawns, we should very much expect—very much *hope*—to encounter someone serving as our guide, our Virgil." Christopher squints at you from the other end of the couch. "You're surprised by that? You thought we just toddled off towards our next rebirth? No. We each have within our Buddha Nature a Bardo escort. The escort's packaging doesn't really matter. It could be Jesus or the Virgin Mary or Elijah or Shiva. They're all faces of the same essence, really. I read a story about a young bloke, seven or eight years of age, terribly sick, whose heart quit beating on the operating table for a few moments. When he awoke from the anesthesia, he told the doctors how he'd been led into the light by his favorite Mutant Ninja Turtle."

The two of you remained quiet for a little while, each of you thinking about death, about your time together, about having to say good-bye. Christopher's eyes gradually filled with tears. With a sigh he looked down and placed a palsied hand to his throat. "Thank you for your kindness, Carter," he continued hoarsely. "I know these Sunday evenings have been challenging for you. But you've handled my grouchiness with grace and compassion. And I must confess, my handsome young friend, that—despite our lack of mindfulness tonight—I've taken quite a fancy to your spinach lasagna."

You tilted your head back and held your gaze on the Malaysian shadow puppets hanging on the far wall. With difficulty you cleared your throat and huskily answered, "It's been my honor, Christopher. You've been an inspiration."

Raising the trembling hand from his throat, Christopher beckoned with a finger for you to come closer. "Please," he whispered, sensing your hesitation.

Tightening your jaw, you inched up the couch until your knees touched. Christopher turned fully towards you, sniffed, dried his tears, and leaned forward. Tensing your muscles at the sensation of his breath against your face, vowing not to pull away, you closed your eyes and readied yourself for whatever was about to happen. But after another sniff, Christopher's lips brushed against your cheek and advanced—as delicately as the touch of a butterfly's wing—to bestow a light, chaste kiss on your forehead. A spasm of grief escaped your mouth as you opened your eyes. Christopher smiled sadly and took your hand. "I sometimes fear that men like us—*bachelors* like us—shall be blown from this life into the realm of Hungry Ghosts. Be mindful, Carter. Lust is interested only in the satisfaction of its own craving. Follow your Buddha Nature, in whatever form it takes. And know this: Your Buddha Nature is true. The Dharma is true." Gently touching his fingertips to your chest, Christopher whispered, "You've a good heart, Carter. Keep it filled with love."

In the computer screen's milky red light you move aside the empty highball glass, remove your suit jacket, and bring your palms together beneath your unshaven chin, prayer-fashion, to offer Christopher's spirit a final bow. When you straighten and open your tear-filled eyes, you blink and turn your head and strain in the darkness to find your meditation cushion on the floor across the room. With a rattling wag of your mala beads, you sniff and wipe your eyes and gaze at Mia's picture again and then over at the brown-and-green Javanese Buddha statue, at its magical, ring-chipped finger.

Rousing yourself with a long, deep exhalation and a hand through your uncombed hair, you push yourself from the computer keyboard and onto your feet. Marley watches as you kick off your shoes and untuck your white dress shirt. You light the three votive candles on the altar, unbuckle your belt, and lower yourself with a groan onto the zabuton. You close your eyes and cross your legs, bowing to the Buddha statue and taking refuge in the Three Jewels. You let go of your breath. And then another, and another, gradually surrendering your weight to gravity, repeatedly whispering as your mantra for this midnight meditation: *We will sit here, the Buddha and I, until only the Buddha remains.*

Forty minutes later the phone rings. Normally you ignore calls while meditating, but tonight you quit chanting, cock your head, and listen as the answering machine in your bedroom clicks on and beeps. "Hi, Carter," comes the staticky voice on what is evidently a long-distance connection. "It's Mia. I hope that I'm not phoning too late, but I was concerned—I just had the *oddest* experience. A few minutes ago, I could have sworn I heard a voice whisper in my ear, 'Call Carter. Call Carter. Call—' "

"—*Mia?* Hey—it's me—I'm home. I was in the other room."

"Oh, Carter, I'm so glad you're there. I hope it's not too late, but I just had the strangest premonition that I should call you. Is everything all right?"

"Everything's fine—I just wanted . . . I just wanted to talk. I've been trying to get in touch with you."

"What time is it there?"

You stretch out across the width of your unmade bed and glance at the alarm clock on the nightstand. "A little after twelve. There's a lot of static—where *are* you?"

"Hold on, let me look at the matches. I'm at . . . the Hotel Santa Clara."

"And where might the Hotel Santa Clara be?"

"The Hotel Santa Clara might be in Antigua."

"The city or the island?"

"The city."

Your jaw loosens. "As in—*Guatemala?*"

"*Sí, señor.* I've come from Guatemala City for a few days of R&R. It's heavenly, Carter. Did you come here during your visit? Cobblestone roads and pastel-colored houses. Fresh mountain air, though there's been some concern about the volcano erupting."

A strange trembling runs through your body. "What are you doing in Guatemala? Wait—wait—listen—give me the number there at the hotel and I'll call you right back. This is costing you a fortune, I know, and we *definitely* have some catching up to do."

It takes considerable effort for the international operator to reconnect you with the local service in Antigua, and when Mia finally answers after the third attempt you're sitting on the edge of your bed, head in hand, upright and fully sober. The line still crackles with static. Sighing with relief, shoulders relaxing, you gush, "So—Mia—what on earth are you doing in Guatemala?"

"Well, for the last month I've been volunteering for Casa

Alianza, in one of their shelters in Guatemala City—the girls' shelter by the Zone One train station."

"You're working with Casa Alianza?"

"Mm-hmm. After I saw the photographs of the street kids you sent me, I called the Casa Alianza office in Costa Rica and told them that I was interested in taking the semester off to do some volunteer work in Central America. They invited me to come teach in the girls' shelter. Which is what I've been doing. And it's been great. Guatemala City is the *ugliest* place on the planet—and there are men with guns *everywhere*—but the girls are *so* responsive to any sort of care or attention. Most of them are orphans from the civil war, living on the streets and in the parks—my Lord, the *stories* they tell. The other teacher in the shelter is a lovely Guatemalan woman, a Jesuit nun, who must be at least seventy, but she has enough spirit and energy for the both of us. And she's teaching me Spanish. *¿Como está usted? Estoy bien, gracias*."

"I'm—I'm amazed, Mia. I assumed you were in Austin working on your thesis."

"Oh, I'm most likely going back. But your photographs *inspired* me, Carter. *You* inspired me—your work, your traveling. I'd been wanting to do something like this for so long. It's tough—don't get me wrong—and there are moments, really tragic moments, that test my faith. The things that poverty can do to people is just unbelievable. Do you know what the Guatemalan police call the street children? *Basura.* Trash. Sometimes, they round the kids up and shoot them. It's just . . . I can't express how sad it is. But *you* saw it. You know what I'm talking about. It's easy to understand why these kids sniff glue all day and night—their lives are *miserable.* But you know what, Carter? I wouldn't trade this experience for anything in the world."

"Jeez . . . good thing I didn't show you the slides from my trip to Rwanda."

"So—you're well? You're healthy and happy and still living the good life in Manhattan?

"Oh—yeah—sure—I'm doing fine."

"I think of you *constantly,* Carter."

"Yeah? Me too. Think of *you,* that is. All the time."

"Truly?"

"Yes. Definitely."

"So . . . you mentioned that you've been trying to get a hold of me?"

"I was. I am. There's a—I have a proposition for you." You pause for a moment to steady your breathing. "How would you like to take a break from your work for a few days and go with me to Morocco?"

". . . Morocco?"

"Five days in Marrakesh and Essaouira—leaving on Monday, April 9th. I've contracted with *Men's Agenda* for a pair of assignments."

"I thought you said you'd never work for them again."

"Well, I changed my mind. And I need an assistant. And I would love for you to go with me, Mia. It'll be a hoot. Have you ever been to Africa?"

"Not in this lifetime, no."

"Well, here's the deal: I'll fly you and a backpack from Guatemala City to New York, New York to Morocco, Morocco to wherever you want to go—Austin, Guatemala City, Timbuktu, it doesn't matter. I'll cover all of your expenses *and* pay you twelve hundred dollars to help load the cameras."

"Goodness."

"Same arrangement as your visit last time—same understanding. I don't see this trip being anything too hot and heavy. Just two good friends riding in the desert side by side on their respective camels."

For several moments the line crackles and pops.

"You still there?"

". . . I'm here."

"So—Mia—what d'you think?"

"I don't know, Carter. It sounds tempting, but you know what the Buddha said about temptation."

"No—it'll be fun. Five days in Morocco with a guy who doesn't speak a word of Arabic. What more could a gal want?"

"April 9th. That's pretty soon, Carter."

You flip open your Handspring Visor and confirm the calendar dates. "Nah—you have plenty of time. The Casa Alianza folks will give you a week off, I'm sure. I mean, you're *volunteering,* right?"

"Yes. But . . . I don't know."

"Oh, c'mon. Jump in. The water's warm."

"I would need to come to New York first?"

"We fly out of JFK on that Monday. I'll get you a direct flight from Guatemala City on Sunday night."

You stare at Marley's wagging tail for the fifteen seconds it takes Mia to respond.

". . . Carter?"

"Yes ma'am?"

"May I have the night to think about it?"

You thrust the phone towards the ceiling, clamp your eyes shut, grind your teeth, and jerk your head sideways—hard—left then right. Gathering yourself, you exhale silently and with eyes still closed reply evenly, quietly, and with pitch-perfect patience, "Of course. I'll call you first thing in the morning."

7

SITTING STIFFLY BENEATH THE READING LAMP at the far end of your couch, you flip restlessly through a lapful of new magazines, some still in their shrink-wrapped covers. *Maxim. Details. GQ. Playboy. Esquire. Men's Agenda.* Each magazine has a mailing label stamped with your name and address near the bottom right-hand corner, and smells of men's cologne. You note that for most of the magazines, masculine blues and blacks serve as the predominant background and caption colors. When you squint to blur your eyes and lean back, you can't tell the air-brushed actress on *Maxim*'s glossy cover from the surgically enhanced model on *Esquire*'s. You glance at a breast or bellybutton or bared leg for no more than the duration of a shallow breath before tossing one magazine to the floor and moving on to the next, driven by some subliminal, culturally conditioned yearning for—for what? you wonder. A rounder breast? A thinner thigh? More skin? *Less* skin? *Any* sort of humanizing flaw? You shake your head miserably. How on earth can real women compete with images like these?

You glance over at Nick again, sigh at the empty cellophane package crumpled in his lap. "Let me know if I need to resuscitate you, okay?"

As if feverishly inserting quarters into a slot machine, over the last fifteen minutes Nick has noisily consumed the entire contents of a $3.95, eight-ounce bag of organic El Diablo "blue corn" tortilla chips he found in your cupboard. Rolling Rock in one hand, the April issue of *Playboy* in the other, he stifles a belch and from the computer console across the den asks, "What time was her flight supposed to get here?"

"She said nine, but she had a connection in Miami."

"To La Guardia?"

"Newark. She's on some rinky-dink Costa Rican airline I've never heard of."

"You couldn't meet her at the airport like a gentleman?"

You grunt and adjust the collar of your new black cashmere polo shirt, purchased last weekend at Nick's favorite vintage apparel shop in Williamsburg. The thought had not occurred to you. Shrugging, you reply dismissively, "Chivalry's dead, baby." Even so, you shoot him another irritated look. Reeking of pomade and one slap too many of aftershave, decked out for a night on the town in distressed-leather Donna Karan boots and Miu Miu topcoat with upturned collar (too James Deanish for your sartorial tastes), Nick arrived at your apartment, uninvited, over an hour ago—apparently for the express reason of seeing what he calls "the sexy vestal virgin" with his own eyes—and already he's devoured the bag of corn chips, drained three beers, and downloaded a porn site. "She's a grown woman," you add with a defensive sniff. "She knows how to hail a cab."

Nick wags his head and turns the *Playboy* sideways to unfurl the three-foot-long Miss April. "You're a class act, Cox."

"A deep bow of thanks, my friend."

"You got anything in here?"

"No. I won't shoot for *Playboy*."

Nick closes the magazine. "I respect that."

Of spending the better part of the next week with Mia in Morocco, you say, "I'm gonna fuck this up, man. I know it."

"With women I always assume the worst. Lower the bar and it won't hurt so much."

The downstairs ringer jolts you from the couch. You rub your chest to relax your thumping heart. "That's her." The forceful, nerve-rattled breath you expel through your lips makes Nick snicker. You re-stack the tossed periodicals on top of the coffee table and dry your palms against your corduroy trousers. After turning the music down you motion impatiently for Nick to put away the *Playboy.* "C'mon, man—be cool. Work with me here."

In the hallway you check your pepperminted breath with a cupped hand and then lean towards the door to listen for footsteps, Marley yelping and circling between your legs as Mia approaches up the hallway, lowers her backpack to the floor, and confirms with a neatly folded slip of paper from her pocket that she has remembered the correct apartment. Before she raises her arm to knock, you open the already unbolted door. "Hey there, stranger," you say. She beams at the sight of you. With a kiss to her cheek, you squeeze her shoulders, inhale deeply, and step back to take in her dramatically new appearance. She's gone a little . . . jungle. And you like it. Dirt-smeared Levi's, hiking boots, and beneath her unzipped parka a faded red T-shirt and tight leather necklace laced through a small white seashell. Though Mia has the same jewel-green eyes, the same delicate nose, the Guatemalan sun has left her skin rosy with color. Biting your bottom lip, you reach up to touch her now boyishly short hair—the thick black mane has been stylishly hacked down to a six-inch bob. You shake your head and exhale, "You look terrific, Mia."

"I *feel* exhausted. But thank you. Hello there, Marley."

"I like the do."

"Really?" She sighs and self-consciously pulls one side of her shortened tresses, then the other, behind her ears. "I wasn't certain what you would think. I know you're a man who likes a healthy head of hair."

After setting down his beer, puffing himself to his full height, Nick clears his throat and lumbers through the den directly towards Mia and her backpack. Squeezed against the foyer wall, you turn and raise a hand for the introductions. "Nick—Mia. Mia, this is Nick. Be careful: if you ignore him, he bites."

Mia blinks at Nick's impressive sweep of hair. "How do you do?" she replies, still standing in the dimly lit hallway, smiling unsurely and extending a hand. "Nice to meet you."

Nick grasps her palm with both of his. "Good grip," he croons in his bartender's voice, half an octave lower than normal, nodding at you his approval, though still staring at your guest. "'Mia Malone.' It's so nice to finally put a face to the name. Old Man Cox here speaks the world of you. And I for one think what you're doing with the kids down there in South America is God's work. Really. I mean that."

"Oh . . . it's just a break from my school work. But—thank you. That's nice of you to say."

Nick releases Mia's fingers with an appreciative cluck of his tongue. "Look at that, Carter—she's blushing. Wow. That's so God-durn refreshing. Hey—listen—are you guys hungry? I'm starving. How 'bout I take you two kids out for a bite to eat before the big trip. My treat. You like sushi, Mia?"

Still out in the hallway, smiling awkwardly, wondering what she's gotten herself into, Mia glances at you and offers a shrug. "Sure. Whatever you two have planned is fine by me. Carter, may I use your bathroom?"

"Of course. Please. You know where it is."

You step back and glare at Nick as he mimics with his chin the movement of Mia's blue jeaned bottom after she slides between the two of you and disappears down the hall. Marley follows her with perked ears around the corner.

"Okay. You've seen her—now *go*." With two hands to his chest you shove Nick into the hallway. He stumbles over Mia's backpack as he backpedals towards the stairs, wide-eyed but amused by your fervor. "Pool when we return," you promise, retreating with Mia's bag into your apartment. "Peace."

Because of nervousness and excitement, neither you nor Mia is particularly hungry, but you decide thirty minutes after her arrival that it might be more comfortable for the two of you to converse, at least initially, separated by a table and with drinks in hand. Both of you are quiet and reflective as you leave the apartment. The thunder shower from earlier in the evening has ended and the cool night air has grown frigid enough to breathe steam. En route around the corner to Pistol's Café on First Avenue, Mia takes your hand and squeezes. She *does* have a good grip. You smile and kiss her cheek. As the two of you walk along the rain-slicked sidewalk, shoulder to shoulder, chuckling between hesitant glances at one another, your heart continues to race with a feeling you can't explain, your chest both light and heavy at once, like a punctured blimp or a train plummeting off the side of a cliff. At the curb you kiss Mia's cheek yet again. "I like the short hair," you tell her. "Put you on a white horse, give you a French flag, and you could be leading the troops to Reims."

You ignore the red light at Seventh Street, stopping short to allow a gypsy cab to turn uptown, its tires whooshing and creating mist, its lowbeams splashing yellow across the wet pavement. "I can't believe I'm actually doing this, Carter," Mia says, shaking her head, shivering, blowing a stray bang with an upward puff. "I can't believe we're going to Africa. *Africa.* How did this happen?"

A bell tinkles against the tinted glass door as you enter Pistol's, a tiny restaurant dark enough for you both to squint and pause before spying and approaching the bar. You smell something burning in the kitchen, and beneath it, subtly, the sweet odor of marijuana. Just one of Pistol's nine tables is occupied. The two whispering, similarly dressed male diners glance up as you take a seat in the far corner. The place is strangely hushed. No music. No television. Little movement behind the bar. You wonder if people have stayed home tonight because it's Palm Sunday.

Surrounded by empty stools, a white-aproned busboy speaks inaudibly near the swinging kitchen door with a Japanese waiter, dressed in a yellow T-shirt and black carpenter's apron, who eventually wanders over to your table with a pair of laminated white menus. "Anything but rice and red beans," Mia replies when the waiter asks her what she's hungry for. Leaning forward, elbows on the metal table, she sighs and continues to examine the back of the small white menu with heavy-lidded eyes, her left leg folded beneath her right haunch: the posture of a bright twelve-year-old growing weary from all the homework.

"Get the ginger-carrot soup," the waiter advises so decisively that you do a double take.

Mia looks up, locks eyes with the young Asian, lowers the menu, and nods. "Sounds good," she says. "And a cup of herbal tea, please. Chamomile if you have it."

You order the same. The waiter brings your food and hot water almost immediately. Lighting a cigarette, wishing you'd gotten a bourbon instead of the tea, you ask Mia about her work at the Casa Alianza shelter. After a couple of self-deprecating anecdotes (how she got lost her first night in Guatemala City, silly mistakes with her fledgling Spanish), she deflects the attention back to you. Between sips of the soup you get her caught up on the details of your life during the eleven weeks since her last visit. Remembering Christopher from the Woodstock retreat, Mia lowers her spoon with the news of his death.

By the time the bowls and teacups are removed from the table (you glance at your watch, surprised to see that it's only eleven), it's clear that Mia is feeling the full impact of a day's worth of travel. Her smile is sleepy, and she's having difficulty keeping her eyes fully focused. You look again at your watch. Your flight leaves tomorrow evening at seven, which means almost an entire day to rest, pack, get a workout at the gym, haul Marley down to Mrs. Pierno's apartment (you pray that the old woman will answer the door), eat a good late lunch, hail a cab, and get to JFK by five. Five-thirty at the latest.

"You ready to call it a night?" you ask. Mia nods with a charmingly stifled yawn, her eyes glistening in the candlelight. You help her with her parka, drop a twenty and a five to the table, thank the grinning waiter—who bows as you leave—and walk back home, hand in hand, in complete but comfortable silence.

As soon as you get inside the apartment and take off your coats, both of you realize that you've not yet formally discussed tonight's sleeping arrangements. Mia's backpack rests against a wall in the hallway: the netherworld between den and bedroom. You refrain from moving the bag in either direction.

Mia shuts herself in the bathroom. "I'm gonna take Marley out," you announce through the bathroom door. "You got everything you need in there?" Mia assures you that she's all set. She's still showering when you return from the walk and continues to shower while you top off your clothes bag with a few more items of springtime apparel—a light sweater, a windbreaker, another linen shirt or two. According to the *Men's Agenda* travel office, Casablanca will be in the seventies tomorrow, the upcoming nights along the coast south to Essaouira no cooler than fifty. On the edge of your bed, leaning over, you double-check the locks on each of the five cases of your photo equipment and then set up the charger for your ThinkPad—all the while cocking your head to better hear Mia's naked feet squeak in the tub, the hot water bounce off her bared shoulders and back and bottom. Ah, you muse, to be a bar of soap. Marley sits facing the bathroom, nose almost touching the door, until Mia, dressed in sky-blue flannel pajamas, a white towel turbaned around her wet hair, emerges from the steam.

You follow Mia into the den, where she wanders to the far bookshelf, bends over, and examines the old Rolleiflex, a pink-blushed conch shell from Costa Rica, the framed photograph you took of her posing beneath the snowy branches of Central Park. "Explain this to me," she says, the towel now draped over her shoulder, turning and extending in your direction a ceramic sculpture, taken from the bookcase's lowest shelf, of Samantabhadra, a Mahayana bodhisattva venerated as the protector of those who teach the Dharma and regarded as the embodiment of wisdom, his naked blue torso sexually intertwined with an equally naked white consort. "Why are these sexual partners necessary for Buddhists?"

"They're not."

"Well, this to me looks like a Buddha, and this is either Mrs. Buddha or a consort, and they are most surely getting in touch with each other's Buddha Nature."

"Well—yeah, that's exactly it. For a Buddha—not a Bud*dhist*, mind you, like me or most Dharma practitioners, but a fully awakened Buddha—all tastes are one. Sex is prayer. Penetration becomes union. For a Buddha, during tantric intercourse the phallus, spiritually and physically aroused, engorges and connects with the feminine principle."

"'The feminine principle.'" Mia smirks, returns the statue to the shelf, and steps over your meditation cushion. "I like the additions to your altar," she says, leaning closer. "Is this a picture of your mom?"

"Yep. That's her. A self-portrait she took when I was about twelve. I think she'd just turned thirty."

"She's pretty, Carter."

"Thanks."

"Are you still meditating every day?"

"Mostly, yeah. How come?"

"Your Buddha's dusty."

You remove the towel from Mia's shoulder and, standing face-to-face, robustly dry her hair. Though she stiffens a little as the towel-drying slows, she dips her chin and presses her forehead against your shoulder.

"You smell good," she whispers into your chest.

"So do you."

You toss the towel to the couch and with your fingertips comb Mia's hair from side to side. "You sleepy?"

"Mmm . . . I'm not sure. That feels good."

"I'm glad you decided to come," you whisper, lowering your fingers between the flannel pajama collar and the moist skin of her neck. You massage her shoulders until they relax their grip on themselves. "We'll have fun together. We should make a good team."

Mia opens her eyes, lets out a long breath, and leans back. Your hands remain clasped around her neck, her mouth so close you can smell her toothpaste. "I hope so."

Brushing your lips against her ear, you whisper, "You know, our last make-out session was one of the hottest two hours of my life. Perhaps second only to kissing Holly Vaccaro in the deep end of her parents' swimming pool when I was in seventh grade."

With a groan, Mia lifts her shoulders and steps out from under your arms, gently poking you in the chest. *"You."*

". . . What?"

"You're dangerous."

"Dangerous?"

"Decidedly so."

You sigh and pick up from the hallway Mia's sweat-stained backpack, which is free of books but surprisingly heavy—apparently she's brought all of her belongings from Guatemala—trudge into the bedroom, and return to the den carrying in your arms a pillow, spare sheets, and a blanket. "Take the bed. I'll keep Marley company out here on the couch."

"You were out here last time."

"Take the bedroom, Mia. Please. I insist."

She gazes up at you for several seconds with a wistful, almost melancholy smile. "You're a gentleman, Carter."

You drop the pillow and bed linen to the couch. "Whatever."

"Hey—" She blinks and steps forward, smiling, rising to her tiptoes to place her hands—lightly—on your shoulders. Clamping her eyes shut, she gives you a short but impassioned kiss. When she lowers herself to the ground, a little out of breath, wide-eyed at what she's done, she says, "Thank you for dinner tonight. And thank you for taking care of the travel arrangements—the flight here. Tomorrow. Being so dear."

"No sweat," you reply, pressing your wet lips with a forearm, exasperated that your loins are prickling so. You smile without showing any teeth.

"The next five days—Morocco—I am *very* excited."

You check the impulse to throw Mia onto the couch, and instead chastely kiss her forehead. "As am I," you confess, stepping safely towards the kitchen.

Despite waking up before nine and having over eight hours to get to the airport, you and Mia are running thirty minutes behind schedule by the time you're ready to lock up the apartment and depart. The day has been a blur. You haven't eaten since breakfast, your new virgin-calfskin Josef Seibel huaraches pinch your toes, and you don't like what your hair is doing. Suitcases and photo equipment stacked by the stairs, you drag whimpering Marley down the hall by the collar and pound on Mrs. Pierno's door until the old woman unlocks the dead bolt and answers. "I'm afraid I didn't get a chance to take him out," you admit. Mrs. Pierno snorts, wags her tiny head—her faint mustache darker than usual—ushers Marley into her naphthalene-smelling apartment, and slams the door. "I owe you big time," you shout at the peep hole.

Somehow on your way to JFK the cab driver winds up getting lost in Park Slope. The check-in at the airport, however, looks like it might go smoothly: only two other passengers stand in line at the Royal Air Maroc counter. After overtipping the porter, you open your passport and check your watch again—you and Mia have only seventeen minutes before the plane leaves.

Since you'll be working outdoors for both shoots, you've brought no lighting gear, which limits the number of equipment cases you need to check to the five Anvils waiting in a row between your soft-shell Tumi clothing suitcase and the dark-skinned, red-jacketed Royal Air Maroc counter attendant. You wince as he drops each case onto the scale and conveyor belt. Mia checks nothing. After a quick chat in French with the attendant as he inspects her passport, Mia joins you by the escalator, squeezes your hand, and whispers that the two of you have received an upgrade to First Class. When you ask why, she winks and replies, "Magic." Despite the rush to get on the plane, Mia remains calm and smiling. She has apparently packed five days and five nights' worth of clothing and toiletries into a small green EMS knapsack, which she tosses on tiptoes into the overhead compartment above the aisle seat you've secured. Squeezed within a plump black North Face day bag, you've brought onboard your ThinkPad, a bottle of Evian, moisturizer, anti-jetlag herbs, trail-mix, your travel Buddha, mala beads, a hardback copy of Paul Bowles's Moroccan-set novel *The Spider House*, and your cell phone.

With the concluding slurp of a second Glenlivet on the rocks, you begin to relax. The past few days have been hectic for you, what with the hubbub surrounding Mia's arrival from Guatemala and the difficulty of arranging by phone a meeting place in Marrakesh for your four models (who'll be coming directly from another fashion shoot in Barcelona), their makeup person and stylist, the location scout (coming from Tangiers), and an Arabic-speaking local to run errands. You realize that the next few hours of flight time might be your only respite for a while. For fairly big fashion assignments, *Men's Agenda* pays by the day, plus expenses, which means there'll be precious little time to waste once you arrive in Casablanca. Your itinerary is tight: one day and night at the Dar al-Assad in Marrakesh for preshoot production, two full days and two nights in Essaouira with the French windsurfer, and two final days and nights of "clothes-posing" back in Marrakesh. You anticipate using one hundred and fifty, perhaps two hundred, rolls of film, and to most certainly put Mia to work. Though you're goosey about her lack of experience as an assistant, you're confident—or at least optimistic—that she'll learn quickly.

For the flight's mostly silent first hour, Mia wears a pair of red-framed Lensmaster reading glasses—inexpensive, unapologetically nerdy—which you've not seen on her before, nor knew that she required, and with an orange Hi-Liter busily marks up her Moroccan *Lonely Planet.* She is wearing the same dirt-smeared Levis and leather necklace from yesterday, though she's replaced the red T-shirt with a light green long-sleeved blouse, Indian-looking, with its detailed and gently swooped neckline. As the plane continues to ascend eastward over the Atlantic, you pull out your ThinkPad and conspicuously evaluate each of the *Royal Air Maroc Magazine*'s half-dozen pictorials, handling the magazine's thin pages like a connoisseur of in-flight journalism, typing disjointed notes on the humming laptop less for the sake of documenting your occasional bright idea than to impress Mia. The cropping of a sepia-tone shot of a Sahara dune by someone named Faleek Shabaz catches your attention, as does the graininess of the quarter-page interior of a decaying Rabat kasbah. You earmark three of the magazine's full-page images: a pair of European surfboarders riding camels along the Essaouira beach at dawn; a turbaned carpet dealer in the dusty Fez medina; a surprisingly sensual portrait of a Muslim woman, her age a mystery, framed by a blue-tiled mosque wall and—save for her dark, haunting eyes, which stare defiantly at the camera—completely veiled from head to ankles.

Over the crumbly remains of a resplendent First Class dessert plate (you're already eyeing Mia's coiled serpent cake and almond croissant, both of which she has yet to address), you glance again to your right. The earnestness with which Mia continues to study her travel guide—her head is lowered almost to serving-tray level, her cheeks the color of apricots—makes you smile and gently stroke her knee. You wonder: Are all twenty-six-year-old virgins like this?

Feeling your gaze upon her, Mia sits up, hugs the book to her chest, turns to you, and offers her first words since the plane took flight: "I have a question for you."

"Okay."

"What do you mean when you sign your e-mails to me 'Love, Carter'?"

You swallow your mouthful of cheese and signal the flight attendant to bring another Glenlivet. Before you can formulate an answer, Mia leans back against the plush leather seat, looks at you with a tender but amused slitting of her eyes, and mercifully changes the subject. "Sister Rosa recommended that we buy rugs from Berbers along the mountain roads," she says, opening her travel book again, "rather than in Marrakesh, where prices are twice as expensive."

Your hand remains motionless atop Mia's knee. "This would be Sister Rosa, the globe-trotting Guatemalan nun?"

Mia glances down at your empty plate. "You eat faster than any human being I've ever seen, Carter. It's almost frightening."

You stare at Mia's reading glasses (which are growing on you), her glimmering green eyes, the new boyish bangs, her delicately flared nostrils. With a smile and exhalation you quench a desire, more affectionate than amatory, to lean over and kiss her on the lips. "How'd you guys do it, Mia—your last boyfriend and you? You were with him for how long?"

"Almost three years."

"And you and he . . . *never?* And the two of you would spend the night together?"

"He would occasionally spend the night with me, yes, but I wasn't too keen on staying at his place. He had a roommate."

"Why didn't you get your own place together?"

"Because we weren't married."

"What about the Lutheran minister?"

"What about him?"

"You would never consider living with someone out of wedlock?"

"No—I *have* considered it, and it seems clear to me that it's marriage that makes a serious relationship work. Living together is . . . it's too easy."

"Three years, huh? I tell you—I tip my hat to him, your boyfriend."

"As do I, still. He was extraordinarily patient and gentle. It wasn't easy for him. Nor was it particularly easy for me." Mia raises the book as you reach across her lap for her pastries. "Please don't misunderstand my attitude towards sex, Carter. I have nothing against sexual intimacy. I *like* sexual intimacy. But, for a lot of reasons, not the least of which are Christian in nature, I've vowed to regard sexual intercourse—full sexual penetration, as you so poetically said last night about the statue—as something sacred to be shared exclusively with one life-long partner."

"Like penguins."

"No. Like two people who truly love each other."

Unable to suppress the urge any longer, you lean sideways and noisily plant your lips against Mia's cheek. "You know, you've already earned your keep with the French. We might be using it boo-coo these next five days."

"*De rien.* But—I don't very much like the idea of you paying me, Carter. It seems odd somehow."

"Technically, *Men's Agenda* is paying you."

"Regardless—I already feel guilty." With no trace of irony, she adds: "Spending time with you—watching you work—that should be payment enough."

Passport control and customs formalities in Casablanca's Mohammed V Airport prove to be relatively straightforward, though you're unnerved when the heavily armed soldier guarding the counter points to the mala beads looped around your left wrist, and in broken English asks skeptically, "You are Muslim?" Spooked by the frenetic noise of the jostling, mostly male crowd hovering around the exits, Mia takes your hand. The thick airport air feels fetid, oily. Everywhere people are smoking, which you forget is legal in public outside of the United States. After tying your windbreaker around your waist, gripping Mia's sweaty palm tighter, you point to the oldest of the six gray-haired porters vying for your attention. You lower your head and lead the old fellow through the mob as he wheels your Tumi and five photo cases from the Royal Air Maroc luggage carousel through the international arrivals hall, stopping at a BMCE bank window to exchange five $100 traveler's checks for the equivalent in dirham notes, and then proceed with some effort through the airport chaos to find a car-rental office.

"You have your passport?" you shout over your shoulder. Mia pats her unzipped parka and nods. Her face is damp and flushed. You assume that she's out of breath as much from the heat as from the airport's noise and confusion. "Are you okay?"

The stooped porter—he's missing all but one tooth, you notice—continues to part the crowd with his rickety wooden cart and cries of *"Balak! Balak!"* Though she's inhaling and exhaling hard through her mouth, Mia smiles gamely and gives a thumbs up. She shouts back, "I'm just not used to this smoke."

"Hey, at least I'm not making you carry all the equipment yet."

When you see Mia's stricken reaction, you squeeze her hand and shout, "I'm kidding."

After he stacks your gear outside the door to the first car-rental agency you spot, you tip the porter and give Mia a moment to gather herself. It takes a full hour to fill out the various forms in the cramped car-rental office, a local agency run by a young Moroccan with moderately good English who escorts you to his fleet of five aging Renaults parked in a neat row at the far end of the airport's seemingly endless gravel parking lot. Three teenage porters—one of whom is barefoot—carry atop their shoulders the five Anvils and your Tumi. Looking like a high school tomboy, Mia has secured the straps of her green EMS knapsack around her shoulders. You take the keys to the largest and cleanest of the five cars, a plum-colored, four-door sedan with an eyebrow-raising 94,788 miles on its odometer, a trunk that reeks of gasoline (in which you and Mia nevertheless stuff the luggage and all but one of the equipment cases), ripped upholstery, loose brakes, and a stick-shift that grinds and occasionally slips out of gear as you begin to make your way through Casablanca's crowded and labyrinthine streets.

Even by your relatively well-traveled standards, Casablanca seems otherworldly, almost nightmarish. Despite the traffic and tumult, you can hear the amplified *adhans*, the muslim call for prayer, echoing from the city's mosques. Against a backdrop of whitewashed, three- and four-story buildings, most constructed in the 1930s, the sidewalks overflow with a jarring mixture of black-suited businessmen carrying copies of the Koran and veiled, djellaba-wearing Muslim women bustling about with their over-sized purses and cell phones. There are more pedestrians in the streets than cars, and every few seconds someone bangs a fist against the trunk of your sputtering Renault. Since leaving the airport parking area, you've not yet gotten above second gear. Everyone streaming into or out of the walled medina (which you've hopelessly circled three times) seems to be hawking something stacked on wooden carts or fastened high on sticks. Brass teapots and jars of ink-black henna. Fly-covered goat heads. Buckets filled with blue ceramic tiles. Perched and tethered on top of a stop sign, a tangerine-eating monkey throws his peelings against your dusty windshield.

Mia is already barefoot and once again sits with her left foot tucked beneath her bottom, her attention yo-yoing back and forth between the guidebook and the carnival-like commotion pressing up against the slow-moving Renault. Before taking a sip, Mia offers you a small water bottle taken from her knapsack. "'With a population of three million,'" she reads from her highlighted *Lonely Planet*, " 'Casablanca has a hint of the decadent languor that marks many of the southern European cities it so closely resembles.' " She lowers the book. "Do you think that's a polite way of saying the city's populated by thousands of old men on donkeys?"

Though you would like to get into your hotel room in Marrakesh before dark, once you finally escape Casablanca (which you and Mia agree is almost as ugly and frighteningly crowded as Guatemala City) you choose to take the long, scenic route south along the Atlantic shoreline. A few miles after the turn-off onto the coastal highway, you slow down and gape at the enormous Hassan II Mosque—after Mecca, the largest Muslim monument on the planet—its rocket-shaped, marbled-and-stuccoed minaret thrusting six hundred feet skywards. As you wind through the grassy hills running parallel to the ocean, honking horns and cloudy blasts of diesel smoke gradually give way to squawking seagulls and the smell of brine. With the car humming along in fifth gear, you and Mia float your arms like goose wings out the rolled-down windows. Every few kilometers you slow down and, with a toot of your horn, steer wide of a whip-flicking oxcart-driver or cluster of children. "Is it just my imagination," you ask, coming to a dead stop at a bewilderingly marked fork in the road exactly forty kilometers south of Casablanca, "or are all of Morocco's signs written in Arabic?" You glance in the rearview mirror at the barren stretch of highway behind you. In the course of thirty minutes you've gone from one traffic extreme to the other.

Ignoring Mia's suggestion that you ask one of the oxcart drivers for directions, you eventually find your way to the busy, Portuguese-influenced city of El-Jadida. With little sense of triumph, you point to the city's name on your unfolded road map. "Okay, here it is," you mutter. After steering through El-Jadida's crowded souk—the outdoor marketplace a lively, chaotic mess of food stalls, white-hooded farmers, and stray livestock—your puttering purple rental car getting suspicious glances—you sigh with relief so impassioned that Mia chuckles and pats your arm. Once you exit through the port city's south side, you turn southeast onto a dusty two-lane road marked by a green sign in Arabic and a small, faded-white cement stump that reads: MARRAKESH, 138 KM.

For the next hour you drive with virtually no oncoming traffic, slowly but steadily climbing upwards from the grassy shoreline hills into the browner, more rugged first steps leading into the High Atlas Mountains. You decide to expend a few rolls of the older Fujicolor Reala, and have Mia take from the one Anvil in the backseat your Contax 35-mm Auto Focus SLR, and the heavier, completely manual Leica M4. Keeping one hand on the steering wheel, you talk Mia through the loading and unloading process for both types of camera bodies. The M4, which you rationalized purchasing a year ago because it "is refreshingly devoid of electronically controlled functions" and has "flawless mechanical precision" —in your mind, a *real* photographer's camera—proves for Mia a challenge. "This Leica is a lovely piece of equipment," you say. "But it can be a royal pain in the ass, and—as I see you're discovering there—a royal pain in the wrist."

Shoulder already aching from the click-and-wind film-advance motion, Mia nods and continues working her way through all thirty-six exposures, each shot taken with the lens cap still on and a meaningless upward thrust of the camera towards the dashboard. She asks, "Isn't this wasting film?"

You shake your head. "Nah. I'd rather blow a few rolls now than when we're doing this for real."

Even though it takes her almost ten minutes to load the first three rolls, when you suggest that she return to the fully automatic Contax, Mia grins, levels her eyes on you, and without glancing down, effortlessly slips a fourth roll into the rear of the Leica, which she pops shut with an emphatic *click.*

"Hot damn," you say, nodding, genuinely impressed. "I thought you said this was your first gig."

As you continue towards Marrakesh, the air begins to cool. There's still essentially no oncoming traffic—perhaps one car or truck every twenty minutes. With the cameras put away, Mia feels a new wave of guilt for having abandoned her responsibilities at the Casa Alianza shelter, for leaving Sister Rosa with the burden of an additional daily meal to prepare and clean up after. Despite the fact that the staff were enthusiastic about her going to Morocco—especially when she explained that she'd be working as an assistant for a photographer from a national magazine (though she didn't mention to Sister Rosa the fairly racy *Men's Agenda* by name)—Mia cannot let go of the truth: Her trip here is selfish. And—perhaps, she fears—morally questionable. If not, why did she refrain from mentioning the trip to her mother when she called from the hotel in Antigua? And she certainly didn't ring up Brian with the news.

With a sigh, Mia removes her reading glasses, looks up from her *Lonely Planet*, and announces, "Did you know that Sahara means 'desert' in Arabic? So saying 'Sahara Desert' is—"

"—kind of silly. Have you read this?" you ask, pulling the copy of *The Spider's House* from your North Face bag.

"No," she says with more disdain than she intends. "Just

Sheltering Sky, which I found to be self-indulgent. I'm not a huge Paul Bowles fan."

"I would love to get him for the fashion spread. Isn't he based in Marrakesh?"

"No, he lived in Tangiers."

"I bet we could get him to Marrakesh for an afternoon. He would do a spread in *Men's Agenda* in a heartbeat, especially if he's got a new book coming out."

"I . . . believe Paul Bowles is dead, Carter."

"Ah."

"Would you mind stopping in the next village and let me get us some more water?"

You glance at your watch. You've been driving for three hours, and you estimate, correctly, that Marrakesh is probably no more than thirty kilometers away. The sun will set within the hour. Regardless—finally acknowledging the impulse to stop and smell the roses, or at least slow down a little—you *do* hope to have some fun over the next few days—you down-shift into second gear, pull off the road, and steer through an unnaturally lush oasis of dark green palm trees. About a half kilometer beyond the foliage, the car bouncing along a rocky unpaved trail, you come upon a small village consisting of little more than an open-air market, a few white-washed, earth-walled huts, a scattering of scrawny goats and chickens, and a group of hooded tribesmen carrying bundled firewood on their shoulders, all of whom pause and stare as you bring the car to a sliding halt in the red dirt. You kill the ignition and reply, "Here you go."

Having taken Mia's barefoot lead after leaving El-Jadida, you strap back on your Josef Seibel huaraches, purchased a week ago expressly for the kind of desert walking you're about to encounter. Mia laces up her hiking boots and vows to start searching for a gift to bring back for Sister Rosa. Looking around as you pull yourself from the Renault (which continues to shake and rattle, and smells faintly of burning rubber), the High Atlas Mountains off to the east, nothing but desert beyond the few palm trees behind you to the west, you see no French or English written anywhere in the village, not a blade of grass, no flowers, only a few scraggly, tortured-looking argan trees, and only one place—a garage of sorts—where you find for sale anything to drink. The gusting desert wind forces you to shield your face with a hand. You shout: "You wanta roam around some?"

Mia nods and stretches her arms before strolling through a loosely designated, uncovered market area, clearly indifferent to tourist trade, today offering only three products: saffron; small, unglazed tagine bowls; and a motley assortment of blackened and generally unrecognizable fruit. Two little barefoot girls, both wearing dirty-white head wrappings, pull on Mia's loose green blouse sleeve and extend empty palms. With a sad smile, Mia removes from the front pocket of her jeans a pack of Dentyne, squats down, and offers each girl a piece.

"I don't think they have electricity here," you shout against the wind as you head back to the car. "I don't see any power lines."

"Is that what I think it is?" asks Mia, grabbing your arm.

You stop dead in your tracks. "Oh man," you reply, squinting. "What the—?"

You hand back to her the half-guzzled water bottle, and jog to the trunk to get a loaded camera. As you and Mia quickly but cautiously cross the hundred meters of parched terrain and approach a lone argan tree standing among the tumbling clumps of dried brush, you pause and confirm that, yes, the tree's branches are filled with—you use your finger to count—nine black, leaf-munching goats.

"Goats?" whispers wide-eyed Mia.

Sitting cross-legged in what little shade the solitary, sparsely leafed argan tree provides from the late afternoon sun, a young Berber goatherd—his white hooded djellaba surprisingly clean—

eyes your crouched advance with suspicion, though he accepts without hesitation Mia's extended hand and shyly returns her smile. By way of requesting permission, you point up at the tree and mime taking a picture. The young boy glances above him, unsure why you would want to photograph what he feels is an embarrassingly small herd of embarrassingly underfed goats, but offers no resistance once you start shooting film.

After the first dozen shots you move to the tree's opposite side—the setting sun now at your back, and from where the clamoring of all the cloven hooves clutching at bark sounds to you like some sort of ancient farm machinery. "I like what these shadows are doing," you say to Mia, who stays dutifully at your shoulder, fully absorbed by the peculiar spectacle, though eager to assist if called upon. With your lens you follow three of the tree-climbing goats as they balance with a bizarre and clunky grace on the crooked ends of the swaying branches, where with snuffling breaths and comically large, uneven teeth they tug and tear at the argan's few remaining leaves. Eventually you stop shooting and simply stand and watch as the smallest of the goats gradually works its way up to the tree's top limbs. Once the little goat gets there, perched precariously on a branch no thicker than Mia's forearm as it stretches to reach for the highest, greenest leaf, you and Mia look at one another, shake your heads in disbelief, and offer the young goatherd and his charges a round of polite applause.

An hour later, back on the narrow main road, the sky grows dark enough for you to turn on the Renault's low-beams, one of which seems dimmer than the other. Approaching the outskirts of Marrakesh, you nudge Mia, who raises her cheek from the headrest and sleepily returns your smile, clucking her tongue at the Groucho Marx wiggling of your eyebrows. She sighs, rubs her eyes, and asks more seriously than you expect, "Are you *perpetually* flirtatious, Carter? Should I take *any* of your charm personally?"

You nod once and offer Mia an exaggerated wink. "All of it, baby. It's all for you."

Dusk and smoky fire-lights from the first knot of flat-roofed red adobe huts eliminate much of the desert landscape as you reach the outskirts of Marrakesh. Immediately the road's pavement improves. Dozens of transplanted palm trees—some ten meters high—swoon over the transplanted green grass like fawning guards of the *ville nouvelle.* Though not as claustrophobic as Casablanca, the city's downtown section bustles with honking cars and pedestrians. Flashing red lights hang over modern-looking crosswalks. You pass a whistle-armed, white-gloved policeman directing traffic. With the windows lowered again, you maneuver the rental car around the French-named cafés and hotels, gradually aiming towards the twisting, noisy maze of the city's thousand-year-old, walled-in medina. Within a few blocks Europe becomes Africa. Bistros are replaced by grimy, torch-lit food stalls and dingy-looking lodgings with names like Hotel Souria and The Eddakhla. As you plunge still deeper into the darkness of "the old city," donkeys and cloppity horse-drawn carriages outnumber cars. The predominant smells are kerosene and incense, the nighttime noise a fantastic cacophony of frenzied laughter, Arabic screams, and tribal drum-music. Like some holy Islamic phallus, the minaret of the Koutoubia Mosque penetrates the colossal cloud of spot-lit smoke rising from the fruit-stand lanterns in the surreally crowded Djemma el-Fna, an enormous market square, which Mia's guidebook lauds as "the world's wildest open-air party."

Stalled within the smoky market mob, you can do little but gape through the windshield at the surrounding show. There must be a thousand people gathered around the car, you estimate—almost all of them dark-skinned, djellaba-clad Moroccans. Dozens of flickering yellow oil-lamps cast eerie, dreamlike shadows over the jostling sea of hooded cobra dancers, *gnawa* musicians banging tambourines (and occasionally the Renault's hood), Berber acrobats, Koran-thumping storytellers, limbless beggars, sweating and near-naked fire-breathers, veiled women reading palms, and toothless medicine men hawking magical goat skulls. For the first time all day, you begin to fully appreciate that you and Mia have entered the heart of an ancient and cabalistic continent.

Eventually you find a small, guarded parking area and walk with Mia hand-in-hand from the car through the entrance of the Dar al-Assad, a four-room, $120-a-night, bed-and-breakfast in which the *Men's Agenda* in-house travel agency booked you a room. You were told little about this former "Moroccan family palace" other than that it's owned by a pair of Frenchmen and overlooks a flowered courtyard in a quiet section of the medina. Pausing to catch your breath, your Tumi slung over your shoulder, you and Mia collectively "Oooh" at the foyer's impressively high, blue-tiled walls and intricately carved oak front desk, the brocade couch, the brass urn filled with an explosion of fragrant red roses. A framed photograph of the recently enthroned thirty-seven-year-old King Mohammed VI, the eighteenth monarch of the Sharifia dynasty since 1664, hangs above a row of four dangling, gold-colored keys. Having left most of the photo equipment in the car, you cast an anxious glance back in the darkness in the general direction of the parking area.

"This is heavenly," Mia whispers, letting go of your hand as she leans her head back to look at the octagonal cupola ceiling. "I feel like a character in *The Arabian Nights*."

A second, slightly impatient *ding ding ding* of the bell brings into the candlelit cubicle an effete-looking, thirty-year-old Parisian with slicked-back black hair, rimless spectacles, and a collarless Moroccan tunic so white it seems to glow. Behind him, continuing to swing, is a door connected to a cooking area. *"Madame. Monsieur,"* the clerk says, drying his hands with a kitchen towel, offering Mia and then you a delicate dip of his clean-shaven chin. *"Bonsoir. Bienvenue à Dar al-Assad."*

Your mouth has gone dry. Your heart—as you feared—is pounding in anticipation of what is about to transpire. Clearing your throat, avoiding Mia's eyes, you respond to the Frenchman in hardy English. "Hello there. Good evening. We have a room reserved under the name 'Cox.' It was booked by fax from New York."

The clerk smiles thinly. "Of course. May I see your passports, please?" After signing the registry and the receipt for a credit-card deposit, you're given one of the gold keys and told, "Room 3 can be found at the top of the stairs to your right."

You clear your throat again and place a hand on the counter. It appears as if the plan might work after all. "Do you have someone who could help us with our luggage?"

"Certainly."

Mia touches your arm and whispers, "Are we getting only one room, Carter?"

Without turning to face her, you pinch your perspiring lips and offer a dismal approximation of a casual shrug. "Looks that way. The magazine made the reservations." You sigh. "I guess I'm stuck with you."

"Carter—"

". . . What?"

But seeing Mia's panic-stricken face, you turn back with another sigh and ask the clerk, "Is there any chance you might have a second room?"

"No, *Monsieur.* I am very sorry. With your arrival all four of our rooms are now occupied until tomorrow evening."

"Oh, Carter," Mia exclaims, crossing her arms.

"Okay—okay. *Relax.* We can manage. It's all good. I'm sure it's a *very* big bed." To the clerk: "They're big beds, right?"

"Oui, Monsieur."

"See?"

Mia lowers her head. "This is . . . oh, Carter. I don't know if this is such a good idea. Actually, I *know* this is not a good idea."

"Hey, I'm sorry, buddy, but when in Rome . . . we'll be okay. This is no big deal. Really." You kiss Mia's cheek, step back, and raise a palm. Waiting until she lifts her gaze and meets your eyes, you promise, "It's a big bed, and I'll be good—so help me."

Mia glances mistrustfully at your wiggling fingers and replies with a shudder, "That's what concerns me, Carter."

After you finally fall asleep—your head pulsing with new worries and concerns—you dream that you're a competitive track cyclist, pedaling in interminable circles round and round a velodrome on a painfully small ten-speed bike. Naked, Mia sits in the otherwise empty stands, timing your laps with an enormous silver stopwatch. The dream concludes with you coasting to a stop, exhausted, after the fortieth lap, where—unable to unclip from the pedals—you fall sideways onto the sloped track and crack your skull.

The headache—a dull throbbing in the sinus cavities directly behind your ocular bones—persists throughout Wednesday's breakfast and intensifies during lunch, an odd, late-afternoon combination of chilled beet soup and seafood tagine served in an airless, poorly lit café in the medina a short walk from the Dar al-Assad's wrought-iron-gated entrance. Bare electric light bulbs hang from the café's ceiling. The stench of kerosene—which hovers *everywhere,* it seems, in Marrakesh—mixes thickly with smoke from a spark-showering charcoal fire, a skewered leg of lamb dripping fat onto the sizzling flames. The large, rough-edged windows separating you from the dusty medina are without glass. Across from the café, no more than ten meters away, eyes closed, arms folded, a soft gray tarboosh perched atop his even grayer head of hair, an old potter squats in the doorway to his ancient shop, murmuring prayers beneath his breath, his bowls, dishes, and jars stacked precariously against the unpainted adobe wall.

By the time tea is served, you and Mia are the café's only customers. Both the young, dark-skinned Moroccan waitress and the smiling, gold-toothed owner continue to be obsequious. Though you feel claustrophobic and queasy, Mia seems unfazed by the lack of fresh air, and leans back, beaming generously, as the waitress fills her cup from a tarnished-silver, swanlike spout raised a full meter above the table.

"Merci," Mia says, clasping her hands together below her chin, clearly delighted by the flourish.

When the young Moroccan woman approaches your chair, you mumble your thanks without looking up and continue to massage your forehead.

Still slung heavily around your neck are the Mamiya 645 and the manual Leica. In the four pockets of the khaki-colored Kurnhardt vest that you loaned her, Mia carries sixteen rolls of Fujichrome Velvia film, a light meter, and three tinted filters. The tripod that she's toted without complaint on her shoulder since leaving the hotel rests across her lap. Both of you've already gotten enough North African sun for you to rue not having packed hats. When you increase the weight on your elbows by leaning away from the heat of the charcoal fire, the little table rocks on its lopsided legs. "Jesus Christ," you mutter, glaring over your shoulder at the splattering slab of meat. From all four directions within the medina, muezzins cup an ear and call their fellow Muslims to disengage from all worldly occupations and recite the Salat al-Zuhr, the early afternoon prayer, their plaintive wails prompting thousands throughout the old city—including the potter across the lane—to stop in their tracks, remove their shoes, and collectively bow or prostrate themselves, forehead to rug, towards Mecca. Pushing away the remains of the bread, you sigh and daub a puddle of spilled olive oil with your napkin.

Mia's relentless good cheer and affection continue to irritate you: All morning, while searching through Marrakesh for a location for Saturday's fashion shoot, she insisted on carrying the tripod, insisted on returning the smile and nod of every burnoose-peddling merchant, insisted on taking your hand and stealing a kiss every time the rest of your party trailed behind or wasn't looking. "Carter, are you okay?" she had asked after you crushed your third unfinished cigarette since breakfast. "Why are you so fidgety?" Unable to make eye contact, you glowered at her grungy Levi's and faded red T-shirt (would she be wearing the same damn outfit all week?), and responded with a grunt and a shrug.

The location-scout from Tangiers, Kiki Holtkamp—a busty, bored-acting South African wearing Timberlands, cargo shorts, a black pullover sweater, a man's diving watch, and Prada sunglasses half-hidden in her stylishly tousled blond hair—had arrived at the Dar al-Assad at ten, thirty minutes late, and brought with her a Moroccan boy called Nadar, who, she announced, would serve as "our local eyes and ears." The kid looked to be no more than fourteen or fifteen and wore a white short-sleeved shirt, clip-on tie, and dusty leather sandals. When you asked Nadar how old he was, the boy offered a lopsided grin and made an "okay" sign with a thumb and forefinger.

"Nadar's from Rabat," Ms. Holtkamp said with a thick Afrikaaner accent, squeezing into the back of the Renault, "but he says he has *cuh*-zens in Marrakesh and knows his way 'round. I'm afraid his English is not nearly as good as his French, and his French is not nearly as good as his Arabic, but he claims he can get us into the Saadian Tombs after hours. He seems willin' to work—he knew how to get through the medina to *your* place, at least, *Cah*-tuh." The bosomy, blond location scout reached around the headrest and tweaked your shoulder. "I was pleasantly surprised to see that an American had booked his room *inside* the medina. Most Yanks stay in the *ville nouvelle*. I never got your full itinerary from my boy at *Men's Agenda*, by the way."

As you drove deeper into the old walled city that morning, your baser self slithered its way back into your heart: Almost dar-ing Mia to notice, you twice returned the shamelessly flirtatious Ms. Holtkamp's buttery, blue-eyed gaze in the rearview mirror. You hated yourself for your lecherous thoughts, especially in light of last night, though it didn't keep you from stealing glimpses of the South African's curvy black sweater. Having announced at the outset of the morning that you desired to do Saturday's fashion shoot in a "lush Moroccan-looking garden of some sort," you silently allowed Nadar, who sat cross-legged beside you in the front seat, to guide you first to the Saadian Tombs, which, he explained in halting English, contained the bones of a "mad" sultan named Moulay Yazid and sixty-six of his fellow Saadians. "Too dry," you determined of the tombs' unwatered courtyard. You then drove westward, around the medina's old rampart walls, to the verdant green and obsessively manicured acreage of La Mamounia, which, Nadar exclaimed with a raised forefinger, was "Morocco's number-one big hotel." You parked the car and spent almost an hour wandering among the five-star resort's flower gardens and orange trees, its three deluxe villas, Art Deco–designed casino, two blue-tiled swimming pools, six red-clay tennis courts, and dozens of tuxedoed and uniformly suspicious staff. "Too European," you grumbled. At Ms. Holtkamp's suggestion, you drove back into the more urban, French-influenced *ville nouvelle* and inspected the Jardin Majorelle, a blue-washed art museum—a former villa owned by Yves Saint-Laurent—surrounded by a tropically lush botanical garden filled with lemon and banana trees, yuccas, bougainvilleas, palm trees, water lilies, and jasmine. Excitedly you decided that the garden's blue zellige-tiled, fish-filled ponds would be perfect, with the additional benefit of being comfortably shaded. Alas, you were told by a guard, who wagged his hand at Mia's tripod and your neckful of cameras and light meters, that the museum's director would not allow professional photography. "Too fucking typical," you declared, ripping and flinging into the trash the purple stub of your two-day pass.

Stuck in traffic in the *ville nouvelle*, growing hungrier, more uneasy, more restless, after four hours driving through Marrakesh in the rattling old Renault—your headache now accompanied by a ringing in your left ear—you abruptly informed the car's occupants that you would forgo garden greenery altogether, and instead utilize a location you'd discovered with Mia last night after dinner, before the two of you settled uncomfortably into bed. Slowing the car and pointing up at the twenty-sixth-floor terrace of the Hotel de la Renaissance, you dipped your head, glancing skywards through the windshield, and announced without enthusiasm, "They have a terrace on the roof with a decent view of the Atlas Mountains. Let's just do the damn shoot up there."

Back at the Dar al-Assad's parking lot, you climbed from behind the wheel, stretched, and grumpily bade Nadar and Ms. Holtkamp good-bye. Tapping your Seiko, you decreed that at exactly three o'clock in exactly three days you wished to find the two of them, along with the four models and their entourage from Spain, and the half-dozen players from *Le Liberty*, the semiprofessional soccer team, waiting for you and Mia in the hotel's lobby. "And dress warmer, little dude," you advised Nadar, jabbing his shoulder. "It'll be cool up there on the roof once the sun sets."

Camera gear still in tow (though you didn't take a single picture during the location hunt), you led Mia through the dusty labyrinth of the walled-in medina into Taza, the first café you spotted, in whose smoky confines you now sit clutching your aching head and sipping your second cup of sickly sweet, mint-sprigged tea.

"I have never been in a country where people friggin' *pray* so much," you groan, continuing to clean up the spilled olive oil, the ululating cries of the muezzins growing louder and seemingly more manic in their intensity. "It's amazing anything gets done here." Mia smiles patiently, and beneath the wobbly table playfully presses your toes with her hiking boots. You glance again at your watch. You'd intended to be on the road for the arduous, three-hour trip back to the coast and your two-night stay in Essaouira by four o'clock. You add with more snippiness than you expect, "Even Catholics don't pray this much."

Mia is growing ever more puzzled by your mercurial mood swings. Though stiffening, she replies evenly, "Well, that depends on the Catholic, Carter."

"How often do *you* go to Mass?"

The question comes out sounding confrontational, and Mia leans back in her chair even farther, answering, "In Guatemala I was going to Mass every morning."

You squint at Mia's sunburned cheeks through your splayed fingers. She looks so skinny to you beneath your vest—and that little shell-thing on her choker: who does she think she is—Laurie Partridge? "Really? *Every* morning?"

Mia nods, shrugs. "Is that really so different from you meditating every night?"

You think for a moment but say nothing.

Tilting forward, her good cheer on the verge of vanishing, Mia taps the Mamiya and whispers, "Would you mind asking the waitress to take a picture of us?"

With a sour face, you gaze around at the four bare, smoke-stained walls, and then over your shoulder at the grease-popping fire. "You know—I don't know. I don't think there's enough light in here. You didn't bring a flash, did you?"

She looks down, pats the pockets of the vest. "Not unless you gave me one."

"Nah—I didn't." You signal for the check. "Anyway, we need to hit the road. You about finished with the tea?"

Mia stares at you. She makes a sputtering noise with her lips, withdraws her feet from yours, and with folded arms slumps back in her chair. "What's going on, Carter? Why are you acting this way?"

"What're you talking about?"

Mia gives her head a slow shake. "Have I done something wrong, Carter? Have I upset you somehow?"

"No, you've done nothing wrong. You've been a team player all day. I *appreciate* you lugging the tripod."

Mia cocks her head. "Are you upset about last night?"

"No. Last night was top-notch."

"Then why are you acting this way?"

"Acting *what* way, Mia?"

"Acting like you're disappointed with me."

"Oh, please."

"Please what, Carter? You are. You've been cold and aloof ever since we got up this morning. You grimace every time I touch you. Even now you won't look me in the eye. What's going on?"

"Nothing's going on."

"Then why are you being so brusque with me?"

"I'm not being brusque with you. I'm not being *anything* with you."

Mia chuckles, sighs. "Well . . . yeah. Precisely. What *are* your feelings for me, Carter? How should I interpret my invitation to this trip? How should I interpret what you said in bed last night?"

"Oh, *man.* Let's not go down this path, okay?"

Regardless, you rewind the tape. You venture a guess that Mia is referring to the proposal you made, shortly before she allowed you to unbutton and remove her pajama top, about the possibility of her returning to New York and staying with you during her summer vacation from school.

Leaning low over your tea, you massage your forehead with a damp palm, the details of last night's semisuccessful seduction taunting you like finger-jabs to the sternum: The mosquito netting and slowly-rotating ceiling fan. The jug of water with its submarined slice of lemon. The theater of shadows played against the blue-and-salmon-colored walls. The groaning wooden bedframe as you climbed across the mattress. Your pants and shirt tossed to the floor. The torch-lit, snake-charming chaos of Djemma el-Fna beyond the palm trees right outside the window. You couldn't have asked for a more tempting setting. But poor Mia had looked so nervous, holding her bag against her chest as she slipped inside the tiny bathroom. When she finally unlocked the door and reappeared in the candlelight wearing her blue pajamas, scrubbed and toothbrushed, she smiled grimly and collapsed next to you on the bed with an air of familiarity so painfully innocent and forced, you wondered if perhaps you should throw your clothes back on and go sleep in the car.

"Do you have any idea how pretty you are?" you whispered, adjusting the pillows.

Mia chuckled uneasily. "I fear that such a question, Carter, is among the cut flowers of your bedtop prose."

Wearing nothing but your mala beads and a pair of "midnight black" Diesel cotton briefs you purchased at Bergdorf's the day before Mia's flight from Guatemala, you rolled over and lowered the full length and weight of your body onto Mia's motionless limbs.

"Aren't you cold?" she asked from beneath you, shivering, her fingers spread helplessly against the mattress.

"This is what I sleep in," you answered, lifting your head. "Should I have brought *my* flannel jammies?"

Mia closed her eyes. "I'm not complaining, Carter. I *like* the way you look. And feel. And smell. And . . . mmmm, thank you . . . taste."

In the darkness Mia tentatively returned your kisses and murmurings, touching the muscles in your bare back and shoulders so lightly you couldn't tell her fingers from the bone-colored bed linen. She offered no resistance as you unbuttoned her long-sleeved pajama top, though she tensed and opened her eyes as you loosened the drawstring to her pajama bottoms. Breathing hard, your face buried between Mia's damp hair and pillow, feet and fingers itchy with desire, you reached beneath her pants and forcefully slid a hand between her legs before she had a chance to decline or accept the advance.

Mia gasped and clutched your forearm, startled, both aroused and afraid, moist eyes wide with disbelief. With the shine of tears in her eyes, she stared blindly through the gauzy white mosquito netting at the ceiling, unwilling to breathe, unwilling to surrender her body to what she was feeling. *What am I afraid of?* she silently pleaded to herself, the heat and smell of your skin—the penetrating touch of your hand—as magical as she had imagined, eyes closed again, embarrassed by her moaning, her gently writhing hips raised against her will, praying desperately, until—*yes*—there—there—she felt God's presence in the room and began to relax. *Is it not through love that You are revealed to me?* You sensed her body becoming slack and cool, her hands lifting from your shoulders as she gradually let go of her arousal. Soon it was as if she were no longer there, no longer lying beneath you—as if she had turned to air. You stopped touching her without her asking you to—this you recall clearly—but continued to kiss her neck and breasts as you both sat up. "Carter . . . Carter," Mia whispered heavily, crossing her arms in the flickering candlelight. "Don't do this. We're playing with fire. This isn't what you want." Still out of breath, you leaned back and nodded and nodded, as if this were the wisest, most insightful observation you'd ever heard.

Eyes lowered, and with the same forced playfulness with which Mia had earlier bounced on the bed—grinning to show that this was all in fun, no harm done—you nipped at Mia's earlobes and shoulders (close to drawing blood) as you helped her rebutton her pajama top, urging yourself to let go of your rising irritation and your resentment of her making you feel foolish. When you asked if she was ready for sleep, she offered a nod and tenderly held the palm of your hand against her cheek. Already you felt the distant rumblings of your current headache—*this virginity thing is gonna be the death of me.* Still undressed, you snuffed the candles and dutifully pressed yourself beneath the covers against Mia and her flannel pajamas, your left arm flopped over her narrow hip, murmuring sleepily, reassuringly, that you're still serious—really—about the possibility of her coming to stay with you for the summer.

Gradually the muezzins' call to afternoon prayer dies off. The only noise in the café comes from the oil-popping fire. You drum the tabletop with your fingertips, glance about like a trapped thief, clear your throat, and reply, "As for last night, Mia, you should interpret that, yes, I would like us to flirt some more with the possibility of you coming to work with me in New York this summer. There. I said it. It's official." After hunching over to count out forty dirham to pay the grease-stained, handwritten bill, you straighten back up and give Mia a long, evaluative stare. *Amazing green eyes she has. What am I so afraid of?* "Everything I said last night, Mia, I meant," you assure her, though her face gives no indication how she now feels about this.

Mia twists in her chair and quietly, earnestly, says, "I adore these Moroccan tables. The patterns are mesmerizing."

"Yeah, me too," you respond, running you fingers across the alternating red and gold tiles. "I wonder how much it would cost to ship one back to New York. It would go great in my kitchen."

Instantly you feel something shift in Mia. You can almost hear the grinding of the drawbridge as it rises. Sitting erect, she returns your glazed stare with a cool, impatient semblance of a smile but says nothing. Once again you've been snared by desire, as stupidly as a monkey with his fist in a hunter's box-trap, so covetous of the banana inside that you refuse to let it go to free your hand. Inclining forward, you frown at yourself and say, "Or I could simply enjoy sitting at one for a few minutes, drinking mint tea with a lovely, intelligent woman—a woman who has been much kinder to me today than I deserve—and then let it go."

You run a hand through your hair and try to catch Mia's attention with a big, toothy grin. But she's not biting. You push yourself up from the table, sighing as you walk to the counter to pay the bill. With a small, dignified nod, the owner pockets your money, takes your arm, leans closer, winks, and whispers within earshot of Mia, "Your woman—she is very beautiful."

You nod in agreement and mutter, "Thanks."

After returning to the table, still standing, you ask Mia, "So—what do you feel like doing? We could probably kill a few minutes shopping, if you want."

"Why did you do that?"

"Do what?"

"Why did you thank him, Carter? I don't understand that. For better or worse, you, as a man, deserve neither credit nor blame for a woman's appearance. You even did it when I mentioned how pretty your mother is."

". . . Whoa."

"Men baffle me."

"What? Wait, Mia—hold on."

But she has already stood, politely nodded at the waitress, and left through the café's front door. You, the café owner, and the old squatting potter across the lane collectively watch Mia turn the corner in what you incorrectly assume is the wrong direction back to the hotel. She doesn't even bother to see if you're following her—which, flustered, cameras banging, you quickly do. Once you catch up—panting from the effort, your face red—tight-lipped Mia declines to take your hand, shrugging as if to suggest that the tripod carried across her shoulders requires her full attention.

As you traipse sullenly through the shadowy lanes of the medina, Mia continues to keep her distance. Neither of you says a word. Sweating from the difficulty of keeping up, you stare at Mia's long neck, her narrow waist. Being an American male who has pledged his allegiance to the misguided notion that desirability and attainability are inversely related, you quickly come to regard Mia's coolness as excruciatingly attractive. This you like. This you want to swallow whole before it flies away. Perhaps if you bought her something. A bracelet or a new necklace. There are no accidents, you remind yourself, picking up the pace, convinced now that this complicated young Catholic is a gift, a life lesson waiting to be unwrapped. And from three steps behind, you can't help thinking that those Levi's of hers make a damn nice package.

Back at the Dar al-Assad, watching Mia across the room pack her one small bag—she seems to be growing more radiant right before your eyes—you're half-tempted to throw the black-bobbed virgin onto the unmade bed. Either that or pound your chest and yowl like a heart-speared coyote. *What do I want from this flighty dove? This is maddening!* You feel like you're fifteen again, your chest filled to bursting. Indeed, by the time you and the luminous, infuriatingly taciturn Mia Malone finish hauling all of the Anvils down the hotel's spiral staircase, across the road, and into the trunk of the Renault, you fear that you have fallen in love.

8

DESPITE YOUR ATTEMPTS AT CIVIL, even light-hearted, conversation, Mia remains mostly closemouthed for the duration of the three-hour drive back to the Atlantic coast. You hum, she looks sideways out the window. You turn up the belly-dancing music on the radio, she dons her reading glasses and lowers her head into her earmarked guidebook—her semiofficial notice to you that she's unplugging from your presence for a while.

"At least read the damn thing out loud," you say as you flip off the radio.

Mia intones: "'Built in the 1700s by Sultan Sidi Mohammed Ben Abdullah, the blue-and-white-painted fishing village is populated by 50,000 Portuguese, French, and Berbers. Flanked to the north by a mosque-like lighthouse, and to the south by sand dunes that lead to the Sahara Desert, Essaouira's medina is protected by stone battlements and an impressive assortment of bronzed cannons. Orson Welles filmed *Othello* within the city's whitewashed, Moorish-designed buildings and along its great white scimitar of beach—'"

"Nice metaphor."

"'—and between their concert tours in the 1960s, Jimi Hendrix and Cat Stevens ventured to Essaouira, dropping acid and writing songs in its half-dozen palace-converted Riad hotels.' Songs about heartache and confusion and the *exasperating* inability to make your love-interest as joyful about your blossoming relationship as you are."

"I can hardly wait to get there."

At nine o'clock, well after dusk, one hundred miles due west of Marrakesh, the moon hanging low and bright over the now-visible ocean, you downshift and slowly approach Essaouira's ramparts, gradually looking up at the two-story white bulwark, its fifty-foot, conical-topped parapet the shape of the lid for a bowl of tagine, the popular Moroccan stew. With the windows rolled down, the cool offshore breeze smells refreshingly tangy and is filled, even at this late hour, with the cries of fishermen auctioning the last of their day's catch of spider crabs, jumbo shrimp, and black eels. After parking the overheated Renault in an unguarded public lot near the walled-in medina, you enter the inner city through the nearest gate, known locally as a *bab*, and eventually find the Riad al-Madina on a narrow, poorly lit lane called Darb Laaouj al-Attarin. Mia gasps as the two of you cross the blue portal and approach the flower-framed front desk. The hotel was originally an eighteenth-century pasha's villa, and the twenty-seven rooms of the three-story structure surround a central, open-air courtyard decorated with blue-tiled tables, potted palms, caged birds, and a multitiered water fountain. To the right of the courtyard, you spy a low-ceilinged, candlelit salon filled with dozens of sitting cushions, throw rugs, hookahs, brass pots, and a pair of wooden, table-mounted chessboards. For the first time since leaving Marrakesh Mia touches you. "This is exquisite, Carter," she whispers, taking your arm, virtually swooning at the sight of the villa's resplendent interior.

The Riad al-Madina is decidedly more upscale than you anticipated, and also proves considerably more expensive: even though it will cost an additional 1,900 dirham—roughly $200 a night—

you've determined that, for now at least, the craftiest strategy for wooing Mia is to pay for two separate rooms. The dark-haired, myrrh-scented Moroccan night manager returns from her office, her brown eyes, red lipstick, and swishing nylons drawing your nose across the courtyard in their wake. Flanked behind the counter by two red-vested valets, the young woman hands back your credit card along with a pair of brass keys.

"Thank you," you respond demurely.

"De rien."

Though she says nothing, as Mia realizes the sleeping arrangements she lets go of your arm, squints, and tilts her head, her face scrunched with confusion. It has in it, this lopsided look of hers, equal parts dismay, begrudging respect, and a slight betrayal of her disappointment.

"*Two* rooms?" she asks over her shoulder, as one of the valets assists you up the stairs with your first load of luggage and photo equipment. "Oh, you are a *curious* bodhisattva, Carter."

"I thought it might make things easier—you know, with the threat of fire and all."

Mia's third-floor quarters are directly above yours. Outside each room on the terrace are a table and two chairs, potted flowers, assorted green-and-yellow ceramics. After depositing her bag inside her room, Mia joins you on the second-floor balcony. "This place is amazing," she says. "Have you seen the room yet? Mine's beautiful. They've put fresh roses next to the bed." Leaning over the wrought-iron railing as you gaze into the courtyard, her left shoulder pressed against your right one, Mia asks with a determined grin and an elfin shift in her voice, "You up for a game of chess? I've been practicing."

"Yeah, I saw the boards," you reply, stifling a yawn. "But let's wait till tomorrow."

A gaily colored parakeet twitters in a cage hanging by rope from the balcony railing. "Are you tired?"

"No, I'd just rather play tomorrow. Who've you been practicing with?"

"One of the Casa Alianza counselors. He says that I have a good endgame, whatever that means."

"Oh? Well, we should definitely play, then. Tomorrow, for sure."

Mia sighs, nods, starts to say something but doesn't.

You kiss her cheek, stroke her shoulder, and watch with mild satisfaction as she turns and trudges by herself back up the stairs to the third floor, clearly nonplussed by this sudden change in tactics. You call up to her with a wink, "I'll wake you for breakfast around eight."

Mia looks back, jiggles her key like a voodoo amulet. "Dandy. I look forward to it."

"Sleep well."

". . . Mm-hmm."

You spend a few more minutes by yourself leaning against the railing, smoking a cigarette. Alone in your room, you inspect the traditional Moroccan decor for the first time, groaning miserably at how quixotically romantic the quarters become once illuminated by the two tapered candles standing on the nightstand. The enormous four-poster bed is draped in white muslin. The two French windows open to a skylit view of the medina, the squawking of seagulls, the distant crashing of waves. Fingering your mala beads, skeptical that there *is* a right path with Mia, you expel another long breath, toss a pillow to the purple-tiled floor, and arrange on the nightstand, between the candles and a trio of red roses in their terra cotta vase, your tiny wooden travel Buddha and, unwrapped from a protective handkerchief, the black-framed photograph of Mia in Central Park. Before lowering yourself to the floor to meditate, you run a thumb across Mia's shy smile. "Great," you grumble, suddenly cocking an ear towards the ceiling as you hear the plumbing crank on, the filling bathtub located so close overhead you can hear the water sloshing.

Toes itchy with the thought of Mia, naked and soapy, splashing in the tub, you walk barefoot back onto the balcony to smoke another cigarette. You look at your watch with disappointment—it's not even eleven. The rest of the pasha's villa, however, seems to have already called it a night. The light behind the front desk is turned off. The bird caged below the balcony has fallen asleep. Ghaita flute music drifts from one of the villa's darkened rooms across the moonlit courtyard. Leaning your elbows on an ivy-strewn patch of the railing, you gaze up at the stars and try to turn your attention to the particulars of tomorrow's shoot.

As you finish your cigarette, from the third-floor balcony comes an unexpected whisper: "Carter? Is that you?"

You straighten and whisper in return, "Yeah. What's up?"

"It's Mia."

"I figured that."

"May I have one of your cigarettes?"

Shaking your head, not quite chuckling, you light the second-to-last Marlboro Light of your pack, and on tiptoes reach up and extend the lit cigarette, filter first, to Mia's lowered right hand. You smell on her fingers aloe vera–scented lotion. Starlight catches a wink of Mia's antique gold wedding band before her hand and cigarette disappear.

A little mockingly she replies: "Thank you, sir."

Nothing more is said. You listen to Mia smoke in silence, wondering if she's come out to her balcony wearing her pajamas.

Eventually she whispers again, "Carter?"

"Still here."

"I'm sorry about the car ride this evening. I know I wasn't very good company, that you were only trying to make peace."

"Don't sweat it."

You wait for more. For a full minute you and Mia remain mute. From somewhere deep within the medina a dog howls at the moon.

". . . Carter?"

Jesus, this is ridiculous. Why doesn't she just walk down? "Yeah?"

"I'm looking forward to tomorrow."

"As am I."

"I really want to be a good assistant for you."

"I'm sure you will be, Mia."

The flute music dies off. Another medina dog joins the first one with its baying.

". . . Carter?"

"Mm-hmm?"

"Sleep well. Have good dreams."

Mia closes and latches the door to her room behind her. "Thanks," you mumble towards the empty courtyard. "You too."

When you awake, shortly after dawn, roosters crowing across the medina, you're holding the spare pillow to your chest. Before joining Mia for breakfast, you shower, shave, trim your eyebrows, throw on a pair of new Maui cargo shorts and your faded 1993 NYC Marathon T-shirt, its frayed collar stylishly ruined by bleach, slather sunscreen across your cheeks and forehead, and needlessly rearrange for the third time the contents of the two equipment cases you plan to bring to the beach. *What did Christopher mean when he said that lust is fear? Fear of what?* Maybe you are about to find out, and this could be how.

You gaze at the Buddha statue as you reassess your line of attack with Mia, debating whether you should wear or leave behind your mala—the implications of your decision not to bring the beads felt as soon as you turn your back to the altar and click open your laptop. You assume that much of the day will be spent without shade: according to your computer's bookmarked International Weather site, the temperature on the Moroccan coast is scheduled to rise well into the eighties. You glance at your watch again. The chirping of sparrows draws your attention towards the opened shutters. Poking your head through the window, the warm and busy medina already abuzz with flies and Arabic chatter and the smell of burning olive wood, you drum your belly and see that to the west, over the Atlantic, the morning sky is cloudless and vibrantly blue.

You're restless. You return to the unmade bed and perch on its edge while you reread on the laptop's screen the downloaded copy of the *Men's Agenda* article on young Michel Motroet, the subject for today's shoot:

> *Beating out long-board veteran Jimmy "Bump and Jump" Walters for last year's freestyle world championship bragging rights, Motroet's tournament and endorsement earnings for the season have already topped $350,000! Like Italy's flamboyant slalom skier, Alberto Tomba, the sensationally tattooed, French Riviera–born nineteen-year-old garners as much press for his romantic exploits as he does for his duck-jibing acrobatics on the waves. At this spring's Kitesurf & Freestyle Invitational in Melbourne, for example, the flashy world champ was spotted by local paparazzi schmoozing at the velvet-roped Bar Cabaret with Australian supermodel Heidi King. Now based in the Moroccan resort town of Essaouira—nicknamed by adventure travelers Windy City, Afrika, and where 50-knot winds are as common as the camels—the notorious, aerial-prone cover boy quips of his precocious success and appetite for fun, "Why does everyone think I should act like a forty-year-old? Do you think a forty-year-old could do what I do on the water?"*

Closing the computer file before checking your e-mail, you snort and mutter, "Prick."

You climb the stairs to the third floor and knock on Mia's door five minutes before eight. There's no answer. You move sideways and check through the window, but the blinds are closed.

"Carter—I'm down here."

When you join Mia in the courtyard, you discover that she's already been to the souks and back, and has brought you a gift—an exotic-looking brass-and-camel-bone teapot—which she sets before you on the blue-tiled table. "The shop owner said that I bargain like a Berber," Mia informs you. "Is that good or bad?"

"Oh, that's definitely good," you assure her, holding the small teapot up for a better look. "Thanks—this is terrific."

The waiter initially addresses you in French. Rather than defer to your bilingual table companion, you point to a selection on the top of the menu and order it for both of you. With the pot of thick black coffee already on the table, you fill Mia's unused cup. "Do you want some juice or anything?" Mia shakes her head. Though of course you say nothing, you're a little disappointed to see (and smell) that she's put on the same clothes—the dirty jeans and red T-shirt—that she's worn two of the previous three days and nights. Regardless, you like that she's taken the initiative with a gift—a savvy opening move for your day together (she *has* been practicing her chess). And with her suntanned cheeks, sparkling green eyes, and hopeful smile, Mia looks as pretty as you've ever seen her.

As if reading your thoughts, Mia explains, "Just so you know, Carter, I'm not trying to make any sort of political statement with my wardrobe selection. It's just that I haven't had a chance to do laundry in a while." Mia leans over the table and whispers, "You should get a whiff of the shirts I'm *not* wearing."

You sip the coffee from Mia's cup. The Buddha said, If it is so, say it is so. If it is not so, say it is not so. Nevertheless: "I didn't notice. But there's bound to be a laundry service here. Or—if you're up for it—we could go shopping and get you something new."

"If we had some detergent, I could do it in the sink."

"Nah—let's go get you something new."

The waiter presents the two of you with identical scallion-and-mushroom omelets, sliced mango, and buttered toast—not what you expected, but close enough. You and Mia nibble in silence, glancing about the bougainvillea-lined courtyard, occasionally sharing a sigh and smile in unspoken agreement over the villa's splendor. For the duration of your meal, you make a point of lowering your fork after each bite, not retrieving it again until after you've completely chewed and swallowed. Neither of you can finish the omelet, though Mia takes her coffee cup back and downs the final swig.

With the gear loaded in the trunk, you and your neophyte assistant set off in the Renault by nine, a full hour before you're scheduled to rendezvous with the teenage windsurfing world-champ. Already the morning air is warm and muggy enough to drive with the windows rolled down. Having noticed the paragraph about Eglise Sainte-Anne highlighted in the guidebook, you surprise Mia shortly into the ride by stopping at Essaouira's one and only Catholic church, a small, unassuming, fifty-year-old concrete building on Avenue el-Moukaouama, just south of the post office. "Supposedly they perform Mass here every morning in French and German," you tell her, killing the engine, dipping your head to look up through the windshield at the church's modest, tree-shaded steeple. "If you'd like a few minutes by yourself, I could wait outside. I don't mind."

"Don't be silly. This—this is so sweet of you."

The chapel is separated from the road by a rusty, knee-high gate and a freshly watered garden, three green-leafed bower trees swaying in the ocean breeze. Mia accepts your hand as you walk around the parked, hissing Renault, silently pass through the gate, and enter into Eglise Sainte-Anne's empty, light-filled nave. Her eyes are wide and dancing in the morning sun. With your first step, the mildewy wooden floor gives a little. You both pause, look around—a gust of the Atlantic winds to your backs carries with it the squawking of seagulls. The nave's interior is stuccoed, white, simple. A dozen stiff-backed pews. A low-arched ceiling painted light blue.

A bearded priest informs you in hushed French that Mass will not start until eleven. Nevertheless, Mia is delighted just to wander by herself in a slow circle around the empty pews, hands caressing the aging red hymnals, a paint-flecked statue of Saint Jude, the green velvet cloths covering the railings, the door to the sacristy. "This reminds me of the chapel near the Casa Alianza shelter," she says, tilting her head for another look at the sky-colored ceiling, as she reunites with you near the entrance. "It has the same feel to it. Peaceful. A little sad. Like a child's poem that doesn't quite rhyme." Mia takes your hand again. "My favorite kind." She leans forward, kisses your cheek. "This was so nice of you, Carter. Thank you."

Mia is still smiling, indeed still seems mildly rapturous, thirty minutes later, as you approach and introduce yourself to the bare-chested Michel Motroet, who is basking in the sun at an outdoor café table in the Place Prince Moulay el-Hassan, Essaouira's main square. The muscular teen, who is being gawked at by a handful of local windsurfers in the neighboring café as if he were a member of the Moroccan royal family, and who seems to be on especially good terms with his blond, Rasta-haired Belgian waitress, wears black, skintight wet-suit pants down to his ankles and red flip-flops on his feet. All of Motroet's toenails and fingernails are lacquered with week-old black polish. His naturally brown-rooted hair is bleached a yellowish blond. Pulled behind his head, the boy's beefy, sun-tanned arms sport a number of intricately detailed black tattoos, the most prominent of which, circling the considerable girth of his right bicep, is a Koran verse written in Arabic script.

"Hey, what's up—I'm Carter Cox, from *Men's Agenda*," you tell him, extending a hand. "This is Mia. My assistant."

"You run zeese marathon, yes?" the boy asks, still seated, though bestowing upon you a complicated approximation of an inner-city handshake.

You look down at your damp blue T-shirt. "Yep. Yes I did. Back when I was your age and didn't know any better."

"What does this say?" asks Mia, stepping forward and lightly touching the Arabic lettering circling the young Frenchman's right arm.

The teenager gives Mia a flirtatious bounce of the muscle, though it's clear from his silence that he has no idea what the tattoo means. More amused than intrigued, Mia moves closer and examines an Indian-head tattoo on Motroet's other shoulder. "These are really . . . interesting."

You stick fifty dirham in Mia's back pocket. "Why don't you go inside and grab everyone a Coke?"

Motroet eyes Mia's bottom as she departs, then lifts his unshaven chin in your direction after she disappears in the café's interior, slumps back in his chair, and asks in his affected mix of French and Jamaican accents, "So, mon, where do you want to do zeese?" Before you can reply, the boy—who is clearly going to be a handful—puts on a pair of gold wraparound sunglasses and adds, "Do you mind da Screamers?"

"Ah . . . we can play with different looks. Sure."

"I need da Screamers. To be honest, mon, I ayte zeese sheet. *Ayte* it. Having ma peek-ture taken sucks."

"Yeah, I know what you mean. Listen, I'd like to set up on the beach somewhere. Where do you usually go to windsurf?"

"It suggests vanity, you know?"

"Right. Where do you usually windsurf?"

Motroet blinks at you. "Where do you tink? In da ocean." The answer cracks the kid up. "No—you're okay. I'm jest focking wid you, mon. Da best wave-sailing eese thirty miles to da north at Moulay Bousaktoun, or to da south at Sidi Kaoki. If you want peek-tures of me in da ocean, dat's cool, we can go dere. Do you have car?"

You wonder how long a karate chop delivered to his Adam's apple would put him out of commission. Checking the impulse to strike, you cross your arms and collect yourself by watching a pair of blue-hooded Berbers pass the table and disappear into a tiny shop next to the outdoor café. Orange carpets and bowls made of dark thuya wood are stacked in a window near the shop's door. With a sigh you turn back, glance at the windsurfing champ's muscle-flattened belly, at his flaking black fingernails and bile-colored hair. You find it difficult to believe that a supermodel like Heidi King would allow herself to be seen in public with this guy, much less date him. Though offering a smile and nodding, you decide right then and there that you will not submit to *Men's Agenda* a single shot of Motroet in or anywhere near the ocean. In fact, you're already plotting how to get the kid and his obnoxious hair atop a camel and beneath the biggest turban you can find.

"Sorry it took so long," Mia says, setting the three opened bottles of Coke on the table next to Motroet's beer. After returning Motroet's nod, she takes a step backwards directly into you, so that her upper back presses against your chest. You say nothing and tentatively rest a hand on her shoulder, wondering, How does *this* fit into the cat-and-mouse game? The ripeness of Mia's damp shirt, the swelling of her back as she breathes, makes your toes prickle, and you imagine her suddenly turning around, the wetness of her mouth against your throat, her pale breasts cupped within the warmth of your palms. Men's greatest fear is to be laughed at by a woman, you once read—women's greatest fear is to be murdered by a man. Which is more likely, you ask yourself, gently pinching Mia's waist and stepping sideways: Mia laughing at you, or you doing Mia harm?

"My art director suggested we do something funky, something . . . offbeat."

Motroet snorts. "Funky, mon. Whadever."

"Preferably with you *holding* your board."

When you suggest reuniting in an hour on the sand dunes of Cap Sim, five kilometers to the south of the harbor, and setting up for the shoot on the beach near the ruin of an old, sand-covered galleon wreck you spotted from the car last evening, the young Frenchman swigs his Coke and offers a skeptical shrug. "No problem. I know da spot." To Mia he asks: "Do you want to drive dere wid me, yes? I have air-conditioned Jeep."

Mia smiles, clears her throat. "No . . . thank you. I should probably stay with the photographer."

It takes almost twenty minutes for you and Mia to carry the equipment from the Renault's trunk down to the sand dunes. Shielding your eyes, you look around the nearly empty beach, which smells of brine and the ammonia-soaked hay bundled beneath the one palm tree in sight. The first pair of white-hooded camel drivers who approach you along the shoreline speak only Arabic. When you point in the direction of the galleon wreck, the older of the two drivers indicates with his hands that a trip there will cost fifty dirham. Mia shies back a step, protecting her eyes from the wind, nervous about both the single-humped camels' cud-chewing teeth and their rickety saddles. Hump to sand, you estimate, is high enough to do some serious damage were either of you to fall. Without asking Mia how she feels about simultaneously riding a camel and carrying one of the two Anvils, you agree to the price and squint again, unsure, at the distant galleon. "Bet you never imagined you'd be doing this a month ago," you shout into the ocean breeze, stepping back from a frothy roll of the incoming tide.

With tugs of their leashes and a tongue-clucking from their drivers, the two snorting, ivory-colored camels soddenly collapse forward into a kneeling posture. You climb aboard, one hand struggling with an equipment case, the other clutching the pommel, and are abruptly hoisted high into the air. *"Whoa,"* you cry, almost tumbling backwards, your sandaled feet slung skywards. Directly to your right, atop a slightly shorter camel, Mia works hard to stay balanced—even with some gentlemanly assistance from the younger driver, the equipment case in her left hand bangs against the camel's matted hair.

Barefoot in the dark brown sand, the older driver leads both animals with two short stretches of rope. You nod your approval at

Mia's stoic efforts and yell into the wind, "You're a tough little bird, Malone!"

The stretch of beach to Cap Sim ends up being almost completely deserted. There are no shade trees, no thatched umbrellas, no long-legged girls in bikinis. The novelty of the lurching, arrhythmic camel ride wears off after the first kilometer or two, especially once the powerful Atlantic wind reverses direction and the sand drives at you head-on. You're worried about having Mia load and unload the cameras—it would take just one grain of sand to scratch and ruin a whole roll of film, and you won't know if she's made any mistakes until you get back to New York and the rolls are returned from the lab. Regardless, you're going to need her help. "At the beginning, once we set up, I'm gonna shoot a few Polaroids," you shout over at her. "When I hand you one, time it for two minutes and then slip it back to me as discreetly as you can. I don't want the kid to see any of his Polaroids. They'll just make him more tense, and this dude's definitely not a team player."

"Aye-aye."

After a half an hour you pass a tiny, clapboard windsurfer rental shop and, nearby, a small group of local boys playing soccer. Seagulls circle overhead, cawing at the two camels. On a dune near the galleon a lone Moroccan family eats watermelon slices on a white bedsheet. The father and two sons are dripping wet in their soaked underwear, the wife and daughter sweating miserably in their fully-veiled, weekday djellabas. To your right offshore a trio of blue-sailed windsurfers fly across the whitecaps back towards Essaouira's main harbor. It looks to you like the windsurfers are going thirty knots or more—so fast you shout to Mia, "Man, they look like they have *motors* on those things."

As the wind dies down near the remains of the beached ship, you ask Mia in a more subdued voice what she thinks of Motroet. "The kid's in pretty good shape, huh?"

Mia shrugs. "Regardless, his not wearing a shirt in public in a

Muslim country exhibits poor taste. He lives here, right? He should know better."

"Do you like his tattoos?"

Mia bats her eyes. "I didn't notice any tattoos."

You had hoped to arrive at the Cap Sim galleon well before Motroet, but—alas—there he stands, still half-naked, brawny arms folded across his brawny chest, snickering and shaking his head at the sight of you and your squire comically astride the two snorting, flea-infested camels. Parked in the sand behind him is a cherry-red, fully loaded Jeep Cherokee Sport. A matching pair of maroon sail-tubes and two yellow JP Freeride boards, black fins pointed towards the clouds, are strapped to the new Jeep's expensive-looking roof-rack. After an ugly dismount—you bang your shin with the Anvil—you give the camel drivers an additional fifty dirham to stand by for a few minutes, but the windsurfing champ makes it clear with a dismissive wag of his head that he's unwilling to pose for a picture anywhere near a camel, much less on top of one.

"What can I do?" Mia asks, her Anvil lowered with both hands to the sand.

"Pray."

It takes almost twenty more minutes for you to unlock the Anvils and prepare the equipment—which, you hope, will be protected from the wind by the hull of the old boat.

"Come stand over here," you instruct the teen as Mia, nurselike, hands you the requested Mamiya 645. "Turn—squint back at the harbor."

"Squint?"

"Like a pirate. You're looking for a ship to rob."

"Why would I robe a sheep?"

"Just turn and face the harbor, okay?"

To Mia you grumble, "I left my softbox in New York, so we're gonna rely exclusively on natural light, though—shit—this friggin' sun is already getting too high." You try having Motroet stand with his bare back against the remains of the galleon's wooden stern. When you ask him to remove his Screamers, he hesitates but, with a grunt, flips the sunglasses into the wet sand.

You mumble over your shoulder to Mia, who cradles with both hands the still-unused Fuji medium-format, "Go grab the silver Litedisc."

"The what?"

"The collapsible light reflector over there."

Mia hustles around the side of the galleon. "This one?" she calls back from the stack of Anvils.

"What color is it?"

"Blue."

You answer testily, "No, not the tube. What color's the reflector? It's inside."

Nose in the opening, Mia shouts, "It looks sort of gold, maybe?"

"No, get the *silver* Litedisc." You glance again over your shoulder. "It's in the other tube."

When Mia returns to your side, out of breath but enjoying her responsibilities, you position her in the sand, kneeling just beyond the camera's field of vision, with the round 42-inch reflector aimed up at Michel's smug face. As you continue shooting, Mia asks, "What's the gold reflector for?"

You lower the camera, finger still on the shutter. "The gold gives the shot a softer touch—it would diffuse the light on his face some. But you're using the silver one because I'm shooting black-and-white right now, which I kind of need to stay focused on, okay?"

Mia's cheeks redden. "Okay. Sorry."

You sigh and lower the camera again. "No, please, I don't mean to snap. Let's just—hey, Michel, look at me—this way—no *this* way—yeah—just like that—good—stay there, just like that. Look down at Mia like she's lunch—*there* you go. Give me another snarl. Yeah. Like you want to take a big bite out of her." You're ashamed for taking this tack, but at least you've got his attention.

Another onslaught of wind almost topples Mia and the oversized reflector. Regaining her balance, she continues squatting uncomfortably in the bright sun. She doesn't complain, though. She doesn't even make a face. Glancing at the sand, you would swear that the hardworking, angelic Mia is not even casting a shadow.

Motroet stifles another yawn. After seven rolls of film it becomes evident that your reluctant model's range of facial expressions is limited to two: bored and theatrically bored. You run a hand through your windblown hair. Though you've not yet panicked, you feel as if you're flailing. You refuse to make eye contact with Mia, who realizes that you're embarrassed and fears that she's to blame. Were you more mindful and less self-centered, you'd recognize that Mia regards your embarrassment not with disdain but with sympathy. She's not blind—she sees how difficult Motroet is making himself and can well imagine how frustrating this must be for you, especially with the heat, the wind, and a novice assistant. Mia doesn't think less of you. She's actually impressed that you haven't yet lost your cool. But you don't recognize, much less acknowledge, her hang-in-there smiles, don't see the cocked eyebrow as she stares Motroet down after he makes a face at you behind your back, don't accept the possibility that a woman could still be fond of you after discovering that you're not perfect.

Embarrassment escalates to shame. Even the camels have drifted away. So what you do is get sloppy on purpose, sometimes not even bothering to check the light meter or fully frame the shot. Fuck it, you decide. Fuck this Tupac-prissy-ass-Rastafarian wannabe. Fuck his Jeep. Fuck *Men's Agenda*. Fuck Hal Ticket and his limp-dick speakerphone. Fuck—

"Arvoire."

Having grown hopelessly restless with you, the windsurfing champ harrumphs, retrieves his sunglasses from the sand, and struts towards his SUV.

"What's up?" you shout into the wind, hands on your hips.

"I go too da waves, mon."

"Come again?"

He snorts. "Da waves. I want da waves."

"What?" You stare at Mia, who, now standing, offers a commiserating and equally bewildered shrug. "We just *started,*" you shout even louder, your voice rising an octave. You do a quick count: if the shoot ends now, you'll have exposed only nine rolls of film, all of them black-and-white. "Dude, you can't just walk off in the middle of a shoot. We have a *contract.*"

You tromp barefoot towards the red SUV, but pull up short before actually grabbing Motroet. Though you know he can feel the heat of your breath on his thick neck, the kid ignores you as he rummages through the back of his Jeep. He doesn't even bother to look over his shoulder at the two fists you've clenched childishly at your sides. "This is bad," you groan, though you're not sure to whom. Certainly not to Mia, whom you refuse to face. "This is . . . not right." But what can you do? Humiliated, helplessly shaking your head at the wet sand, you just stand there, arms limp, camera dangling, unwilling to watch the tattooed teen unfurl and erect a sail in the longer of his two yellow boards, stroll with it into the breakers, and within a minute transform himself into nothing more than a taunting flash of maroon flying with the African breeze across the waves back towards the harbor.

"Do you want to have children?" you ask drunkenly, leaning forward on your elbows, your aching sunburned head hanging close to the table.

It's almost midnight. You've showered and put on a sports jacket and led Mia through the medina to Chez Toufik—according to the Riad al-Madina's concierge "the most expensive restaurant in Essaouira, and deservedly so." Decorated in the fashion of a Berber salon, the elegant, outdoor restaurant has but six tables on its torch-lit patio, the other five occupied by fashionably dressed Europeans.

A pair of stout, white-aproned Moroccan waiters stand stiffly beneath the nearby proscenium arch. You and Mia are both exhausted, dehydrated from the wine, and by the minute growing more sore from the shoreline camel ride and long walk back to the medina. Because of today's miserable shoot—perhaps your worst professional experience ever—you indulged yourself tonight with a spicy lamb tagine (the first meat you've tasted in nearly a year) and, for dessert, three deep-fried doughnuts and a slice of serpent cake. Before replenishing her wine glass, you offer Mia a cigarette, which she declines.

Something has shifted again between you and Mia, and you sense it's for the worse.

Mia has never looked more stunning. She is wearing the new blue sarong (tied low at the hip, per your suggestion), the new sandals, the new French-cut, white cotton Moroccan blouse with hand-embroidered filigree (which, as you expected, accentuates the bangs of her short hair, her long neck, and the high, gentle curve of her breasts), and the new silver bracelet—all of which she reluctantly allowed you to purchase for her this afternoon, without bargaining, at three successive beachfront souks near the villa. After your question, Mia takes another sip of wine—you're halfway through a second bottle of an Algerian rosé recommended by the waiter. Her green eyes are closing like a young flower's petals at nightfall. Fingers caressing the stem of her wine glass, tilting her head back, remaining deep within herself, she makes a little groan and touches the hollow of her throat as she swallows.

". . . Children?" she asks. Mia opens her sleepy eyes, crosses her arms. "Hmm, I'm not sure, Carter. Some women are built to be mothers. I fear I was designed to be a consumptive on the shores of Italy."

You continue staring at Mia's upturned face through the candlelight.

She strains for a moment to focus, the irises glistening, and says, "I hope I didn't make things more difficult today on the beach."

"No—it's me who should apologize. You were fine. *More* than fine. And I'm sorry we had to lug everything back by foot. I guess my impatience pretty much savaged the whole shoot from the start."

"I'm sure you managed to get at least *one* good picture of him, Carter."

"I'm not holding my breath. I just don't think it was meant to be today."

"Allah's will, eh?"

"Yeah . . . Allah's will." You swirl your glass, fix your eyes on the white blouse's neckline filigree. "Did you like the church this morning?"

Mia answers dreamily, her words slurring slightly, "Yes. Very much so."

In a voice lowered and husky, you lean forward, look straight into Mia's eyes, and whisper, "You know, you're gonna make a terrific mother."

"I don't know. Terrific mothers usually don't imbibe this much wine on a weeknight."

Your unblinking stare grows so intense Mia eventually closes her eyes again and leans back.

"*Your* mother put no pressure on you to become a Catholic, right?"

A little dizzy, baffled by this series of non sequiturs, Mia opens her eyes, lays her napkin on the table, and debates how to answer. "No," she replies skeptically. "I came to Catholicism on my own. I thought we'd covered this, Carter."

"But why? Why Catholicism?"

She's unsure how seriously she should take you and your questions and replies wearily, "Because Jesus is God. Because I dig the Bible."

"Good stuff, huh?"

"Yeah. It's exceptionally good stuff."

"What do you particularly dig about it?"

Mia straightens and squints at you suspiciously. "Carter—what's brought all this on?"

"No—truly—I wanta know: what's the appeal?"

"Well, when's the last time you read the Epistles of Paul?"

"Before breakfast."

"Then you know—the Bible's incredibly intriguing and beautiful. Have you really read Paul?"

"Ah . . . no."

Mia places her right palm against her chest, her eyes locked on yours as she recites, "'I appeal to you therefore brethren, by the mercies of God, to present your bodies as a living sacrifice, holy and acceptable to God, which is your spiritual worship. Do not be conformed to this world, but be transformed by the renewal of your mind, that you may prove what is the will of God, what is good and acceptable and perfect.'"

Eyes softening, you look down at your hands. "Wow."

Mia asks, "Have you read the *Bhagavad Gita*?"

". . . No. I haven't."

"You would like it, Carter. It's short. And you would see where Buddhism comes from. The new Stephen Mitchell translation is excellent."

"No doubt."

"The Sutras. The Bible. The Mahabharata. The Koran. They're all pretty much paths to the same kingdom. At least it seems so to me."

You look up. "The kingdom of love."

Mia smiles and nods approvingly. "Yes. The kingdom of love. And of peace through renunciation."

After paying the check, you place your coat around Mia's shoulders and take her hand for the short stroll through the narrow lanes of the medina back to the pasha's villa. Despite its being after midnight, several of the souks surrounding Place Prince Moulay el-Hassan are still open. Though smaller and less chaotic than the Djemma el-Fna in Marrakesh, Essaouira's central square bustles gently with a mixed crowd of locals—mostly young, platonically affectionate Muslim males (their arms linked or slung over a companion's shoulders, an unusual sight for an American)—and a handful of beer-swilling blond tourists bobbing their heads to the softly playing Moroccan drum music. As you pass the now-empty café where you first encountered Michel Motroet this morning, the turbaned owner of a spice shop hobbles out of the darkness and with a perverse cackle plants a foot-long lizard on Mia's upper arm. Too worn out to be afraid, Mia lowers her head and allows the green reptile to crawl across her neck and shoulders before you pluck it away by the tail.

As you turn the corner, you squeeze Mia's hand. A conversation in the shadows is interrupted by a woman's giggle. Overhead someone plays a lute. From another window comes the purring of a cat. In a dark alley near the villa, you suddenly turn Mia sideways and press her body against the damp stone wall. Hands clamped to her arms, you kiss her neck and mouth, both of you moaning and pulling tighter, startled by the intensity of the embrace. When you eventually lean back to catch your breath, Mia's eyes are still closed, and though she smiles and her hands continue to stroke your waist, she whispers, gradually nudging herself away from you, "I think I *will* take that cigarette, please."

You adjust the coat around Mia's shoulders and lead her by the hand around the corner. She lowers her head against your chest—her eyes closed again—as you knock on the Riad al-Madina's locked entrance.

Your heart is your Buddha Nature, you remind yourself. It's the voice speaking to you right now, reminding you that karma is in play at all times, in all places. Karma does not punish. It does not reward. But it always leads to either pain or joy.

Karma will lead Olaf Ferguson in room 7, awakened by your door-pounding, to discover his wife weeping again in their candlelit bathroom. His heart will whisper to him to remove his hands from his hips, to step into the flickering light and lift his sobbing wife from the floor and into his arms, to understand that tonight she needs only to be held and listened to, not given more of his advice. Karma will be in play in the morning, when the kiss Mr. Ferguson receives from Mrs. Ferguson during their courtyard breakfast leads Philip Beck, a Brit checking out after a four-day stay in room 13, to smile and tip Ahmed Youssef Abidjan, one of the villa's young Berber valets, an additional four hundred dirham—three days' salary. The unanticipated sum suddenly makes it possible for Ahmed to attend a music festival in Rabat this coming week with his girlfriend, Fatima, his first love about whom tonight he will dream. Untouched and folded safely in his pocket, the unexpected four hundred dirham will also make Ahmed careless carrying your luggage to the car during your abrupt departure from the villa tomorrow afternoon, and will result in your stopping dead in your tracks, cursing the sight of the last Anvil flopped over sideways in an oily puddle behind the idling Renault.

Not knowing this, of course, you thank the young Berber valet, his thick black hair creased upwards from a pillow, as he drowsily unlocks the hotel entrance, yawns, and without prompting gives you and Mia your room keys. Save for the bathroom candle in room seven and Ahmed's torch-lamp behind the front desk, all the villa is dark.

Your three-night-long seduction of Mia accelerates with her accepting your invitation to join you on the second-floor balcony for a cigarette. She waits, teetering, fingers clasped self-consciously behind her back, as you unlock the door to your room, applauding silently once you find a crumpled half-pack of Marlboro Lights in the bottom of the Tumi. You leave the bedside lamp lit, the door to your room ajar, the better to see each other in the balcony's moonlit shadows. Sitting side by side on a wrought-iron loveseat, staring down into the villa's darkened central patio, you're halfway through your cigarettes before either of you speaks.

"If I were a tree," Mia announces, "I fear that all my life would be in the leaves."

Nodding sagely, you respond, "I have no idea what that means."

Mia brushes away a nonexistent mosquito. She's still wearing your coat, her lips puffy and wine-purpled, her unfocused eyes half-closed, though she seems to you now more sleepy than inebriated. Chuckling, she pinches what's left of her cigarette between a thumb and forefinger and blows a plume of smoke towards the stars.

As the two of you stare into the empty courtyard, shoulders and hips pressed firmly together, Mia continues lightly chuckling to herself at some private joke. You start to ask her what's so funny, but choose to play it cool: she'll tell you if she wants you to know.

As the chuckling persists, you finally turn your head and inquire, "Have I done something to amuse you?"

"Yes, yes," she says, *"—constantly."* The giggling intensifies into muted, hand-covered laughter until, with a shake of her head, Mia silences herself.

You clear your throat and shift your weight and glance down at Mia's right hand—her cigarette hand—which is now resting on your thigh. You ask, "Have you thought any more about this summer?"

Mia smiles knowingly at the sexy deepening of your voice. "I have indeed."

"And?"

"Perhaps we should see if we first survive Morocco."

A mirthless grin creeps over your face. After glancing at your watch, you lean forward and crush the remains of your cigarette against the balcony railing. "It's getting late," you say. "We should call it a night."

"Did I do something wrong?" asks Mia, her hand retreating back to her lap.

"Nah—you look sleepy, that's all."

"I'm *fine,* Carter. I assure you. And I want another cigarette. May I have another cigarette, please?"

"No. Let's call it a night." You pat your knees, stand, tug Mia to her feet, and silently escort her up to the third floor. For a moment on the stairs you consider calling off your plans. "I'll wake you for breakfast," you whisper beside her door, your lips grazing her ear. "Sleep well." With an audible kiss to both cheeks and forehead you bid Mia good night.

Once in your room, you remove your sandals and lie in bed flat on your back, wide awake, fully dressed, glumly staring at the ceiling as you wait for the thirty minutes of "squirm time" to pass. The wine has completely worn off, and already your mouth is so parched your lips taste of blood. Your eyes focus on the area of ceiling stucco you assume, accurately, to be the flipside of the floor directly below Mia's bed, and you try to ignore the cockney voice inside your heart that says, *You're in one of your states, Carter. Let it pass. Don't make this trip a weepy.* You work hard not to look at your nightstand altar—the framed photograph, the travel Buddha, the coiled mala beads. You would sell your soul for a joint. Blinking, cocking your head, you remind yourself that you don't *have* a soul—that's where you part ways with the good Christian above you. *We are our karma*, Christopher once explained. *We are omniscient Buddha Nature packaged in a body. Nothing more. Nothing less. Buddha Nature surfing a wave of karma from one lifetime to the next.*

"Whatever," you mutter. "How seriously can I take a Dharma teacher who munched psychedelic mushrooms?" You glance again at your watch. "No, Mia *wants* this," you tell yourself as you get out of bed. You repeat it to the mirror as you brush your teeth, run a comb through your hair. "She does. Think about it. The hand on the leg. The tongue in the alley. The bump and grind at the café this morning. Playing hardball with all the slobbering over Motroet's tattoos. And she didn't put up much of a fight wrestling around half naked in bed in Marrakesh. No, this is part of the deal. We're humans. We've been—*whatever* we've been—*involved*—for almost three months. She's a grown woman. If she doesn't want to go for the gold, then we back off, but . . . nah, she wants this. She does. This is what humans *do,* for Chrissakes."

Overhead, Mia sits cross-legged on her red-and-gold quilted blanket, sleepless, face contorted with emotion. Her room is illuminated by a single votive candle sputtering on a corner of the nightstand. The one book that she brought from Guatemala (in addition to a weather-worn New Testament as tiny as your deck of cards)—a slim paperback edition of G. K. Chesterton's biography of Thomas Aquinas—lies open, face-down, across her lap. The blue shutters to her two French windows are latched shut, the dying commotion from the medina barely audible now. Although she feels almost fully sober, her head swims as she stares into the white muslin draped around the four-poster bed. She replays in her mind the blur of events over these past three days and nights, wondering what has led her to feel so dreadfully helpless and confused. Though she anticipates your knock on the door, understands the implications of allowing you to enter, she cannot determine what it is that she ultimately desires from you, and—because of that—how much of herself she is tonight prepared to give.

"What am I to think of a man who claims to be a vegetarian," she asks herself, "but who tonight ate a pot of lamb?" Around and around her wrist she spins her new silver bracelet, wondering whether she is indeed falling in love with you. She tells herself, forcefully, that her wish for security, comfort, approval, consistency, affection—namely, reciprocated love—is not outrageous, and is certainly within the framework of her Christian precepts. "Could I marry this man?" she asks, recalling her first impression of you in Woodstock as you sat alone in the very rear of the meditation hall, self-conscious, working hard to look relaxed, a sweet lost soul embarrassed to make public the noble pursuits of his heart. "God made us as we are," she reminds herself. "Isn't the one unforgivable sin to not fully live our own lives?"

Barefoot, shirt untucked, you leave your door unlocked and tiptoe up the stairs to the third-floor balcony. Surprised by the shadowy candlelight you spy through Mia's window blinds, you lean your ear against the thin glass, take a deep breath, and with a single knuckle tap twice.

Mia checks again to see how far down the Moroccan blouse you bought her goes over her bare legs ("See, no more 'jammies,' Mr. Cox"). Having put on her only pair of thong underwear (which will *stay* on, she has vowed, no matter what), hand-washed and hung to dry before dinner, wishing that yesterday she had shaved her bikini line better, she panics and reluctantly pulls the blanket and sheet over her outstretched legs all the way up to her waist. After flipping the book over, Mia clears her throat, sits up straighter, and replies evenly, "Come in."

Curious why the bolt is not fastened, still on your tiptoes, you turn the knob and gently, noiselessly, enter. In the soft orange light you drift towards the bed like a sea creature, silently gazing all the while at Mia's form, partially obscured behind the parted, white muslin scrim and sitting up against the pillows, eyes wide open, the lower half of her body hidden beneath the covers.

"Couldn't sleep," you whisper.

"Nor I."

You pause at the foot of the bed, pinch Mia's toes through the quilted blanket. With a tilt of your head, you read the title of the text held in her lap. Though you refrain from smiling, the fact that her bedside lamp is turned off and only a single votive candle is lit betrays the fact that Mia—presumably out of nervousness—is holding the book as a prop. A good sign, you decide.

"Nice shirt. Someone must have a crush on you."

Mia glances down at herself but says nothing. From the surprising amount of flesh revealed by the blouse's drooping neckline, it appears that Mia is wearing nothing beneath the stiff white cotton.

"You look cozy," you continue, glancing around self-consciously at the room's details: the purple kilim pinned to the far wall, the darkened horse-hair lamp, the rose-filled brass pot. "You got some color this afternoon. It looks good. Are you sore?"

"Only in my arms and back and legs and feet and bottom. And, come morning, no doubt in my head as well." Squinting her eyes at you, Mia adds pointedly, "You dispense wine too freely."

"Are you okay?"

"Mm-hmm."

You step closer. "Are you trembling?"

"No. A little, maybe."

"You cold?"

". . . No."

"Nervous?"

"Of course. Aren't you?"

"I don't get this, Mia. Aren't you comfortable with me by now?" You come around to the side of the bed, sit on the edge of the mattress, rest a hand on the wooden beam. "Don't you know how I feel about you?"

"I have no idea."

"None?"

"No. You perplex me, Carter. One moment I feel close to you, am close to you—am in bed with you—am positively *glowing*—and then . . . I don't know what happens. You treat me like you've lost a bet. I visit you in New York, convince myself that something might blossom between us, and then I don't hear from you for weeks. Every night in Guatemala I thought about you, Carter. Every. Single. Night. And half the time I was doubled over imagining you trotting around naked in your apartment with one of your gaggle of bisexual, rock-climbing sex-partners."

"Don't say that."

"I can't help it. I appreciate the sentiment conveyed with this visit, don't get me wrong. I was rather hoping you'd take advantage of the unlocked door. But—" Eyes filling with tears, Mia crosses her arms and gathers herself before continuing. "I believe God speaks to me most often through circumstance, Carter. I further believe He prompted me to act on my urge to call you from Antigua. And I am thankful that I did. But I'm left wondering: How often do you find yourself in this situation? How often are you barefoot, with your lovely blue shirt unbuttoned just so, sitting on the side of the bed of some hapless travel companion in the wilds of an exotic country? Giving her that look—yes, *that* look, Carter. Making her feel so uneasy she can't think straight. What do you *want* from me?"

"Your respect. Your trust. Your friendship."

"And my third eye winks at your third eye. Play fair, Carter. *Please.* You're so . . . infuriating. *I'm* the one who's supposed to be thirteen years younger. Just be honest with me. What do you want?"

". . . I want to make love with you, I suppose."

Mia says nothing.

You lower your eyes to the candle. "What's the secret? How do you do it?"

"What—do what, Carter?"

"Walk the walk. Stay on the path so well. Really. I feel blessed to have met you. You *inspire* me, Mia. I think you're the most virtuous person I've ever known."

"Hardly. Carter, I'm no saint. I drink in my share of sensual pleasures. I like to be looked at. I like to be held. And kissed. And touched. Do you suppose that just because I'm Catholic and fairly intelligent, I don't wish to be desired? That I haven't sinned?" Mia pulls the blanket tighter. "I, too, have lied. Just like you I've objectified members of the opposite sex, cheated and connived and played dumb about how much I meant to them. Don't romanticize me, Carter."

You push away the long, gauzy white muslin. "Look at me. Mia, *look* at me." You wait, unblinking, until her damp eyes meet and lock with yours. So close now that you can feel the heat of her breath against your cheeks, you say, "Listen. I didn't come up here to upset you."

". . . I know."

"This isn't what I wanted." You sigh. "Maybe I should go." You squeeze her hand, rise from the bed, and move towards the door.

"Wait, Carter. Please. Hold on. Don't leave like this."

On cue, you nod dutifully, realizing that you have reprised, almost by the book, Count de Valmont's systematic seduction of Madame de Tourvelle. You return from the door, and situate yourself on the side of the bed again, closer this time, your knee resting against her pillows. Leaning forward, you smooth Mia's hair, kiss her cheek. "Do you *want* me to stay with you?"

Mia sighs, touches your fingers.

"This needn't be complicated, Mia. I just want us to be happy. To enjoy our time in Morocco together."

"As do I." Mia looks into your eyes, studying your face, as she implores, "Right now—us—is this the truth, Carter?"

Willing yourself not to blink or lean back from the question, you respond, "I would say . . . yes. It certainly feels like the truth, if I understand what you're asking."

As Mia continues staring at you, her glimmering green eyes leveled squarely with yours, the only noise in the room is your heart pumping and Mia's labored breathing.

Taking Mia's hand again, you ask, "Would you mind if I kissed you?"

She searches even deeper in your eyes. "No. I would like that. But promise me—*promise* me, Carter—that we'll be mindful."

You answer by silently unbuttoning and parting the white filigreed blouse, gently moving Mia's body sideways past the stack of silken pillows. Her skin is warm. Closing her eyes, Mia stiffens but offers no resistance as you lay her on her back, caress her neck and breasts, gradually lower the sheet and quilted blanket down her legs. "God, you're beautiful," you whisper. Your heart thrums with a mingling of guilt, tenderness, and the tingling undertow of sexual arousal. One foot still on the floor, you feel yourself bend over and kiss the hollow of Mia's throat, and with your lips and tongue circle the hardened nipple of each of Mia's dovelike breasts.

Mia remains silent for the first few moments of your nuzzling, breathing through her mouth, tremors rippling through her legs and across her shoulders, her fingers clutching your forearm as her pleasure intensifies. She stares up through the mosquito netting at the ceiling fan before closing her eyes and forcing herself to confront what she cannot quite believe is happening, the sensations that she's feeling. It's as if her flesh has turned to warm liquid.

"Carter—"

"—Shhhh . . . it's okay."

Mia lets out a little puff of breath, her jaw thrust forward, holding herself rigid for fear of melting into oblivion. As you lick her breastbone, lay your cheek against her skin, she blinks, strains for a moment against your weight and touch. "*. . . Carter.*"

"It's okay," you whisper, jolted by the sound of Mia's heart beating against her chest, but not enough to cease and desist. "It's okay."

Desperately, fingernails digging into the skin of your arm, teetering on the brink of disaster: "Kiss me. Please just kiss me, Carter. *Please—*"

Groaning hungrily, eyes clamped tight, an awful calm bathing your heart with a squirt of squid-ink, you tell her, "I am," and quickly work your way with your parched mouth down the short runway of her goose-bumped belly.

9

WITH BOTH HANDS YOU GRIP the sink and stare at yourself in the black-framed bathroom mirror, your face swollen and waxy. Normally by eleven A.M. you're starving, but so far this morning you've had no appetite. Even your coffee was hard to get down. Though you've showered twice (the second time with cold water), you remain bleary-eyed. And you're still unshaven. Your head is throbbing—you can *hear* the blood pulsing across your temples—your mouth tastes of metal, your cheeks are sunburned, and the muscles in your neck and shoulders feel as tight as piano wire.

After splashing your face with more cold water, you run a wet comb through your hair, and then, wearing only pants, you step out again onto the balcony opposite the stairs and look up to see that Mia has still not raised her blinds. You glance at your watch. 11:16. Several people in the courtyard stare up at you and your bare chest as you walk back to your room, hands sunk deep in your pockets, eyes averted from a neighbor's opened door, and look over the railing to confirm that Mia's not waiting for you at the front desk. "Could she really still be asleep?" you wonder.

Back in your room, restless, nagged by guilt, pacing in tight circles before the bed, you abruptly halt, reach deep within your clothes bag, and retrieve your Dharma journal, running a fidgety hand over its beige, coffee-stained cover, decorated during your first meditation retreat with black, felt-tipped Tibetan calligraphy copied from a meditation-hall *thangka.* Hoping for inspiration or guidance, you open the journal for the first time since arriving in Morocco and scan at random the six entries you made on the yellow, blue-lined sheets between March 29th and April 10th—the days between Mia's call from Central America and Tuesday's arrival in Casablanca. Because of your dyslexia (manifested chiefly as a dizzying reversal of most asymmetrical letters), you've come to appreciate the pithiness of Buddhist teachings. Of the scrawlings in your notebook, those that are not excerpts from Dharma texts are assorted questions or insights scribbled by candlelight on your zabuton during sitting meditations, or while lounging on your couch after a Sunday evening spent with Christopher.

You shake your head at your childlike handwriting and penchant for exclamation points, shut your left eye to better focus, and read out loud:

> *Recognize ego! Scoop the ego out with the Six Perfections (daily!). Recognize what is not ego: Buddha Nature. Rest in the non-ego when meditating, the "emptiness" between the thoughts. The more scooping, the more expansive the emptiness. The more emptiness, the easier it is to rest in it. The more you rest in it, the more you become it!*
>
> *"When you meditate all day, you are Buddha all day!"*
>
> *Is the ego caused by fear of death? If we eliminate our fear of death, do we eliminate our ego?*
>
> *"All beings by their nature are Buddha, as ice by its nature is water."*
>
> *"Allow Buddha Nature to rise naturally during meditation. Relax—Buddha Nature will teach itself!"*
>
> *Jesus was a Buddha!*

Fluttering your lips, you close the journal and try, with limited success, to drive from your soul the dark business of last night by busying your brain with plans for the afternoon. As if wearing blinders, you direct all of your attention towards the immediate future, the steps immediately in front of you, reminding yourself that it is with good reason that man's eyes are located in his forehead and not his hindhead—that what's done is done. You sink back on the bed, tossing the Dharma journal towards the Tumi, wincing at its page-sprawled landing against the wall. *Damn. Why don't I just flush my mala beads down the toilet while I'm at it?* Sitting cross-legged on the mattress, you flip open the ThinkPad and double-check your Moroccan itinerary file: the only task marked down for today, Friday, April 13th, is to return to Marrakesh before dusk. After closing your Moroccan contact-numbers file, you buzz the front desk and ask the concierge to call the Dar al-Assad to confirm your return, but she promptly buzzes back and informs you that she's unable to make a connection with Marrakesh over the villa's land line. You try e-mailing an arrival-time confirmation to the Dar al-Assad's Web site, but this too proves fruitless: your AOL Inbox indicates that your message was returned as undeliverable.

You close the ThinkPad and stare at the wall. You're about to burst. With almost two hours to go before your one o'clock rendezvous with Mia, you put on a shirt, strap up your sandals, secure your passport and money-clip in a back pocket, don your sunglasses, and head for the medina to expose some film. For an hour you wander through the crowded market with your light meter and Leica halfheartedly raised, bending over and sniffing with unusual poignancy the fragrance of bundled cypress twigs and kevda flowers, pyramids of turmeric, gur spice, and black tulsi. Few of the souk owners invite you to examine their wares. A white-robed potter averts his leathery face and angrily waves his hand when you try to take his picture. The furtive scowls you receive from several veiled Moroccan women chill you. Somehow, you fear, everyone in the market knows about last night.

After killing thirty more minutes meandering along the shoreline, joylessly smoking your fourth and fifth cigarettes of the day, you return to the villa shortly before one. You realize that since coming to Morocco you haven't gone out once without buying something—beneath the Leica in your camera bag are now a dozen "Wind City, Afrika" postcards, purchased at a kiosk on Place Prince Moulay el-Hassan, and, wrapped in pink tissue as a present for Mia, a silver-and-amber-crested hand-of-Fatima necklace, procured despite intense bargaining at a price that required using your American Express card, in the same jasmine-scented shop where yesterday afternoon you bought the silver bracelet.

Neither you nor Mia was able to sleep last night. Self-consciously pressed against her unmoving body, your breathing seemed to both of you the loudest noise in the world. As sunrise approached, Mia agreed that it might be best if you went back down to your own room. You hated what came next: for almost a minute you crawled on your hands and knees, fumbling on the rug beneath Mia's bed for your sandals before remembering that you hadn't worn them. "Please—feel good about this," you pleaded awkwardly, standing and shuffling to leave in the predawn darkness, a hand alighting on her hip hidden beneath the covers as you steered towards the door. "We were careful," you added. "There's zero to be worried about." Mia said nothing in response—or, more precisely, what she mumbled into the mattress you were unable to hear. As you were pulling the door shut behind you, Mia still lay unmoving under the blanket, fully clothed in her pajamas, her body curved like a question mark around the extra pillow.

Twenty minutes later, as hazy morning light began spreading over the courtyard, you tiptoed barefoot back up to the third-floor balcony and slipped a note beneath Mia's door:

Dearest Mia,

Thank you for a warm and tender evening. My heart is still fluttering from how beautiful you looked in the candle-light. Please trust that what we shared was fueled by love and respect, and that I fully understand the significance of our embrace.

Please feel free to sleep late today. It's Good Friday, after all. Let's plan to rendezvous at 1:00 at the front desk and try to leave for Marrakesh by 1:30.

I very much look forward to our remaining days (and nights?) together in Morocco. Thanks again for all your hard work and patience.

Love, C

12:38. Your room is getting uncomfortably warm. While washing your hands and rebrushing your teeth, you avoid making eye contact in the mirror with your Buddha statue, which seems to be staring at you from the nightstand. With exaggerated mindfulness you dry your hands and lay the postcards and Mia's latest gift on the bed, now made. You stare blankly at the pot of red roses to your right until—enough: you decide to go up and investigate. Rebuttoning your shirt, you leave the door ajar and ascend the balcony stairs two steps at a time. On the third floor you see that the woman from room 7, arms cradling a folded stack of fresh white towels, is standing on the balcony terrace outside Mia's room, her head tilted towards the door, eyes narrowed, troubled by something she hears inside. Startled as you bound around the corner, she straightens and continues walking.

You look over both shoulders and gently place your fingertips, then an ear, against Mia's lone window, its lowered wooden blinds the same bay-tinted brown as the door three feet to the right. None of her lights are on. Pressing your ear closer to the glass, you make out the muffled sounds of a conversation in the bathroom, Mia's voice choked with pain. *What on earth is going on?* You close your eyes and strain to hear—*who is she talking to?*—and jump backwards as the bathroom door slams shut. A glass shatters in the sink. You try to open the door, but it's bolted.

Fearing that Mia has harmed herself, you give up wrestling with the door knob and move back to the window, and shield your eyes as you peer into the room through a small gap in the blinds. Dressed in her pajamas, the top to which is misbuttoned, the collar askew, Mia comes out of the bathroom and drifts slowly, zombie-like, across the room. Her hair is wet, her face red from crying. Silently moving her lips in prayer, she stumbles towards the dresser, which she shoves with both palms—hard—before wheeling around, the shape of her mouth suggesting that with the push she has hurt her wrists. Groaning like a wounded animal, she falls heavily to her knees. She begins to weep, her eyes clamped shut, head bowed, fingers interlaced beneath her quivering chin.

Your eyes fill with tears as you stare through the blinds at Mia's genuflected body, frightened (though not surprised) by the intensity of her distress. Even as you touched her last night, you knew in your heart that this might happen, but somehow—somehow you talked yourself through it. Stepping backwards from Mia's room as if pushed, torn between banging on her door and marching off to the battlements to hurl yourself into the ocean, you realize, sickeningly, that you are a thief, and the worst kind of thief, because what you have stolen cannot be returned.

At one o'clock you drift down to the courtyard in a haze of bewilderment and worry, your untucked blue linen shirt damp with sweat, your head swimming from the muggy air and the scornful cry of the muezzin in a nearby mosque calling the faithful to the early afternoon prayer. You wait for Mia in the empty salon across from the villa's front desk atop a pile of red-and-yellow cushions, not surprised that she hasn't yet come down. Twenty, thirty minutes pass by with no sight of her. By one-forty, crushing out another cigarette, you give up hope that she will join you.

You glare down at your mala beads, which you desperately draped around your left wrist after spying on Mia so upset in her room—a final gasp for a spiritual life that now seems dead in the water. The rarefied world of Tibetan Buddhism, with its Medicine Taras and "perfect" stupas and endless prattle about *bodhicitta,* suddenly seems ridiculous to you. What good is *any* spiritual path, you wonder, for someone completely devoid of patience and generosity and love? Hands clasped behind your back, eyes lowered, stifling each new wave of angst as it rises, you circle listlessly around the courtyard's potted palms and stone columns, past the central fountain and the few remaining tea-drinkers, and slowly mount the stairs.

On the second balcony a peek of yellow: a note written on three folded sheets of the hotel stationery awaits you under the door to your room.

Carter,

You have given me permission before to be honest with you, so here goes: In the Scriptures, we are urged time and again not to place our trust, our faith, in man. Jesus didn't, "for he knew man's heart," how devious it is. And, indeed, I have never really trusted you to any great extent, so I ought not to pretend. (It seemed that you even instructed me not to trust you too fully.) As a result, I am left Utterly Confused about last night.

I have tried not to write this letter, for I fear it will do irreparable damage to our relationship—friendship, romance, soulmatehood, whatever it is we've shared these past three months. We have come full circle: a relationship initiated by a pair of notes shall end with a pair of notes. I will be gone by the time you read this dismally crafted missive (I am tired, so am rendered incapable of finding better words with which to express myself), carrying with me the hope that I will arrive by bus tonight in Casablanca, and the assumption that my passport and a smile will be enough to get me through customs. If I find I must hold my ticket until the original departure date, then I shall spend the night in Casablanca, or perhaps venture to Tangiers and look up the ghost of poor Mr. Bowles, and thus see you on the plane Sunday morning.

I bear you no grudge, Carter. I have learned much from your carefree spirit, your spontaneity, and your ability to see the beauty in almost everything you encounter. Though I'm certain nostalgia is the death knell for a relationship, I must nonetheless say that I shall never forget the sight of you meditating before your lovely altar with Marley in your lap, nor the joy I felt during our surprise visit to the church yesterday morning. I also know that once I return to Sister Rosa and the children, I will miss you more than ever.

I'm sorry for leaving you in the lurch with your responsibilities tomorrow back in Marrakesh, but we both know that you will manage swimmingly—I fear most of my bungled debut as your Assistant yesterday was spent simply getting in the way.

You're a truth seeker, Carter. That is what drew me towards you in the beginning, and still draws me towards you even as I write this. I feel foolish for being so confused, and apologize for being so intemperate in my behavior with you. But I sense that I have fallen stupidly, hopelessly, into something that I fear might not be love. Until I know for certain, we should be apart—for your sake as well as mine.

Thank you for bringing me here, Carter. I pray that one day in the future we shall discover our truest selves on new ground, and take our places at the great banquet table (the Eucharist, you may know, is also known as the Love Feast) and experience deeper, purer Communion.

God bless you,
Mia

The speedy taxi ride across town to the small CTM bus station is over before you can locate your money clip. The surrounding buildings, dark and empty, are stained gray by the relentless bursts of diesel exhaust. A young beggar, propped with his wooden crutch against a wall in the shadows, tosses a pebble at a stray dog sniffing a puddle near the ticket window. Only one vehicle is in sight—a rickety blue-and-white school bus. Its ancient engine is rumbling, and dozens of dark-skinned faces and arms dangle loosely from the windows. "El-Jadida" is marked in white soap at the top of its cracked windshield. Surely Mia couldn't have caught an earlier bus, you tell yourself—she had to have fled the villa sometime between 12:45 and 1:00, otherwise you would have seen her pass the front desk while you waited in the salon.

As you step from the taxi you spot Mia standing with her bag in front of one of the curbside food stalls surrounding the tiny bus station. She turns her back when she sees you coming towards her. She has hoped, despite herself, that you might follow, but is still surprised to see the urgency in your eyes. She glances again at the idling bus as you trot across the dusty street, stop several feet short of the curb, place your hands on your hips, shake your head with mock exasperation, and shout: "What is your *deal,* soldier?"

She turns fully around to face you. "Consider this a backhanded compliment, Carter. You've won. I don't have the strength to fight you off anymore."

"No, don't say that. Listen. Hey—*look* at me." Lowering your voice, you take a step closer, tentatively touch her arm. "Let's go someplace and sit down and talk about this. Okay? I want to discuss last night as much as you do."

The bus belches more black smoke and folds its door shut as it prepares to depart.

"I can't. I need to be away from you for a while."

"No—you can't just *leave*."

"Oh?"

"No. Last night was—last night was—whew—I don't know. It was *amazing,* Mia. The last thing I want is for you to feel bad about it."

"I don't know what 'it' *is,* Carter."

"It is *us*—our feelings for each other. Listen—I want things to work out between you and me. For us to be together. I want this to be a *good* thing."

Sighing, her eyes still red and puffy, Mia reaches out a hand, but pulls it back before touching you. "I can't be with you right now. I'm sorry. I need to catch my breath—I'm so tired I don't know what's up or down."

"No. I *want* you to stay here, with me. I want you to *be* with me. I want last night to be . . . *okay* with us. This is what people *do,* Mia. We're adults. We're humans. Last night is nothing to be afraid of. If you want our time together here to be romantic, I would love that. *Love* it. I'll give you whatever you need. And if you need some space—you know—your own bed, your own room—that's fine, too."

"I don't *want* it to be fine, Carter. That's—you have absolutely no idea how much you confound me, do you? None."

"I'm *trying* to understand."

Mia straightens, wipes her eyes. "I have to go. I'm sorry. I know this will make it difficult for you tomorrow, but—"

"—Mia . . . *please.*"

"Don't, Carter. Oh Lord, the bus is leaving."

She tugs, forcing you to release her arm. You step backwards and watch helplessly as she hoists her bag over a shoulder and hurries towards the squealing, slowly reversing bus. "Mia," you shout. *"Mia."* But she refuses to look back.

She waves at the bus until it shudders to a halt. After she boards and disappears into the dark interior jumble, the Moroccan driver glares at you across the station yard as he folds the door shut. You can do nothing but stand there as the old school bus lurches backwards down the oil-slicked incline, slowly screeches to a stop, grinds into first gear, and heads forward around the corner onto the road heading north along the coast to Casablanca.

Just like that, Mia is gone.

For several minutes you remain by the food stalls, fingers interlaced on your head like a winded sprinter. Your throat feels squeezed by an invisible hand, and your neck and shoulders are so tense you fear that soon you'll be unable to pivot your head.

This is not the story you'd written for yourself. This is not the path you assumed you were traveling. You'd long fancied yourself a talented juggler of pleasure and ethics—*prided* yourself on the ability to have loads of fun and presumably do the world no harm. So how did you drop such an important ball? If you were to pursue yesterday's question about lust and fear, you might get some answers. But that would mean taking a breath and seizing this moment as an opportunity to awaken, and right now you're too full of self-pity to see straight, much less recognize the truth.

Ignoring the pair of old cream-colored Mercedes idling behind a signpost reading TAXIAT KEBIRA, you stagger the three kilometers back to the villa on foot. It takes almost an hour before you come to the whitewashed medina walls. As you plod past the parked Renault and veer towards the opened *bab* nearest the Riad al-Madina's entrance—the waves of the Atlantic crashing like thunder against the shore break—a gust of hot wind blows sand into your eyes and mouth and nostrils. "God damn it. God *damn* it." Wiping your face with your shirt, you spit and shake off the urge to cry and stoically trudge forward, one foot in front of the other, a mourner in a funeral procession for your own fallen ego.

Once in your room, you pack brusquely, sloppily, driven by the need to load the rental car and escape Essaouira as hastily as possible. With a flicker of pain in your chest, you stuff the mala beads, the Buddha statue, and the picture of Mia into a side pocket of your toilet kit. After paying your bill at the front desk, you reluctantly give your keys to Ahmed Youssef Abidjan, the same young Berber valet who assisted with your arrival two days ago. The grinning teenager volunteers to carry your Tumi and all five cases of photo equipment down the stairs and out to the parking area by himself.

"Merci, monsieur," says the girl at the front desk as you lift a hand and exit the pasha's villa for the last time. You readjust your sunglasses as you march through the forty-foot *bab* and turn towards the now partially shaded parking area, then you see with alarm that the Renault's engine is already running, the exhaust pipe smoking heavily, and that behind the steering wheel Ahmed is dancing his shoulders in the driver's seat, ostensibly warming the motor for you, though in fact completely lost in reverie about the wad of unexpected dirham notes in his back pocket, his girlfriend, Fatima, and their upcoming voyage to Rabat. As you pass in front of the windshield, the boy smiles, gives you a thumbs up, and races the engine so loudly you cover your ears. "What the *fuck,*" you mutter, the color draining from your face, as you see that because of the young valet's carelessness one of the five Anvils has fallen sideways into a puddle. You bang the hood, and with an index finger slice your throat until the boy kills the engine.

Abashed, eyes lowered in the sudden silence, Ahmed sprints back to the villa before you can give him his tip.

You stand before the car, blow out a breath, run a hand through your hair. "Great," you mumble, "just great."

As you start loading the gear into the trunk, you hear the crunching of gravel behind you. Fists clenched, you spin around as three kaftan-clad Moroccans—an elderly father and his bearded son, both of whom need to get home to Aztendara, and a tall, darker-skinned Berber who has joined them with hopes of hitching a ride back to his village near Tafraoute—cautiously advance from the shadows towards you and the Renault with their right palms placed respectfully against their chests. All three men wear sandals and white, sweat-stained Koofi skull caps. Stepping forward, his brown eyes nervous but steady, the middle-aged son asks in a mix of Arabic and broken French if you'd be willing to drive them as far east as you intend to travel today. Though you make out "Marrakesh" and guess that the men want a lift, you shrug that you don't understand what they're asking, glancing uneasily at the long, black knife-handle protruding from a sheepskin bag draped over the Berber's bony shoulder.

"I'm sorry," you say, arranging your face sympathetically. Though you're in no mood to play chauffeur, the least you can do is refuse them politely. But before you can foolishly offer them the dirham notes you'd pulled from your money clip to give to the valet, the gray-haired father—his leathery brown face creased by deep wrinkles—apologizes in Arabic for disturbing you and silently leads the other two men back into the shade of the palm trees.

You loathe yourself for serving the unholy trinity of gluttony, intemperance, and lust, and vow on this first morning back in Marrakesh—out loud, with a self-conscious bow to the Buddha statue you've finally unpacked—that by your fortieth birthday you'll put away all childish things and return to the spiritual path you've somehow lost. Nevertheless, you return to the hotel room two hours later, after a feverish shopping spree in the souks surrounding the Djemma el-Fna, in possession of a set of Safi dinner plates, a leather pouf, an Argine canister, a henna-stained Duizi vase, and a traditional Moroccan bone mirror. In retaliation for Mia's desertion, you were even tempted to return to Taza, the smoky medina café, and purchase one of the gold-toothed owner's dining tables for your kitchen. With disgust, you drop the unwrapped bone mirror to the dresser and search the room for the bottle of red wine you brought with you from Essaouira yesterday. When you eventually find it—under the bed, uncorked, essentially empty—you shake the bottle's final ounce to clear the sediment, and, leaning your head back as far as you can manage with your stiff neck, pour the vinegary wine directly down your throat.

3:40 P.M. You park the Renault on a bustling, café-lined side street in Marrakesh's *ville nouvelle,* lift your sunglasses, and do a final vanity check in the rearview mirror. "Great," you grumble. Your sunburned nose is peeling, your eyes are bloodshot, your teeth look gray, and your unwashed hair is so greasy you have to dry your hand. Other than that, you look and feel just dandy.

With a single photo case in tow (you're not even sure which camera bodies are inside), sunglasses back on, stupefied by unhappiness and self-abhorrence, you slowly ascend by portered elevator to the twenty-sixth-floor terrace of the Hotel de la Renaissance. As you approach the outdoor bar, you offer a joyless wave and join Kiki Holtkamp, the South African location scout, who is wearing a tight black T-shirt, a pair of self-cuffed cargo shorts, and hiking boots. With narrowed blue eyes she glances with suspicion at the one photo case you've brought and asks with her thick Afrikaner accent, "Ware's yuh lil helpah?"

"Where's your lackey from Rabat?"

"He's watching the gulls lace up their frawks." With a smirk Kiki points towards a small crowd clustered beneath a canopy on the far side of the terrace. "So are the soccer players, pervies all."

Because of the synthesized Arabic pop music playing on the bar stereo and the breeze gusting at this altitude, you can no longer hear the car traffic down below. "How long've you guys been up here?" you ask, wiping dried scum from the corners of your lips.

"Since three. Splendid job buttoning, Carter." You look down at your wrinkled white silk shirt, thrown over a gray tank-top, one of the rolled sleeves no longer rolled, as Kiki corrects the misaligned buttons. "Rough night?"

"I need a drink."

"No, you be a good boy. We have *work* to do."

You unlatch and open the Anvil and see that you have but two camera options: the cumbersome Hasselblad or a $200 Minolta point-and-shoot. You pinch the bridge of your nose. Loading the Hasselblad as you plod across the roof—your self-loathing is quickly turning into irritation and impatience—you see that all four of the models' eyes are puffy and dilated, and snort with disbelief when Kiki explains that the strangely torpid women are not heat-fatigued or jet-lagged from their trip from Spain but are stoned on ecstasy tablets provided by the makeup artist. "They showed up this way," Kiki mutters. "Stupid gulls. All they seem interested in is stroking one another's arm hair."

In other circumstances you might be amused by the gelatinous grins you get as you place your light meter near the four models' noses. But today you are way beyond amusement. Simple instructions—"turn to the right, please—no, your *other* right"—soon become an exercise in futility. It doesn't help either that one of the models is Claire Minor, a histrionic brunette boasting a handful of B-movie acting credits, with whom you had a weekend-long fling after shooting a Beefeater Gin ad in Chicago three years ago. Claire, like the rest of the giggling, long-legged quartet, is barefoot and wears a blue bathing suit bottom, a red bandeau, and a white Lawrence of Arabia–style headdress. Despite the romantic tryst (or, you fear, because of it), Claire refuses to make eye contact with you unless your camera is raised, and snorts sarcastically each time you suggest that she stare off at the mountains.

To further complicate things, you've been provided with only three local soccer players, none of whom speaks English nor will listen to young Nadar's timid translations into Arabic. With their bushy black hair, thick necks, short legs, and broken noses (the only one willing to smile for the camera is missing a front tooth), the three burly Moroccans seem an unlikely choice to model Joseph Abboud's summer line of linen shirts and slacks. And they are ogling the four droopy-limbed, scantily clad females throughout the entire shoot with such a libidinous hunger that all of the $200 designer shirts—the chief reason you've come to Marrakesh—become saturated with sweat almost as soon as the men put them on.

An assignment that would typically take two full days (even with the aid of an assistant), you finish in just under seven hours, because of your indifference to its outcome. Over the course of the afternoon and evening you're mindful of little more than your desire for this appalling African excursion to conclude. Occasionally your attention strays over to Kiki, who, with spread legs and arms akimbo, black cell phone holstered to her hip like a sheriff's six-shooter, holds back murmuring onlookers who wander over from the bar area to watch you work. You shoot exclusively with the single-lens Hasselblad, knowing all the while that the folks at *Men's Agenda* will be displeased to receive from you nothing but 70-mm black-and-white film to process.

The panoramic views from the twenty-sixth-floor terrace prove photogenic enough, especially as the sun begins to set, and you arrange the motley group of models and athletes first in front of the Atlas Mountains to the west, and then in front of the minaret of the Koutoubia Mosque towering above the Djemma el-Fna to the east. As the moon rises and sky darkens and you abruptly lose all of your natural light, you realize what a serious blunder it was to have brought only one case of gear. No tripod. No color film. No light-box or flash. Mixing self-penance with professional responsibilities, you decide, will do little to promote your spiritual salvation.

Indeed, the cause-and-effect of the day will result in Bruce Wetzler, *Men's Agenda*'s executive editor, greenlighting for June's "Yummy Gals" issue only one of your images from Marrakesh—a grainy headshot of Claire Minor he will salvage as "Yummy Gal #16" and pair with 250 words of text by Roy Blount Jr. The original "Man and Morocco" fashion section will be pushed back a month and then killed. Should you still be alive in June when the magazine cuts its quarterly checks, you will receive full reimbursement for your Marrakesh expenses but only a fourth of the contracted fee for the unused photos. As well you'll be told formally by young Harold Ticket via his speakerphone that you'll never again be asked to work for *Men's Agenda*, nor for any of the six other publications owned by The Deerbok Group, the magazine's London-based parent company.

A long Saturday night slides slowly into the early hours of Easter Sunday. A northerly breeze has cooled the hotel terrace. Twenty-six stories below, Avenue Mohammed V is empty save for a few taxis and late-night pedestrians. Fifty blocks to the east, the smoke-shrouded Koutoubia Mosque is spotlit with beams of yellow. Near the railing, three French-speaking Moroccan couples slow-dance under an unmoving silver disco ball hung from the canvas awning.

Alone at the terrace bar with Kiki after everyone else from the shoot has departed, you swallow the backwash from your lukewarm Guiluxe and call for two more bottles. The long day and dim lights and gentle rhythm of Marrakesh at night have lulled you into a near stupor. Sunburned, bleary-eyed, bloated with despair, you lean heavily on your elbows and gaze drunkenly through the cigarette haze at the contours of the thirty-seven-year-old location scout's tight, black T-shirt.

"It's getting cooluh," Kiki observes, though she refrains from donning her windbreaker, which—along with the proximity of her bared knees to yours—you take as a favorable sign, in so far as anything about the future can look favorable.

With the arrival of the new beers, Kiki lifts her chin, turns her head as if interested in the bartender's tumbler glass, and with both hands pulls her blond locks up and behind her ears, flaunting in one fell swoop her gym-sculpted biceps, a rarely seen stretch of her neck, and a left earlobe modishly festooned with one two three four five *six* tiny silver loops.

You reach up to give the row of diminutive earrings a jiggle and note, "You could hang a little shower-curtain from these."

Kiki nods and drops her hair. "Clever."

Though you've only been talking to Kiki for thirty minutes, you've already forgotten whether she said she grew up in Johannesburg or Cape Town, is separated or divorced, and is scheduled for an upcoming trip to New York or recently concluded one. After you explain to her your relationship with Christopher Wolf, whom you describe as a "mentor" and "inspiration," and begin a not-so-interesting anecdote about your first assignment for *Men's Agenda*, Kiki's attention drifts. The breeze picks up. You quit speaking in midsentence and stare down at your beer bottle, as if the ghost of witless banter has cursed your tongue. Pressing the Guiluxe against your forehead, you try a different route. "So . . . Kiki. What's your story, professionally speaking? Are you a *freelance* location scout?"

"No, I'm full-time. On the masthead, with benefits and all whatnot. Wetzler gives me three or four assignments a month. I'm based out of London, as I believe I mentioned."

"Do you have to deal with Harold Ticket at all?"

"The awt director? Rarely, though he seems sweet enough. No, I report directly to Wetzler, who's a doll. At least when he's on his lithium."

You sneak a peek at Kiki's exposed midriff as she reaches across your lap and pulls closer the monogrammed container for her sunglasses. Discreetly, you dip your nose into her cherry-scented mane for a quick sniff before she straightens. The alcohol is softening her looks, you decide, though the muscles in her legs, especially the calf muscles right above the Timberlands, frighten you—you've seen lumberjacks with less sturdy gams. Regardless, it seems fairly evident to you that naked and atop a mattress, the strapping South African would prove an astounding sight. You light another cigarette and ask quietly, "Where're you staying again?"

"The Hotel Toulousain. It's nice enough, I suppose. I was tempted to take a room at La Mamounia, but I doubt I could square that on my expense account. Ahh you still at that bed-and-breakfast in the Old City?"

"Room number 3."

"Is it agreeable? Can you sleep through all the hurly-burly of the Djemma el-Fna?"

"I've got a balcony with two chairs. Come decide for yourself."

Kiki grins knowingly, clinks your beer bottle, and stands up to leave. "Not tonight, I'm afraid. It's tempting. *You're* tempting. But—not tonight." She places fifty dirham beneath her unfinished beer and holds out a hand for you to shake. "Well. Thank you for the company, *Cah*-tuh. I look forward to seeing the results of what we did today. The spread is slated for June, right?"

You shrug. "I'm not sure. Either June or July."

"Well . . . at any rate, good luck. Be careful going back to the medina."

Two beers later a taxi deposits you in front of the Dar al-Assad. Carrying the lone Anvil over your shoulder, you take the key from the desk clerk and mount the stairs to the same juniper-scented, second-floor room you shared with Mia four nights ago. It seems a lifetime has passed since then.

Though you're not particularly aroused, not even particularly drunk, you decide to cater to the prickling in your toes. Stripped down to your boxer shorts, you close the blinds, lower yourself onto the end of the unmade bed, and with a smack of your lips plug the ThinkPad into a phone line, leaning back on your elbows as you await a connection to the Internet and the cyberspace world of naked women. Prompted by the spirit of Mia's absence, you rationalize your vow-breaking indulgence as a kind of self-mortification. Hyper-gluttony as purification.

Though your AOL account announces that you have mail, without explanation your computer's server refuses you access to the oldest of your bookmarked Web sites, the salaciously titled, Amsterdam-based, *Sweet Girls 4U.* You search for hits to Web sites containing the words "lick" and "nasty." No luck. You punch in "Tiffany St. Cloud" and "naked." Nothing. The blue-and-white AOL screen just sits there. You try the Dutch porn address again, drumming your fingers for two or three minutes before the cursor freezes. You make explosion noises with your lips as you decide whether to reboot. Enough. Apparently *something* doesn't want you to break your vow. You snap shut the laptop's lid, feeling—surprisingly—more relieved by your failure than rankled. You put your computer on the floor, slump back against the pillows, close your eyes, and count twenty slow breaths. The toe-prickling gradually subsides. With a yawn, you reach over and snuff the bedside candle and re-cover yourself with the sheet, curious to know which is the most likely cause of the mysterious Internet censorship: your benevolent Buddha Nature, the ghost of Mia's lost virginity, or Morocco's Muslim government.

Late Easter Sunday. The New York night air feels as cold and dank as it did seven days ago. The few East Village pedestrians braving the rain-slicked sidewalks are bundled and hunched beneath dripping black umbrellas buffeted by a southeasterly wind. When the yellow cab slides to a stop in front of your apartment building, the drizzle hastily turns into a downpour. You're drenched before you make it to the door. Gasping, heart thudding from your pack-a-day cigarette habit and the mountainous ascent up the five flights of stairs, you pay the Chinese cab driver the additional $20 you promised for helping with your luggage and photo gear and halfheartedly return his bow before he turns and trots down the hall.

You massage your chest, wrinkle your nose, and sniff: the sweaty brown walls stink of pesticide and bad-weather dreariness. Slumping at the sight, you see that the door to the trash chute is once again locked. You flip through your mail and then fumble for your keys, and you note for the first time in all the years that you've lived in this pitiful building that yours is the only apartment on the sixth floor without a welcome mat outside its door. Actually, you've noticed it several times before, but tonight you're thriving on gloom. You then see that a brown cardboard box—roughly the size of a computer monitor—has been placed against the wall to your right. *Hmmm.* You cradle the mail against your rain-soaked chest and bend over for a look. The plain brown package has your name on it, but there's no return address nor any markings on the box's exterior that hint at the contents. On the box's left side is a white UPS 2nd-Day Air label, a bar code, and a yellow sticker marked: "UPS Driver: Do Not Redirect or Release This Package Without a Signature." You don't remember ordering any new software or desktop gear from your guy at Computer Mania, and, besides, the store's shipping cartons always come printed with black zebra stripes and the company logo.

No—you don't like the looks of this. *Who would've signed for the delivery? Mrs. Pierno?* You glance over your shoulder, squat down, and listen for ticking. Recalling the story of T-Bone Cuthridge, a freelance investigative reporter blinded last summer when he opened a letter bomb sent from Miami, you finish unlocking your door and carefully nudge the box into the den with the side of a foot, debating from the safety of your couch—Rolling Rock in one hand, damp Marlboro Light in the other—what to do next. There *are* certain individuals implicated in the Resistoleros exposé angry enough to perhaps wish you and the author harm—but then you remind yourself that the article and your photos were never published. Regardless, you get up, rummage through the hall closet for your old motorcycle helmet, and return from the kitchen wearing a pair of black oven-mitts. Squinting, inhaling noisily through the helmet's chin vent, you squat down again and with a butcher knife gingerly slice through the brown-paper seal securing the box's cardboard flaps. You move the box forward to get better light from the table lamp, and with a deep breath drain yourself of everything not needed to stay utterly focused. As soon as you see what's beneath the white Styrofoam peanuts, however, you shake off the oven mitts and flip open the helmet's plastic face shield.

"Oh man," you mumble. You remove and lower the motorcycle helmet to the floor. "Unbelievable." With both hands you lift from the box a shrink-wrapped white wicker Easter basket. Jelly beans, six chocolate gold-foiled eggs, and a stuffed bunny lie in the green stuffing. Taped to the basket's curved handle is a pink, computer-printed note: BLESS YOU ON EASTER. ALL MY LOVE, MIA

Silently you carry to the couch the unexpected gift and sit down, all the while shaking your head with disbelief. You're touched, indeed are close to tears, but you also now feel even more lost and hopeless. Goodness is something you don't deserve. You refuse to reread the pink note. With the Easter basket resting heavily in your lap, you finish your beer and stare out the window at the rain. You can't bring yourself to tear through the basket's shrink-wrapped covering, and are so conflicted in your emotions that you can no longer stay seated. "Why would she do this?" You carry the unopened basket into the kitchen, stow it out of sight behind a cupboard door, and with a fresh Rolling Rock plod back out into the hall to get your luggage.

Five minutes later, using an elbow, the Tumi between your legs, the photo gear stacked behind you by the bathroom, you flip on the bedroom light. What you see is not good. The potted granadilla on the windowsill has wilted. So has the gillyflower by the bed, which, now that you look at it, seems different—the four pillows are puffed unusually high against the headboard, your 275-thread count, crocus-colored Egyptian cotton sheet is folded crisply at an angle over your $350 Calvin Klein down comforter. Then you recall that Mia was the last person to sleep in here, that it was she who made the bed. Clothes still soggy, head throbbing, you leave your suitcase and move forward into the room, write SOS in the dust on your dresser, with a ratchety crank of the cord pull open your blinds, and settle yourself on the edge of the mattress. Through the rain-streaked windows the thunderstorm shows no sign of letting up. You massage your temples and catch a glimpse of the flashing red to your right: there are six messages on your answering machine. You ignore them. You glance behind you again at the neatly stacked quartet of lilac-colored pillows, and with a sad half-chuckle inhale deeply, ruefully, eyes closed, hoping for a scent of Mia's pajama-clad body still lingering in the air.

After finishing the second beer, you move back into the den, push the empty Easter basket carton to a corner, and walk down the hall to Mrs. Pierno's apartment to retrieve Marley. You knock twice on your elderly neighbor's door before she finally unlatches the bolt, gives you a withering look, and reluctantly allows you to step into her darkened foyer. "You said you were gonna be gone just a few days," she grumbles. "You've been gone a week. I'm too old to be carrying ten-pound bags of dog food all the way from D'Agostino's, Carter. And you need to button your shirt when you come to my door."

The old woman's apartment smells strongly of the cabbage boiling in a white pot on her stove. *The Tonight Show* plays softly on a black-and-white, rabbit-eared television pulled on its cart to within a yard of her recliner. You leave the door cracked behind you as Mrs. Pierno, tightening her faded blue robe, disappears into the steamy kitchen. Buttoning and tucking in your shirt, you take a tentative step deeper into the TV-lit den and look around for Marley—you've never been this far inside Mrs. Pierno's apartment before, and its colorless, cluttered decor makes you even sadder. Aside from the tiny television and lopsided recliner, there's a pale, claw-footed sofa that takes up the nearest wall, and a round end-table on which sit a porcelain turtle, a sewing kit, a chipped statue of St. Ignatius, and a framed snapshot of Mrs. Pierno's two balding, pot-bellied sons proudly posing in their snug blue firefighter uniforms. A tear in the yellow lampshade at the far end of the couch is covered with masking tape.

"*There* you are. Come here, boy." You bend down and clap your hands as Marley, tongue lolling, hesitates and then scrambles from the kitchen straight past you, out the door, and up the hallway, paws clicking wildly as he slides around the corner.

"Your dog ate my slippers," Mrs. Pierno informs you as she returns from the kitchen. She's scowling and carrying a wooden cooking spoon in one hand, Marley's leash and water bowl in the other. You stand. Age and widowhood have battered your tiny neighbor's face into a clenched fist of wrinkles, chapped lips, and shrunken, colorless eyes. "My *good* slippers," she clarifies, shuffling forward, her robe now tightly sashed, dropping Marley's supplies into your outstretched arms.

"I apologize. I know he can be a handful." As you move into the hallway, you struggle to remove from a front pocket the hand-of-Fatima necklace you bought for Mia. "Here—I brought this from Morocco." You turn back and press into Mrs. Pierno's palm the small, amber-crested necklace.

"What is it? This is for me?"

". . . Yeah. I want you to have it."

"What? Oh, it's a *pretty* little thing."

Flustered by the unexpected gift, she adjusts the collar of her robe and quietly closes the door in your face.

Midafternoon Monday, after thirteen hours of fitful sleep, you send by bike messenger the unprocessed shots of Michel Motroet and the Marrakesh models to Harold Ticket's assistant at *Men's Agenda*'s midtown office. Though it's quit raining, it remains, as Christopher would say, "a day of iron skies and cold creeps," and you endure most of it inside, traipsing through your greenhouse-warm apartment in sweatpants, wrinkled T-shirt, and mismatched socks, sluggishly moving from kitchen to den to bathroom, as if wounded in the knees and corroded by inner rust. You don't meditate. You don't bother shaving or brushing your unwashed, brine-smelling hair, which is topknotted beneath a red, tortoiseshell hairclip. You drink the last two Rolling Rocks and a stray Dos Equis, and then smoke a hand-rolled cigarette of mixed tobacco and marijuana lit with a front burner of the stove. You watch much of a three-hour marathon of VH1's *Where Are They Now?*, your television's "surround sound" control cranked up so corybantically loud that the Fordham freshman baby-sitting the Cisneros twins in 6D twice pounds on your shared wall with a broom handle.

"'Hell is where the damned are completely absorbed in their own frustrated self-love,'" you respond slurringly to Def Leppard's forty-year-old one-armed drummer as he reminisces about the band's early success, your comment apropos of you're not sure what. Flipping between channels during the marathon's next commercial break (". . . and sugar pill. People with certain kinds of myeloid tumors should not . . . gives you a good night's sleep without the . . . because you don't get a second chance to make a first impression. That's the reason why . . . Today at *four.* Right here, on *chan*-nel . . . slip-slip-slip-slip-slip-*slip*-pery soft—just like your own—but *better!*"), without warning feeling a wave of déjà vu wooziness that leaves you lightheaded and sweaty, you sit up on the couch and concur with yourself that you are indeed at this moment more stoned than you'd last convinced yourself that you thought you might be. Or were. Are. Now. Whoa . . . that's . . . *intense.*

After a few minutes with your head and shoulders hanging out the opened top-left window (the only one willing to unlock), the fresh air finally does you some good, and you vow that you will do as you promised yourself earlier and deliver Mia's untouched Easter basket to 6D before dark. Once your vertigo dissipates, you turn back, still squatting on the warm and ticking radiator, and take in your cramped apartment from this unusual perspective. How *ridiculous* this place is, you conclude, glancing around the den with disgust. The *waste* of it all. All the unused computer equipment. All the stacks of unread magazines. On the bookshelf (briefly satisfying your craving last autumn for the latest in navigation technology), sits a pocket-size, waterproof GPS with a barometric altimeter and electronic compass. Against the kitchen nook's far wall, a rarely used $1,600 Shankmire mountainbike. Hung from the bike's handle, a wireless MP3 NeckPhone so futuristic-looking you're too embarrassed to wear it in public. Somewhere above the refrigerator there's a polymer-gripped Kenero oyster knife that's never known the snap of a cracked shell. Somewhere beneath your bedroom dresser lies a Citizen sportswatch that will measure and report your body temperature. In the back of your crowded bedroom closet hangs, unworn, a Burberry wool-flannel overcoat (a Barney's "winter warehouse sale" impulse purchase), and below it, collecting dust, a pair of $400 Ermenegildo Zegna leather boots. And right there, sitting before you as proudly as an IMAX movie screen, a 65-inch Toshiba Theaterwide High Definition TV whose volume is still turned up so loud the windows are rattling in protest. "Who *needs* this shit?" you shout. "Plant a tree or deflower a virgin—none of it matters to you, does it? *Does* it?" But before you can answer, the commercial ends and you lose your train of thought.

Having let go of Mia as well as three days will allow, you refocus your attention on satiating your growing cannabis-induced hunger, which you more than manage by consuming an entire microwave-softened pint of Choco-Cherry ice cream, followed by half a box of Snyder's salted sourdough pretzels. Belly stuffed, the rest of your body bloated with self-contempt and aggrandized self-pity, you further numb your brain and soothe your flesh with a Valium and a steaming, thirty-minute shower. Forehead pressed against the tiles directly beneath the pulsating showerhead, you gradually come to recognize that there is little difference between your various soul-clouding thirsts and the addiction of the Resistoleros, the orphaned street children of Central America, to their narcotic cobbler's glue. All afternoon long your ego has squalled like an infant: *Feed me. Feed me.* For your self-imposed house-arrest-cum-bacchanalia, there seems to be no middle way. Spitting out shower water, you accept the disheartening fact: you're like an alcoholic who punishes himself by drinking more.

As the afternoon becomes night, your cravings intensify. You cater to each with little thought of the consequences. Having stepped off the spiritual path, you stumble deeper into the woods, deciding while rolling another joint that you've lost your patience for Buddhism's grueling honesty, and that the only payback that you've received for your charity work with Christopher is a fucking broken heart over his death.

Were you tonight to sit on your zabuton and surrender yourself for a few minutes to something *other* than yourself, you'd realize that what you've done with Mia is behavior symptomatic of the unawakened soul, an exercise of vanity and loneliness by someone who seeks sanctuary in the shadows. You'd realize that you're not sad and confused because you took Mia's virginity—you took Mia's virginity because a life-long slavery to your ego has beaten you, the ache so deep in your bones you've convinced yourself that it's simply the human condition. And, perhaps most important, you'd realize that if you don't change your ways, and soon, the emptiness in your heart will eventually make it collapse upon itself.

After dinner (a dry ham sandwich, the rest of the pretzels), you phone Visheen Asrani with the intention of a little Monday-night hokey, but your long-nailed Indian consort is out, and you choose not to leave a message on her strangely echoing answering machine. Opening a $30 bottle of Merlot, you call Preta, Nick's Gothic-looking, bar-owning girlfriend, who sounds tempted by your invitation to come get high and watch *Taxicab Confessions* on HBO but claims that she's needed for last call at her club. "Whatever," you reply, hanging up louder than you expect. With a stifled wine-belch you dial up the number from the back-page ad in last week's *Village Voice.* After three rings you get a recording of a young woman's voice: "*Welcome* to New York's *hottest—all live—all adult*—phone line. Where ladies call *free* to talk dirty to *you.* Just *sixty*-nine cents a minute, ninety-nine cents for the first. You'll need a touch-tone phone. If you're under eighteen, please hang up. Now, get ready. *Guys*—main menu: press *one* to leave steamy dateline personals. Press *two* to connect *live—one-on-one*—with a *lady* anxious to speak just to *you.*"

You sniff and beep the 2 key, waiting through several seconds of static before hearing a muffled *click.*

". . . Yeah? Who's that?"

You sit up a little. "Hello?"

". . . I can't hear nuthin'. Is somebody on the line?"

You clear your throat. "*Hello?* Who's this?"

"Score. This is Dominique. Who's that?"

"This would be . . . Frank."

"Hey, Frank. Where you callin' from, baby?"

"Upper West Side. Broadway and Eighty-first. You?"

"From under the covers in my queen-size bed."

". . . Ouch."

"Whutcha *wearin'*, Frank?"

". . . Sweat pants. Socks."

"Oooooh. That's *hot.* You wanta git down with me for a while? My husband's got the kids till midnight."

The ringing phone wakes you shortly after one. You're still slumped on the couch, still wearing your sweatpants and ridiculous tortoiseshell hair-clip, still holding an empty wine glass in your lap. Unnerved, Marley has moved away from you into the kitchen. In the dream you were having, your head had swollen to the size of a party balloon, your throat constricted into a foot-long straw, your moistened lips chomping at air as you floated, Tantalus-like, over an excruciatingly tempting buffet of refrigerated desserts: chilled strawberries, lime sorbet, peach hamantaschen, chocolate-pudding cake, a slice of Boston cream pie.

You pick up the receiver after the third ring. "Yeah?"

"What the fuck is your *deal*, bud?"

Loud, staticky nightclub noise pounds through your skull. "Who's this?"

"*Nick*, asshole. And don't tell me you didn't think I'd find out."

You massage your eyes. "Yo—what's shaking, *Nick?"*

"The pool cue I'm gonna shove up your ass, that's what. I should bitch-slap you silly, dog. First you push me down your fucking stairs, now you're hitting on my lady."

"Whoa, *Nick.* She's no lady. She's our wife."

"You're—I don't get you, Cox. What is your *fucking problem?"*

"My fucking problem, *Nick* . . . is that I am not a very good person."

You hang up, light another cigarette, secure the wine glass, and test the nearest beer bottle. With the remote control you change channels to a local cable station, where, for the next hour, you watch a sad parade of poorly lit, naked, and partially naked women dance alone and with strained sultriness for a jittery, hand-held camera, one after another, atop *The Robin Byrd Show*'s tiny pinewood stage.

Still in bed at eleven Tuesday morning when the phone rings with more bad news, you lift your head from beneath the pillow as Hal Ticket addresses your answering machine. "*Carter*," the adolescent-sounding art director yells into his speakerphone, "listen—I'm big-time confused, buddy. Why'd you send me unprocessed film? I thought I was gonna get transparencies, or at least contact sheets. And there's no *color,* Carter. You spend a *week* in fucking Morocco and this is all you got? There's, like, twelve rolls of color, tops. And there isn't *squat* of the windsurfer kid. I don't know, man, we need to talk. Call me. Pronto."

The answering machine shuts off and with a clickety whir rewinds.

". . . Shit."

Over the next half hour, before you can come up with a single reason to pull yourself from bed, you endure two more bad-news phone calls, both of which you screen while hidden beneath the comforter. The first is from Tess, your oldest sister in Tucson, who reprimands you for neglecting yesterday to call Samantha, the youngest of your two sisters in Atlanta, to wish her a happy thirtieth birthday. The second is from someone named Mary Beth Koontz, who proclaims in a friendly but unfamiliar voice that she's finally made it to New York City to see you ("y'all thought I was kidding about coming, didn't ya"), and leaves the number of a midtown hotel where she can be reached for the next six days.

By noon, trudging back to the kitchen, you've begun to feel cotton-mouthed and gummy-eyed from the bedside joint you smoked after hearing Hal Ticket's rant, the rest of last night's Merlot, a second Valium, and one of the Codeine tablets you stole from Visheen Asrani's pocketbook last month, a head-wobbling combination almost as potent as the drugs-and-alcohol mix that landed you in Century City Hospital as a UCLA undergraduate. Your sweatpants and stained white T-shirt stink of day-old cigarette smoke. Your skin is so oily you don't want to touch yourself. Marley—ears perked, softly yelping—eyes you from where he waits by the front door. "Two minutes, okay?" you mutter, tossing in his general direction a pink rubber chew-bone.

The squalor in the kitchen makes you turn the overhead light back off with a groan. Leaning heavily, dizzily, on the cluttered counter, side-stepping a white puddle of congealed potato-leek soup on the floor, you fan your nose and glower, in turn, at the uncovered garbage pail, an overturned ashtray concealed behind the toaster, the six unrinsed green Rolling Rock bottles lined up like soldiers before the blue recycling bin, and on the opposite counter a black Pottery Barn bowl sticky with the remains of the Choco-Cherry ice cream scooped into it sometime late Sunday night. Ignoring the whining dog and smelly kitchen mess, you open the nearest cupboard door and devour straight from the box a crumbly handful of Golden Grahams cereal.

In midchomp you pause, cock your head. Out in the hallway, Mrs. Pierno laughs and playfully shouts in Italian at one of her firefighter sons. You close your right eye and stare at the microwave clock: 12:14. You close your left eye: 12:19. You open both eyes: 12:14. Either way it's lunchtime. You extract from the refrigerator a papaya-flavored Seymour's Smoothie and, from among the various tools of mischief lying next to the toaster on the counter, a reclosable, grease-stained, sixteen-count package of Entenmann's white-chocolate-macadamia-nut "soft-baked" cookies. Practically giddy with indifference, no longer even beginning to reproach yourself for your indulgences, and certainly not worrying about the karmic consequences of your misbehavior, no longer caring much about anything, you transport the cookies and the fruit drink into the den and with a grunt sink backwards onto the couch.

You avoid eye contact with Marley, who continues to whine with his nose to the door, and bring to your parched lips the largest of the macadamia-nut cookies, so buttery moist you're made woozy as it slowly folds forward while you prepare to bite it. You stack the cookie's two soft halves onto your extended tongue. The subtle tapestry of tastes—white chocolate, sugar, unsalted butter—leads you to close your eyes and list sideways against the couch. As you chew in open-mouthed slow motion, eyes still shut, you reach down and search by touch for the smallest of the many magazines scattered on the throw rug beneath the coffee table. You shout: "Marley—have you seen the *TV Guide?*" The dog barks, advances towards your knees, barks again, circles back towards the door.

You swallow hard. You feel your brain growing muzzier and muzzier from the cocktail of cannabis, Valium, Codeine, Merlot, Golden Grahams, and macadamia-nut coursing through your veins. "*Jesus,* boy. Hold your horses."

You find your *TV Guide* under some socks as you stuff a second soft-baked cookie into your mouth. You reach for a third before you even begin chewing. After perusing your options for Tuesday afternoon TV-viewing, you lower the magazine, sit up, stare out the window, and wonder aloud, germane to nothing you were thinking up to this moment: *How did Mia know I'm dyslexic?* The unanswered question leads you to look over at Mia's photograph from Central Park. Dreamily you hear again the January snow crunching beneath your winter boots as you pass through the gate to Sheep Meadow, smell again the street vendor's roasted chestnuts and sugar-glazed pecans, feel again Mia's mittened hand affectionately squeezing your arm as Marley fetches the wrong stick.

"*Marley!*" you cry.

You reach back into the Entenmann's carton. Mia. *Men's Agenda*. Marley. You're thinking about all three things at once, none of them clearly, when you start to choke. The initial impelling hack spews cookie bits and saliva across the coffee table. You grab your throat. *Fuck.* You lean forward, panic-stricken, and pat your chest. Your eyes water as you realize that a sizable chunk of the third cookie, unchewed, has lodged in your windpipe right below your Adam's apple. Eyes bulging, you rise from the couch to a half crouch. You can swallow, but—*fuck fuck fuck*—you can no longer breathe. Marley's ears stick up at the high-pitched crowing sound coming from your larynx.

Not knowing that a self-administered Heimlich maneuver would be made possible by using the back of your cushioned desk chair, you freeze, cautiously bend over—hands on your knees, nose running, mouth filling with saliva—and waddle in this peculiar short-stop posture out the door and down the hallway to Mrs. Pierno's apartment. You trust—you *pray*—that your neighbor's EMT-trained son will know what to do.

By the time you reach your neighbor's door and knock, the trapped breath burning in your chest causes the aperture of your peripheral vision to shrink. Over a minute has passed since the cookie went down the wrong pipe. This is not good—and you hear nothing from within the apartment. Ears ringing, a sheen of sweat flushing your blue-tinged face, you knock again, frantically, and position yourself before the door's peephole so that anyone inside can see who it is.

Mrs. Pierno tiptoes out of the den into the kitchen, still wearing her brown raincoat, having only minutes earlier returned from her weekly lunch date with Anthony, the elder of her two firefighter progeny, a first-line supervisor at FDNY's Engine Company 118 in Queens, currently browsing through a *Reader's Digest* out of earshot in the bathroom. The old woman doesn't even bother to look through the peephole. She knows all too well that impatient, single-knuckle knock of yours and has sworn that hell will freeze over before she ever again agrees to take care of your dog. "No longer will I be taken advantage of," she whispers to herself as she continues to hide out against the stove.

Your eyeballs feel close to bursting—the pressure in your brain is unlike anything you've ever experienced. With your left fist you pound the center of your chest—repeatedly—desperately—and then, as if strangling yourself, you clutch with both hands at your throat and attempt, unsuccessfully, to somehow squeeze the cookie chunk upwards from your windpipe, like toothpaste from the tube. Eyes whirling, bowels loosening, you strain to stay focused as you fight the onslaught of weariness. You collapse cumbrously onto your knees in the pallid hallway light, the impact snapping your head backwards and rattling your teeth, your legs and arms weighed down by the airless diving bell your body has become. Your field of vision goes blurry-black at the top and bottom as the curtain begins to close.

You lower your head, limply drop your hands to your hips. The last thing you see before everything turns dark is the yellow, water-stained ceiling panel above the stairwell.

Already unconscious, dead weight sinking upon itself as the puppet strings dissolve, you kneel unsupported for a second or two before slumping sideways, the crack of your cheekbone as it smacks the hallway floor registering as a dull, muffled thump somewhere off in the distance.

10

YOU REMEMBER YOUR THREE SISTERS as little girls, barefoot and pigtailed, squealing as your father spun them on the tire-swing in Sheaffer Park. You remember your mother's nervous smile as she pulled from behind her back and bestowed upon your outstretched, twelve-year-old hands the gift-wrapped, twin-lens Rolleiflex: "Happy birthday, sweetheart." You remember your father at fifty, lying in his hammock with his shirt peeled off, sweaty from mowing the yard, reading the *Sacramento Bee*'s classifieds with a Heineken pressed to his forehead. You remember the ferocity with which you fingered Nancy Suhkotai, the drill-team captain, whose white boots stank of sweat and whose last name you couldn't pronounce, the first Friday night after you were diagnosed as a dyslexic. You remember a fist fight in the high school cafeteria with Alex McPhillips over his girlfriend, Ellen Lawson-Meyers, your former best friend declaring tearfully with each of his feeble punches: "You *suck,* man."

You remember holding shivering, six-week-old Marley in your lap on the Lexington Avenue Express train as you brought him home from the pound. You remember the taste of a fresh cup of Fairway's southern-pecan coffee and a cigarette. You remember the satisfying *ta-click* of a secured zoom lens, the motorized hum and vibration of auto-rewind. You remember shoplifting from Computer Mania an Elvis Presley mousepad. You remember confessing, sotto voce, to the sleekly suited Barney's salesclerk, while charging a $120 four-pack of Paul Stewart white-silk pocket squares, "God, I'm *addicted* to this shit." You remember the piquant perfume-stench of Visheen Asrani's dark skin, her red fingernails crawling over your shoulders. You remember gawking, open-mouthed, at Greta Hüber's black bikini top as she leaned over the chessboard and with a shrug reluctantly forked your queen: "Check. *Puh*—you're not paying good attention, Carter."

You remember porn starlet Tiffany St. Cloud's bruised arms. You remember the crinkling sound of Preta Moore's black leather pants. You remember the emptiness you felt waking up in the morning on Nick's couch across from auburn-haired Hannah Weaver, still asleep, gently snoring, her Tibetan fur hat discarded on the floor among the empty champagne bottles.

You remember why the roll of film containing the shots of Mrs. Pierno is still in your refrigerator.

You remember the strawberry smell of Mia's ponytail. You remember whispering in Mia's ear the first night in Morocco, your voice as light as rose petals: "You have *no idea* how pretty you are, do you?" You remember Mia, naked, trembling beneath you in her bed your last night together at the Riad al-Madina, her eyes pleading for you not to betray her trust, her flushed face turning, eyes shutting, as you finally shuddered and fell away.

This is what you take with you.

Death is a mirror, Carter—we reap what we have sown. Fueled by karma, worshippers of ghosts are condemned to the realm of ghosts.

"The floor's all wet," observes Mrs. Pierno from her doorway. "Did he slip and fall down?"

In the hallway Mrs. Pierno's son shakes his head, removes his raincoat, kneels, with effort finds and removes the obstruction in your throat, takes a deep breath and lowers his lips to your mouth. Your blue-tinged cheeks and forehead are cold to the touch. If his mother weren't watching, he'd probably not bother trying to resuscitate you.

Near the stairwell, nose to the floor, ears flattened, Marley sniffs and yelps nervously. He knows that his master has died and fears that he's somehow to blame.

Mrs. Pierno's son answers over his shoulder between halfhearted pumps to your chest. "Nah—choked. He's been here awhile."

"Should I call an ambulance?"

"Yeah—but take your time, Ma. He's gone."

As we discussed, Carter, death is an exact reversal of the stages of conception. First the earth element is reabsorbed into the water element, its migration accompanied by the sensation of physical weakness, the sluggishness and weight that brought you so heavily to your knees twenty minutes ago. Your eyes have rolled back in your head. Your bowels and bladder have loosened. Because you were born in late February, under the sign of Pisces, a water sign, your physical makeup is dominated by liquid: that's why the drowning sensation continued unabated for what seemed to you an eternity. If you could have moved or breathed, you would have screamed.

Next, the water element reabsorbs into the fire element. Everywhere there's smoke, as if the walls, the ceiling, everything is burning, everything is consumed by flames. You're here but not here as the fire element dissolves into the air element: the only remaining warmth in your body hovers unsurely around the lining of your heart. With these last few thrusts of the fireman's palms against your sternum, your body lets loose of what little tension is still clenched upon itself.

"Oh, Lord—he's *dead?*" asks Mrs. Pierno, her voice faltering with the realization of what she's done.

Out of breath, sweating under the arms, her son glances at the skittish dog, back down at the floor. "Is this the guy you were complaining about?"

Your eyelids flutter. Your fingers uncurl. Your mouth opens with a final spasmic yawn as the air element returns to empty space.

Mrs. Pierno covers her mouth. "Oh, God."

Yes, Carter, those are fireflies behind you. No, you are *not* a thief—not in your heart. Don't think that. The state of your mind from here on is crucial. Abandon grasping as best you can. Try—as mindfully as you're able—to let go of these memories. *Try* to have no regrets. Remember our practice. Remember the *samadhi* of meditation. Recognize the Buddha within you. *Surrender* to this inner divinity.

Your body seems separate from your awareness of it, doesn't it? Strange, eh? That's because your awareness is now physically unfettered and floating free in space. That's right. You are *not* that body down there, my friend. You're the light—this force that *animated* the body. Allow the light to bathe in its own warmth, to grow brighter and brighter as the masculine and feminine forces from your parents' sperm and egg separate, leaving nothing in their wake but Buddha Nature's pure awareness, the clear luminosity of your higher Self. If you'd tried a little harder as a human and were enlightened, you'd recognize this stage as an opportunity for freedom, a potential break from the samsaric cycle of birth and death, and could remain in this light—fully *return* to this light—*be* nirvana.

With his death Buddha Shakyamuni let go of *dukkha*—of human suffering—and remained forever in the pristine light of *Dharmata.* His Holiness the Fourteenth Dalai Lama has passed through this Bardo of Dying thirteen times since his enlightenment six hundred years ago, choosing to sacrifice his own eternal freedom by being reborn again and again as a human for the welfare of all sentient beings.

But you, my vain, self-cherishing friend, continue to clutch at the corpse down there, afraid to let it go. Why are you refusing to release yourself? Just let it be. You've been through this Bardo so many times before—don't you remember? Carter Cox was a dream. *This* is a dream. You are the light. You *must* let go of the body—let go of *everything*—in order to be free. *Wake up, man!* You're a Buddha—we're *all* Buddhas!

"The soul lives by that which it loves rather than in the body which it animates." Saint John of the Cross said that. A Christian. *He* understood.

Twenty-five hundred years ago Buddha Shakyamuni understood this as well. He said: "The man who gathers only the flowers of sense pleasures, whose Mind is entangled, death carries him away as a great flood a sleeping village." Gandhi's last words were, "Oh God." *He* understood. His entire life was embodied in that final breath.

Your last words? "Fuck fuck fuck."

Oh well. We never know when we'll be struck down. Death *always* takes us by surprise.

No—*this* way. You're missing the boat. *Ignore* the water, and don't get in a paddy about rushing so much. Just come back into the light. Calmly. Yes. *Into* the light.

Pay attention and *listen* to me.

Drop the body.

Drop the body.

Drop the *bloody body.*

There. Yes. That's the stuff! Just let it go. Rise up. Do you see? *You* remember this.

Now follow me along the path—we talked about this part in front of the gigglebox on *several* occasions. I'm only here to remind you of what you already know. Since you *persist* in interacting with the universe dualistically, you're stuck with yours truly: the embodiment of your Buddha Nature packaged, as it were, in the interactive form of one of the few folks in your decidedly self-centered life to whom you opened your heart and shared, as Master Merton so poetically phrased it, "disinterested love." Remember: *you* invoked *me.* When *I* died, I was dealt a Bardo-guide triumvirate of Padmasambhava, Jamyang Khyentse Rinpoche, and His Holiness the Dalai Lama, who would speak to me only in Tibetan. Mia Malone will summon the Virgin Mary. Had you been a God-fearing Jew, you might have conjured up Elijah or Moses.

It's frightening, I know, but try to relax. *You* have it relatively easy: rather than a shaggy Charlton Heston or a thousand-headed Krishna, your higher-Self omniscience comes to you courtesy of a prissy old East Ender with a Kensington cockney.

This way. Mind the puddles. Yes. *Now* we're moving. It's been forty days and forty nights since your neighbor pretended not to hear you knocking on her door. Truly. I know it's hard to believe—it's gone by in a snap—but your body has been buried in a cemetery in Sacramento, your sisters and parents have gathered and cried, and your apartment, as of the first of the month, is now rented to a newlywed couple from Albany. Mia finally found out about your death this past Sunday. Karma has propelled you—*you*—this awareness—through the Bardo of Dying and the Bardo of Becoming, the transitional stages between death and rebirth, realms no more or less real than the Human realm or the Hell realm or the Dream realm into which you ventured nightly during your life as Carter. My first Dharma teacher used to say that karma is weight, that in order to break free of the samsaric cycle of rebirth we must shed that weight with an experience of equal, self-negating heft in the next life. Tit for tat, as it were. To cut to the chase, my karma-heavy friend, you're obliged to spend some time ridding yourself of the extra baggage you've accrued.

It's too bad, really. You were on the right track with your fine work down in Central America. But you rather blew it with Miss Malone, I must say. Rinpoche told me once: "Whosoever offends an innocent person, pure and guiltless, his guilt comes back on him like dust thrown against the wind." Mia had taken a Christian *vow*—a vow she'd worked *very* hard to keep. But that's been your modus operandi, eh? One saucy swot after another—never enough. Eyeing the next bite before you swallow the one you're chewing. Did you know that Carter Cox slept with more women during his thirties than the number of times Mia Malone's ever been kissed? Of *course* you know that. You know *everything*—you just choose to ignore it.

I wouldn't swallow that if I were you. And be mindful of the smoke.

Yes, this is the Hungry Ghost realm. Here in this wasteland you'll find there's no water fit to drink, though there's an endless supply of gnarled and leafless trees, bent and crimped, semi-petrified in perpetual autumn. It's a foul and arid plain, sunken in gloom, whose faint moonlight remains forever trapped in dusk. The Bardo of Becoming has ended and you're now stuck here for a while. Sorry. If it's any consolation, the only thing that suffers here is the ego. In the Hungry Ghost realm you're reborn but not reborn, alive but not alive, dead but not dead. Though you've entered this realm without a body, you'll feel physical sensations—in your instance, mostly unquenchable thirst. Dehydration up the wazoo. Parched lips, cracked tongue, endless edentate smacking—that sort of thing. The only sound for miles and miles will be your own labored breathing, amplified tenfold by virtue of this echo. No, relax—*relax*—if you don't fight it, it won't drive you so batty. And that stench is from—well, you see them. Ooh—be careful—those are pointy.

There were six possibilities for your rebirth: The Hell realm, which is *decidedly* unpleasant. Dante knew of what he spoke. The Animal realm, which is essentially a jungle—always looking over your shoulder for bigger animals aiming to eat you. No fun. Your pool mate, Nick, still has a bit of the wolf in him from his last go-round there. There are a couple of higher, semidivine realms—very Caribbean-beachy, no worries, mate—but you're a good ways from either, so I won't torture you with the details. The Human realm, which—quite frankly—is an opportunity you wasted. And last, but certainly not least (for that would be Hell), that in which we are presently ensconced: the Hungry Ghost realm. This particular version I've fashioned for you as a never-ending horizon of concentric moats of undrinkable muck, a dash of Samuel Beckett with a pinch of T. S. Eliot—subterranean steam purling up from the scorched ground, gray escarpments, relentlessly dry air, some token fire and brimstone—yikes, watch your step—you shouldn't have watched *Nosferatu* so many times—the occasional yawing pit of sulfurous smoke-wisps and ash, and that empty mudcracked hut which, from this moment on, shall serve as your home. Here, alas, as I've mentioned, you'll find there's no water fit to sip. It's a graveless graveyard; you'll want to die, but you can't. The Hungry Ghost realm is an expiatory place, so be patient. You must *suffer* the karma in order to slough it off, I'm afraid. It could be worse—though I wouldn't lick any more of that if I were you—seriously—it's only going to make you thirstier. *Seriously*. Don't be a dimbo.

You needn't crawl, just try not to retrace your steps. Keep moving forward. Do you spy that pile of bones over there? Those are from your previous lives. All of them. Even the fishbones. Yes, it's this way in all directions—nothing but desiccated earth and gloomy shadows and the occasional mudcracked hut. Living in the hut behind you is Winifred Sinclair. Died in 1907 at the age of fifty-two. Born just a mile or so from your flat in a *very* nice Greenwich Village brownstone. Hanged herself after her husband left her. She was more attached to his money than his love, turned out, though she refuses to admit it. She's doing her time stacking silver dollars she's got nowhere to spend. Poor thing. In that hut up on the peak is Cecil Leavell, a divorce lawyer from Brooklyn Heights. *Loved* to drink bourbon and gamble. Loved it, loved it, loved it. Dropped dead after folding a hand of seven-card stud with an ulcerated belly and a bloated debt-line with the bank. He's eyeing you like that because he fears you're planning to steal his slot machines. He's got a baker's dozen of them lining his walls—it's all he ever does, walking 'round in circles in his hut, cranking their arms, one after another, waiting for a jackpot that never comes. Most likely neither Winifred nor Cecil will ever speak to you. *Nobody* says much in the Hungry Ghost realm.

Do you find these set details a bit heavy-handed? Well, it's *your* imagination.

Yes, I realize that it's hot. I'm sorry. And yes, I *see* the water. I *know* you're thirsty. But you can't drink from any of these ridiculous buckets—their bottoms have all gone rusty. I know it's terrible: they're *everywhere.* That's the point.

What? Okay—fine—*ignore* me—do as you will—in the end it's all the same to me.

By virtue of the weight of your accrued karma, you're due to stay here for one third of a minor *kalpa:* approximately three hundred years. Not a good hand to be dealt, I admit. Bleak as a midnight scourge. But remember: When you realize the nightmare you're stuck in is an illusion, the nightmare dissolves. Easier said than done, I'll grant you, but that's pretty much the brass ring.

I *know* your lips are dry, but use your loaf, man—it's *salt* water.

Listen—*you* know what to do. Be patient with yourself. Be generous to your heart. And whenever you need some sound advice, you know where to find me.

Until then,

Cheers.

11

BUT THAT'S NOT WHAT HAPPENS.

When you awake in the Essaouira hotel, shortly after dawn, roosters crowing across the medina, you're holding the spare pillow to your chest. Before joining Mia for breakfast, you shower, shave, trim your eyebrows, throw on your mala beads, a pair of new Maui cargo shorts, and your faded 1993 NYC Marathon T-shirt, its frayed collar stylishly ruined by bleach, slather sunscreen across your cheeks and forehead, and needlessly rearrange for the third time the contents of the two equipment cases you plan to bring to the beach. You assume that much of the day will be spent without shade: according to your laptop's bookmarked International Weather site the temperature on the Moroccan coast is scheduled to rise well into the eighties.

The chirping of sparrows draws your attention towards the opened shutters. You wander across the room and poke your head through the window. The warm and busy medina is already abuzz with flies and Arabic chatter. To the west, over the Atlantic, the sky is cloudless and vibrantly blue.

At eight-thirty, the rendezvous time agreed upon before last evening's goodnight kiss, you climb the stairs to the third floor and gently knock on Mia's door. There's no answer. You move sideways and check through the window, but the blinds are closed.

"Carter—I'm down here."

When you join Mia in the courtyard, you discover that she has already been to the souks and back and has brought you a gift—an exotic-looking, brass-and-camel-bone teapot, which she sets before you on the blue-tiled table. She still seems as breathless about staying in an eighteenth-century pasha's villa as she'd been yesterday when, stepping from the Darb Laaouj al-Attarin through the villa's blue-framed door, she first caught sight of the Riad al-Madina's lavish, fountain-centered courtyard. "The shop owner said that I bargain like a Berber," Mia informs you. "Is that good or bad?"

"Oh, that's definitely good," you assure her, holding the small teapot up for a better look.

Mia is still smiling, indeed seems mildly rapturous, as you depart an hour later from Eglise Sainte-Anne's empty, light-filled nave. Carrying the photo equipment, the two of you reenter on foot the northern end of the medina shortly before ten, and with some effort proceed with the photo gear through the crowded, narrow lanes leading to Essaouira's Portuguese-styled central square.

"Hey, Carter, why didn't we just fly directly to Marrakesh?"

You shrug. "Guess I figured driving down the coast from Casablanca would be more scenic, more Thelma-and-Louise-y. Besides, Essaouira doesn't have an airport, and if we'd flown straight to Marrakesh, well, we wouldn't have seen our flying goats."

Mia smiles, her face softening as she repeats dreamily, stressing the fricatives with playful puffs, "Our fabulous flying goats."

Already perspiring, gesturing with your chin towards the thirty-pound, brushed-silver Anvil Mia has hoisted to her shoulder, you ask between breaths, "Is that too heavy for you?"

"I'm not the one huffing."

As you continue towards the square, Mia infers correctly that your thoughts are turning towards the upcoming photo session. So are hers. Growing nervous about what her responsibilities will be as your assistant, Mia gamely asks, "Do you, as they say, plan to shoot digital today, Carter?"

You must catch your breath before you can answer. "Nah. I don't even like shooting color."

"So . . . who are *your* favorite photographers?"

You sigh and come to a stop in the shade of a souk's awning, and glance up at an orange kilim rug hanging from a second-floor window. "Oh, hell, I don't know. Name some."

Mia lowers the Anvil to the hay-strewn ground and secures the case between her knees. She wishes that you would be gentler with her, would see that she's trying, that she wants to be helpful but is afraid of making a mistake, that you would understand that few things distress her more acutely than the fear of being a burden. "What do you think of Andrew Goldsworthy?"

"Don't know his stuff."

"Paul Strand?"

"A poor man's Frederick Sommer."

"Sebastio Selgado?"

"Good to very good."

"Alfred Stieglitz?"

"Overrated."

"Really? Did you know that his art gallery was the first to show Cezanne, Picasso, and Brancusi in the United States? Not to mention, of course, Georgia O'Keeffe. Stieglitz was *very* influential in shaping the twentieth-century American visual aesthetic. I think he's—*what?*" she asks, her Louisiana drawl sneaking through, embarrassed but smiling as you chuckle and shake your head. "Am I being an art-history geek again?"

"Yes. And I love it."

You and Mia step flat against the souk's adobe wall as an elderly potter and his bowl-laden donkey clop past.

"So, I'm curious, Carter—who among you freelance photographers is considered the most successful in America right now?"

"Money-wise?"

"Sure."

"Oh, man. The top tier—Bruce, Herb, Annie—they're all filthy rich. They can pull in fifty K for a one-day shoot and not even squeeze the shutter. Second-tier folks, someone like Michael Deveritti or Chance Anders—any of the guys who have regular gigs with Deerbok or Condé Nast—they all gross, I'm guessing, a quarter-million a year."

"Where do you fit in?"

"Where do I fit in?" You snort. "*Do* I fit in?" You pick up your case and continue walking. For a moment you're a senior in high school again, trudging from the boys' locker room into the cafeteria after failing to find your name listed on the roster for the varsity football team for the second straight year. You turn the corner, with Mia trailing a few steps behind, raise your head, and look back at your earnestly smiling, bewitchingly self-conscious companion, and offer a self-deprecating shrug.

"Am I being crass?"

"No. It's just—I'm not sure what my answer is." You slow down, let Mia catch up. "I suppose you could say that I'm midlevel successful. Perhaps lower midlevel."

"No. You're being modest, Carter. You are *very* successful. And *very* talented. Your Resistolero pictures, for example—those are terrifically powerful images. Selgado would be proud."

"Oh please." But you remind yourself that Mia was apparently moved enough by your photography to take a sabbatical from grad school and move to Guatemala City to become a volunteer.

Three steps later you come to a halt again, lower the photo case against one of Essaouira's ubiquitous blue wooden doors, and turn fully to Mia, who, holding the Anvil now on her left shoulder, gazes at you with an upturned face, smiling blissfully as you take her free hand and squeeze its palm with a surge of affection and trust. She's dreamed of you looking at her in such a tender manner since the afternoon she read your first note in Woodstock. Moved by your awakening heart, you stare into Mia's eyes and blurt forth in confession, "Actually, I could do better. Much better. I'm *lazy*. And not just professionally. I mean, I smoke too much. I drink too much. I'm addicted to sensual pleasures—physically addicted—I would whore myself for a hot shower if I had to. My memory's shot. There are whole relationships I can't recall." You take your hand back, sheepishly slip it into a pocket. "I don't know. I'm not sure what I'm trying to say here."

Embarrassed, you pick up your gear before moist-eyed Mia can respond. Up ahead you spy two little dark-skinned Berber girls, barefoot and filthy in buttonless white frocks, slowly leading an elderly blind beggar towards the entrance to a souk. The girls—perhaps as young as six or seven—have beautiful brown eyes, but their thick black hair is matted and dusty. They look and act like they've not slept in days, seemingly aware of nothing but their exhaustion and their grip on the old man's kaftan. You trot forward a few steps, crouching in the shadows as you follow the two girls through the lens of the Leica slung around your neck while they position the elderly man, who you assume correctly is their grandfather, on a stool near the mud-cracked stoop. Squatting against the wall where they flank their charge, in whose lap rests a tiny wooden alms bowl, neither of the girls speaks nor acknowledges the mid-morning shoppers, even the one or two who drop coins. "Good Lord," you mutter as the reality of what you're looking at sinks in. That children of this age—of *any* age—should endure this sort of degradation breaks your heart.

You spend almost fifteen minutes exposing film. Mia watches you affectionately from several steps behind as she leans against a door, the photo case secured between her legs. She admires the fact that you're taking your time—indeed, she senses you're so absorbed that you've forgotten your responsibilities with the windsurfer—and she's impressed that you're managing to photograph the old man and girls so unobtrusively.

You expose two rolls before you're ready to move on. Mia squeezes your arm but refrains from voicing her thoughts, and the two of you continue walking in silence after you place a folded ten-dirham note in the blind man's bowl. When you turn the corner and plunge into Place Prince Moulay el-Hassan, the small but bustling central square, European pop music is blasting from a radio on the balcony of a nearby restaurant. Smoky from a line of grilled-seafood kiosks, the square is framed by four outdoor cafés half-filled with young Moroccan males, almost all of whom are holding American cigarettes and sipping cups of mint tea or coffee. You shade your eyes and scout for the young windsurfer. You decide on a young man in the middle of the busy, noisy café to your left. "That must be him," you say over your shoulder to Mia, of a deeply tanned, bare-chested teenager wearing black wet-suit pants with his feet propped up on a chair.

Three steps behind you as you approach the boy's table, Mia is still smiling from your confession and the sight of you photographing the children. The nineteen-year-old world champ squints up at you unsurely as you lower the photo equipment between his two chairs.

"Michel?"

The young man reluctantly removes his Walkman earphones.

"Are you Michel Motroet?"

The boy gives an affirmative upward nod of his unshaven chin, scratches his chest as he eyes Mia's jeans and tight red T-shirt. Though handsome and athletically built, he has brown-rooted hair bleached yellowish blond, haphazardly tattooed skin, and toenails and fingernails lacquered with chipped black polish.

"I'm Carter." You extend a hand. "This is Mia, my assistant."

The windsurfing champ cocks his jaw in your direction, slumps in his chair, and asks unenthusiastically in his affected mix of French and Jamaican accents, "So, mon, where do you want to do zeese?"

You remind yourself that the kid's only nineteen, that you too hated having your picture taken when you were his age—hell, you *still* hate having your picture taken. He slips on a pair of gaudy, wraparound sunglasses—he clearly feels uncomfortable making eye contact with you, perhaps because you're twice his age and three inches taller—and submits that the best wave-sailing spot in all of Morocco is fifty kilometers to the north at Moulay Bousaktoun, though he says that he'd prefer to meet up with his friends at Sidi Kaoki twenty kilometers to the south, and asks if you'd be willing to take his pictures there. Both locations strike you as needlessly inconvenient. For a moment you flirt with the possibility of using the Cap Sim galleon wreck you spied last evening as a backdrop—sticking the kid on a camel and having him wear a turban, with his board tucked beneath an arm like an oversized school book. Let him show *that* image to Heidi King. But it's a beautiful morning, you decide, and since Motroet is presumably the finest windsurfer on the planet you might as well do the shoot in his most comfortable element.

"Go grab one of your boards and whatever gear you'll need for the day," you tell him, as Mia—whose amused regard for the half-dressed teen now borders on mild disgust—not-so-subtly steps backwards and presses her shoulders against your chest, lowering her eyes as she imagines your arms protectively wrapped around her waist. "We'll take my rental car to Sidi Kaoki. What the hell. Let's have some fun."

It's midnight. You've showered and put on a sports jacket and walked with Mia, hand-in-hand, through the labyrinth of the medina to Chez Toufik, a quiet and elegantly decorated outdoor restaurant designed in the fashion of a Berber salon. Its six torch-lit tables are manned by a pair of stout, white-aproned Moroccan waiters, one of whom approaches out of the shadows, clears what's left of your vegetable tagine, and asks in broken English if you'd like to order a second bottle of the Algerian rosé he first recommended almost two hours ago.

Leaning forward on your elbows, head close to the table, you stare at Mia's face through the candlelight as you decide. She's never looked lovelier. A little intoxicated—and not entirely from the wine—you drink Mia in with your gaze. She wears her jeans and one of your long-sleeved cotton shirts, loaned to her before she showered for dinner, the soft white sleeves rolled up into enormous cuffs. Around her left wrist she absently spins the silver bracelet she reluctantly allowed you to purchase for her at a beachfront souk after the shoot with Motroet. Mia averts her face sideways an inch, and, remaining deep within herself, continues to caress the stem of her empty wine glass. She's clearly tired from working in the unshaded Sidi Kaoki cove all afternoon, sunburned, a little dehydrated. A second bottle of wine could very well do her in. You raise your head, cast the hint of an apologetic smile up at the waiter. "No thanks," you tell him. "We're fine."

Though equally exhausted, you feel sanguine, potent, confident that your relationship with Mia will continue to blossom. Professionally, the day went well: Motroet proved more receptive to your directions than you'd expected, chiefly because you used his five windsurfer friends as an audience. (If you've learned anything during your tenure as a professional photographer, it's that celebrities and athletes, peacocks all, like to show off for one another.) The kid didn't even seem to mind that the Renault's bungee-corded trunk took a chip out of his $1,600 fiberglass board. The unexpectedly photogenic dunes of Sidi Kaoki made the winding, forty-minute drive along the coast worth the effort. You exposed twenty-six rolls of film in just under four hours. And Mia—bless her heart—didn't miss a beat loading the camera bodies, drying the Polaroid test shots, or holding the reflectors.

Over the remains of your vegetable tagine, you ask, "Do you plan to have children?"

Mia slowly opens her sleepy eyes. "That's an interesting segue."

"Do you?"

"Hmm . . . I'm not sure." She moves her empty wine glass to the left. Having struggled with her sexual feelings for you ever since her visit to New York, Mia is nervous about where tonight might be heading, but—like you—is also cautiously optimistic about your relationship. Regardless, she decides to cut off your seduction at the pass: "Quick game of Royal Air Maroc?" she asks. Her eyes self-mockingly widen over the prospect of reprising your silly word-bluffing game—its format a loose variation of Fool's Choice—which the two of you invented during the transatlantic flight to Casablanca. "First one to three gets to pick dessert. You go first."

"Oh God," you groan. But you accept the challenge and sit up straighter and drum your lips with your fingers as you struggle to come up with a word whose definition the frighteningly literate Mia will not know. "Okay. Atlatl."

"Come again?"

"Atl-atl." You spell the word for her. For the first of your two proffered definitions, one real, one imaginary (much of the fun of the game comes from trying to keep a straight face while delivering the fictional explanation), you clear your throat and say in a matter-of-fact voice, "An atlatl is a device used by tribal spear-throwers. A throwing device, that attaches to the spear. It's about a foot long, is held in the spear-thrower's throwing hand, so that the spear-thrower is, in fact, *slinging* the atlatl to give his spear added velocity and, I would assume, added accuracy. That's what an atlatl is."

". . . Okay."

"*Or,* in fact, an atlatl is that protective area at the bottom of car's stick-shift—"

Mia snickers. "Uh-huh."

"—accordion-like, in the fact that it has *tiers,* usually made out of rubber, and it is *out* of that—out of the atlatl—that the stick-shift arises. I don't know what the American equivalent would be, but in European sports cars that's what it's called. The stick-shift base."

"In a Triumph or Fiat."

"Precisely."

Mia laughs. "No atlatls in Fords."

"No."

"That's fabulous." Mia wipes her eyes. "Mmm . . . I'll go with . . . definition number one."

"You are correct."

She is fully present again (she'd hoped the game would *diminish* the sexual tension), and her Irish green eyes dance as she thinks of a word you won't know. "Okay. I have one. Do you know what a troglodyte is?"

"Hmm . . . no. Don't believe so."

"Okay, a troglodyte is either . . . a prearchaic insect—a *beetle* sort of insect—found in African jungles."

You put a finger to your pursed lips.

"*What?*" she asks.

"No, go ahead. You're doing fine."

"*Or* . . . a troglodyte is a metaphor used for—the *denotation* of the word is 'an ancient cave dweller,' but the *connotation* now is like a Luddite, someone who is fearful of technology."

You hold up two fingers.

"You knew."

"Nope. Score's tied," you say. "Next word: *Loupe.* A photography term. A loupe refers to the small plastic apparatus within which is a magnifying lens, so that a photographer or a magazine editor or jeweler can more closely examine—or *through* which one of those guys can more closely examine—"

"'Guys?'"

"—the images—or girls—on—"

"'Girls?'"

"—or women—on a proof sheet. It's called a loupe. It's sort of the same size as the image on the contact sheet and *loops* around it, I guess. But that's not what a loop is."

"No?"

"Oh no. A loop, in fact—"

"Do tell."

"—is a cooking term that refers to a unit of one hundred rotations of a whisk—one hundred *beats* of a whisk—when preparing a sauce or eggs, whatever it might be. So, if the recipe calls for, say, the flan or omelet to be *looped* three times, that simply means that it needs to be beaten three times a loop, which is three hundred times."

Mia's snort draws looks from a neighboring table, which prompts a louder snort from both of you. She covers her face with her napkin and waves her hand for mercy as the game dissolves into laughter.

After composing yourselves and paying the check (without ordering dessert), you place your coat around Mia's shoulders and take her hand for the short stroll through the narrow lanes of the medina back to the pasha's villa. Even though it's after midnight, several of the souks surrounding Place Prince Moulay el-Hassan are still open. As you pass the now-empty café where you met Motroet this morning, the turbaned owner of a spice shop hobbles out of the darkness, and with a perverse cackle, plants on Mia's upper arm a foot-long lizard, which you pluck away by its tail before Mia even knows that it's there.

As you round the corner, you squeeze Mia's right hand—her ring hand. Behind you, an Arabic conversation in the shadows is interrupted by a woman's giggle. Overhead a cat meows. In a dark alley near the villa, you suddenly spin Mia around and press her against the damp stone wall. Hands clamped to her slender arms, you kiss her neck and mouth, both of you moaning and pulling tighter, startled by the intensity and heat of the embrace. When you eventually lean back to catch your breath, Mia's eyes are still closed, and though she smiles and her hands continue to stroke your waist, she whispers, as she gradually inches herself away from you, "I think I need a cigarette."

You adjust the coat around Mia's shoulders and lead her by the hand around the corner. Her head is lowered against your chest—and her eyes are closed once more—as you knock on the Riad al-Madina's locked entrance. You thank the young Berber valet, his thick black hair mussed from his pillow, as he drowsily unbolts the hotel entrance, yawns, and without prompting gives to you and Mia your respective room keys. Save for the bathroom candle in room 7 and Ahmed's torch-lamp behind the front desk, all the villa is dark.

Silently, you escort Mia directly up the stairs to the third floor. As soon as you enter her room—still uncertain of your intentions—you excuse yourself to the bathroom.

Mia hangs up your coat and with a complicated sigh lowers herself onto the edge of her bed, pushing on the mattress as if browsing in a bed store. With a match she lights the votive candle resting on her nightstand, cupping the flame with a palm as she situates the candle between the roses and her Thomas Aquinas biography. The blue shutters to the two French windows overlooking the medina have blown open. Plaintive-sounding buoy-groans from a lone trawler fishing under the stars waft with the breeze over the medina rooftops. From where she sits, Mia can see the bottom half of the moon. Although she's sober and less sleepy than she was an hour ago, her head swims as she gazes through the white muslin draped over the four-poster bed.

Staring at the closed bathroom door as you continue to wash your hands and face, Mia wonders: What would Brian Castle,

Lutheran minister and occasional swing-dance partner (who kissed her good-bye after driving her to the Austin airport when she flew to Guatemala), say about her present imbroglio? Has she betrayed Brian? Surely she must have, if for no other reason than he doesn't know that she's here. What would Monsignor Olinski say? If she loses her head, and thus her faith in the sanctity of romantic love, who would she more egregiously betray? God or herself?

Mia debates whether upon your exit from the bathroom you should find her standing safely beside the bed or seductively tucked beneath its covers. She compromises by assuming a side-saddle posture atop the red-and-gold quilt. Subconsciously inspired by the young woman sitting on the shore in John Singer Sargent's 1909 oil painting *The Black Brook,* a print of which hangs on a wall in the UT graduate-student art library, Mia sits stiffly upright and leans on her right haunch, eyes lowered, head cocked demurely, coyly, as if listening to the babbling stream of the bathroom faucet, trembling hands clasped on her left knee, in a fashion that she trusts is at once languorous and feminine.

Perched thus on the middle of her bed beneath the slowly circling ceiling fan, a pillow against her hip, the lone candle sputtering on the nightstand, Mia takes a deep breath and waits. "Could I marry this man?" she asks. She recalls her first impression of you in Woodstock, sitting alone in the very rear of the meditation hall, self-conscious, working hard to look relaxed, a sweet lost soul embarrassed to make public the noble pursuits of his heart. "God made us as we are," she reminds herself. "Isn't the one unforgivable sin to not fully live our lives?"

When you come out of the bathroom, you push away the white scrim and, with your sandals still on, join Mia on her bed. You like how she looks in your shirt. Sitting cross-legged facing her, close enough to feel the heat of her breath, you see that the wine, the walk from the café, and the brief kissing session in the alley have brought a sheen to her sun-reddened cheeks.

"If I were a tree," Mia announces, "I fear that all my life would be in the leaves."

Nodding sagely, you respond, "I have no idea what that means."

"Neither do I." Mia looks you straight in the eye and whispers, "Right now—us—is this the truth, Carter? Is this real?"

You lean over to smooth Mia's hair, kiss her cheek. Warmth spreads through your loins. "I would say yes. It certainly feels like it."

Closing her eyes but tensing, Mia asks, "Should we smoke a cigarette, do you think?"

You lean back. "I'll leave you the pack. I'm gonna call it a night."

". . . Really?"

"Really. It's getting late." You smile and pat Mia's hip, stand, head for the door. "Thanks for all your help today. You were great."

"Yeah?"

"Yeah. You really were. Listen, why don't you sleep in tomorrow? Get some rest. I'll meet you in the courtyard for lunch around one."

"Are you sure?"

"Yeah."

After placing the pack of cigarettes on the dresser, you open the door, step out onto the balcony.

". . . Carter?"

"Hmm?"

". . . Thanks."

You offer a little bow and then wink. "Sleep well."

"You too."

You decide to spend Good Friday morning drifting with your Leica through the high-walled lanes of Essaouira's medina. As you leave the villa, Mia is sitting barefoot on her balcony reading and smoking one of your cigarettes, still wearing the billowy white shirt you lent her last evening. Smiling contentedly, not needing to say a word, you feel yourself float down the stairs and stroll across the courtyard, where the bubbling central fountain is filled with dozens of day-old red rose petals. When you turn to look back up at the third-floor balcony, you see—with a surge of affection that brings with it a sigh of happiness—that Mia's eyes are locked on you, and remain locked on you—unblinking, fully alive, confident enough not to turn away—even as you lift your camera and press the shutter.

Upwind from the beach, free from the smoke that comes with the evening food-stall grills, the medina's morning air smells pleasantly of orange blossoms and coconut oil. Every few minutes during your walk you pause, lower yourself onto your haunches, and take in through your lens the various vignettes unfolding around you: An outdoor barber snipping the thinning gray hair of a dozing Sufi cleric bibbed beneath a white bed sheet. *Click.* Two Portuguese brothers, black-haired and muscular, surrounded by powdery heaps of saffron, crushed licorice root, and dried crocus flowers, leaning with concentration over a backgammon board, the boys' scale, mortar, and pestle hidden beneath their table. *Click.* A parrot in a brass cage swinging on a clothesline slung between a pair of opposing fourth-story windows. *Click.* Near the square, watched by a semicircle of tourists, an acrobat troupe juggling and somersaulting and singing in Arabic across an arrangement of nine burnt-orange kilims. *Click.* A purring black cat tiptoeing across the long rows of neatly paired sandals outside the proscenium-arched entrance to a mosque. *Click.* A group of Moroccan schoolchildren who pose for you in a giddy, arm-linked cluster. *Click.*

As you turn the last corner of the lane on your return to the villa, a barefoot fisherman sloshes the red-stained water from a bucket of baby eels into the alley where last night you kissed Mia.

Click.

The muezzins conclude their call for early afternoon prayer as you secure the Leica's lens cap and circle around the courtyard's potted palms and stone columns, past a pair of wicker baskets piled high with lemons, and a lone table of European tea-drinkers who smile and raise their cups as you ascend the stairs. When you knock on her door, you see that Mia has already packed and is perched cross-legged, still barefoot, on the unmade bed beneath the parted canopy. Her hair is slicked back from a bath. After you drop the Leica and camera bag on the mattress, she asks, "When should we get ready to leave?"

"There's no pressing need to hurry back to Marrakesh—we're not scheduled to meet up with the soccer team for the fashion shoot until tomorrow afternoon." You glance at your watch. It's almost one and neither of you has eaten since dinner last night. "Are you getting hungry?"

"Not yet. You?"

"Nah, I'm good. Though I could use a cigarette."

Mia grins and tosses you the pack. Flywheels of affection and desire twirl behind her eyes. "Did you take some good pictures?"

"Hope so."

Mia lifts the lit cigarette from your hand and indulges herself with a puff. Coughing, patting her chest as she hands the cigarette back, she says, teary-eyed, "I haven't yet quite figured out the appeal of these things."

You look at your watch again. "I'll meet you downstairs in twenty minutes."

"Righty-oh."

Back in your room, you hum as you pull your Tumi from the closet and start rolling up your clothes, and you're still humming as you amble down the stairs to the front desk and settle the bill. The two nights in Essaouira have flown by. As the manager phones the Dar al-Assad to confirm your return, you lean against her desk in a haze of bewilderment and joy. After you hand him the keys to the room and Renault, Ahmed, the villa's young valet, bounds up the stairs to get the Tumi and five cases of photo equipment. Pinching your waist as she sneaks up from behind, Mia takes your hand and follows you across the terrace, pausing to inhale the fragrance of the roses floating in the fountain and for one final look at your ivy-strewn balcony, pocketing a tiny loosened blue floor tile as a souvenir. *"Merci, monsieur"* bids a girl from the kitchen as you exit the villa for the last time.

As you pass through the medina's gated entrance and approach the parking area, you see that the Renault is already running, smoking heavily from the exhaust pipe, and that Ahmed is dancing his shoulders in the driver's seat, thoroughly enjoying his attempt to warm the engine for you. You and Mia stop in front of the car, and the boy smiles, gives you a thumbs up through the windshield, and races the motor so loudly that you and Mia let go of each other's hands to cover your ears. "Okay, okay," you shout at Ahmed, slicing your throat with a finger until he kills the engine. You move around the side of the car towards the opened trunk, chuckling and shaking your head, ears ringing, and you note that the last in the line of Anvils has flopped over sideways into a puddle. Though you lower your head and pinch the bridge of your nose, you say nothing.

After pocketing your tip, the boy jogs back towards the medina. Mia bends down to pick up the soaked photo case. The crunching of gravel in the palm-tree shadows directs your attention to three kaftan-clad Moroccans—an elderly father, his bearded son, and a tall, darker-skinned Berber who has joined them with hopes of hitching a ride back to his village near Tafraoute. They cautiously advance towards the Renault with their right palms placed respectfully against their chests. All three men wear sandals and white, sweat-stained Koofi skull caps. The middle-aged son nods to Mia as she stands on the other side of the car. His brown eyes are nervous but steady as he steps forward and asks in a mix of Arabic and French if you'd be willing to drive them as far east as you intend to travel today. Though you make out "Marrakesh" and gather that the men want a lift, you shrug to indicate that you don't understand what they're asking, glancing uneasily at the long black knife-handle protruding from a sheepskin bag draped over the Berber's bony shoulder. "Hey, Mia—can you help me out over here?"

After a brief discussion in halting French, Mia explains to you that the three Muslims have no money and are stuck without a ride back to their village of Aztendara.

"Aztendara?"

Mia shrugs. "That's what it sounded like."

You whisper, "What about the tall dude?" You look away from the Berber and grin awkwardly at the gray-haired father, whose leathery brown face is creased by deep wrinkles. You estimate that the old man must be close to eighty. He and his bearded son are as thin as boards and identically stiff-legged.

"Apparently he just wants to go as far as the other two are going," Mia replies. "I don't think they know each other."

"The middle guy's the oldest guy's son?"

"I believe that's what he said, yes."

You unfold your road map across the warmed hood of the rental car and find the tiny town of Aztendara deep in the High Atlas Mountains, 130 kilometers south of Marrakesh. You glance at your watch and then back up at the tall, gaunt-looking Berber—surely if he intends to do you harm, his weapon would be concealed. Although Aztendara is considerably out of the way, you like the idea of driving into the High Atlas Mountains in a car filled with real live Moroccans. Mia seems comfortable enough with the idea. And the mountain road might give you an opportunity to use your new zoom lens. "You're fine with this?" you ask Mia, who nods without hesitation. "Okay—why not?" You fold the map back up, secure your sunglasses, and gesture for the trio of Moroccans to climb into the Renault's back seat. "Next stop, gentlemen: Aztendara."

• • •

For the first hour the five of you drive east on the road to Marrakesh in comfortable silence, watching through the dusty windows as the flat Moroccan landscape whizzes past. The afternoon sky is perfectly blue and cloudless, and there is little oncoming traffic with which to contend. Though you can get nothing on the radio other than static, and the temperamental ten-year-old Renault's engine rattles whenever you accelerate, and your lower back aches from hauling the photo equipment along the beach yesterday, and you are self-conscious speaking to Mia within earshot of your non-English-speaking passengers, and then self-conscious when the two of you whisper, all in all you feel pretty damn terrific—perhaps as light and carefree as you've felt in weeks.

The more you think about it, the more you like how last night unfolded. Restraint apparently has its virtues. All day you've been almost magically invigorated, as if a spell on your body has either been cast or broken.

As you climb higher and higher into the Atlas Mountains, the air begins to cool. You downshift to second gear and wind slowly along the Nfis Gorge through the desolate trekkers' hamlet of Imlil, thankful that you pretty much have the narrow road to yourself—at certain spots it would be impossible for two vehicles to pass one another. You reason that the car's creeping pace must account for the good gas mileage—the gauge hasn't moved in over an hour. In the Ourika Valley near the Mizane River, you crane your neck to see the crumbling kasbah on the promontory overhead and then slow the car and crawl through a tiny, unnamed settlement, without electricity or phones, populated solely, it seems, by scraggly juniper trees and untethered mules.

"Some view, huh?" you say, as you drive through the next pass, whose elevation is seven thousand feet. You laugh nervously at how little room there is for error. The road has no shoulder, and the gravel and loose rocks—some large enough to do damage to an oil pan—force you to stay in second gear. You try not to look sideways into the gorge, try not to mind that there are no guardrails, try not to imagine too precisely what causes the death of a person who plunges off a cliff behind the wheel of a four-door sedan filled with gasoline.

As Mia floats her hand out the window, staring at the mountains that surround the car on all four sides on this last stretch to Aztendara, she wonders how long your kindness will last. Your warmth and gentleness seem to her provisional. Though she's grateful for last night, she suspects that you might resent her for it. She fears that muzzling your libido had less to do with her and more with some confounding Buddhist precept, doubts that you're serious about wanting her to visit New York this summer, dreads the prospect of returning to Guatemala, hates feeling out of control like this, hates that she wants you to desire her as much as she does, *really* hates that tomorrow you'll be working with Kiki Holtkamp, with the accent and the breasts and the thick blond hair and those absurd hiking boots. Taking a deep breath, Mia looks down into the rocky valley below, her ears popping, and realizes that she can't see the bottom. She notes with concern that both of your hands are clamped to the steering wheel.

"How ya doing?" you ask.

Mia squints at you beneath her windblown hair. "Why is there no guardrail?"

You smile. "Is my driving making you nervous?"

"No. You're doing fine. It's just—I don't know—this road is spooky high. I don't think I've ever been above the clouds like this."

You lean over and kiss Mia's cheek. When she turns back to the window, relaxing a little, grinning despite herself, she likes that she can feel your gaze lingering on her neck.

The three backseat passengers seem oblivious to the perils of the narrow mountain road. Indeed, every time you glance in the rearview mirror all three of the Moroccans look half asleep.

Khalid Chirat, the elderly gray-haired father, who has never before ridden in a European car, continues to be delighted that Allah would let him cross paths with such a beautiful automobile—and with an American who would allow him to enjoy its plush comfort. Eyes shut, napping lightly, Rouk Chirat, Khalid's forty-five-year-old son and sole heir, continues estimating in his dreams how much of his leatherwork he'd have to sell in Essaouira and Agadir to one day replace his stable of donkeys with a car like this. The young Berber continues staring down at his hands. Though relieved to be moving in the general direction of his village, the Maghreb-born Sunni Muslim—named Tayo by his father—prays that it will take at least another full day to get from Aztendara to Tafraoute, which is ninety kilometers farther to the south. The forlorn twenty-year-old, who speaks little French and works sporadically in his village as a knife-grinder, had been traveling along the coast for a week, selling a season's worth of his uncle's thuya-wood chessboards to the various tourist shops along the way, before losing all of his uncle's profits this morning when he mislaid his clothes bag in the medina. No worse fate could've befallen Tayo or his family: three months' worth of his uncle's revenue—not to mention his own commission and a change of clothes—disappeared into thin air no sooner than he'd turned his back. Though he trusts that Allah will provide, the rattled knife-grinder worries that for his carelessness he'll be forced by his father to leave the village and asked not to return.

Without warning, drying your cramped palms on your thighs, you bring the Renault to a stop in the middle of the mountain road and kill the ignition. "I need a breather," you explain, double-checking the emergency brake, and leaving the car door open in case a vehicle appears around the bend without warning. "Holler if you hear someone coming," you say across the hood to Mia, who walks around the front of the car and puts her arms around your shoulders, embracing you with a kiss to the ear.

"You want to take some pictures?"

You check the time. You assume, inaccurately, that Aztendara is only fifteen or twenty kilometers away. "Good call."

Remaining in the back seat, their hands folded in their laps, the three Moroccans turn and look out the rear window as you take a carbon fiber tripod from the trunk. Atop it you secure a Canon EOS-3, already loaded with film, and with a double snap attach to it your new foot-long USM zoom. You steady the tripod's legs and, with Mia standing quietly at your side, focus through the lens on a distant, snow-covered peak of what you'll later learn is Mount Toubkal, the highest point in all of Morocco.

You shoot two full rolls before closing the trunk and returning to the car's interior. "You gentlemen doing okay back there?" you ask over your shoulder before you attempt, with no success at first, to restart the engine.

"Vous allez bien, derrière?" Mia clarifies for you.

All three men smile and nod.

You're perspiring by the time the gagging car returns to life. Mia works hard not to look relieved as she offers you the water bottle, which you decline with a curt shake of your chin. Though the sputtering Renault is moving forward, it sounds and feels close to stalling. The ache in your lower back returns, and is exacerbated by the odor of gasoline—you fear that pumping the accelerator has flooded the engine.

"You okay?" asks Mia.

The color drains from your face as the car, with a rattling shiver, coughs, gasps, and dies, slowly—silently—rolling to a halt over the popping gravel. ". . . Shit."

"What's wrong? Are we out of gas?"

According to the fuel gauge, you still have half a tank. "I don't think so."

Because of the incline, the car begins inching backwards towards the rocky mountainside. You force the stick-shift back into gear and yank the emergency brake. Once the car is safely stopped, you take a deep breath to calm yourself. Concerned that the car is now angled towards the road's shoulderless edge, you pump the accelerator—fast—and repeatedly turn the ignition, but to no avail. The starter cranks, but the engine refuses to turn over.

"Could we have overheated, do you think?"

You sniff and search the Renault's control panel for red lights. "I don't smell anything." You let go of the key and massage the back of your neck. "This . . . is not good."

You look into the rearview mirror and make eye contact with the three grimly smiling backseat passengers, all of whom are unsure what is happening. The Chirats are so rarely in automobiles, they believe it's possible that stalling like this is routine. The young Berber, who has never owned a car, rarely drives, but occasionally changes the oil on his village's forty-year-old tractor, presumes that either the Renault is out of gas or its fuel-line is clogged. Because of this morning's debacle in the market, however, he is reluctant to voice his diagnosis.

"How far are we from their village?" asks Mia.

"I don't know," you admit. "A ways."

You and Mia lean to the right and scan the gorge and adjacent mountain top in search of anything that looks like civilization. You estimate that you have less than three hours until dusk. Making a mental checklist of available provisions in the car in case the five of you are stuck on this deserted mountain road overnight, you poke and shake your cell phone but are unable to get a dial tone.

"I guess we could wait until somebody comes by," Mia suggests.

"There's nobody *out* here's the problem."

Once you finally figure out how to open the hood, you and Mia stand before the car's hissing innards, hands on hips, squinting from the vaporous heat of the oil-smeared engine block. You haven't the slightest idea what to do—you're a New Yorker who hasn't owned a car in almost a decade, and the maintenance on your one and only motorcycle consisted of occasionally spraying WD-40 on the chain and polishing the exhaust pipes.

You're relieved when the backseat door opens and Tayo joins you beneath the raised hood. Frowning seriously, lightly patting his chest, he steps closer after a moment's hesitation and announces in what little French he knows, *"Je suis mécanicien."*

You look at Mia for a translation.

"He says that he's a mechanic."

Turning back to the long-legged Berber, glancing at his gray hooded kaftan and dirty skull cap, the grime beneath his fingernails, the redness in his tired eyes: "Yeah? You're a mechanic?"

"Oui."

"We're out of gas—right?"

Without prompting, Mia restates, *"Pas d'essence—oui?"*

The young knife-grinder nods with growing confidence. *"Oui. Oui."*

You shrug. "The gauge says we got half a tank." Regardless, you step back against the mountainside as Tayo gently lowers the hood, positions himself behind the steering wheel, and disengages the clutch so that the car rolls backwards—slowly gaining speed—the driver's door flinging wide open. Khalid and Rouk, who've barely breathed since the Renault died, turn to each other in the back seat and exchange worried looks. Approaching dangerously close to the cliff, the Berber pops the clutch: with a jolt the engine roars to life and propels the Renault forward for thirty meters or so, directly past you and Mia, flattened against the towering rocks, before stalling again.

After two more stop-and-go passes, it becomes clear to you and Tayo both that the rental car is indeed out of gas—or, probably, down to about a pint, which is sipped forward into the engine only when the vehicle rolls downhill.

Out of breath but exhilarated, Tayo hands back the key and confirms: *"Pas d'essence."*

Impressed with the young Moroccan's initiative, you point across the hood in the direction of the upcoming bend and ask, "Aztendara—*oui?* In this direction? The way we're going?"

"*Oui.* Aztendara."

"There's petrol in Aztendara—yes? *Oui?* Petrol?"

"*Oui. Oui.*"

You make a clucking noise with your tongue and nod. "All right," you announce, leaning on the opened driver's door, though Mia is the only one who can understand you, "here's what we're gonna do. The mechanic and I are gonna walk till we find some gas. The three of you stay here with the car. I think that's the safest thing. You keep the key. You've got plenty of food and water, and there's a flashlight in one of the photo cases, in case you need it. I *trust* we'll be back before dark." You kiss Mia's forehead and give her shoulders a squeeze. "If someone comes along, flag 'em down."

"You really think it's out of gas?"

"Yeah. The gauge must be busted." You lower your chin as you meet Mia's eyes. "You okay with this?"

". . . I guess so."

"Everything's gonna be fine," you assure her, lowering your sunglasses and squaring your shoulders. "This is the *adventure* part of adventure travel."

"Do you want to take some water?" she asks meekly.

"Nah. You keep it. Everything's gonna be fine. We'll be back before you know it."

An arduous hour later you and the Berber finally stop to rest. Both of you are soaked with sweat. Winded from the altitude and incline, you've been lagging several steps behind and are growing increasingly dispirited not to have seen any signs of life. *Where the hell is Aztendara?* It was foolish not to bring water. And your cigarette habit is killing you.

Tayo squats in the shade beneath a boulder with the hood of his kaftan pulled forward over his head and his eyes averted. He takes a bruised apple from the sheepskin bag slung over his shoulder and slices it in two, worried that his bravado back at the car might be leading to further trouble. Popping the clutch to start an engine was a trick he'd performed solely with his village's old tractor—initially he wasn't even sure which of the three foot pedals operated the Renault's brake. Though he wanted to impress you and your American wife, he fears that he's not only led you to believe that he knows more about cars than he actually does, but that he knows where the two of you are heading. Falling back on his native Arabic, the young knife-grinder—an *unemployed* knife-grinder, he reminds himself miserably—looks up and says, with half-hearted hope, that surely the two of you will soon come upon the village.

You shrug, unsure of what he's said. You note nervously the length of the glistening blade and wave off his invitation to share the fruit.

"No English, huh?" you mumble over your shoulder, once the two of you start trudging forward again. "You just parlay-voo French. And you're a mechanic, right? You work in a garage? *Voo un mechanique, oui?*"

You raise your fists and pretend to turn a steering wheel.

The Berber smiles thinly. *". . . Oui."*

You plod around the next bend, working hard to stay ahead of the young Moroccan. Both of you are determined to keep moving until you reach Aztendara. The crumbling road is steep enough for you to push during each step with both palms against your knee.

After a few more minutes, you stop, straighten, and listen to what sounds like an approaching engine. *Could it be?* You turn around. You and the knife-grinder wave both arms overhead until a dusty red-and-white diesel truck, loaded with rattling racks of empty cola bottles, squeals its brakes and rumbles to a halt.

You hop onto the truck's rusty running board. "We're from that car you passed a few miles back that ran out of gas," you shout over the smoky muffler. The Algerian-born driver, who speaks neither French nor English and is sweating profusely beneath his oil-smeared *dupatta* headwrap, shrugs. "*Petrol, petrol*—back that way, five miles or so," you explain, holding onto his half-lowered window with one hand, and with the other wagging your money clip. The driver continues shrugging, though you sense he knows exactly what you're talking about and is abashed for having not bothered to stop.

After Tayo clarifies your predicament in Arabic, he turns and indicates with ten flashes of his long brown hands that you must pay the driver one hundred dirham. You snort with disbelief at the pirate's fee but shake your head and follow the slope-shouldered driver around to the back of his truck, where he unstraps from beneath the spare tire a twenty-gallon plastic container of diesel fuel and sloppily fills eight empty twelve-ounce cola bottles.

Ninety minutes later, struggling with your share of the sloshing bottles in various configurations of your sweat-slicked fingers, dirt-grimed and dehydrated, virtually stumbling from exhaustion, you're greeted with applause and a hug of relief from Mia, who hops down from the Renault's purple hood when she sees you and Tayo approaching.

Rouk and Khalid have not moved from the back seat.

The young Berber walks directly to the side of the car and empties his four bottles into the gas tank. When he glances over his shoulder, you give him a weary thumbs up. You draw an arm across your mouth after gulping the water Mia offers, and you admit to her that you fear this might not work. "When we were walking, I think he was trying to tell me that this diesel fuel could screw up the Renault's engine."

Once Tayo finishes pouring in the remaining four bottles of fuel, you hand him the water jug. "If we go slow, we can make it to Aztendara—yes?" You mime driving the car in first gear. "Very careful—*oui?*"

The knife-grinder crosses his arms, nods his head unsurely.

You assume that the Berber grew up in these mountains, that he's well-acquainted with the terrain, knows where to go to get a tankful of proper unleaded gasoline. And with French cars popular in Morocco, you trust that he, as a Moroccan mechanic, must be familiar with how Renaults handle—at least more so than you are—and thus decide to defer to his driving skills, which, presumably, go hand in hand with his employment in a garage. Besides, you could use a nap.

With an extended palm, you invite Tayo to get into the driver's seat and try the ignition.

"I insist," you say when he hesitates.

The refueled rental car starts up with his first attempt, which surprises no one more than the young knife-grinder. While the car sputters but remains alive, you jump into the back next to Rouk and his father and grab hold of the headrest. "Let's do it," you say, drumming the padded cushion.

Mia frowns, clears her throat. Already buckled up in the front passenger seat, she's perplexed by your choice not to drive, and concerned by the Berber's odd behavior. He looks as wide-eyed as a boy given the controls of a spaceship. But she's reluctant to question your decision out loud, especially in front of three other men, so she bites her lip, says a little prayer, and discreetly tightens her seat belt.

Tayo is even more perplexed. Although he's never before attempted to drive a vehicle this fast or powerful, and certainly not on a narrow mountain road, after the disgrace of losing his uncle's money in Essaouira he's eager to prove himself. And he's flattered by your trust.

The young Berber looks down and presses the gas pedal hard with his sandal, and the car jerks forward so dramatically that Mia's head snaps back against her headrest. With the sheepskin bag still slung around his neck, the adrenaline-fueled knife-grinder forces the whirring Renault into second gear without using the brake or clutch, and accelerates. He leans towards the windshield, eyes set. His bony shoulders are so tense beneath his kaftan that they almost touch his ears.

On the first turn, which the young Moroccan takes without slowing, both rear tires momentarily lose their grip on the road, gray dust rising as the speeding car corrects itself.

Mia closes her eyes.

Blinking, you murmur, "Whoa."

Alarmed by the car's increasing velocity, Mia secures her right elbow on the window frame, reaches up and grabs hold of the roof.

"How ya doing up there?" you shout, the wind rushing through the windows.

"Okay . . . okay," replies Mia, lifting a little from her seat. "Should he be going this fast, Carter?"

The straining engine sounds like it's about to explode.

You pull yourself forward and look at the speedometer: though it's still in second gear, the furiously vibrating rental car is going seventy-five kilometers an hour. The tachometer is well into the red.

Tayo's long brown fingers are squeezed so tightly around the steering wheel that his knuckles have turned white.

You glance into the gorge. "Uh . . . no," you answer dully, grabbing hold of the driver's seat headrest, the color draining from your face again, as the out-of-control Renault loses traction on the turn, slides sideways across the gravel, fishtails towards the cliff's edge, and flips.

12

SWIRLING SULTAN AND COBRA TONGUES, camel's hump and parrot dung. *Something* like that." Mia listens to herself repeat the rhyme, her first-person perspective shifting to third as her awareness comes close to catapulting itself from her traumatized body. She can still touch her torso's front and back, still wiggle all ten fingers and all ten toes, but there seems to be nothing inside of her, nothing between the bones, and as she hears herself explain from a distant part of her brain what has happened, she feels uncertain whether she's doing the telling or only listening, if her death has already occurred or is about to.

"'Swirling sultan and cobra tongues, camel's hump and parrot dung.' What does that *mean?*"

Upended, hanging upside down from her seat belt, Mia drowsily smacks and stretches her dried lips into a yawning, teeth-baring *O,* still unable to swallow the metal taste stuck on her cotton-mouthed tongue. Though most of her body has gone numb, she's thankful that she's not in much pain.

"Swirling sultan and cobra tongues, camel's hump and parrot dung. Who on earth is *singing* that?

"Oh . . . that's *me.*"

Mia closes her eyes and continues letting go of her body. *Take me if you're ready*, she whispers to Jesus, her voice lifting up farther, rising like a smile: *Here I am, here we are, here I am with you.* She surrenders herself to the warmth—a kind of bathing within the darkness—and from the center of the warmth she sees a light, and in the center of the light she's an infant again, as naked and pink as the day she was born, exactly seven months old, splashing in warm bathwater pouring hard from the spigot. She catches her breath as her father lifts her from the suds and tosses her gently towards the bathroom ceiling. Weightless, suspended in air, she catches her breath again and looks down, eyes wide—there's nothing to hold on to!—and with a scared smile of hope feels her body begin to fall back into the warm water and the safety of her father's hands.

Next to her, loosened from his seat belt, no longer hanging upside down, the frightened and humiliated Berber mouths a noise that goes *ungh ungh ungh ungh ungh ungh,* cutting himself badly on the broken window as he crawls from the overturned car. Stumbling to his feet, losing a sandal, he jogs sobbing through the gray dust cloud still hovering over the wreck, trotting and flailing his arms up the road in the direction the car had been aimed before he lost control.

Your first thought: *He's not going for help.* The second: *He's not coming back.*

You stay focused, fully conscious, strangely calm, crouched and unmoving on the ceiling of the flipped Renault. Your head and left shoulder hurt from hitting the window frame as the car's slow roll slung you upside down, but it doesn't feel as if anything's been broken and your breath remains steady and relatively relaxed. The reading lamp—somehow illuminated—lies between your feet. The stick-shift and steering wheel descend from above. Though your fingernails are dug into the headrest pad, to which you clung as the car overturned, they remain there by choice as you decide how best to proceed. You sniff again: the smell of gas is getting worse. The car has been wrong-side up for no more than ten or fifteen seconds, you estimate. The engine is still running—*roaring,* actually—the two front tires are engaged and spinning madly in second gear, searching for something to grip. Though you're concerned about the gas tank exploding, you realize that your movements must be mindful. *Stay calm.* You lower your breath back into your belly, let go of the headrest and squeeze a shoulder between the two front seats, fumbling with the key until you manage to kill the ignition.

Behind you: the white of skull caps and kaftans as Khalid and Rouk climb through the other backseat window. You can only see the men's legs and feet and therefore don't notice that once they stand and turn back to face the overturned car, Khalid shakes his head in disbelief, mumbles a prayer, and thumbs a short strand of his cedarwood prayer beads. His cheek is bleeding lightly, and his son pulls him by the arm away from the cliff. Though bewildered, neither man is seriously injured.

The windshield is fissured from the car's upended tonnage. Gray dust and soot are still settling over the gravel-strewn road and groaning chassis. Mia continues to hang upside down, mumbling to herself, her eyes closed, her head tilted at an unnatural-looking angle. Her right upper arm sticks out the lowered front passenger window, perpendicular to the frame, and her right hand clutches the roof.

The air crackles as you pull yourself through the broken backseat window and push yourself to your feet. You trot around the front, drop to your belly on Mia's side, and confirm that since she was holding on to the roof as the Renault rolled over, Mia's trapped hand is now being crushed by the car's weight.

You reach into the interior and turn Mia's face. Her skin is cold. "Mia," you whisper. *"Mia."*

When you get no answer, you stand and motion for Khalid and Rouk to join you with their shoulders against the chassis. The three of you push and push and push, pleading for a surge of adrenaline that refuses to come. Finally you must stop: the Renault won't budge. Out of breath, his kaftan soaked through with sweat, close to tears from the sight of Mia's pale arm and pale wrist and what little is visible of her pale hand, Rouk continues to shove upwards against the door frame by himself, his sandals slipping in the dirt and gravel, until his father lays a hand on his shoulder.

You fall to the ground again, reach through the window, and attempt to rouse Mia by squeezing her arm. Her face is red and swollen. Her lips are parted. "Mia. Can you hear me?" At the touch of your hand her eyes flutter. She feels you reaching through her dream as the front doorbell rings, hearing herself shout to her mother in the kitchen, *I'll get that—it's for me.* She flings the front door open with both hands. The Louisiana heat whooshes in and slaps her hard in the face with a blast that brings a splash of bright light and burning pain into her flattened hand, a fiery lava-like sensation that snaps awareness back into her body with a sharp intake of breath. "Oh . . . *my God,*" she gasps. She blinks her eyes as she, for the second time, realizes with alarm where she is, what has happened—that she's hanging upside down in the seat belt with her arm out the window and her palm compressed beneath the weight of the car.

Stretched across the road flat on your belly, your feet hanging over the cliff, you scratch and claw and dig into the loose tarmacadam surface, trying to make space beneath Mia's knuckles. "You're gonna be okay," you assure her. "We're getting you out."

"Get it off. Get it off."

"Hang in there."

"Oh God—get it off. Please get it off."

"It's okay."

As her voice trails off, Mia closes her eyes. Her lips continue to move, but you can't make out what she's trying to say.

"Keep your eyes open, Mia. That's *important.* You gotta stay awake."

Mia nods, but her eyes remain shut. She clenches her teeth and begins blowing out breaths like a woman in labor.

"That's good," you whisper, still scratching into the tarmac between her hand and the rooftop. "Keep pushing the breaths out. Slow 'em down a bit. Yeah. Just like that. That's good. Just let 'em go."

You hear a truck approaching from around the bend. Khalid and Rouk move away from the cliff and turn to see what's coming. Still lying on the ground, clawed fingers torn and bleeding, you glance over your shoulder as a dusty white Ford pickup truck brakes to a halt within an arm's length of the shadow cast eastward by the Renault's rear bumper. With the engine still running, the truck's driver—a middle-aged Moroccan construction worker en route to Aztendara—secures the emergency brake, swings open his door, and strolls over to the wreck, surveying the scene with a casualness that suggests that an automobile lying on its roof in the middle of the High Atlas Mountains is for him a routine sight. He tucks his white, long-sleeved shirt into white painter's pants speckled with dirt and various shades of dried paint. He eyes with interest the Renault's cracked windshield and exposed underbelly.

Filthy, scraped on your forearms by the broken glass and gravel, you push yourself to your feet and join the truck driver and the two Chirats with their shoulders against the side of the rental car. On the count of three the four of you shove upwards. This time you manage to get better traction, and with the help of the additional pair of legs the automobile lifts from Mia's hand.

The three Moroccans stand back, watching silently. Khalid continues fingering his prayer beads as you drop to the ground and slide halfway through the window to unbuckle Mia's seat belt. Using all of your arm and upper-body strength, you lower Mia sideways and pull her, awkwardly, shoulders first, from the car's interior. As you stand and lift her to her feet, she groans and retracts the wounded hand to her chest before going limp in your arms, dead weight. Her face is ashen. Her head lolls to the side. "Mia—you gotta stay awake." You lower her to the ground and kneel beside her shoulders, cradling her head in your hands. Her lips have turned blue.

"Mia?" You smack both sides of her face with your fingertips. You can't tell if she's breathing. *"Mia?"*

You lower an ear towards her mouth and listen.

Nothing.

"—Mia?"

Rouk steps forward and tentatively offers a water bottle. "No—no water," you tell him, shaking your head emphatically. You fear that she's gone into shock. You search the road before pointing towards the Berber's sheepskin bag and knife. "Yes—*that.*" Rouk hands you the bag, and you discard its contents and roll the sheepskin into a ball and secure it beneath Mia's head. You move down to her feet, lifting and holding them by the ankles near your chest so that gravity will aid the flow of blood to her brain. "She needs a doctor," you say, beseeching the construction worker with your eyes as you struggle to keep Mia's feet as high as possible. You gesture with your chin down the road. "*Hos*-pital? *Oui?* Do you understand? Do you know where we can find a doctor? Yes?"

The driver says nothing as you lift and carry Mia in your arms to his pickup truck. Her cheek bounces limply against your shoulder, and her eyes remain closed as you buckle her into the truck's passenger seat, her body sagging against the closed door. Calmly, the driver climbs in on the other side, takes his seat before the steering wheel and engages the clutch. "You know where to go?" you ask, out of breath, through the lowered window. Again, no response other than an odd half-smile. Quickly you assist Rouk and his father up and over the pickup's tailgate into the empty flatbed. You squeeze Khalid's bony shoulders, stare deeply into his dark brown eyes. "Are you okay?" you ask, nodding until the old man pats your arm.

Hands on your hips, breathing hard, you turn back and stare at the Renault's crumpled trunk. It contains everything you've brought with you to Morocco: your clothes, your laptop computer, tens of thousands of dollars' worth of camera equipment, all the film you shot in Essaouira. Much of your life as you presently know it is in that trunk. If you leave without it, most likely you'll never see any of it again. But you need to get Mia to a hospital, and soon—there's no time to unload *any* of your belongings. "Shit shit shit," you mutter, running over to the Renault's front passenger window, dropping to your knees to grab from the glove compartment your money clip, an unopened bottle of water, and the two passports. You leave the key in the ignition. To the contents in the trunk you say good-bye.

Ten minutes later: "You *must* stay awake—okay?" Squeezed in the pickup truck's front seat between Mia and the driver, you tighten your arm around Mia's shoulder and pat her cheek after her head falls forward, passing . . . right . . . *now* . . . the spot where less than two hours ago you and the Berber flagged down the cola truck and bought the diesel-laced gasoline that fueled much of your present predicament. You gaze at Mia's face with tender sympathy and raise the volume of your voice: "Are you with me on that?"

". . . Mm-hmm."

"Yeah? How old are you, Mia?"

When she doesn't answer, you turn down the truck's radio, which is playing a surreally frenetic Arabic soundtrack of clarinets and tambourines.

"Mia—tell me how old you are."

". . . Hmm?"

"How old are you?"

". . . A hundred and eight."

"Where are we?"

Dully, softly, she begins to cry and asks, "Am I going to lose my hand, Carter? Are they going to have to take my hand?"

She winces as you lift her right palm for a look. Gingerly you turn the hand over. If there are broken bones, none of them has pierced the skin. The flesh across her knuckles and wrist is torn and bloodied—the wounds are deep and in need of medical attention—but you sense that the damage is repairable. "Can you wiggle your fingers?"

The movement causes Mia to scrunch her face and moan—but this is good: pain will keep her conscious.

"You're gonna be okay," you tell her, brushing away her tears. "It's not that bad. You didn't hit your head, did you?"

" . . . No."

"Did you hit your neck or chest or anything against the windshield? All of your insides feel like they're where they're supposed to be?"

Mia nods sleepily and shuts her eyes again, her head bouncing along with the bumps in the road.

"Mia—" With three fingertips you slap a spot on Mia's injured hand, just below her grandmother's wedding ring, where the ripped skin is pink and oozy.

". . . Ouch."

"Stay awake, Mia."

When again you smack her torn knuckles, she raises her head and opens her eyes.

"*Damn,* Carter."

Thirty minutes pass without any signs of civilization. The truck driver's forearm remains draped nonchalantly over the top of the steering wheel, and with his free hand he occasionally grooms his thick black mustache. Slowly but steadily he heads east. At a fork in the road at the crest of the mountain he steers away from the direction of Aztendara onto an old caravan trail that descends into a valley to the north, glancing over his shoulder at the two passengers bouncing in the flatbed. Following a pair of faintly visible Jeep tracks carved into the red dust, he maneuvers the old Ford pickup over the desert terrain, between wilting palm trees and sparse patches of brown grass, slowing as he reaches a parched plateau. The valley's dry, rocky terrain appears almost lunar to you.

In the near distance are some primitive buildings: the village of Amen, a tiny, medieval-looking hamlet named, with more wishful thinking than irony, after the Arabic word for water. As the pickup truck comes to a stop, you glance sideways and ask incredulously, "There's a hospital here?"

At first glance Amen seems to consist of little more than a dozen or so adobe huts clustered along the road, a small souk (which is boarded up), and a handful of thatch-roofed farmhouses scattered on the slope of the mountain. There are no other cars or trucks anywhere in sight. No telephone or power lines. Several stray goats, baying for food, gather around the front of the Ford as it idles near a square, cinder-block building, easily the most modern structure around, though its two windows are without screens or shutters and its rusty tin roof is peeling at one of the corners. With a palm the driver toots the truck's horn.

Beneath a faded red cross painted above the narrow doorway appears a young Moroccan woman, wearing a long white smock—a makeshift nurse's uniform. Her black hair is tied in a bun, and she shields her eyes from the setting sun and watches from the cement doorstep as you help the still-woozy Mia from the truck.

"Do you want me to carry you?" you ask.

Mia smiles gamely. "May I have a rain check?"

Clutching her bloodied hand near her throat, her face furrowed in pain, she allows you to guide her past the nurse and through the door into what is apparently a combination one-chair barbershop and medical clinic. The crude cinder-block building, which is unlit, surprisingly cool in temperature, and smells of kerosene, is divided into two halves: To the right are a barber's stool, a horsehair broom, and a circular wall-mirror framed by a pair of black shears and a folded straight-edge razor, hanging on hooks. To the left, in a slightly larger, more cluttered and darker space, you make out an unmade cot and three small wooden tables, atop the nearest of which lies an infant's scale, a coiled stethoscope, a jar of balsawood tongue depressors, and an uncapped syringe. In a shallow alcove, a curtained drainage hole and plastic bucket half-filled with soapy water serve as the building's toilet facilities. The fumes from the kerosene force you to breathe through your mouth as you take a seat next to Mia on the cot. On the wall across the room, above an unlit lantern, hang a framed photograph of the previous King Mohammed, an Arabic eye chart, and a poster of a Moroccan baby boy being immunized for smallpox.

"Whatever happens, you are *not* getting a shot."

A pair of dusty orange chickens cackle in the doorway. Mia smiles sleepily, blinking back tears as she closes her eyes and lays her head against your chest.

A small crowd gathers outside the clinic to see if you and Mia are wounded badly enough to die. The young woman in the white smock has disappeared—so too the godsend Ford and its enigmatic driver. Through the unscreened window you see across the road a young villager sitting on his haunches before a small house made of yellowish mud, half-hidden in the greasy smoke wafting from a coal-burning cooking brazier. He watches the commotion as he winnows barley stubble, a tethered black goat munching straw at his side. In the nominal shade of the *tizi* trees behind the cluster of curious locals, Rouk and his father kneel side by side. They lower their foreheads to the ground with a prayer of thanks to Allah for keeping them alive. The sight of the two men in full prostration gives you pause. *Just how close did we come to driving off the mountain?*

You stroke Mia's hair. "How are you feeling?"

She shrugs. "I've been better."

"You look beautiful."

"Hmm . . . I think you banged *your* head."

Eventually the nurse returns with a lighter-skinned, Spanish-born "doc-*tor*," who introduces himself as such with an enthusiastic pumping of your hand. You make out only the man's first name: Mañuel. Over his wrinkled trousers and collared green shirt the young medic wears an unbuttoned white barber's coat that smells of hair tonic. Despite his thinning black hair, terrible posture, and a nervous twitch in his left eyelid, you estimate, accurately, that his age is no more than thirty. Ignoring Mia's injury, straining to continue in English, he either gushes that you and Mia are his first American visitors of the year, or that sometime last year he visited America. His rudimentary English fails completely when you ask what kind of medicine he practices.

"She shows no signs of internal injury," you assure him, after describing the details of the wreck and what happened to Mia's hand, "and she doesn't think she hit her skull." To Mia: "Are you allergic to any medicines?" She shakes her head. "No allergies. She may have some broken bones, so if you could X-ray her that would be great."

The medic looks at the cement floor and then over his shoulder at the bucket of water. He's moved back two steps and is perspiring heavily across his upper lip.

"Perhaps you should check her blood pressure?" you suggest.

The young nurse applies a wet cloth to Mia's wounds and then moves away as the Spanish doctor-cum-barber inspects Mia's neck with two of his fingers, closing his eyes as he feels her forehead for signs of fever. "Is she your wife?" he asks, stepping away from the cot.

You and Mia glance at one another. You hesitate, then nod. "Yes."

"Is she with child?"

You shake your head and hold back a smile. "I don't believe so, no."

Without knocking, Amen's imperious, pear-shaped *caid*—the local equivalent of a mayor or administrating chief—enters the cinder-block building, dressed in his most official-looking yellow slippers and saffron-colored djellaba, and in Arabic gruffly addresses the doctor. The nurse appears startled by what she hears. You're made nervous by the round-waisted *caid*'s conspicuous lack of eye contact with either you or Mia—even more so after he departs with a spin of the barber's stool and the discomfited medic sheepishly explains that you and Mia are not to leave the clinic until officers from the Sureté Nationale, Morocco's civil police, summoned by the *caid* from their mountain gendarmerie in Fermoud, arrive to file a report on the accident and the whereabouts of your "missing" rental car.

"The police?"

"They have questions of you. I am sorry. This is all I know."

Night falls. You and Mia have been waiting for hours. Four or five gray-haired villagers, wearing identical beige-colored kaftans with lowered hoods, hover silently around the clinic and the closed souk, their hands clasped behind their backs, their heads collectively turning whenever you move from the doorstep for a look up the road. Since wrapping Mia's wrist with white gauze, the fidgety young doctor has not returned.

The dry evening air is cool and there is little wind. Agitated crickets buzz in the darkness. The interior of the clinic is lit softly by two hissing, moth-shadowed lanterns brought in shortly after dusk by the sweetly smiling nurse, who has returned every half hour to check on Mia. The last time she carried a tray topped with a pot of hot mint tea and a plate of beignets, half of which you gave to Khalid and Rouk, who continue to sit without speaking outside the building against the trunk of a *tizi* tree. The *caid* made clear to them that they too are forbidden to leave. Not that any of you could. The only vehicle to have passed through mountain-locked Amen since the pickup truck's departure was a mule-drawn cart carrying bundled turnips.

Mia continues to rest on the cot curled up on her side, fully dressed, her injured hand tucked beneath her chin: an exhausted and bloodied gamin taking refuge from the night. You are hunkered in the doorway with your chin on your hands and your legs loosely crossed. You've been trying to meditate but find yourself more interested in the magnificence of the Moroccan sky, mesmerized by the blood-orange moon, the bounty of pulsating stars, and the rhythmical, otherworldly sounds spilling out of a pair of hillside, lantern-lit buildings—the two brightest lights in the entire valley. One hut is occupied by village males. The other, pink-mud *dar,* perched a few meters higher on the slope, is occupied by a larger assemblage of village females. For the past half hour the two segregated groups have been responding to the other's chants with vigorous hand-clapping and Arabic song in a kind of ritualized call-and-answer.

You wonder again about the frightened Berber, for whom you feel only pity and sadness—the thought of him cowering alone in the mountains gives you no solace. It was a terrible, *selfish* mistake to let him drive, you realize, and you continue to debate whether it was wrong to pick up hitchhikers in the first place. Without the extra passengers, presumably, you wouldn't have gotten into a wreck. But, then again, had Khalid and Rouk not been along for the ride, chances are the car would still be on Mia's hand.

You glance at your watch for what seems like the hundredth time. In five minutes it will be midnight. The wait for the gendarmes has been interminable. Were Mia in *really* serious shape, you're not certain what you would do. Along with your American Express and Visa cards, you have $180 in American twenties and approximately $200 worth of dirham notes. Though you assume the Renault is a lost cause, you trust that whatever paperwork the rental agency will require for its damage can wait a few days. And you've thought little about the implications of missing the photo shoot in Marrakesh, which is scheduled to begin—you look at your watch yet again—in just over fifteen hours. Your plan is to find a way back to the airport in Casablanca, board the first plane to New York, and get Mia to a hospital as expeditiously as possible. Surely, you trust, the Moroccan police will see that Mia's injuries require more medical attention than Amen's hapless young medic can provide. Beyond making a formal statement about the accident, and perhaps paying a fine for leaving the scene, what more could they want?

Mia rests on her side in the shadows of the cot-side lantern. She's awakened by the distant rhythms of the hillside religious ceremony, and now stares fondly at your profile as you gaze at the sky. "How are you doing over there?" she asks.

"Okay. A little restless. You?"

"Better." She adjusts the pillow. "Do you think we'll be able to get your photo equipment back?"

You shrug. "I don't know. I'm not counting on it."

"Shoot—*shoot.* Carter, I'm so sorry. I feel this is all my doing."

"Please."

Mia blows on the back of her bandaged hand. In the darkness around the cinder-block clinic, crickets continue to chirp and buzz. "You know, I lost all my luggage like this once before," she says. "The summer after my sophomore year in college. A friend from my dorm and I were backpacking through Egypt. She and I were swimming in a pond near our hostel one day—we'd just left Alexandria—when a boy with a knife came up and demanded our backpacks. He couldn't have been more than twelve or thirteen, but the local Egyptian police knew who he was. When they brought him to the police station, the boy said he'd traded our bags for a soccer ball. We were left with nothing but the clothes on our backs and our bathing suits."

"What'd you do?"

"The police gave us three options: Let the boy go. Press charges and wait in Egypt another month for a trial. Or agree to have one of the policemen *dissuade* him from his burgeoning life of crime."

"Which meant?"

"Which meant letting the police tie the boy up with rope, hang him from the ceiling, and beat the bottoms of his feet with a truncheon. And if we agreed to this, we had to *witness* it."

"Damn."

Your attention shifts to a commotion among the elderly men mingling between the clinic and the road: their heads turn in sync to the east as a pair of headlights approaches.

"That must be the police," you announce, standing. "*Finally.* How's your hand?"

"I'm not sure. It feels strange. It doesn't hurt quite so much." Mia struggles to sit up. "But my arm and shoulder are beginning to ache—*ahh*—pretty badly."

You pat your chin. This is not good news. You wonder if the wounds are infected. You turn back in the doorway as a brown-and-white military Jeep rolls to a stop, a pair of village dogs barking and snapping at the tires. The Jeep's interior light clicks on, and the darkened halogen headlights are replaced by red hazard beams silently rotating on the roof. Beneath a black beret, the driver squints at a clipboard propped against the steering wheel.

Over your shoulder you whisper to Mia, "You ever done any acting?"

"In high school I was Town Person Number Three in *Finnian's Rainbow*."

"Perfect. From this moment on you need to be in a great deal of pain, if you know what I mean."

The Jeep doors creak open and the two gendarmes step out. Both are tall, clean-shaven, and solidly built. Neither looks older than twenty or twenty-one. Both pause outside the clinic for a moment to stretch their backs. They wear matching blue uniforms, rakishly cocked black berets and heavy military boots, and carry holstered side arms and black batons. With his arms crossed and legs spread, the driver listens to the *caid* and bed-roused doctor, both of whom have magically reappeared in the clinic's scraggly front courtyard, and are busy embellishing the details of your puzzling, carless arrival in Amen.

After glancing at the doorway, their eyes flickering with distrust, the gendarmes flip on their flashlights and motion with a puffing movement of their left hands for you to step backwards into the clinic. Mia on the cot has assumed a dramatically slumped posture—clutching her bandaged hand, she's clamped her eyes shut and, swaying slightly from side to side, begun to moan. As the gendarmes and their entourage enter the building, you shield your face from the flashlights as Mia's bent figure is briefly illuminated. Her bandaged hand, strategically placed near her forehead for easier viewing, is for several seconds spotlit, though neither gendarme seems particularly concerned about her condition. The *caid* speaks in Arabic to the doctor, who then whispers something to the two gendarmes, which prompts them to look sideways at one another and snort. The driver asks the *caid* another question, in response to which he points a stubby finger at the nurse and grumbles something that causes everyone in the room to grow hushed and turn expectantly in your direction.

Again you're blinded by the flashlights.

"They want to see your papers," the young medic announces.

Squinting: "Okay. Sure, no problem."

In the light from Mia's lantern, the driver examines your passports. Snapping his fingers, the second gendarme makes you raise your hands and interlace them on your head as he searches your pockets. With a surprisingly forceful shove to your shoulder, he spins you around so that you face the wall, and with the sides of a boot he widens the distance between your feet. Mia stops moaning and straightens up. The worried nurse shakes her head in disapproval at how you're being treated.

The Spanish doctor clears his throat and says, "They want to know who is the driver of the missing car."

Over your shoulder you answer, "First of all, the car is not 'missing.' It's wrecked. Secondly, I have no idea—the guy who was driving took off for the hills. He ran." Fingers still interlaced on your head, you gesture with an upward nod of your chin towards Rouk and his father. "I don't think they know who he was either."

"None of you is the driver of the car?"

"That's correct."

The doctor translates this for the gendarmes and *caid* and then glances back. "It is your car though, yes?"

"It was a rental car I got at the airport."

"But you are not the driver?"

"No."

"And where is the driver?"

"I have no idea. Listen—what's this all about? My wife, as you *know* and they can surely *see,* needs to get to a hospital."

After your answers are translated with an apologetic shrug, the *caid* sucks in his gut, grunts, and turns his back and looks at himself in the barber's mirror. Though he harbors no ill will towards you for being an American, he is a recent widower prone to high drama and low forms of mischief—if his speculation that you're a drug smuggler or a spy proves false, at least the proving process shall provide him with some entertainment. He's already spoken twice this evening on his British-made ham radio with the police commandant in Fermoud. In the morning he'll dispatch a wrecker from Aztendara to find and tow your rental car to Amen, after which he'll personally search the trunk and interior for contraband or weapons and file further reports, via his radio, to the Sureté Nationale's regional outpost, though he'll not mention his decision to keep your laptop computer and camera cases at his home.

"Whatever we need to do to get this show on the road," you say, making eye contact with everyone, "let's get it done."

No one moves or speaks. Beneath your sandals the cement floor feels electrified. Your heart is beating so hard you're worried about it giving out on you. Still facing the wall, you glare sideways at the taller gendarme, silently demanding an explanation for the delay. The other gendarme taps his clipboard, pockets the two passports and your money clip, and motions for you, Mia, and the Chirats to follow him outside.

You glance imploringly at the doctor, who shrugs and replies as you and the others are shepherded through the door, "You must go in the Jeep with them to the gendarmerie in Fermoud."

"What?"

"I am sorry. This is all I know."

"You've gotta be kidding."

You shake your head and look up at the moon and stars with open-mouthed wonder as you lead the others, single-file, from the building and crunch across the dusty courtyard towards the caravan trail and Jeep's rotating red lights. Tense and breathy behind you, Mia whispers, "What is going *on,* Carter?"

You feel a wave of vertigo, as if you're watching yourself in a movie that you don't remember making. One of the village dogs continues to bark in the darkness. Scrunching your eyes, trying unsuccessfully to avoid the red hazard beams, you sigh and answer Mia over your shoulder: "It looks like we're being arrested."

After two grueling hours of being squeezed in the military Jeep's tiny back seat, the lining of your cerebellum throbs from impatience, anger, exhaustion, nicotine withdrawal, and lack of oxygen. Because there's so little leg-room, you're turned sideways and are pressed painfully tight against the front seats' metallic-framed backing. Rouk leans his forehead against the ripped upholstery of the driver's headrest, Khalid is jammed halfway behind his son's back, and Mia sits on your lap, her injured arm slung over your shoulder, her cheek pressed against your chest. The bumpy terrain has been jostling her hand so badly that the white gauze is soaked through with blood.

The Jeep's stifling interior—the gendarmes refuse to lower the windows—stinks of the Chirats' unwashed kaftans and the diesel fuel that stains your jeans. You've given up fighting to keep your head from knocking against the empty rifle rack, and are simply working to keep your shoulders and neck loose and relaxed, to *become* the bounces. The entire journey thus far has been over relentlessly rocky ground—the lunar mountain landscape seems to you to have transformed into something apocalyptic. You've not seen a single vehicle, village, or hut since leaving Amen. So uneven and precarious is the narrow road—if you can call it a road—that the gendarmes have stopped the Jeep twice and debated over which crumbling crag they should proceed. To make matters worse, with each of the Jeep's abrupt swerves you relive the sickening sensation of the Renault losing control and lifting into the air. Shielding her face with your hand, you do your best to keep Mia from looking sideways into the seemingly bottomless gorge to the left.

Rouk is fending off nausea. You're not doing much better. From what the otherwise useless medic managed to impart before the Jeep whisked you away, you gathered that you and the others are being transported to the regional gendarmerie in Fermoud, presumably to be questioned about the car wreck. Though still apprehensive about what awaits you at the police station, your initial anxiety about being robbed, shot, and left for dead has dissipated—had crime been the gendarmes' chief intention, chances are they would have forced you from the Jeep during the first half hour. You've only the vaguest notion where you are, but you can tell that you're ascending, because your eardrums keep popping. The steep mountain wall—so close you could reach through the window, if it were open, and touch its protuberances without fully extending your arm—rises so high above you that you can no longer see the moon or much of the sky.

The two gendarmes are proving to be menacing jerks. For no other reason than to frighten you, both times the driver stopped for a cigarette he veered the Jeep directly towards the edge of the shoulderless road and slammed on the brakes, snickering as he killed the headlights. The gendarme in the passenger seat has been especially brusque with Rouk and Khalid, frequently glaring backwards in the rearview mirror and snapping at them in Arabic. You intuit, correctly, that the young policemen disdain you and Mia because they see you as feckless Americans, citizens of a land they know solely from the barracks' television—that they despise your culture's arrogance, its fast-food imperialism, its abject disdain for everything but its own insatiable hunger. In their eyes you are arrogant Westerners who discard a rental car as easily as a McDonald's wrapper. Were they not in uniform, you trust, the crew-cut gendarmes would snatch your Visa and American Express cards and titanium-clasped Seiko and then beat you to a pulp with their batons.

You kiss Mia's sweaty temple, touched by how tough she's being, saddened by all the suffering that you've caused her, about which she has yet to complain. You dry her upper lip with a finger and gently blow on her lowered lids and reddened cheeks. You consider again just how close all of you came to being killed this afternoon, suddenly overwhelmed by the prospect of this woman you hold in your arms no longer being among the living. You kiss Mia's damp cheek again. The thought of her someday dying, as she must, brings tears to your eyes.

Hearing you sniff, she whispers, "Are you okay?"

You pull her tighter. "Mm-hmm."

As you sniff again, Mia presses the side of her face more firmly against your shoulder. "I love you, Carter."

"I love you, too."

The Jeep finally arrives in Fermoud, pop. 5,000, a town on the northern edge of the Ourzazate Valley, around four in the morning. Sunrise is still two hours away, and the dusty, potholed streets are empty. After passing the Es Saada kasbah, a deserted bus station, and several dilapidated hotels and restaurants flanking the town's palm tree–lined central square, the Jeep grinds into first gear and slows to a stop before an orange-lit guard's booth in front of the gendarmerie. You nudge Mia awake.

The driver and guard converse in hushed tones through the Jeep's lowered window. Straightening and adjusting their dirt-smeared kaftans and skull caps, Rouk and Khalid rouse themselves. You dislike the strange look this third gendarme is giving Mia, and are made even more nervous when he steps onto the Jeep's rear bumper and rides with you around the now-unmanned guard hut, back into the deserted street, and into the rear, unlit parking area of an adjacent two-story building. "What is going on?" you ask, but you get no reply. There are no other police vehicles here—no vehicles, period—and there's nothing on the cement building's exterior to indicate what's inside, no windows through which you can get a sense of what awaits you. Clearly, however, this is not the police station.

Guided solely by the light of the moon and the driver's jangling holster, you walk stiff-legged and sore from the Jeep to the building's back door. The other two gendarmes trail behind Khalid, who is so worn out he can barely walk and must be assisted by his son. Mia clutches your hand as the driver knocks twice with his baton against the metal door, which, after almost a full minute, accompanied by an electronic buzz, is eventually unlocked from inside.

The metal door yawns shut behind you with an emphatic deadbolt *thunk*. The three policemen seem startled to find the gendarmerie's commanding officer awaiting them, and quickly come to attention and salute. The commandant sits behind a large wooden desk, one of only two pieces of furniture in a space that looks like a small, unused warehouse. The empty, shadowy chamber is perfectly square—approximately forty by forty feet—and through an open door near the desk is connected to a dimly lit hallway that veers sharply to the right. The bare walls are cement, wet-looking, cold to the touch, and smell of disinfectant. A bare hallway bulb and a reading lamp on the commandant's desk provide the only interior light.

The grim-looking room is made even more ominous by the second piece of furniture: to your right, positioned over a small drainage hole, stripped of its blanket and mattress, metallically skeletal, is a cot. What appear to be leather restraining devices are loosely fastened to each of the bare frame's four rusty legs.

You press three fingertips into your forehead and mutter, "My God."

Mia asks, "*Carter?* Where *are* we?"

". . . It's okay. Just stay calm."

Overcome with fear, succumbing to the terror-muffling drowsiness that often falls over condemned prisoners as they walk to the gallows, Rouk lets go of his father's arm and sinks to the floor against the wall, lowers his head, and covers his face with his knees. In his last life, Rouk's failure in the caravan business led him to move to a village near Mount Hira, on the outskirts of Mecca, where he studied the Koran with a local mullah and progressively surrendered himself to the Five Pillars of Islam. Lucid at the moment of his passing at the age of seventy in December of 1955 (he died reciting the opening surah of the Koran: "Praise be to Allah, Creator of the worlds, the Merciful, the Compassionate, Ruler of the Day of Judgment"), fueled by his karma, the continuum of his consciousness took rebirth in January of 1956 as Khalid's first and only son. With a déjà vu–induced shudder and groan, Rouk recalls the grisly details of the final moments preceding his *first* human death, in 1571, after nine hours of torture in a regional prison in what is now present-day Mauritania, in an interrogation room not unlike this one.

From behind the desk the regional commander glances with little interest at Rouk's crumpled body. As a peasant he is only the appetizer. You and Mia are the entrée, the American main course, for which he has stayed up all night waiting to be served.

The commandant is a large, muscular man with short black hair, a strong nose, a refined tilt to his jaw, and dark brooding eyes—were he not in a Moroccan police uniform, he could be an Arabian sultan or Roman proconsul. On the short sleeves of his crisply pressed blue shirt he wears red epaulets and a tiny red-and-green Moroccan flag. His black beret and gun holster sit neatly on the desktop next to a stack of French paperbacks and a silver pot of mint tea spiked with anisette. He was trained at the Royal Institute for a military career that never materialized, and from 1993 until 1998 he served as the *chargé d'affaires* in the notorious Galaat Magouna Prison, where he presided over the summary executions of political prisoners and Algerian refugees and developed an ironic, self-loathing taste for dark-skinned Saharan prostitutes. He has never married, never led soldiers in combat, never felt comfortable wearing on his chest the gold-crested Distinguished Service badge. He resents terribly this gendarmerie posting in the wasteland of Fermoud, and *loathes* his ragtag company of thirteen gendarmes, most of whom are a third his age and essentially illiterate.

In his last life the commandant was a female black-haired mastiff, a domesticated guard dog, propelled by karma at her death in 1952 into the Human realm by virtue of her loyalty to her master, the senior muezzin of the Irkoubeline Mosque in Tafraoute. The karmic residue from this canine incarnation has made the commandant fond of ritual and ceremony but averse to the subservience he feels is implicit in Muslim prayer and prostrations (an antipathy that has led to alcoholism and the first signs of madness), and routinely compels him during the most violent stages of his prisoner interrogations to bare his incisors and growl.

The commandant eyes Mia and asks in an affected baritone deepened further by the anisette, *"Vous parlez français?"*

You intuit that it's unwise for Mia to talk to this man, that an imagined rapport with an attractive American woman will only embolden him. Before she can respond, you shake your head and say firmly, "No. We both speak only English."

After a whispering exchange in Arabic, the commandant takes from the young gendarmes your money clip and passports, which he inspects carefully beneath his reading lamp, thumbing through the pages, examining each of the entry stamps, sniffing the money clip twice, presumably for any scent of marijuana or hashish, before storing it all in a drawer. His dark eyes flash at Khalid, then over at Rouk. With a wave of his manicured fingers the commandant directs the hut guard to return to his post, and for the remaining two gendarmes to escort you and Mia from the dank interrogation room.

You refuse to move. "She needs a doctor," you tell the commandant as he stands. You lift Mia's bloodied hand towards the lamp light. "Talk to me if you want—but she needs to get to a hospital."

The commandant ignores you and walks over to the still-seated Rouk, prodding him with the toe of his boot to straighten. Forcefully you and Mia are separated from the Chirats and shoved by the two gendarmes out of the interrogation room, around the corner, and into the long hallway. As you're marched down the corridor, your mind spins wildly as you consider your options, none of which is good. The hall connects with three other doors, you see, the farthest of which leads to an opened and emptied utility closet, towards which you and Mia are ushered. Sensing that you're preparing to strike or bolt, Mia turns and pulls you gently by the hand with her into the closet. "Come. Let's just do as they say."

After you step inside next to Mia, the taller gendarme lifts the single-sided dummy handle and shuts the metal door behind you.

In the darkness you look down at the cement floor, which is wet, slippery. The cramped space is rife with a clammy, enteric stench—evidently you are not the first to be detained in here. Squeezed shoulder-to-shoulder, you and Mia turn and stare straight ahead, your fingertips pressed against the metal door. Assisted by the hall light bleeding through a ventilation grate near the door's top, your eyes gradually grow accustomed to the darkness.

Mia clutches her bandaged hand to her chest and asks, "Are they going to hurt us, Carter?"

"No. I think they just want to fuck with Khalid and Rouk a little."

"Why?"

You sigh. "I don't know. Maybe because they can."

But the door suddenly reopens, and with a thrust from behind Khalid stumbles forward into the closet. The elderly Moroccan falls into your arms as the door latches shut behind him. Trembling terribly, he seems near tears, but once he regains his balance his eyes immediately seek and find Mia's bandaged hand, which he is careful not to touch as he gathers himself and turns to face the door and whatever fate awaits the three of you.

Over the next few minutes your mind continues to race with fears of torture and unlikely plans for escape. Your heart is beating so hard you can hear it through your shirt. Taking a deep breath, you look up at the ceiling and think, "I take refuge in the Buddha, right? Okay—if the Buddha were stuck in here, what would *he* do?" You close your eyes and wait for an answer, surrendering to your omniscient Buddha Nature by shifting your point of view to second person.

The first thing you feel me suggest is that you should take a few more deep breaths and try to harness your adrenaline as an accelerant for mindfulness rather than panic. As Mia continues to quietly pray, you lean an ear towards the ventilation panel: the building's back door buzzes again and is unlocked. A muffled conversation, a bark of disdainful laughter, departing pats on the back. You guess correctly that having come to the end of their nightlong shift, the two young gendarmes have been dismissed by the commandant and allowed to return to their barrack bunks back at the gendarmerie proper. You wait, motionless, for any sound indicating the arrival of replacements, but none comes.

Two locked doors. One policeman. One gun.

With Rouk sequestered alone in the interrogation room with the commandant, you decipher the various noises coming through the grate once the questioning begins: boots squeaking against the floor, the commandant's holster dropped to the desktop, the jangling of keys, the scratching of something metallic against one of the walls. Mia flinches when the commandant begins shouting, his anisette-fueled roars punctuated by a succession of heavy fist-blows to the desk. When Rouk attempts to say something in his defense, he's cut off in midsentence with a slap to the face.

"Okay," you whisper calmly. "I have a plan."

Once you've explained to Mia your intentions, you step back against Khalid and look up at the ventilation plate. Though the grating space is too narrow for any of you to squeeze through, you stand on your tiptoes, reach up, and with surprising ease loosen and remove the grating's four screws. A gasket-like layer of mildew and grime keeps the unfastened metal in place. Squatting, you instruct Mia to give you her rosary beads and then stand on your thighs. "If no one's in the hall," you say, grasping her knees once she lifts herself, "remove the grating and look down to see if the door handle swings upwards or downwards."

"How can I tell?" she asks, pinching the plate, carefully lifting it from its rectangular slot.

"Quietly—quietly. Is the hallway clear?"

Mia nods and places her cheek to the ventilation slot, straining to see down the door's other side. "It's just a flat brass handle."

"Is it curved on the top or bottom?"

"On the bottom, it looks like."

"Good. Okay, put the grating back. Shhh—be careful. Will it stay without the screws?"

Mia pulls her hand back and waits a moment before answering. "I think so."

"Okay. Good job."

After Mia lowers herself, you continue wrapping a section of the ten small ave beads and a larger paternoster of her rosary around the red-tasseled gourd of your mala. Once linked and secured by the little metal crucifix, the two strands of prayer beads reach in length from your extended hand down to your knees—almost three full feet. "Yeah, this is gonna work," you whisper. Before you can ask for it, smart old bird that he is, Khalid reaches into his kaftan's front pocket and uncoils from the leather *tasbih* bag his cedarwood prayer strand. Glancing up at the ventilation slot with a nod, he evidently understands what you have in mind.

"All clear?" you ask, after Mia secures herself atop your bent legs again, her opened palms flattened on either side of the grating. This time you hold on to her hips and lean back to balance her weight.

Khalid winces at the scuffling sounds coming from the interrogation room.

"It's going to be okay," you tell him. "We're gonna get Rouk out of there."

Mia takes a deep breath, nods affirmatively. "It's all clear."

"Okay—quickly," you tell her. "Just leave the top in—yeah—like that. Good. I got you. Do they reach?"

"I can't tell." She labors to keep her eyes on the mala's red tassel, the pain from her injured hand showing in her face, her hair damp with sweat. She's breathing hard through her mouth. At the bottom of the three linked prayer strands, the paternosters and crucifix of her rosary clink against the closet's brass dummy handle. "Oh . . . *damn* it."

"It's okay. Take your time."

"There: it reaches."

"Okay. Good. Just try to loop the bottom around the latch. Do you have enough room?"

"I think so."

"You have it secured? Let me know when you have it secured."

". . . Yes yes yes."

"Keep it tight. Ready? Yank up on three. One. Two. Three."

As Mia lifts the handle, you reach around her leg and push forward a quarter of an inch, just far enough for the unlatched door to remain in the jamb. Hopefully, for someone approaching up the hall towards the closet, the door still looks shut.

"Got it. Hop down."

Mia unloops the rosary from the handle and reels the linked prayer strands in through the ventilation slot, replaces the grating, and then lowers herself to the floor. Holding your breath—you hear nothing but silence from the interrogation room—*did he hear?*—you straighten up and quickly fasten the four screws back into the door, and then, with raised palms, position yourself into a crouch.

The hallway, you estimate, is just under forty feet long. Presumably the other two doors along the corridor are locked, and there's no guarantee that either would lead to safe passage from the building were they not. There's no way out except past the commandant, who has a loaded pistol and perhaps thirty pounds on you and whose snarling voice rises again as he continues to berate and strike Khalid's son.

"Okay," you whisper, "let's go ahead and do this before we talk ourselves out of it. On three. You ready?"

Mia mutters, "No."

Still cocked like a Greco wrestler, relaxing your knees and shoulders, bracing yourself to blast forward, you count: "One. Two. Three."

With a huge intake of breath, Mia shuts her eyes. The extended, blood-curdling scream that lets loose from her small body is so astonishingly loud, Khalid covers his ears. You nod strenuously for her to continue. Gasping, eyes watering, face red, she leans over, brings her damaged hand to her forehead, and screams again—the sound tearing at her throat until she finally runs out of breath.

You tilt your head, raise a finger for Mia to be still. From the interrogation room you hear hurried boot steps, the commandant fastening his holster around his waist as he impatiently turns the corner and stomps up the hall to investigate.

"Ready?"

Mia nods.

The moment the commandant's shadow is visible on the floor at your feet, you kick open the unlatched door and shove it forward with all the force you can muster, the metal making contact with your captor's nose and chin with a resounding, bone-snapping *crack.* You cock a fist but restrain yourself from delivering the punch. Instead you push and drive hard with your legs, forcing the stunned commandant to lurch backwards with a yelp. As his palms rise protectively to the blood spilling from his nostrils, partially obscuring his view, Mia and Khalid—whom she tugs by his kaftan—rush forward, turn, and assist you in shoving the dazed police commander into the closet, whose door you slam shut and secure before he can turn around.

You grab Mia's left hand and pull. "Let's go. Let's go. Let's go."

Bent low in the event bullets start flying through the closet door, you hurry Mia and Khalid down the hall and around the corner, exhilarated but fearful of the condition in which you'll find Rouk. Entering the shadowy warehouse room, Mia yanks your hand and skids to a halt. The empty cot is no longer over the drainage hole. The commandant's black beret is on the floor. *"Rouk,"* she cries. Khalid lets out a gasp of relief at the sight of his son standing behind the table lamp, unbound, very much alive, though his right eye and cheek are swollen and red. He is breathing loudly through clenched teeth and nods as he reaches for his father and realizes what has happened.

After Mia finds the two passports in the top drawer of the desk, you bring an index finger to your lips and motion for the others to wait as you press the button beside the door and buzz it unlocked. Cracking the door open a few inches, you peek outside. It's still dark. You glance at your watch: 4:35. The parking lot is empty. The military Jeep in which you journeyed from Amen is nowhere in sight.

With your hands you indicate that everyone should move slowly, calmly. "Walk like you own the place" is your silent mantra as you and the others stroll from the building, through the parking lot, around the corner, and back onto the empty street, heading as nonchalantly as possible in pairings of two along the sidewalk in the opposite direction from the guard's hut and police station. Mia keeps her bandaged hand hidden beneath her shirt. As you veer onto a parallel street at the first opportunity, your pace quickens slightly, but you manage to keep yourself in check by counting breaths. You sling an arm around Mia's shoulder, point up tourist-fashion at a mosque's minaret. All goes well: the few predawn peddlers you pass as they set up shop among the shuttered souks either nod good morning or ignore you altogether.

Staying a safe distance from the gendarmerie, you circle back through the gradually awakening Fermoud towards the bus station you passed earlier. There are few cars on the streets. "Keep your fingers crossed," you advise Mia. "It might still be too early."

Alas, once you reach the station there are no buses in sight, and the ticket window is still bolted shut. Even the fruit stands surrounding the garage are boarded up.

But at the next corner you *do* see a tan-colored Mercedes taxi, smoking and idling noisily with its interior light flipped on. The lone passenger—a well-dressed Moroccan who looks eerily similar to the owner of the white Ford pickup truck who delivered you to Amen—smiles and holds the door open for Mia after he steps out from the back. You gently bang twice on the trunk to alert the taxi driver that he has another fare. After Mia, Khalid, and Rouk scoot across the back seat, you close the rear door and hop into the front passenger seat, locking the door behind you. You glance over your shoulder to the left and then to the right: in all directions the coast appears to be clear.

So that the taxi driver will not hesitate to accept what you assume will be an arduous, day-long trip, you drop into his lap, with a flourish, unfolded from your money clip one bill at a time, all of your dirham notes and then each and every one of your American twenties. The driver's eyes alternately widen and narrow as the final bill floats into his possession. After the longest, most heartfelt sigh of your entire life, you lean your head back against the headrest, and with two words make clear your request: "Casablanca, please."

13

OUT OF THE DARKNESS ONE of the trilingual Royal Air Maroc flight attendants leans low over the empty aisle seat and asks in a whisper if you'd like another Dewar's and water, her mouth close enough for you to smell her cinnamon TicTac. The orange glow of Mia's reading lamp, one of only two lights still turned on in the airliner's twin-aisle cabin, illuminates her light brown face. With her thick, Western-styled hair, mink black and glistening with myrrh-scented oil, cinnabar lipstick, smartly tailored blue blazer and white silk blouse, its oversized collar flattened and separated to reveal a delicate silver necklace, the congenial Moroccan stewardess looks like she could be a sales manager for the Deerbok Group. You glance at her winged, silver nametag, which is imprinted in both Arabic script and English: FARIBA. Even though it's after midnight and already the third hour of this transatlantic flight to the United States, she maintains an easy, professionally attentive smile as she waits for your answer.

You place a palm over the highball glass. "Thanks, no. I'm good."

After Fariba nods and returns to the aft galley, you hold your watch up to the reading lamp and check the time. Most of your fellow passengers are tucked under green blankets, asleep, but you and Mia remain wide awake. Despite being physically worn out, the two of you are so energized with excitement and relief that neither of you can keep your eyes shut or even manage to eat—an hour ago your dinner trays were removed untouched. For the last thirty minutes Mia has flipped restlessly through the in-flight magazine, and you've chewed your ice and watched her. A second drink would relax you, but you're not ready to relax. You're enjoying this sensation, this newfound sense of freedom, wherein everything—the shimmering fabric of the tunics you're both wearing, the air in your lungs, the simple fact that you and Mia are alive—seems remarkable. The level of your happiness is so primal, all you can do is shake your head and giggle.

"Hey—look," you whisper. You turn your wrist over and show Mia the watch face: it's precisely seven minutes and thirty-five seconds into Sunday morning. "Happy Easter."

Mia nods—and does a double take, surprised that you would remember. She smiles and kisses your stubbly cheek. "And to you."

With a collective *ding* throughout the darkened cabin, the overhead seatbelt lights turn off. You lean across Mia's lap, mindful of her blue sling, and raise the oval window shade—outside there's nothing to see but endless nighttime sky.

"So, what did you end up doing?"

"With whom?"

"With the Egyptian police and your pubescent thug."

"Oh. That proved to be a tough choice actually, but we decided that if the boy was released unpunished he'd likely continue to rob people, perhaps even hurt somebody. We didn't have the money to stay another month in Egypt for a trial—we didn't have *any* money—so—reluctantly—we agreed to let the police cane his feet. They made us go into the cell and watch it, and it was *terrible.* He cried out for his mother the whole time. But I believe that it was the right thing to do, given our limited options."

You stare at Mia's profile as she looks back down and continues reading an article in the magazine. Without her glasses, she must squint, which stirs your heart. You laugh quietly and wag your head again at the wonder of it all. *Carter Cox and Mia Malone: spiritual compatriots and conspirators in temerity—the Bonnie and Clyde of North Africa. What on earth will happen next?* You're giddy with exhaustion, tremulous and slightly stupefied with love. You feel like a gawky young hawk during its first migration south—unsettled, excited, cautiously acquiescing to the instinctive gut-tug to take flight to warmer climes. Since lifting off at the Casablanca airport, you've not once let go of Mia's left hand, which you now raise to your pursed lips for a kiss.

With the stop in Aztendara, the taxi ride through the mountains to the coast and then north to Casablanca took almost twelve hours, roughly the full span of the day from dawn until dusk. You're pleased that you allowed for a detour that took the Chirats safely home. Az-*ten*-dara—Rouk gently corrected your pronunciation—proved to be a nondescript village in the mountains southeast of Marrakesh, its sparsely vegetated outskirts here and there nibbled upon by unsupervised herds of scraggly-looking goats, none of which had apparently learned to climb trees. The town's center consisted of an outdoor food market, an ancient one-pump petrol station, and the foul-smelling Fenouch Tannery, a hivelike series of medieval mud-brick vats and hide-skiving stalls, manned by a dozen bare-legged workers whose lower torsos were stained maroon and saffron from their dyes.

Struggling with his French, Rouk nonetheless made clear that you and Mia and the taxi driver must join him and his father for lunch in their small adobe home, an invitation that Mia—despite the discomfort of her injured hand and an unvoiced concern that the police might be following—insisted that you accept. After a quick, comfortably quiet meal consisting of warmed potato soup and mint tea, Rouk led you behind the house into his work shed and shyly showed off examples of his original leatherwork: coiled piles of belts, a wicker basket half-filled with small brown purses, and a stack of soft, exquisitely detailed goatskin wallets, dyed russet. He took the largest of the wallets, dusted it against his kaftan, and offered it with his heartfelt thanks, spoken softly in Arabic, for the kindness you showed his father. "I'm sorry for all that happened," you replied, a hand to your chest and lowered eyes serving adequately as translation. The realization that you would most likely never again see Rouk and Khalid after you said good-bye made it difficult to do so. As you waved farewell through the taxi's rear window, both you and Mia blinked back tears.

The moon had come out by the time you arrived at the Mohammed V airport. The early-evening sky was clear and cool and already filling with stars. At your direction, the taxi stopped and idled at the end of a short line of identical, tan-colored Mercedeses beneath a rectangular sign pulsating with white, five-foot-high fluorescent letters: BIENVENUE A L'AEROPORT DE CASABLANCA. Having spent a *very* long day together, before disembarking you reached across the seat and shook the driver's hand, and then insisted with a raised palm that he keep all the money you'd dropped in his lap that morning. Mia took your arm as you stepped, stiff-legged and sore, onto the curb. "I can't believe we made it," you said. Seeing that the two of you carried no luggage and wore clothing that reeked of petrol and was stained with blood, the white-turbaned porters who'd crowded around with their pull-carts moved on to the next taxi, leaving you and Mia to enter through the airport doors alone.

Though you were wary of the handful of black-booted gendarmes patrolling the terminal, you nevertheless approached a pair who were eyeing girls by the Lufthansa ticket counter. You lifted Mia's wounded paw and nudged her to ask in French if there might be a medical clinic somewhere in the airport. The two round-waisted policemen, both of them pushing fifty, stepped closer for a look at Mia's poorly bandaged hand and reluctantly escorted the two of you past a series of clothing and tobacco kiosks, around a corner into the international terminal's relatively empty east wing, and through a pair of swinging doors marked in red UNITE MEDICALE D'URGENCE.

Once inside the little airport clinic, Mia was tended to by a polite, multilingual, native-born physician named Abdel Karim Harouni. He wore a custom-tailored sports coat and wine-colored tie and breathed quietly through his nose as he examined Mia's eyes, neck, right elbow, and forearm. Behind him in the small but well-equipped clinic, a white-uniformed nurse took the temperature of a little boy resting quietly on a cot beside his mother. With Mia on the end of his examination table, her feet dangling a few inches above the floor, Dr. Harouni patiently swabbed, inspected, and tested each finger and seemingly every square millimeter of her right hand. "I would like to have my technician take X-rays of the wrist and forearm," he suggested, gently daubing hydrocortisone ointment along Mia's torn knuckles. "And we should consider giving you a tetanus booster."

When the three processed X-ray sheets were delivered to him twenty minutes later, Dr. Harouni assured Mia that she was "free of any fractures that I can see—*miraculously* so, considering your story." He gauzed and bandaged and placed her hand and forearm in a blue sling and then dropped into her lap a packet of extra-strength Tylenol tablets, given free of charge, as was the rest of her care at the airport clinic.

Mia squeezed your fingers and hummed as the two of you passed back through the swinging doors and wound your way through the warm, smoky terminal to the Royal Air Maroc ticket counter. Since you had nothing in your possession but your passports and a couple of credit cards, you expected difficulty getting on a flight. But after a conversation with an English-speaking shift supervisor that lasted no more than five minutes, you and Mia were charged a nominal rescheduling fee and given two boarding passes for the nine o'clock flight to JFK.

"Unbelievable."

"Please don't feel we have to get back to the States straight away on *my* account," Mia insisted. "I feel fine—truly."

You jiggled the two tickets. "Nah, I'm ready to go home. Everyone who showed up in Marrakesh is long gone by now anyway."

"Are you sure? You won't get in trouble?"

You offered a nonchalant shrug. "There'll be other fashion shoots. *Alas*. We've got some time before the plane leaves, though. You wanta get a change of clothes? Maybe wash up a little?"

After only a couple minutes of browsing, you purchased at the nearest garments kiosk, with what little credit remained on your American Express card, two knee-length blue tunics, small and extra-large, and a pair of baggy pajama-style cotton trousers to replace your filthy blue jeans. Despite a slight nicotine-withdrawal headache, you refrained from buying any cigarettes. Mia lingered a few steps behind as you signed the receipt, warmly gazing at the muscles in your back and shoulders, having over the previous twenty-four hours discovered in you the white knight she'd trusted would one day surface.

Moved by the tenderness in your gaze as you handed her the smaller tunic, she caressed your cheek before the two of you disappeared into adjoining bathrooms to change clothes. You ignored the stares while you undressed and splashed yourself clean at the men's-room sink. With little hesitation you dropped your rolled-up jeans and shirt into the trash. Cigarettes, cell phone, laptop computer, five cases of camera gear, and now the last of your clothes—all were gone. "Tweedle Dee and Tweedle Dum," you joked as you reemerged from the bathroom moments after Mia. Her damp hair, like yours, had been finger-combed back with cold water.

As you and Mia began to walk towards the international terminal's security check, smiling at the swishing sound of your matching Moroccan blouses, you noted out of the corner of your eye that the two gendarmes who'd escorted you to the clinic—accompanied now by a younger, carbine-wielding third—were staring at you from near the Royal Air Maroc ticket counter. At first you didn't notice that they'd turned and begun to trail you, but the crackle of a walkie-talkie got your attention.

"Let's pick it up a little," you said, pulling Mia deeper into the noisy chaos outside the domestic-arrivals gate, the crowd mostly Moroccan djellaba-clad females awaiting their husbands and fathers, the mala beads beneath your shirt bouncing against your chest as you pushed through all of the cart-pulling porters.

"Are they still following us?" asked Mia.

You refused to look back. Close to trotting, mindful of Mia's injured hand, the two of you weaved around the car-rental booths and then circled the food kiosks, heads low. "This way," you said, ascending a set of stairs that led back to the international terminal. You paused on the top step to catch your breath and check Mia's sling. "You good?" you asked. Mia nodded, her cheeks flushed with color. You glanced over both shoulders, and then down the stairs—the three gendarmes were nowhere in sight.

Confident that you'd given the police the slip but wanting to take no chances, you lingered among a swarm of Europeans queued loosely before a money-exchange office's Plexiglas window, your backs turned towards the busy walkway. For several minutes the two of you held hands and gazed down at the floor. Had you been alone and worried exclusively about your own safety, rather than making Mia's welfare your chief concern, you doubted that you'd feel this relaxed and confident. The insight—a revelation of sorts—made you lift your head and offer Mia a half smile, a smile you managed to maintain for a moment or two even after you spotted the three gendarmes, flanked shoulder to shoulder, stomping through the crowd of tourists straight for the money exchange.

"Back the way we came," you whispered, leading Mia by the hand towards the stairs. "Don't stop."

With a glance over your shoulder you saw that the policemen were parting businessmen left and right, briefcases flailing. One of the gendarmes shouted, *"Attendez! Arrêtez!"*

"Keep walking."

But on the stairs' top step a large, red-coated security official—walkie-talkie in one hand, clipboard in the other—blocked your way. "*Monsieur Cox*?" he asked.

You and Mia stopped, turned. Several of the European tourists lowered their cigarettes to watch. You knew that Mia could not run with her injuries, and it would be madness to fight. There was nothing to do but square your shoulders and wait. The gendarmes, all of whom were out of breath and irritated, surrounded you within seconds.

"Monsieur Cox?" demanded the largest of the three as he adjusted his holster.

"Yep," you replied, crossing your arms. "What do you want?"

Before anyone could say anything else, Mia stepped forward and situated herself between you and the policemen, her green eyes blazing. Like Joan of Arc ignoring her battle wounds, she slipped her right arm from the sling, planted both hands on her hips, and announced righteously to the policeman who'd spoken, "Sir, you are mistaken. We are not criminals. We have done *nothing* wrong. We found ourselves in a situation that—"

The gendarme cut her off. *"Monsieur Cox,"* he repeated, gently waving a blue passport in front of Mia's nose—a blue passport which you recognized as yours and suddenly remembered leaving on the Royal Air Maroc shift supervisor's desk.

"Ah." With a sheepish nod you accepted and pocketed your identification.

The third gendarme—the youngest but highest ranking of the trio—lowered his carbine and stepped in front of his junior partners. He jabbed a finger in the direction of Mia's bandages.

Struggling with his limited English, he asked, "Madame, what is the cause of your injury?"

Mia tensed. She swallowed hard but didn't so much as blink. She realized that the other two policemen had most likely not understood one word she'd said. With a sigh she reslung her thickly padded hand, the skin puffy but clean, gingerly bent her elbow, and, wincing dramatically as if from the memory, turned and pointed at you. "I slapped Monsieur Cox last night and sprained it."

"It is serious?" he teased.

Mia nodded. "Very."

Once again baffled by the behavior of Americans, the three gendarmes offered perfunctory salutes and without another word followed the red-coated security director back down the stairs.

"How much do you remember of the wreck?" you ask.

Mia closes the in-flight magazine. She's barefoot, with her legs crossed beneath her in the seat, her jeans almost completely hidden under the loose-fitting blue tunic. She thinks for a moment before answering. "Not much. I remember the car lifting into the air. I remember praying. I remember you carrying me in your arms to the pickup truck."

"You know, maybe you oughta call your mom when we get back to New York," you suggest. "Let her know that you're okay."

Mia covers her eyes. "Good Lord. She still thinks I'm in *Austin*."

"Oh, before I forget." You pat your tunic (which you've decided is the softest, most comfortable item of clothing you've ever worn) and retrieve from its breast pocket the gold wedding band, given to you by Dr. Harouni for safekeeping while Mia got her X-rays. "Are you ready for this?"

Mia checks her bandaged right wrist with a slow wiggle of her fingers. "Sure. Bring it on."

After you slip the ring back on Mia's injured hand, you give the loop a little prayer-wheel spin for luck and recall with a déjà vu shiver the night your Javanese Buddha statue's right ring-finger developed its magical nick.

Across the aisle, half hidden in his mother's arms beneath their green blanket, a Moroccan baby drowsily offers you a smile.

"Look at that," whispers Mia. "My fingers are so swollen, now it actually fits."

You glance again at the cooing baby as you consider the implications of what you're about to say. ". . . Mia, about what I said in the Jeep yesterday? Do you remember?"

Mia lowers her head and smiles. "I do."

"Well . . . I meant it."

"I meant it too. I *love* you, Carter. With all of my heart." Mia's face softens and her eyes well up with tears.

"Come live with me, Mia. Come stay with me in New York."

"Oh, Carter . . . I can't do that. You should understand that by now."

"Not even for the summer?"

"Not even for the summer. I *love* you, Carter. I don't want to be your roommate."

"Well . . . then . . ." With a fingernail you clink the empty highball glass. You take another long, very deep breath, making certain that you're truly ready for what you're about to propose.

After resetting the orange-lit call button above the elderly woman in 24B, Fariba moves up the aisle past you and Mia towards the thick blue curtains partitioning First Class from coach. She pretends not to hear the *ding* coming from a seat along the other aisle. She has news, and she's eager to deliver the news to Salah, her friend and coworker, whose similarly coifed head is peeking between the parted blue curtains.

"I'm *bored,*" whispers Salah in their native Arabic. "Everyone up here is asleep."

With her back to the darkened coach section, Fariba whispers breathlessly, "Don't look up. Do you see that couple with the reading light on in 14B and C?"

"Mm-hmm."

"*Don't* be so obvious."

"I'm *not*."

"Do you see them?"

"Mm-hmm."

"The man just asked the woman to marry him."

"No."

"Yes. I'm almost positive."

Salah scrunches her dark feline features into a pretend scowl. "I'm jealous. Did he give her a ring?"

"He did. It was gold. I saw him put it on her finger."

"Daggers."

"*Please.* It's not as if Octavio hasn't asked you a *hundred times* to marry him. On his knees. Asked your *father*."

Salah groans and pulls the parted curtains closer to her cheeks. She is three years younger than Fariba, though twice as experienced with Spanish men. "I know, I know," Salah whispers. "But I *told* you—I want his older brother. And they *both* refuse to leave Tangiers."

"No. *You* refuse to say 'I do.'"

"I don't."

"You do."

"I *don't*."

"Yes—you *do*."

With a playful, self-mocking snap of the curtain, Salah whirls around and returns through the darkness to the dimly lit First Class galley. "What if what Fariba says of me is *true?*" she thinks with a deliciously devious grin. Moved by a spasm of mirth and a squirm-inducing memory of her last night in Tangiers, Salah dances her shoulders beside the empty food carousel and pinches the blue-blazered bottom of Layoune, the senior flight attendant, whom she met for the first time only a few hours ago.

"Would you like a break?" asks Salah. "I'll cover things for a while, if you'd like."

A seventeen-year veteran with Royal Air Maroc, supporting a son in private school in Agadir and an aging mother with whom she shares a one-bedroom home near the airport in Casablanca, Layoune normally works the afternoon shuttles to Las Palmas and Dakar. She's used to flying with different cabin crews, but in recent weeks a growing sense of doom and a rash of insecurities have troubled her so much she's found it difficult to maintain eye contact with her coworkers, especially the younger females. Tonight she has felt especially tense and nervous.

"Thanks, no," Layoune replies, blushing more from Salah's kindness than the pinch. "I'm fine. How is it back there?"

"Dead. I like your perfume, by the way. It's nice. It smells of lemons."

Layoune offers her first heartfelt smile of the evening and steps forward and confides, "That's what it is. After my baths I squeeze over my body a sliced lemon."

"Before you dry off or after?"

"Before."

Salah shifts her weight onto her other leg and imagines the sensation of citric acid massaged into her wet skin. "I *like* that."

Layoune begins to hum to herself after Salah leaves the First Class galley. She removes from the microwave oven a plate of apple-filled croissants with which she has decided to surprise the pilots. She continues humming, grinning in anticipation, as she fills two large Styrofoam cups from the fresher of the two pots of coffee, and with a knuckle knocks lightly on the cockpit door.

Within the locked interior, the two pilots wear wrinkled, short-sleeved white shirts, blue ties, and identical Breitling Colt Automatic chronometer watches, awarded them in December by the Rabat-based aviators' union. After checking the cabin-pressure altimeter, Vladimir Gray, the plane's fifty-five-year-old Cheshire-born captain (newly arrived to Royal Air Maroc after a successful but unpleasant stint at British Airways), unlatches and cracks open the cockpit portal, acknowledging the unexpected treat in a hearty voice, similar to Christopher's cockney, with a hand to his chest and an effusive, "Well, fancy this. Thank you, luv."

The aroma of steaming coffee immediately suffuses the stuffy cockpit. In the seat on the right, manning the helm for the past hour while Captain Gray read his April issue of *The Economist*, the copilot, Estragon Louisant, a thirty-three-year-old former major in the Seychellois Air Force, licks his lips and eyes the warmed pastries. Like bears revived from hibernation, both men, from deep within their throats, make low rumbles of pleasure. Captain Gray secures the plate and napkins away from the instrument panel, extends to First Officer Louisant the fuller of the two coffee cups, winks, and raises his own in salute after an initial slurp. "Cheers."

First Officer Louisant is pleased to remain at the helm once Captain Gray returns to his magazine. With the plane under his guidance, he takes his time nibbling the croissants: their tart but tasty apple filling reminds him of his newlywed wife's attempt to bake a pie during his father's first visit to their Rabat apartment—a hilariously failed effort that filled their little kitchen with smoke, set off the hallway fire alarm, and prompted snorts of laughter from both him and his wife as his father politely insisted on slicing for himself a piece of the blackened, double-crusted fruit pie. First Officer Louisant sighs with each bite: it's been three nights since he last spoke to his wife, four nights since he last held her in his arms. Because of the new, semistaggered transatlantic schedule out of Casablanca, it will be three more nights before he returns to Rabat, which leads the wistful copilot to sigh yet again, close his long-lashed eyes, and resolve to telephone his wife—even if it means waking her—as soon as the plane touches down in New York. The decision makes him swallow the last of his coffee, loosen his tie, and disengage the autopilot. He manually and visually confirms that the Boeing 767–200's altitude is holding steady at 35,000 feet. He then pushes the yoke forward to nose the plane down a couple of degrees, and with his left hand—his fingertips sticky with pastry glaze—nudges the throttle and accelerates to the maximum cruising speed of 580 mph.

The surge in the plane's velocity is accompanied by a half-octave shift in the whining of the two enormous Pratt & Whitney engines, and it gently forces you and Mia backwards against your seats. "*Whoa,*" you say. Your heart is pounding: the formal proposal you heard yourself make Mia a few minutes earlier—not to mention her surprisingly swift acceptance—lingers in the air like a canyon echo. There's no going back. You squint into the overhead light. "Do you *feel* that?"

Both of you seem to be lifting out of the seat belts. Still dazed and gazing forward, Mia smiles nervously, nods a little, squeezes your hand, and whispers, "I do."

ACKNOWLEDGMENTS

My thanks to Daniel Menaker for his terrific editing, and to William Clark for being such a mindful literary agent. For their generous contributions to this book, my gratitude to Plaegian Alexander, Deirdre Faughey, Lydia Weaver, Olga Gardner Galvin, Christine Heike, Vanessa Scanes, Elizabeth Mutton, Rebecca Tolmach, Bill Albrecht, Michael Silverwise, David Gunter, Darden Smith, Dr. Anne C. Klein, Evan Smith, Quita McMath, Bill Magness, Flint Sparks, Dr. June Idzal, Garchen Rinpoche, Sogyal Rinpoche, Lama Surya Das, Charles Genoud, Jack Kornfield, Huston Smith, my students and colleagues at Trinity, and everyone at the Lineage Project.